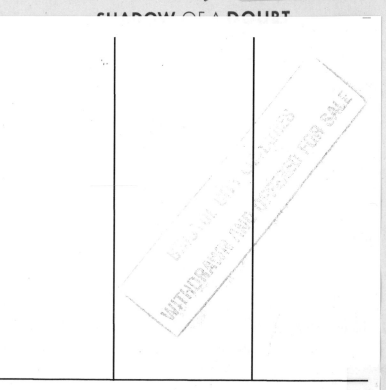

logical thriller which grips from page one
Amanda Jennings

Michelle Davies was born in Middlesex, raised in Buckinghamshire and now lives in north London.

When she's not turning her hand to crime, Michelle writes as a freelance journalist for women's magazines, including *Marie Claire*, *YOU* and *Stylist*. Her last staff job before going freelance was as Editor-at-Large at *Grazia* and she was previously Features Editor at *Heat*. She began her career straight from school at eighteen, working as a trainee reporter on her home-town newspaper, the *Bucks Free Press*.

Also by Michelle Davies

DC MAGGIE NEVILLE SERIES

Gone Astray
Wrong Place
False Witness
Dead Guilty

SHADOW
OF A
DOUBT

MICHELLE DAVIES

ORION

An Orion paperback

First published in Great Britain in 2020
by Orion Fiction,
This paperback edition published in 2021
by Orion Fiction,
an imprint of The Orion Publishing Group Ltd.,
Carmelite House, 50 Victoria Embankment
London EC4Y 0DZ

An Hachette UK Company

1 3 5 7 9 10 8 6 4 2

A CIP catalogue record for this book is
available from the British Library.

ISBN (Paperback) 978 1 4091 9343 2

Typeset by Input Data Services Ltd, Somerset

Printed and bound in Great Britain by Clays Ltd, Elcograf S.p.A.

MIX
Paper from
responsible sources
FSC
www.fsc.org   FSC® C104740

www.orionbooks.co.uk

To Nan

16 July 1994

Cara must've fallen asleep at some point, but she can't remember closing her eyes. She rolls over and peers at the luminous dial of her alarm clock. Telling the time is a relatively new skill and it takes a few seconds of concentration before she is sure the hands are pointing to half past midnight. Time to get up and catch Limey Stan, she grins to herself, her mind buzzing with her plan of how they are going to do it.

The early-hours temperature is mild, so she doesn't bother to pull her robe over her nightie, nor stuff her bare feet into slippers. Yet outside it is raining. Heavily, she guesses, judging by the noise it makes pelting against her bedroom window.

Her bravado begins to wane as she creeps along the landing towards Matty's room. Her parents' bedroom door is firmly shut and the house is pitch-black, just the way Limey Stan likes it. Is he already downstairs, crouching in the shadows in the hallway, waiting to pounce? Shuddering from tip to toe, Cara wishes she'd included using a torch in her plan.

Matty is in such a deep sleep, it takes three attempts to rouse him. When he finally does wake, he takes one look at Cara, flips onto his front and buries his face in his pillow.

'I know you're scared,' she tells him, 'but that's why we need to get rid of Limey Stan. So we can stop being scared.' When he shakes his head, face still hidden, she pokes him hard in the back with her finger. 'Come on, it'll be an adventure. Isn't that what the Power Rangers do? Fight the nasty men and have adventures?'

Referencing her little brother's favourite TV show does the trick and a few minutes later, after a heart-pounding dash downstairs and along the hallway where Limey Stan usually prowls, the children have hidden themselves behind the full-length curtains in the front room.

'Did you see him?' Matty asks her breathlessly as they assume their places. He's not heard Limey Stan speak yet, let alone caught a glimpse of him. Cara wakes him up whenever Limey Stan wakes her, but by the time Matty gets to the top of the stairs, to her frustration, he's always gone.

'No, he's not here yet.'

But he will be, soon, and when Matty sees him too, everyone will know she is telling the truth about what's been disturbing her night-times for the past few months.

Boredom quickly sets in while they wait for him to materialise, however. Then Matty, who is only six, gets the giggles and his entire body begins to shake, making the curtain ripple. Cara tries to be annoyed that he's not taking it seriously, but secretly she welcomes the break in tension and soon she's giggling uncontrollably too and the two of them are shaking so much, they wind themselves in the folds in the curtain. Plunged into even deeper darkness, Matty stops laughing and begins to panic.

'I'm stuck.'

Cara blindly reaches forward until she makes contact with her little brother's familiar form. She pulls at the fabric that's now wrapped tightly around him, but as she does, she hears a creak in the hallway next door, quickly followed by another.

She yelps. 'I can hear him, he's coming!'

Frantic now, Cara pulls at the curtain again, but her hands are sweaty and Matty's writhing too much.

'Stay still,' she implores him. 'I can't get it off if you don't stop moving.'

But as he finally obeys, she senses they are not alone in the room. She swears she hears breathing and it's getting louder.

'It's Limey Stan,' she wails. 'He's going to get us!'

Matty screams, but the curtain muffles the sound. Cara tries to make another grab for her brother, but it's too late.

Limey Stan has beaten her to it.

Part One

Chapter One

Cara, now

The Brimsdown Arms isn't the closest pub to our office, but it holds the distinction of being the nicest in the vicinity. Fashionably muted grey walls, an array of absurdly named craft beers and scrubbed wooden tables large enough to seat all eleven of us. Towards the end of the evening, if they've been vacated in time, we'll migrate to the two leather sofas at the back of the room, grateful to lower our wearied selves into their bowed cushions.

Invariably, someone will doze off, alcohol limit breached, and phones will be whipped out to enshrine their slack-mouthed inebriation on social media. For this reason, I make sure it's never me who drinks too much, sticking to vodka tonic and alternating with fizzy water whenever it's my turn to go to the bar.

Tonight, the sofas are still taken and I'm sandwiched at a table between Donna, one pay grade above me and hardwired to never let me forget it, and Jeannie, head of our department and one of the most generous people I know. She buys the first round without fail every Friday after work and never minds when the same three people peel off home immediately after their free glass of whatever is drained.

She's telling me about her plans for the weekend, but I'm

struggling to hear what she's saying over the music blasting from the speaker above our table. Earlier, we'd asked the manager to lower the volume, but he claimed it was designed to rise and fall with the pitch of customers' voices and turning it off would mean shutting down the pub's entire music system. We decided to test his theory and lower it ourselves by whispering for five minutes, but then Leo, the office junior, began to snigger and the spread of laughter around the table sent the decibel level soaring again and that's where it's remained.

As I strain to hear Jeannie, someone reaches between us to grab the empty glasses littering the table and I jolt as they lean a little too heavily against my shoulder for it to be accidental. My colleagues' faces break into sly, knowing grins and immediately I know it's him, the new bartender I went home with last week and whose name doesn't easily spring to mind.

Donna theatrically digs me in the ribs. 'Aren't you going to say hello?' she hollers above the music.

I shrug non-committally but do steal a glance up at him, then wish I hadn't. He's younger than I recall, his skin gloriously unmarked by any signs of creeping age, and I'll admit I'm taken aback: how could I not have noticed how boyish he was? He's really not my type. Then my memory crudely reminds me that our interaction was too urgent to allow for lingering looks, and my face reddens.

He stares down at me, waiting, a hank of messy blond hair flopping over his forehead. Acutely aware everyone's watching us, I flash him a smile, which he returns, then I beckon him closer. His eyes light up, until I speak.

'You've missed one.'

'What?'

'That one over there.'

I point across the table to the empty pint glass next to Leo, who has reached the swaying-in-his-seat stage of drunkenness.

My one-night stand snatches the glass up, his cheeks now a vivid shade of crimson to match mine, and he disappears into the crowd in the direction of the bar.

A couple of the others laugh at his retreating back, but Donna clicks her tongue disapprovingly. 'You could've been nicer to him, Cara.' Her voice is still raised to counter the music.

Jeannie catches the comment and leans across me to respond, forcing me to sit back in my seat. 'Why should she?'

'Yes, why should I?' I mirror.

'Because you went home with him last week,' Donna bristles.

'So?' Jeannie shrugs. 'This is 2019, not 1950. Not every sexual encounter has to lead to something. No need to get your knickers in a twist if Cara's not bothered.'

It's a paper cut of a remark, designed to sting. We both know Donna is unhealthily invested in my private life, regularly making it the focus of office chat, and I've complained to Jeannie about it more than once. Why should it matter to Donna, or anyone else, that I'm thirty-four and still single and content to be so? Jeannie gets it, and has cautioned Donna to stop prying, but it hasn't deterred her. Then again, it hasn't deterred me either, hence last week's liaison after closing time.

'But sleeping around is so dangerous. She might catch something.' Donna is discussing me as though I'm not here. 'Not that I'm saying you've got an STD,' she adds, finally addressing me. 'But you know what I mean.'

I bite back a retort. She makes it sound as though I'm with a different man every night, when the bartender is the first person I've slept with in three months. I would never share these simple truths with Donna, or even Jeannie, but I'm usually more discerning about whose bed I get into – the bartender is definitely the lower end of my age limit. I also have a rule, which Jeannie is aware of, never to have sex with anyone who might want to see me again afterwards. This is not the act of self-preservation people may assume – be the dumper, not the dumpee – I just struggle to entertain what a serious relationship entails and I've got so used to being on my own that I can't imagine committing to someone long-term. Being loved unstintingly for years on end is a concept I am unfamiliar with.

'I'm sure Cara is being sensible,' says Jeannie, catching my eye and smiling. 'We've talked about this before, Donna. Marriage isn't for everyone.'

Donna scowls. She finds it impossible to believe I don't want to settle down and that no relationship is worth relinquishing the privacy and lack of intrusion that being on my own gives me. She and 'my Martin' met at school, were married at twenty-two and had three children by the time she was my age. The way she talks about her husband though, I'm not sure she even likes him any more, let alone loves him. But broach the idea of them separating and you'll get short shrift and a lecture on marriage vows being unbreakable.

'Maybe if you seriously changed the way you look you'd attract a better standard of man,' Donna sighs, washing down the insult with the dregs in her glass.

'You think I should have plastic surgery?' I laugh.

She eye-rolls as she reaches across the table for the bottle of wine in the ice bucket, then grimaces when she realises it's empty. She plonks it back in the bucket neck-first, then hollers across the table at the others that it's someone else's round.

'I doubt you could afford it on your wage, but that's not what I meant,' she says. 'Your face is fine, but I think you should grow your hair long and wear more make-up. A pixie crop might be trendy, but it isn't very feminine.'

She's so drunk now it comes out as 'femininny'. Reflexively, I fold my right hand over the nape of my neck, where the shortest hairs taper to a velveteen point.

'I like my hair this length and, besides, you were telling me only three –' I release my hand to check my watch to be sure, and am surprised to see it's nearly ten '– actually, four hours ago as we left the office that you like the way I do my eyeliner. You even asked me to show you how I flick it up at the ends.'

I'm baiting Donna into continuing our quarrel because it's a variation of the same one we have every Friday night and not to have it would be weird. However irritating she might be, and however much she crosses the line with my personal life, I do find a strange comfort in the repetition of how we are with each other and the way we bicker. I suppose it's because routine is something I cleave to and have done for years. Having your life turned upside down as a child can do that to a person.

Jeannie leans across me again.

'Give it a rest, Donna. If I had my time again, I wouldn't rush to settle down either. I'd have kept my options open too.' She looks over at the bartender, who's now serving someone. 'Are you sure you don't want a repeat performance with that one though? He's lovely-looking.'

'He's way too young; don't encourage her!' Donna drunkenly shouts.

I don't respond to either of them. I can't. Their physical proximity is starting to make me feel hemmed in: their arms are pressed solidly against mine and I don't like it. It's overbearing, too intimate. I tense my body to prevent myself elbowing them off me, because I don't want to cause a scene. The stark physicality of one-night stands I can cope with, affectionate embraces and touching I can't.

They continue chatting, seemingly unaware of my discomfort, and I've just reached the point where I'm about to jump to my feet to escape their confinement when I receive an unexpected text. Unexpected because the people who usually text me are all seated at the table. I feel the message before I see it, in the vibration of my mobile in my handbag rammed between my feet beneath the table.

Grateful for the excuse to move, I reach down and rummage blindly in my bag, lifting out the phone just as the screen goes dark again, but not before I see what the text says. The words are succinct, the tone brisk – yet the emotional impact of them combined is so colossal it punches the breath from my lungs.

I scrabble to activate the screen again, my heart thudding so frantically it's a wonder Donna and Jeannie can't hear it. I read the text again and the clamour of the pub recedes to a low muffle as I try to take in the news that I am unutterably shocked to receive.

My mother is dead.

Chapter Two

Cara

The text isn't from anyone in my contacts. Then again, it wouldn't be. The people I count as friends and associates these days don't know my mum. But this person does, right down to the last minute of her life.

CARA, YOUR MUM DIED AT 12.33 TODAY. WE
THOUGHT YOU SHOULD KNOW. KAREN.

I grip the phone tightly, a necessary anchor as my thoughts clamber over themselves to be heard. Mum's dead? How? Was it expected, sudden . . . even planned?

Did she die at the house?

Jeannie and Donna have turned away to talk to the others and I am grateful to be ignored. Light-headed, I check the text again, lifting the phone up to my face for a better view, but the wording hasn't changed. My mum is dead and has been for almost ten hours.

Illuminated against the backdrop of the dimly lit pub, the text glares back at me, challenging me to disbelieve it. And I do. I just don't get how she can be dead: she is – was – no age at all. Mentally, I calculate exactly how old. If I'm thirty-four now and she had me at twenty-seven, that would make her sixty-one. That's relatively young still, isn't it?

Jeannie nudges me. 'You okay?' she asks, eyeing my phone. I flip it over in my hand so she can't see the screen. 'You've gone really pale.'

'I'm fine.' I do a passable impression of smiling, then rise to my feet. 'I need the loo. I'll be back in a minute.'

I take my phone with me and push through the throng towards the toilets. There is a queue outside the ladies' and I recognise the woman at its rear as someone from our firm's marketing team, but she doesn't acknowledge me as I slot in behind her. I don't merit her attention because I'm 'only' in accounts, but for once I don't mind being snubbed. I can't make small talk now, not when my mind is racing at a million miles an hour and my pulse is matching it step for step.

Mum died and I wasn't there.

I should've guessed Karen would be the one to tell me. My father aside, she was the person Mum was closest to. Sisters born only eighteen months apart, they bought houses in the next street from one another and had their children around the same time so they could raise them together. Unless Mum had remarried, I expect Auntie Karen was with her at the end, holding her hand until the last . . . unless, it hits me, her death really was sudden and no one was. The thought of Mum being alone like that makes my knees buckle and I stumble into the marketing woman, who shoots me a look over her shoulder. I mumble an apology, blaming it on the heeled boots I'm wearing. She probably thinks I'm drunk and I'm happy to let her.

A few minutes later, it's my turn for an empty cubicle. I shut the door with a bang and rest my forehead against the sign on the back of it advertising the pub's Christmas menu, even though it's still only mid-October. I let out a sob, then another, but my eyes remain dry. I've shed so many tears for

14

my mum over the past two decades that now, when she's finally deserving of them, there are none to give.

Our estrangement was her doing. She made the decision, along with my dad, to pretend I didn't exist. I read somewhere once that on a person's deathbed his or her overriding regret isn't failing to land their dream job, own their own house or earn enough money, it's losing contact with loved ones. Did Mum, in her dying moments, wish we'd reconciled? My heart steels a fraction as I count up the years I've been on my own and I wonder if it's too much to hope she was bereft that we hadn't.

I peel myself away from the door, lower the toilet lid and gingerly sit down. Cradling my phone in both hands, I wonder how to answer my aunt's messages. Does she even expect me to? The lack of warmth suggests she might not, nor are there any 'hope you're well' or 'take care' platitudes I can boomerang back. Then again, I silently scold myself, she's hardly going to be concerned about niceties after her sister's died and I won't have been the only relative she'd have had to break the news to, which in itself gives me pause. I wonder where I ranked on her list of people to contact. It's probably too much to hope that I might've been first, and the time lapse would suggest not.

I try to formulate a response, my fingers hovering over the keypad, but I keep coming up blank. Calling my aunt is out of the question, I decide – because what do you say to someone you haven't seen or spoken to in twenty-five years?

The last memory I have of Auntie Karen is standing on the front doorstep of our house with her arm around Mum's shoulders as she sobbed, convincing her that my departure was for the best. That left Dad to walk beside me as they rolled me away; I can still hear his voice breaking as he asked the doctor whether the restraints pinning me to the stretcher were really necessary. I shall also never forget how his face sagged with despair when they lifted me into the back of the ambulance and his fingers were wrenched from mine. It was the last time we ever held hands.

Suddenly I'm angry. Screw Auntie Karen and what she said that day. If she hadn't stuck her oar in, filling my parents' ears with poison, my life would've turned out differently. I wouldn't be hiding in a pub toilet in Colchester, slightly tipsy and devastated to find out my mum is dead – I would be at home in Heldean with my cousins, raising a glass to her memory and choosing which songs to play at her funeral.

There's a bang on the cubicle door.

'What are you doing in there?' a woman shouts, an edge to her voice. 'People are waiting out here and you've been in there ages.'

I look at the time on my phone and I'm startled to see half an hour has passed since I received the first text.

I hear another voice, this one familiar.

'Cara? Are you in here?' Jeannie calls out.

'Is that your friend in there? Tell her to get a bloody move on.'

Knuckles rap softly on the cubicle door. 'Cara? Are you okay?'

Rising to my feet, I slip my phone into my trouser pocket and open the door. One look at Jeannie's concerned expression and I fall helplessly into her arms. Still the tears won't come, but I howl as though my heart is breaking – which I think it might be.

Jeannie's voice rings in my ear. 'Christ, what's happened?'

I can't find the words.

'Cara, tell me what's wrong.'

Eventually, I lift my head from my boss's shoulder. The women waiting in line have melted back to a respectable distance.

'It's my mum,' I stutter. 'She died today. I just found out.'

Jeannie's mouth falls opens in shock and a rumble of sympathy reverberates among the women watching us.

'Oh, Cara, I'm so sorry.' Jeannie's eyes brim easily with the tears that mine can't produce. 'Was it sudden?'

I don't want to admit I haven't a clue, so I lie and say yes.

'Let's get you out of here. With a bit of luck, we can get you on a train to Morecambe tonight.'

That pulls me up short. 'Morecambe?'

'To be with your dad.'

Her comment baffles me, because Dad's been dead for almost two decades. He was killed in a car accident not long before my sixteenth birthday.

Then the penny drops.

'I don't mean Anne,' I say quietly.

Now Jeannie is confused. 'I thought that was her name?'

She's heard me mention Anne and has assumed she's my mum. I've never told anyone at work what I tell Jeannie next.

'Anne's my foster mum. It's my real mum who's died.'

Jeannie stares at me, palpably stunned. One of the women in the queue has reached bursting point and squeezes past us apologetically to use my vacated cubicle. This propels Jeannie into taking my hand and leading me outside into the corridor separating the toilets from the rest of the pub. It's busy, with people going back and forth, but there's a quiet spot at the end, by the fire exit. As we stand there, I feel a draught sneaking under the door and it's a reminder that while the pub is warm enough for us to shed our layers down to our shirtsleeves, outside autumn's making its mark.

I can see Jeannie is brimming with questions for me, but she's astute enough to realise I'm in no state to be forthcoming right now, so she sticks to the practicalities a situation like this requires.

'Where does – did – your mum live?' she asks.

'Heldean, on the Herts–Essex border.'

She frowns. 'That's about an hour away, if I'm thinking of the right place. Maybe we could get you a taxi there. It'll cost, but it'll be quicker than going by train at this hour.'

I shake my head. 'I'm not going back there.'

'Oh, Cara, I know this must be a huge shock, but are you sure? Who let you know that she died?'

'My aunt, but she won't want me turning up.'

'It's not up to her – she was your mum,' she says fiercely. 'If you want to go back to pay your respects, she can't stop you.'

I feel a surge of affection for Jeannie for saying that. She doesn't have children of her own – never could, she'll cheerfully tell anyone impertinent enough to ask – and instead she helms our office like the mother hen she never had the chance to be. She cheers on our triumphs, counsels our failures, disciplines us when we step out of line and never for a second do we doubt she cares. I've often thought she'd make a great foster carer, but I fear the boards which approve them might not be enlightened enough to look past the sheath-like blouses, skyscraper stilettos and eighties-era make-up to see what a remarkable person she is.

'I honestly don't think I could face it,' I say, which is an understatement and a half.

Jeannie looks pained on my behalf. 'When was the last time you saw your mum?'

I hesitate. If I'm honest with her, it means risking her finding out my real identity.

It was decided early on, while I was still in the Peachick, that I should keep my first name because the distress of adopting a new one might impede my recovery. It's perhaps the only thing I am grateful to the Peachick for. Actually, that's not entirely true. Two years locked up in that hospital taught me the art of being still – when everything around you is chaotic and frightening and loud, when the adults around you are strangers you can't trust, learning how to quiet yourself so you go unnoticed is quite the skill and one I still use to great effect.

But while I stayed as Cara, I changed my surname from Belling to Marshall, which I plucked from a book. The day I left foster care, I vowed never to reveal to another living soul who I used to be – why should I go through life being judged for what people thought was the truth about me, and if they looked me up online, they would only assume the worst. Cara Belling and the events of July 1994 have their own Wikipedia entry.

Yet this news about my mum has broken me in a way I could never have predicted. I feel alone and lost again in the same way I did coming round my first morning in the Peachick and wondering why my parents had put me there. A dedicated psychiatric unit for children and adolescents, it is a place I remember mostly for its outward cheeriness – every wall was covered in artwork and murals, as though that might be enough to distract us from where we were. It didn't work.

'Cara?'

Jeannie startles me from my reverie. She's only a few years younger than Mum was and is gazing at me with such tenderness that suddenly I decide I should tell her at least some of the truth. I need to tell someone.

'The last time I saw my mum I was nine years old. Once I was in foster care, I never saw or spoke to her again.'

Chapter Three

MEMORANDUM

To: Dr Patrick Malloy, head of clinical services
From: Dr Stacey Ardern, consultant child and adolescent
    psychiatrist
Subject: Cara Belling
Date: Friday 22 July 1994

As requested, this is the abridged version of my first assessment
– full report to follow by end of day.

Cara has presented with signs of acute emotional distress since
her admittance three days ago. She appears to have no grasp of
the nature of her surroundings and repeatedly asks to go home.
She so far refuses to engage in conversation about what happened to her brother and any mention, however abstract, of the
entity known as Limey Stan that she identified to police officers
at the scene of the fatality induces hysteria. Trust-building may
be a challenging and drawn-out process and pushing too hard
on the subject at this early stage may be deleterious for her.
Therefore, a cautious approach by all professionals coming into
contact with the child must be heeded.

Chapter Four

Karen

The kettle is almost at boiling point, the sound of gurgling water reaching its crescendo. Karen stares at it groggily. She can't remember coming into the kitchen to switch it on or why she has – the time for soothing cups of tea has long passed and everyone in the living room is on either red wine or neat spirits now. None of them has requested another hot drink and neither does she want one. She reaches over and switches the kettle off and as it is silenced, she hears her husband, Gary, let out a peal of laughter in the next room, which sets them all off.

The sound of their merriment rakes at her insides like a fork scraping a plate and she wishes they would leave. She'd been happy to see them when she arrived back from the hospice and was grateful for the fierce embraces and salving words and the tears of solidarity for her loss, but already she can sense their veils of sadness beginning to lift. Only by a fraction, and abetted by the alcohol, but enough to make her feel as though she is the only one who still cares that her sister died today.

The door between the kitchen and hallway swings open and Ryan enters, empty bottle of Cabernet in his grasp. Without prompting, he goes straight to the recycling bin to deposit it.

'Dad's asked me to open another one,' he says.

Karen nods and he pulls another bottle of red from the rack by the fridge.

'Don't you want a glass?' her son asks.

She shakes her head. 'No, absolutely not.'

Right now she can't imagine drinking wine of any colour ever again.

Twice a day, volunteers brought a trolley round the hospice, offering free alcoholic drinks to patients and their relatives. An unorthodox form of palliative care, but one that made the waiting that bit more bearable. Anita had been conscious for occasional moments during her final twenty-four hours and it was during one of those moments she suggested the two of them enjoy a last glass of white wine together 'to toast me on my way'. She'd only managed a sip of hers before weakly shoving it away, so Karen had downed both glasses in quick succession and now she has to live with the memory that while her sister took her last, shuddering breath, she'd sat there feeling horribly woozy.

'Why don't you come and sit with us, Mum? Everyone's talking about their favourite memories of Auntie Neet.'

Karen swallows hard. She has so many, she wouldn't know where to begin. She and Anita were two halves of the same coin their entire lives, companionably intertwined in a way that belied many sibling relationships. Blind panic rises up in her at the thought of never seeing her sister again and she covers her mouth with her hand to stop herself crying out.

'Mum?'

She shakes her head, too upset to manage a reply. Ryan reaches over and squeezes her shoulder.

'I wish we could've been with you at the end. It must've been so hard going through it alone.'

Karen nods, tears coming quickly. It was Anita's emphatic wish that only she be at her bedside when she died and so Karen

22

spent three days at the hospice on her own watching her sister ebb away, the hardest thing she has ever had to do. She would have given anything to have Gary be there to support her, even for an hour or so, but Anita would not be swayed. Gary was not welcome and nor was anyone else.

Ryan eyes his mum's phone, which is lying on the countertop next to the kettle. 'Has Cara texted you back?'

Karen lowers her hand from her mouth. 'No, not yet.'

'The woman you spoke to definitely gave you the right number for her?'

'Yes, she did. She was very nice about it. She even offered to tell Cara herself, but I said no.'

'You should've let her,' says Ryan, his voice hardening. 'The less any of us have to do with her, the better.'

'It's not that simple,' Karen replies stiffly.

'Isn't it? Auntie Neet never wanted to see her, so why should we bother with her now?'

'Your aunt wanted me to tell her.'

'But why? Cara meant nothing to her.'

'Please, Ryan, let's not go through this now. Not tonight.'

Karen is too exhausted to deal with her son's anger right now, but she accepts it isn't misplaced, because she feels exactly the same. Having to make contact with Cara bothers her immensely – as far as she is concerned, her niece lost the right to be involved in any family matters a long time ago.

'Sorry, Mum, I don't mean for you to get upset again. It's just when I think about what Cara did . . .' He grimaces and his hand tightens around the neck of the wine bottle. 'It's wrong that we have to take her feelings into consideration now.'

'I know. The best outcome all round would be that she doesn't care her mum's died and she leaves us alone.'

But she won't, Karen thinks bitterly. Cara's return to Heldean is guaranteed, because before Anita died she made sure of it.

Chapter Five

Cara

I wake the next morning to a voicemail message from Anne saying my aunt Karen has been in touch with her, that she and John are very sorry for my loss and could I call them back please? It was almost eleven the previous evening when she rang me, but I was already in bed by then – after I told her about my mum, Jeannie sent me home in a taxi she paid for upfront and as soon as I reached my flat, I put my phone on silent and crawled into bed with a half-full bottle of vodka for company.

Wrenching my head off the pillow takes some effort: my brain feels like it's been nailed to the inside of my skull. The now-empty vodka bottle is on the floor beside the bed where I must've dropped it and I nudge it out of the way with my foot as I stagger to the bathroom. Mustard is waiting outside the door for me when I've finished, his baleful stare compounding the shame I feel. He rallies when I feed him though, and I wish, not for the first time, that people were as easily placated as dogs.

I adopted him from a dog-rescue charity six years ago and he was there for eighteen months before that. A veritable canine soup – my vet reckons he is part Alsatian, collie and boxer – poor Mustard kept being overlooked for prettier dogs, but I loved him at first sight because I could see he was desperate for some permanency in his life and I knew all about that myself.

Phone in hand, I clamber back into bed. Anne picks up on the first ring.

'Oh, kiddo. We've been worried about you.'

Just hearing her voice lifts my mood. 'I'm sorry. I know I should've called you last night, but my head was all over the place.'

'I'm not surprised. It must've come as a terrible shock after all this time. I can only begin to imagine how you must be feeling.'

I picture her sitting in the hallway of their terraced house, one street back from the Morecambe seafront. She and John, my foster dad, have one of those old-fashioned telephone benches with a seat upholstered in a busy floral fabric. As a teenager, I used to be embarrassed by how naff it was and would purposely perch on the stairs to use the phone to avoid sitting on it – now I love it because it's so them.

'I'm okay. I mean, it is a shock, but it's not like I knew her.'

'That's as may be, Cara, but losing a parent, whether you were close to them or not, is still difficult,' says Anne. 'We just wanted you to know we're here for you, for whatever you need.'

My heart expands with gratitude. Anne and her husband, John, are the only people I feel I can truly rely on and knowing I have their support now means a lot.

I was two months past my eleventh birthday when I pitched up on their doorstep for the first time, tired and desperate for the toilet after the long train journey from London with my social worker. What's always stuck in my mind from that day is how they let me find my own way to the bathroom, encouraging me to roam about upstairs as though the house was mine and always had been. After two years of constant supervision at the Peachick, it was like being let off a leash and as I came downstairs on that first occasion, I remember I was smiling in a way I hadn't for many months.

Anne and John are also the only grown-ups who ever listened

to my side of the story about Matty's death and believed I was being genuine. They also gave short shrift to anyone who questioned whether I should be allowed near their other foster children. My past, or rather what I was accused of, has never been a concern for them, and over time, I've come to realise what a huge act of love it was to foster me when so many others were reluctant to.

'Your aunt called me again just now,' Anne continues. 'She was worried you hadn't received her message yesterday and wanted to check I'd given her the right number.'

'Worried?'

I once again call to mind Karen standing on the doorstep with Mum the day I left and I find it hard to believe she is bothered about my welfare now. She certainly wasn't the last time she saw me. It dawns on me I can no longer even bring myself to call her Auntie Karen, because that sounds like a person who is kind and loving and she was neither of those things.

'Well, more like agitated,' says Anne.

That makes more sense.

'You don't have to talk to her if you don't want to,' Anne continues, 'but the polite thing to do is to acknowledge she's contacted you.'

This makes me smile for the first time since yesterday evening. Growing up in Anne's house, 'the polite thing to do' was the number one rule. She stayed calm when we got angry and lost our shit, which happened a lot, or when I tried to run away once, but if any of us were rude to people, her disapproval could be felt from miles away.

'I'll text her back once I'm off the phone,' I promise. 'Was it you who gave her my number in the first place?'

'Yes. She called at about seven o'clock last night. I suggested the news might be better coming from us, but she wanted to be the one to tell you. She was concerned about how you'd take it.'

More concern for me, yet Karen's text was bereft of any. Funny, that.

'How did she get your number?' I ask.

'Your mum had our address written down, so Karen was able to get our landline number through directory enquiries.'

'Really?'

'I know. I was surprised she kept it too.'

I was told that social services had informed my parents where I'd been placed after my discharge from the Peachick and that contact would be initiated if they requested it, but they never did. So if Mum had had Anne and John's address all this time, why did she never get in touch? Not a single word from her in all those years. Did she ever come close, I wonder – write out a birthday card, then think twice about sending it? Was she ever tempted to visit, or even just to stand outside the house to catch a glimpse of the daughter she'd disowned?

I let out a long sigh. Second-guessing the whys and wherefores of a woman who became a stranger to me isn't something I'm capable of this morning. I feel out of kilter and so do my surroundings, which bothers me immensely, because for so long my flat has been my haven, the one place where I can be myself and forget about who I was. It's as though real life is seeping through its protective walls and the safe space I've spent all these years carefully constructing is being eroded brick by brick. I think this is upsetting me as much as her dying.

I live on a peninsula of the Essex coast that's cut off from the mainland twice a day by the tide. It's a twenty-minute drive from my workplace in Colchester and I chose to settle here when I was eighteen because it's one of those blissfully subdued places that old people like to retire to and was the environment I needed after two years in hospital and another seven in foster care. Less touristy than Morecambe, it is calm and quiet and I can breathe here. I go for daily walks along the coastal path and spend my weekends treading a familiar route through the nearby nature reserve. Mustard, who is now sprawled on my bedroom floor watching me, loves the walks as much as I do, but loves diving into the estuary more.

It's also only an hour's drive from where I grew up. An unquenchable need to be close to Heldean was another reason I didn't stay in Morecambe, much as Anne and John hoped I would. They even offered to apply for a 'staying put' order on my behalf so I could remain in their foster care until the age of twenty-one, but I said no. I wanted to come back down south as soon as I was free to and so my social worker arranged for me to be set up in independent accommodation with the support of a carer for the first year, until I felt confident enough to go it alone. Anne and John understood why I wanted to move down south, I think, after I made it clear they were my family now and I would never lose touch with them. True to my word, I still visit once every other month and spend every Christmas and Easter with them.

'Do you think I should go to the funeral?' I ask.

'Do you want to?' Anne parries back.

'I don't know. I think so, but I don't want to go anywhere near that house.'

Even the mere thought of returning to 16 Parsons Close inspires a terror that makes me shudder violently. I will never understand what possessed my parents to continue living there after what happened. Even after Dad died – which I was only informed about by my social worker – Mum still refused to relinquish the house and its hideous memories. I know that because I regularly check online to see if it's been listed for sale, but it never has.

'You wouldn't have to. You could go to the funeral, pay your respects, then leave. You won't be alone either – I'm coming with you,' says Anne decisively.

Relief floods through me. I had a feeling she might offer, but I didn't want to ask. She doesn't drive, so John would need to stay with their current charges, and it's a long way on the train from Morecambe to Heldean, with at least two changes and a crossover on the Tube between mainline stations in London. But Anne knows what returning to Heldean will mean for me, which is why she wants to come.

'I would love you to, thank you.'

'Once your aunt lets you know when the funeral is, I'll sort out my ticket.'

'I'll pay for it,' I say hastily.

'I can pay my way, kiddo.'

The nickname 'kiddo' is not exclusive to me; it's the default title Anne gives all the children in her care. Dozens of youngsters have crossed her and John's threshold over the years and it stops her inadvertently forgetting anyone's name and inflicting the kind of hurt that is magnified a million times when you're new to foster care and already feel displaced and forgotten. She and John are both edging towards seventy but refuse to retire, saying that while there are children who need a place where they can feel safe, and for as long as the local authority will allow it, they'll carry on fostering. At the moment, they have two girls staying, one of ten and another of thirteen. Both a handful, they have yet to realise how lucky they are to have landed on Anne and John's doorstep. But they will, eventually, just as I did.

I can easily cover Anne's ticket. I will happily pay out hundreds if it means she will come with me to Heldean.

'Let's see how much it costs first, then we can argue about who pays,' says Anne. 'But I can come down sooner, if you want some company?'

'There's no need. I mean – there's nothing to talk about really, is there? She was my mum, but I didn't know her.'

We both know my feelings towards Anita Belling are far more complicated than my casual tone suggests, and that our relationship cannot be so easily downplayed, but Anne knows me well enough to let it drop.

We talk for a bit longer, then I say I need to take Mustard out for a walk and we hang up. He starts circling by my bedroom door in anticipation.

'You need to wait a minute, mate. I have to send this message first.'

I draft and send the text quickly, because if I give myself any more time to think about it, I'll chicken out.

HI KAREN. THANK YOU FOR THE TEXT. THE NEWS
HAS COME AS A GREAT SHOCK. I WOULD LIKE TO
ATTEND THE FUNERAL – PLEASE CAN YOU LET ME
KNOW DATE/TIME/CHURCH. CARA.

The reply is instantaneous, as though Karen's been waiting all night and all morning for me to message her back.

THE FAMILY FEELS IT WOULD BE INAPPROPRIATE
FOR YOU TO BE THERE.

Instantly I'm annoyed. Why bother to tell me my mum is dead if it changes nothing?

I furiously tap out a response, but before I can send it, another message comes in.

PLEASE UNDERSTAND THIS IS A VERY DIFFICULT
TIME FOR US AND YOUR COMING WILL ONLY CAUSE
MORE DISTRESS.

I draft a curt response but promptly delete it. Karen has no right to ban me from attending and I really should fight my corner, but what's the point? I don't need the added stress.

OK.

I'm not expecting any response to that, but my phone pings again and this time her reply floors me.

WILL READING IS TUES 5TH AT FAIRLOP'S, HIGH ST. 11.30 A.M. YOUR MUM LEFT INSTRUCTIONS SAYING YOU MUST ATTEND.

I sit bolt upright on the bed. Why do I need to be there? My frown deepens as I read the text again: attending a meeting slap bang in the middle of Heldean High Street is not the same as slipping unobtrusively into the back of a church to attend a funeral. I don't know if I want to be that exposed. Heldean is a small town where things don't go unnoticed, and my turning up at Fairlop's to hear my mum's will being read would be big news for locals. Someone might even tip off the media, a thought that floods me with anxiety. I have read every awful, nasty word that has been written about me over the years and I dread to think how much worse it could be in this age of trial by social media. As my possible exposure looms large, I struggle to catch my breath, the palisades of my haven crumbling faster around me.

After a few moments, Mustard whines louder to remind me he's still waiting and I clamber off the bed to reassure him, grateful for the distraction. Crossing the room, my gaze strays to the photograph in a tiny blue frame on the chest of drawers beside the door. Barely bigger than a passport headshot, it's the only picture I have of my brother Matty and its inferior quality compared to the photograph alongside it, of Anne and John, reflects the fact it was cut from a newspaper. Matty is smiling impishly in the picture and as I draw nearer, it hits me that it's not for Mum that I must swallow my fears and return to Heldean – it's for him.

Chapter Six

The Heldean Advertiser

ONLINE EXCLUSIVE
1 HR AGO

The Heldean Haunting: mother dies 25 years after infamous hoax

By Beth Jenkins, Senior Reporter
@Beth_ HelAdv

The mother at the centre of the Heldean Haunting has died after losing her battle with cancer, her family has confirmed.

Anita Belling, 61, passed away on Friday at St Bernadette's Hospice, ten months after she was diagnosed with cancer of the liver.

It was in 1994 that Mrs Belling's family made headline news when her son, Matty, six, was smothered to death by his nine-year-old sister, Cara, at their home in Parsons Close. The inquest into Matty's death revealed he suffocated when Cara wrapped him in a full-length curtain in the front room of their home and he was unable to escape.

Afterwards, Cara famously tried to blame his death on a ghost called Limey Stan, who she claimed was haunting the family's three-bedroom property for months preceding the killing.

The case came to be known as the Heldean Haunting and has been the subject of various books over the years, including one by Heldean resident and self-proclaimed paranormal expert, Timothy Pitt. He remains the only person to ever support Cara's claim that Limey Stan existed.

Cara was below the age of criminality at the time of the killing and therefore too young to be tried. Instead, she was admitted to the Peachick Children and Young Person's Psychiatric Hospital in London, where, according to an interview her parents gave to the BBC at the time, she was diagnosed with delusional disorder. On her discharge two years later, she was taken into foster care somewhere in the north of England.

Mrs Belling's husband, Paul, died in a road traffic accident on the M11 in 2001. She never remarried. Her sister, Karen Johnson, issued an appeal for privacy via *The Heldean Advertiser* on behalf of their family.

'Whilst we understand there is still considerable interest locally in what happened twenty-five years ago, I ask that we be left alone to mourn in peace,' she said. 'We shall be making no further statement beyond this.'

Details for the funeral are not yet known, but Mrs Johnson, of Dargets Road, confirmed it would be a private service for close family and friends only. Cara Belling will not be among the attendees.

RELATED STORIES

- The Heldean Haunting: the fatal hoax that shocked a nation
- Debunking the myth of Limey Stan – local paranormal expert claims ghost DID exist
- Whatever happened to Cara Belling?

Chapter Seven

Cara

They blamed two specific events for planting the seed of what happened – 'they' being the doctors and psychiatrists who examined me in the immediate aftermath of my brother's death and put me under continuous observation at the Peachick for the next two years. So determined were they to make sense of what had happened, they searched long and hard to identify the so-called triggers that, in their opinion, had precipitated me developing a form of psychosis known as delusional disorder.

But they all got it so, so wrong.

The first supposed trigger they identified I have a vague recollection of, although not in the way they recorded it in my medical notes, which I requested access to a few years ago when I was still trying to unpick what I had experienced and why. At some point in April 1994, my parents had bought some new furniture for the front room and Mum insisted she no longer wanted copious rows of video tapes on display, so she asked Dad to sort through his collection and throw out the ones he was no longer interested in keeping. According to my notes from the Peachick, I sat with Dad as he went about his task and we spent an enjoyable hour or so discussing what films he liked and why.

Among the cassettes were blank tapes on which he'd recorded

programmes previously aired on TV – and among them was *Ghostwatch*, a 1992 spoof 'mockumentary' that involved three famous TV presenters of the day investigating a haunted house and somehow managing to trick 11 million viewers into thinking it was genuine. Dad loved anything scary and apparently told me – I have no recollection of this, I am going by what is in my notes – that it was one of the scariest things he'd ever watched. He wasn't alone, either. The BBC was flooded with complaints from thousands of people utterly traumatised by the broadcast that was billed as a drama: I've since read up on the programme and it ended with the so-called poltergeist seizing control of the TV cameras and one of the presenters disappearing into a 'void'.

Dad had written '*Ghostwatch* – NOT FOR CHILDREN!' on the spine of the tape and at the Peachick they determined it was that which piqued my own obsession with ghosts and our house being haunted. In my notes, it says that 'learning about *Ghostwatch* had an adverse effect on Cara's mental reasoning that eventually manifested as delusional disorder', which I swear is rubbish, because after helping Dad sort out his tapes, I never gave the programme a second thought until they started asking me about it a few weeks after I was admitted to the Peachick. Or badgered me about it, more like.

Although my notes paint a picture otherwise, it felt as though the hospital's agenda was already set. The police saw me as guilty of killing Matty and so my doctor's job was to get me to admit I was lying about Limey Stan and it felt as though little thought was given to how traumatised I was at being separated from my family. Until I was hospitalised, I'd never spent more than three nights away from home and that was to stay with my grandparents, only an hour's drive away. I had been due, however, to go on a school residential trip in the October of that year, to an Outward Bound centre close to where I now live on the coast. But when the time of the trip came round and my classmates were squabbling over bunk beds and learning how to build a campfire and keep a canoe upright, I was trying to convince a bunch of strangers I hadn't lost my mind.

There were six beds in my ward at the Peachick and I was the second youngest occupant by a month. The youngest was a boy who had shown signs of depression since the age of three and had tried to kill himself three days before his eighth birthday. We never became friends because I didn't want to. I wasn't the same as him, I wasn't ill. The only thing wrong with me was that I couldn't get people to listen to me. So I succumbed to the Peachick's rigid routine and endured the creative workshops designed to tease out my deepest feelings that put me off sharing them for life and the long, painful sessions with my psychiatrist talking about Matty, until finally someone did listen and determined I was no longer a risk to anyone else or myself, and they let me out. To say I'm still angry about the two years I lost in the Peachick is an understatement.

The second trigger they claimed to have identified took place on a Thursday after school, about a month ahead of us breaking up for the summer holidays and just before my ninth birthday. I cannot confirm the timing is correct, however, because this incident I don't remember. Instead, the timing was based on conversations the doctors had with my dad, and if his memory was correct and it was Thursday teatime, then I at least know what I would've been doing – Thursdays were special because it was chips-for-tea day and the only time Mum let us eat in front of the TV. Matty and I would sit on cushions on the floor in front of the coffee table with the spindly legs and the shiny black lacquered surface and watch *Scooby-Doo* while we shovelled fat, salty chips from the deep fat fryer into our mouths in rapid succession like they were coming off a conveyor belt.

According to the notes, neither of us looked up when Dad

came into the room, which didn't surprise me to read: Daphne tied to roller-coaster tracks was always far more interesting than whatever moan he'd brought home from work. Usually it involved the area sales manager for the stationery supplies firm where he worked being a wally and Dad being in the right. This time, though, the gripe involved me. Dad was furious because I had been naughty at school and the head teacher had to call Mum in, so, as a punishment, my planned Barbie-themed birthday party was cancelled and I apparently became so upset I took it out on Matty. Again, I cannot argue against what I do not recall, but what I can dispute is that even if this incident did take place, it had nothing to do with what came to pass a few weeks later. I did not plot revenge on anyone, least of all the little brother I adored.

Anne suddenly touches my arm and I jump in fright and whip my gaze from the window.

'Sorry, I didn't mean to scare you,' she says. 'You were miles away. Penny for them?'

I drag my focus away from the blur of countryside streaming past the window and give her my full attention. I know I've been quiet since we met at Liverpool Street to catch the train to Heldean and it's not fair of me.

'I was thinking about what happened . . . I can't get him out of my head.' Anne knows which 'him' I mean, and it's not Matty.

It's been a while since Limey Stan has given me the kind of nightmares that rouse me from my sleep in a cold sweat, but in the three weeks since Mum died, he has visited me nightly, reaching from the shadows to grab at me, his fingers ice-cold and spindly, as he hisses his name. He looks exactly as I remember him: he has no face, only a blur where his features should be, but he is tall and broad, dressed in black, and when he looms over me, I feel as small as a child again.

Last night's dream was the worst so far and I am exhausted from the emotional onslaught it triggered – it ended with Limey Stan's fingers wrapping around me like creeping ivy as he cocooned me in a burgundy velvet curtain and I woke up gasping and choking for breath and crying for Matty, who suffered that fate for real and died terrified and in pain while I hid next to him in the darkness, too petrified to stop it.

'Your mum's death was bound to bring it all up again. But you're not going anywhere near the house, so there's nothing to fear.' Nonetheless, she reaches over and squeezes my hand reassuringly. 'It's going to be okay, Cara. We'll get the will reading over with and then we'll be on our way.'

Mum's funeral has been and gone – I abided by Karen's wishes and stayed away. Instead, I went to work as usual. Jeannie has respected my wishes not to tell anyone else about my bereavement and not to ask intrusive questions. I think she hopes I will tell her in my own time why I ended up in foster care, but I won't. I could not bear her to think badly of me.

Moments later, we pull in to the penultimate station before Heldean and I have an overwhelming urge to get off and double back, before it's too late.

'We can cancel the hotel,' I say to Anne, the fear in my voice making it wobble. 'It's not too late.'

'Your mum asked for you to be there when her will was read,' she answers me gently. 'There must be a reason why and if you don't find out what it is, I think you'll regret it. You might finally get some answers.'

I don't share her expectation, but I nod. Whatever reason my mum had for requesting my presence at the solicitor's tomorrow, I don't think it's something to feel hopeful about.

'We'll have a spot of dinner at the hotel and an early night and you'll feel much more prepared in the morning. One night, that's all you have to stay for.'

A whistle blasts somewhere on the platform and a volley of beeps inside the carriage indicates the doors are closing. The moment to escape has passed.

'I doubt the reading will even take that long . . .'

Anne's voice fades to background noise as my mind drifts back to my medical notes. Among the hundreds of pages of mistruths and supposition was one absolute, incontrovertible fact: no matter how many times they asked me, cajoled me and even threatened me, not once did I concede that I made Limey Stan up.

Chapter Eight

MEMORANDUM

To: Dr Patrick Malloy, head of clinical services
From: Dr Stacey Ardern, consultant child and adolescent
  psychiatrist
Subject: Cara Belling
Date: Monday 16 January 1995

As requested, here is the background into this morning's incident, ahead of you being in receipt of my full report.

Cara has been more lucid in recent weeks, directly correlating, I believe, to an adjustment to her medication. As a consequence, she has allowed me to draw her into conversations about the events leading up to her brother's death, although she will not discuss his actual dying. Her willingness to talk about him is, I consider, the most significant breakthrough since her admittance six months ago.

Today, however, in a bid to better understand her feelings towards her brother, I raised the cancellation of her birthday party in June. Thanks to information provided by her father at the point of her admission, we know that she reacted violently to it being cancelled, pushing over a coffee table and sending plates of food flying at her brother and causing him to sustain a cut and bruising to his face. When I broached the subject today, Cara became highly agitated and assaulted a staff nurse and myself using her fists. Neither of us was injured and the child was restrained in accordance with protocol.

Chapter Nine

Cara

It's a picture-perfect autumn day when we leave the hotel the following morning, the sky a cloudlessly bright shade of cerulean and the air invigoratingly crisp. Yet I pay no heed to its beauty as I scour the faces passing us by on our way down the high street. Every person feels like a potential threat to my well-being, that they might recognise me and expose me for who I really am, and I hate feeling like this. Normally, I go about my business with quiet confidence.

Anne spent breakfast trying to placate me, by reasonably pointing out that it is very doubtful anyone would match the nine-year-old me to how I look now, but I remain on high alert. She does at least agree that we should attend the will reading, then collect our bags from the hotel and get the first train out of here.

'Do you remember the town much?' she asks as we walk along.

'A bit. I remember the Red Lion. The shop below it used to be Woolworths.'

I point at the statue that now preens over a pound shop on the other side of the road. The lion appears freshly painted, its intricately carved mane glossily reflecting the sunshine bouncing off it. A couple of years ago, it had deteriorated to the point of collapse, paint flaked off, plaster crumbling, until the local paper staged a campaign to fund its renovation. I know this because I read the online version of the paper every day; the town may have changed since I last set foot in it, but I am fully versed in how.

'This road's been pedestrianised since I was last here,' I say, nodding at the cobbled paving stones now covering the former expanse of tarmac. 'Cars used to come along there all the time. I remember when the market was on, it used to be a nightmare. Matty almost got run over once, running out from behind a stall.'

It was me who saved him. I saw the car coming before he did and managed to grab his arm and pull him out of its path. Matty was such a scatterbrain, easily distracted, never looking where he was going, so it was down to me to protect him. It was my job as his big sister. Whenever we went out to play, Mum and Dad would issue stern instructions 'to keep an eye on your brother no matter what' and I did. I kept him safe. The only time I couldn't was when Limey Stan came for us.

I dreamt about Limey Stan again last night. This time, Matty was there and he cheered and clapped as Limey Stan put his hands around my neck and squeezed. I woke up clawing at my throat in panic and Anne, who was in the twin bed next to mine, had to get up to calm me down. She kept saying over and over, 'It was just a dream, Cara, it's not real.' But that's the thing, isn't it? People say ghosts aren't real either and yet one managed to kill Matty.

If I'm honest, the adult me who's absorbed reams of studies and read hundreds of books on the paranormal since I was a teenager struggles to believe in ghosts. How could anyone not question whether they exist, when there is so much empirical evidence weighted against it? Yet the nine-year-old me who survived the summer of 1994 makes me believe. To that Cara, who lives constantly in my head, Limey Stan was as real as Anne is walking alongside me now and she refuses to entertain even the tiniest doubt of what I can remember from that day. The rest of the world might think I smothered Matty by wrapping him so tightly in the curtain he couldn't breathe, but the two of us cleave to the truth, refusing to let it go. You didn't kill him, her voice will remind me, and I nod, knowing that I didn't. It was Limey Stan.

'What else has changed?'

Anne's question drags me back to the present and I spend a few seconds absorbing the other alterations to Heldean's centre. Some are more subtle, like the taxi rank moving from opposite the indie DIY store on Queen Street to a slipway round the corner – the DIY store is now a Costa – but, as a whole, it is achingly familiar, and as we continue towards the building where Mum's solicitors are, I feel myself being absorbed into the town's fabric again, as though I am walking into fog.

'What number is it again?' asks Anne.

'Eleven.'

'This is it then.' She halts outside a town house next to a bank. There are wrought-iron railings outside, with a neatly engraved sign attached: Fairlop Solicitors. Est. 1929.

My insides suddenly drop, as though I've been tipped upside down. Almost instinctively, Anne reaches for my hand and I clutch hers in return.

'I can't do this.' My voice is almost a squeak.

Anne doesn't say 'Of course you can' or 'There's nothing to worry about', or express any other sentiment designed to make me pull myself together. She knows me better than that.

'What's worrying you the most, kiddo?'

'Seeing all of them,' I answer honestly.

'I expect they're just as nervous. It's been a long time for you all.'

I'm trembling now and it has nothing to do with how chilly it is today.

'What do I say to them?'

'Whatever feels right. Just remember you're here because your mum wanted you to be. You have her permission.'

She's right. I am not here by default. Whatever emotions have been stirred up within my extended family by her dying, this was Mum's wish. As for how I'm feeling, my emotions currently oscillate between anger that she never sought to end our estrangement before she died and sadness that it's too late now. Being forced to think about her makes me realise I never stopped loving her or my dad, despite them turning their backs on me, and the grief I'm feeling has taken me by surprise.

'Let's go in,' I say.

Still hand in hand, we mount the steps. Someone inside buzzes us through the front door and then, before I have time to catch my breath, there they are, waiting silently together in the reception area, their eyes fixed on the doorway in anticipation of my arrival.

My family.

Chapter Ten

Cara

Isn't it funny how the mind works? My immediate thought on being confronted by my flesh and blood for the first time in a quarter of a century is not how pleased I am to see them, but that I have woefully misjudged what I am wearing. My relatives are in smart funereal black, while I am casual in jeans. Anne did question my choice of attire before we left the hotel, but I didn't have anything more formal with me, and because I've never attended a meeting such as this, I didn't know it was an option I should've considered. But clearly the occasion of a will being read demands tailored formality, not skinny-cut grey denim and beaten-up ankle boots and a man's navy peacoat bought for a fiver from a charity shop. At least Anne's keeping the side up in her M&S slacks, even if she is wearing an anorak with them.

My second thought is that I don't want to say hello first, but fortunately I'm saved from doing so because my aunt gasps out loud on seeing me, which diverts everyone else's stares from me to her.

'Oh my God, you look so much like your mum,' she breathes. 'I – I wasn't expecting you to.'

I am at a loss as to how to respond. Sometimes I struggle to remember what Mum looked like as a whole. Instead, I recall only snatches of her – the blood-red colour she painted her nails, the scratchy, lacquered blondeness of her bobbed hair, a particular T-shirt she wore with a sequinned butterfly on the front. I do have photographs of her – the social workers arranged for me to be sent a couple when I was at the Peachick – but I could be staring at images of an actress, so little recognition do they spark. But I don't believe I resemble anything of the woman in them: she exudes glamour and poise, while I, with my mid-brown 'unfemininny' cropped hair and minimal make-up, will never be described as such.

'So alike,' Karen murmurs again.

As we size each other up, I am struck by how different my aunt looks compared to the memories I have retained of her. She was always the dark to my mother's light, inheriting the height, brunette hair and medium frame of my grandfather, while Mum was petite and fair like Nan. Now Karen is as blonde as Mum used to be and she's rail-thin, which serves to accentuate how much she's aged since I last saw her.

Thrown, I look to Anne. She steps forward.

'You must be Karen. I'm Anne, Cara's foster mum. We spoke on the phone.'

They shake hands, but my aunt doesn't budge from her seat and her gaze never leaves me. I feel the heat of it on my face, warming my cheeks until they go pink. I stare back, wondering what she's thinking. A fraction later she lets me know.

'Thank you for staying away from the funeral.' Then she briskly lifts her handbag from the floor and pulls it onto her lap, a protective barrier between us.

The exchange leaves me winded, as though she's delivered a well-aimed kick to my gut. I suppose I thought she might at least be a bit friendly. But before I can retreat to the opposite side of the reception where there are empty seats, the young man seated to her left catches my eye. I realise who he is and I'm astounded. 'Ryan?'

'Hi, Cara. It's been a while,' he says unsmilingly.

The last time I saw my cousin was the night before Matty died. I remember it being one of the few nice days we'd had that July – sometime later, I looked it up and discovered 1994 had one of the wettest and coldest summers on record, which seems fitting with hindsight – and we'd gone to the Rec with Matty and our other cousin, Ryan's sister, Lisa, after school to play on the swings. Lisa bought us sweets on the way with her pocket money.

As cousins, Ryan and I squabbled like hell and even had fist fights on occasion, but we were close. Not as close as he was to Matty though, being the same age, and as I drink in his appearance, my mind is invaded with questions about what my brother would've looked like now. The dark curls that defined Ryan as a child are now shaved to a bristly shadow to counter a receding hairline – would Matty have lost his hair by now too? Or would his bright blond hair simply have faded to mouse brown, the colour of our dad's? At six, he was short for his age – would the years have given him height to top mine? Would we still adore each other, like we did then?

I swiftly blink back tears, then ask Ryan how he is. He's about to reply when Karen hisses at him to be quiet and he meekly obeys. I look down at her, but she won't meet my gaze again. Thinking about it, her appearance hasn't altered that much from memory – she's still the hard-faced cow I remember she could be.

The third member of their group is a woman with long reddish hair sitting next to Ryan, who I'm certain I've never met – it's not Lisa, put it that way. I assume she's Ryan's partner or wife. Whoever she is, she keeps her head bent and her eyes firmly fixed on the floor.

Finally my gaze falls on Gary, Karen's husband and my step-uncle. He does meet my eye, flashes me a tight smile, then quickly turns away.

Reunion over, I'm about to take a seat across the room when the receptionist pipes up. 'Mr Taylor is ready for you. Third door on the left along the corridor.'

I let Karen and her entourage go first: I wouldn't put it past her to elbow me out of the way if I took the lead. Hostility is emanating from her in waves, but where at first it unsettled me, now it's making me more resolute. Mum wanted me here and there's nothing she can do about it.

'I'll wait out here,' says Anne. 'Come and get me if you need me.'

I nod. We already agreed it wouldn't be appropriate for her, a stranger, to be privy to my mum's final wishes at the same time as her family learns of them. I am nervous about being in the meeting alone, but I know I can walk out any time I want to.

I'm half expecting to be ushered into a vast ornate room with dark walnut-panelled walls and enormous wing chairs for everyone to be seated in, like they do in film scenes when there's a will reading. Stephen Taylor's office is no bigger than a box room, though, overlooking a car park, and only two of us can be seated while the rest stand. I am surprised when Karen takes one of the chairs next to his desk and signals at me to take the other.

Taylor appears flustered by our number. 'Sorry about the lack of seating. We're not used to accommodating larger groups,' he says.

His face is so boyishly youthful that I am tempted to ask how long he's been practising law and does he know what he's doing? Maybe Mum got a cheaper rate for using someone so junior.

He clears his throat.

'These days, we usually divulge the contents of a will to family members individually. The practice of will reading by executors only began because the majority of people years ago were illiterate and needed someone to read it for them.' None of us react to his impromptu history lesson and his face flushes. 'However, my client, Anita Belling, stipulated she wanted family members all to be present at the same time, so here we are.'

He's so nervous, I can see a rash beginning to creep from the rim of his shirt collar towards his chin. Then I realise it's me who's making him nervous. His eyes keep darting in my direction, but it's as though he daren't allow his gaze to settle. I understand: he's labouring under the belief he knows all about me and why I am estranged from these people. I do him a favour and ease his awkwardness by looking away first.

Taylor plucks a single piece of paper from a foolscap envelope on his desk. Karen shifts forward in her chair, but my posture does not alter. I am not expecting anything from my mother in this scenario: I have thought long and hard about why she wanted me here and I have concluded that it's probably that Dad left me something when he died and she's finally passing it to me. Perhaps his treasured collection of ELO vinyl – on the rare occasions he was at home when I was little, he would put his records on for me to dance to and I used to adore twirling around the front room with him, laughing and singing. It was my hallowed time with Dad, when he was my Mr Blue Sky.

'Well, this isn't going to take long,' says Taylor, emitting a chuckle that, on realising its inappropriateness, he tries to cover with a cough.

As Karen shifts again in her seat, he clears his throat to speak.

'I, Anita Belling, residing in Heldean, Essex, do make, publish and declare this to be my Last Will and Testament, hereby revoking all Wills and Codicils heretofore made by me.' Taylor looks up, makes sure we're all paying attention, then continues reading. 'To my sister, Karen Mary Johnson, I leave my collection of jewellery and the sum of £25,000 . . .'

My aunt's face begins to purple. She's not happy. She goes to say something, but Taylor shuts her down by raising his hand.

'I give and bequeath all remaining tangible personal property that I own at the time of my death, including the property at 16 Parsons Close, Heldean, together with all unearned premiums on all policies of insurance and pension in force and effect at my death with respect thereto, to my daughter, Cara Marshall, née Belling.'

My jaw drops. There is a commotion beside me, my aunt is on her feet saying something, Gary's voice has raised too, but I am too stunned to react. I cannot believe Mum's left me the house.

'I don't want it,' I blurt out.

Taylor's eyes widen and the commotion next to me suddenly subsides.

'I beg your pardon?' says the solicitor.

'I don't want it.'

'But these are your mother's wishes,' he says, clearly perturbed that someone would want to turn down a bequest that could amount to hundreds of thousands of pounds.

'You heard her, she doesn't want it,' says Karen sharply. 'And if she doesn't, it goes to the next of kin after her, doesn't it?'

The subtext is painfully obvious: it will go to her.

'I don't want the house. I don't want to ever set foot in there again. And I don't want to stay in Heldean while it gets sorted out,' I state emphatically.

Taylor's face slackens with relief.

'You don't have to. We can arrange for the property to be sold on your behalf – we have a conveyancing department who can handle the transaction for you. It can take up to a year to settle an estate, but there's no need for you to stay in Heldean during that time.'

'That house is my sister's! It belongs to my family. How dare you try to dictate what happens to it!' Karen howls at the poor man.

'It's your niece's now,' he blusters back.

'She's no niece of my mine.' She turns to her husband, who is as aghast as she is. 'I can't believe Anita's done this to me.'

I stand up too. 'Look, we can sort this out. I don't want the house. If you want it, you can have it.'

Taylor tries to interject. 'Wait, it's not that simple—'

'Now hang on a minute and let Cara speak,' my uncle interjects. He throws an encouraging smile my way and I return it gratefully. 'If our niece wants to give it to us, let her,' he adds.

Now Taylor is on his feet too, trying to regain control of the proceedings. 'Actually, I hadn't finished reading.'

We all turn to him, surprised. His hands twitch as he raises the piece of paper again.

'Should my daughter, Cara Marshall, née Belling, wish to rescind her right to my estate, the total value, excluding the sum set aside for my sister, Karen Mary Johnson, shall be split equally between Peachick Hospital in London, for the treatment of children and adolescents with mental health conditions, and The Fostering Network, a charity that supports those in the lives of fostered children.'

Overcome with shock, I clasp my hand to my mouth. I don't believe it. Mum wants to leave money to the institution where she abandoned me and to the organisation that put me back together once I left it? My mind scrabbles to work out why: by recognising their significance to me, what was she trying to say? That she was sorry I needed them in the first place? That she's made her peace with what happened? That she's forgiven me?

I lower my hand from my mouth. I don't need her forgiveness – she should've asked for mine. She should have believed me when I said I didn't kill my brother.

Chapter Eleven

Cara

We miss the next train back to London, then the next one and the one after that. Neither of us is fit to make the journey home yet: Anne is as stunned by my mum's will instructions as I am. We've gone back to the chain hotel where we stayed last night and are sitting in its small, perfunctory bar, me on my second Scotch and Anne sipping on a white wine diluted with lemonade because it is only lunchtime still. Our overnight bags are now in the storeroom behind reception, waiting for whenever we do decide to depart.

Anne hasn't asked me what I plan to do. Instead, she asks me again if I have any idea why Mum wrote her will the way she did.

'Not a clue,' I say, taking another sip and wincing as the fiery liquid burns a path down my throat. I don't even like Scotch that much, but it was the first drink that sprang to mind when the hotel staffer who served us said I looked as though I could do with something strong. 'It feels wrong to even consider keeping the money, but Mum giving me a get-out clause to give it away doesn't make my decision any easier. I could easily give it all to The Fostering Network, but that would screw up any chance of reconciling with the rest of my family.'

'Not to the Peachick as well?'

'You know how I feel about that place,' I mutter darkly.

'You associate it with being removed from your family, but that wasn't the Peachick's fault. You could've ended up somewhere else, you just happened to be sent there. The job of its staff was to get you better and they did. The Peachick has also helped countless other children over the years, so I think it's as deserving of the money,' says Anne sagely. 'Anyhow, is that what you hope might happen with your family – reconciliation?'

I answer carefully, mindful not to bruise her feelings. Fostering is transient and she and John have always understood and accepted that, but it doesn't mean they become any less attached to the children in their care and when a relationship grows to be like ours, it takes on a deep familial significance. The last thing I want is for Anne to think that after all she has done for me I wish to replace her with another mother figure, but I cannot stem the feelings of affection I still have for my wider family, however conflicted those are.

I wouldn't call it love, more like yearning: I never gave up hope that one day Mum would get in touch, especially after Dad died and she was all on her own, and so I did secretly hope that when Karen saw me at Fairlop's she would be pleased to see me and end our estrangement and through her I might be able to reclaim a little of what I lost. Now, witnessing how raw her hostility is, I realise I've been foolish to think that might happen.

But I do not tell Anne any of that. Instead, I lie. 'I only care about seeing my cousins, because we used to be close.'

'It would be nice for you to have family to call on,' Anne nods.

I reach over and take her hand, rubbing the lined, liver-spotted back of it with my thumb pad. Had I not known that she and John were pretty much the only foster carers willing to take me on, I might have wondered if it had been deliberate that

I was placed with them, so the contrast between Anne and my mum would make me forget what I'd lost. Anita Belling was the kind of woman who never went to the corner shop without a face full of make-up and her nails done, whereas Anne saves her dressing up for special occasions, like New Year's Eve, her favourite night out of the year, when she and John book into one of the big hotels in Manchester for a dinner and dance.

'I have you and John for that,' I say, smiling. 'I've lasted this long without them, so if I do decide to give everything away instead of to them and they hate me for it, I think I'll be fine.'

Anne nods appreciatively and I let go of her hand.

'I wonder why Lisa wasn't there, though,' I muse.

Of them all, she was the one I was least worried about seeing. Although four years older, Lisa always made time for me, was a confidante of sorts, and I hero-worshipped her because of it.

'I think there were enough spectres at the feast already.'

I laugh, then let out a groan and rub my temples roughly with my fingertips. 'Why didn't Mum leave a proper explanation with the solicitor about why she decided to write her will like that? She must've realised how upset Karen would be and, in all honesty, I don't blame her. Mum has nothing to do with me for twenty-five years and all of a sudden she's leaving me the bulk of her estate. If I was Karen, I'd be pissed off too.'

'I suspect your mum did leave you an explanation,' Anne remarks.

'If she had, surely she'd have left it with Fairlop's?'

'Perhaps she did, in a fashion.'

I stare at her blankly. 'I don't understand.'

'The keys.'

She's referring to a set of keys Taylor handed me before I left his office. The sight of them made me gasp out loud, because the key ring bunching them together was a cream ceramic heart with the word 'Mummy' etched on it in red, which I bought for my mother with my spending money on holiday on the Isle of Wight when I was seven. She'd been a bit moody all week and I wanted to cheer her up.

I fish the keys out of my coat pocket now and turn them over on my palm. What message was she trying to send by giving me the key ring back? Am I supposed to be grateful she kept it all these years?

'I think if she's left you anything else, perhaps something that she didn't want her sister to be privy to,' Anne adds pointedly, 'then that's where it'll be – at the house.'

The blood drains from my face. 'I can't go back there.'

'I know you don't want to, but I'm starting to think the house might be at the root of all this. Why else leave it to you and hand the keys over like that, if she didn't want you to set foot in it ever again? I don't mean to sound flippant, but perhaps she thought it was time for you to lay the ghost to rest.'

'That's what I'm most worried about,' I mutter, taking another sip. My glass is almost drained and I'm seriously tempted to order another. A Scotch-fuelled slide into oblivion is more appealing right now than dealing with the mess my mum's just dumped at my feet. 'I get what you're saying, but it's a bad idea, sorry. I can't go back there.'

I couldn't even bring myself to send letters to the house, even though I desperately wanted to write to my parents, asking them to visit me after I moved to Morecambe. The thought of writing down that address made me feel faint and I was angry my parents chose that place over me.

'In that case, let's go somewhere you haven't been before.'

I raise an eyebrow. 'Such as?'

'It's time you visited your brother, Cara.'

Chapter Twelve

Karen

Karen goes straight upstairs on arriving home. Her and Gary's bedroom is at the rear of the house and if she looks out of the window to the far right, she can see the brow of the sycamore tree at the end of Anita's garden. Living close by to each other as adults was an ambition they had coveted since they were little and they couldn't believe how lucky they were to find perfect homes in adjoining streets. Gary and Anita's husband, Paul, hadn't been as keen – as brothers-in-law they rubbed along nicely, but they were too dissimilar to be close – but the promise of taking turns babysitting so each couple could enjoy nights out was a persuasive tactic that worked.

Karen grasps the sill to steady herself as a fresh wave of desolation crashes over her. She misses her sister so much it has manifested as a physical pain in her chest. She rubs the area that aches with the heel of her palm, as if that alone might dispel her despair. This grief is nothing like any she has ever experienced – not even her parents dying had made her feel like this. It makes no odds that she had been prepared for it, from sitting with Anita in the consultant's office as he uttered the words 'stage four' and knowing exactly what he wasn't saying, to organising the service at St Mary's to her sister's exact stipulations. The sense of loss is far more visceral, far more brutal, than she could ever have anticipated.

Then there is Cara. Her grip tightens on the sill. The shock of seeing her niece hasn't abated on the journey home: if anything, she is more shaken up now that some time has passed. She hadn't imagined Cara would grow up to resemble Anita to the extent she does, but the chestnut brown eyes, the slope of her nose, the way her mouth moved as she spoke – there is no disputing she is her mother's daughter.

Karen was the third person ever to hold Cara. Her niece was minutes old, still sticky and warm, and Karen was consumed by instant, fierce love for her. She already had Lisa by then, an adorable four-year-old who was the centre of her world, and she was thrilled Anita could now experience that special mother-daughter bond for herself. That both of them ended up being estranged from their daughters is an irony not lost on her now.

Actually, that's an incorrect summation of her relationship with Lisa, she thinks. It's not that they are estranged – Lisa attended Anita's funeral and stayed at theirs – it's that they are strained. Any conversations between them are painfully polite, to the point that they feel more like job interviews, with her the prospective employee asking endless questions and Lisa responding like the reluctant candidate who's decided they no longer want the job. The detachment that now exists between them hurts Karen deeply and she doesn't know what she did wrong to trigger it.

Suddenly a voice booms up the stairs.

'Want a cuppa?' Gary yells.

With a sigh, Karen lets go of the sill.

'Yes, please,' she shouts back.

If he's making tea, that means he's stopped ranting at last, she thinks. His tirade about the injustice of the will had begun on the steps of the solicitor's office and continued all the way to the car park and back home and she knew why – Gary was expecting them to be left the house, because publicly that's what Anita had promised. Her sister had told them she wanted it to be transferred into Karen's name but for Ryan and Natalie to live in it, rent-free, while they saved up enough money to buy out a half-share that would then go straight to Lisa. In the absence of her own children, Anita had told Gary she wanted her niece and nephew to benefit and he was grateful, because he was frustrated he couldn't lend Ryan a deposit himself. Still, his annoyance at Cara now getting everything was preferable to having to listen to Natalie crying in the back of the car that she and Ryan were never going to be able to afford their own house now.

How guilty Karen had felt listening to her son urge Natalie not to give up hope. He said that as a family they should look at ways to challenge the will and Gary immediately seized upon the idea, suggesting Anita must have been mentally impaired to want to leave all that cash to Cara, the daughter she had hated for all these years. Karen had to force herself to agree, because not doing so would make them suspicious.

She glances a final time at the sycamore, then heads out of the bedroom. Descending the stairs, she curses her sister for her honesty. Anita could have easily died without saying a word about rewriting her will, but instead she blurted it out and now Karen feels like she's betraying her family by pretending she knew nothing about it and that she's as shocked as they are to learn Cara gets almost everything. She hopes her outrage was convincing enough, because Gary will never forgive her for not telling him at the time. He'd have tried to change Anita's mind had he known.

But knowing about the amended will doesn't mean she has to go along with what it says. Cara doesn't deserve to inherit Anita's wealth – and Karen will do whatever it takes to make sure she doesn't receive a penny of it.

Chapter Thirteen

Cara

If the man is surprised by my question, he doesn't show it. I suppose working in a cemetery, surrounded by death and grief all day, every day, makes you immune to the unusual and the unexpected. He hasn't introduced himself, but the badge on his breast pocket proclaims him to be Jim Thompson, Cemetery Operative. Working in a place populated by dead bodies is not a job I'd be comfortable doing and my shoulders ripple in a shudder to confirm it.

Jim takes his time to answer, repeating my question as he stares first at the grave we are standing beside, then back at me.

'How many can you fit in? I suppose that depends on whether they're being buried or have already been cremated. If it's ashes in an urn, you can pack quite a few into one plot.'

'Buried,' I say quietly.

Mum hated the thought of being cremated. I must've been only eight at the time, but I remember her telling me, after the service at the crematorium when my great-granddad died, to make sure she was buried when it was her time. Dad would've gone along with what she wanted and agreed the same method for himself. He always did everything she said.

'Well, your standard-size grave can take two interments, but allowances can be made for three, if it's agreed when the plot is purchased. It's so's we know to dig down deeper,' Jim replies. 'If it's more you're wanting to bury, you'll need to buy a bigger plot than standard.'

I want to ask if my parents got to choose the plot's location, or whether it was the job of some faceless clerk at the council to assign it. The biting wind that carried us through the cemetery is less vicious here, tempered by the ancient oak spreading its branches above us. It's the most secluded spot you could find in a place where isolation is king, and while it is only early afternoon still, the shade of the tree makes it seem more like dusk.

But I let the question die on my tongue, scared of saying too much.

Jim is now reading the inscription on the pale marble gravestone, his lips twitching as he says the words back to himself under his breath. I wonder if he reads books in the same way.

Matty Belling 1988–1994

Paul Belling 1958–2001

Loving father and son, reunited in peace

It kills me to see Matty's name etched there next to Dad's when he had only just mastered how to write it himself when he died. His given name was Matthew, but apparently I couldn't pronounce that when he was brought home from the hospital, so my parents shortened it to Matty for my benefit and the nickname stuck. At school, he was Matty B though, because there was another boy in his class called Matthew and Matty didn't want to be confused with him. Dad used to say Matty B sounded like a DJ's name, which was fitting because, like me, my brother loved music and loved to dance.

My mind wanders for a moment and I imagine us in our

twenties, in some dark, sweaty club in Ibiza, lost in the rhythm of a thumping bassline, our arms aloft and grinning madly as we dance side by side, even closer now as adults than we were as kids. Or maybe Dad was right and Matty would have been behind the decks, spinning the tunes to bring the heaving crowd to its feet, me passing him cold beers as he worked.

Then I force the images from my mind because I am perilously close to breaking down and I don't want to. I won't cry, not here, not in front of this stranger.

'There's three in here now, though,' Jim announces. 'Them two mentioned, and the one we put in almost a fortnight ago. Those are her flowers.'

He gestures to the wreaths and bouquets propped up around the grave's marble edging, which is currently moved to one side to allow for Mum's burial. The flowers are wilting now, time and an absence of water robbing them of their richness. The smallest bunch is mine, but you wouldn't know it from the card. I didn't sign my name in case Karen threw them away. I had the florist write 'RIP X' and hoped Mum would know it was me, however dopey that might sound.

'There's definitely not room for any others?' I ask. 'Can you not bury the coffins side by side, rather than on top of each other?'

Jim is becoming exasperated at being forced to labour the point. 'No, it wouldn't be allowed in this plot. Three's all you're going to get in there.'

So they didn't make room for me.

I swallow hard and my disappointment scrapes down my already dry throat. I don't know why I thought my parents might have decided to accommodate me when they bought the plot after Matty's death – until the will reading, nothing that's happened in the past twenty-five years has given me any hope that they would – I just thought maybe.

Jim looks at me, then back at the headstone. I flinch, knowing what's coming, but it's too late to walk away.

'Hang on, are you her – the Belling girl?'

My silence is all the answer he needs.

Jim recoils so violently it's as though he's trying to separate his facial muscles from the skin covering them.

'What you did to that poor family of yours—'

'What exactly did I do?' I snap back. Two neat Scotches on an empty stomach have given me a headache and I'm feeling testy and in no mood to be judged by this stranger. 'Go on, you tell me what you think it is I did.'

Unfortunately, it turns out Jim isn't the kind to back away from a confrontation and his eyes blaze with indignation as he aims his index finger at me, stabbing the air between us to make his point.

'All them lies you told, pretending it wasn't you. Making up all that stuff about Limey Stan to get yourself off the hook.'

My breath catches in my throat at the mention of the name. It's been a long time since anyone other than Anne or John has used it in my presence, but I should not be surprised it trips so easily off Jim's tongue: Limey Stan is part of Heldean's folklore and perhaps the only thing the town is notable for.

'I didn't make it up,' I croak.

Jim looks disgusted. 'How can you stand there after all this time and still say that?'

I realise what a terrible mistake I've made coming to the cemetery – now Jim will tell everyone he knows that Cara Belling is back in Heldean and that she stood by her poor family's grave and spun yet more lies.

'Why don't you just admit what you did?' he barks at me.

I am welded to the spot, trembling like a frightened puppy, when I feel Anne's hand take my arm and I sink gratefully against her. She was waiting on the path for me and must've heard the heated exchange and has come to rescue me.

'It's time to leave,' she says.

'Go on, tell the truth!' Jim roars at me, his face so close to mine, I can see the metal fillings plugging his molars.

The sensible thing would be to ignore him and walk away. But jacked up on 75 per cent-proof alcohol, I suddenly lose all sense of control and what's right. Wrenching my arm from Anne's grasp, I rush towards him and he almost topples backwards onto the grave in fright.

'For the last time, it wasn't me who killed my brother,' I scream in his face, spraying it with spittle. 'Limey Stan did it!'

Chapter Fourteen

MEMORANDUM – STRICTLY CONFIDENTIAL

To: Dr Patrick Malloy, head of clinical services
From: Audrey Shay, senior administrator
Subject: Transcript of session #39 between Dr Stacey Ardern, consultant child and adolescent psychiatrist, and patient 426-001, Cara Belling
Date: Friday 31 March 1995

[Preceding discussion was about a book CB is reading, *The Worst Witch All At Sea*]

SA: Do you also know the story of Aladdin and the genie of the lamp, Cara?
CB: Yes, I saw the film too. I liked the genie.
SA: He was a funny character, yes. You know, I've always wondered what it would be like to be granted three wishes like Aladdin was. I think it would be quite difficult to choose what to spend the wishes on.
CB: I think it would be easy.
SA: What would you choose for your first wish?
CB: To go home. I don't like it here. Why can't I leave?

SA: We've talked about this already, haven't we, Cara. We want you to go home too, but we have to make sure you are better first. You understand that, don't you? Good. So, what would be your second wish?

CB: I'd like a kitten, a black one. I'd call it Smoky.

SA: That's a great name for a cat. Mine's called Trevor.

CB: Trevor? That's a boy's name!

SA: I know, but it suits him. He's a tortoiseshell. Trevor the tortoiseshell.

CB: Mummy wouldn't let me get a kitten.

SA: Did she explain why?

CB: Because they sometimes pee against furniture and she didn't think I'd look after it properly. I would've though. Matty said he'd help me.

SA: Is getting a kitten something you and Matty talked about then?

[CB doesn't answer, but SA's reaction suggests the child nods/ shrugs affirmatively]

SA: That's good. You and Matty talked about a lot of things, didn't you?

CB: Yes. I miss talking to him. [Sounds tearful]

SA: Cara, are you ready to talk to me about what happened to him?

[1.16-min pause while CB cries]

SA: I know this is very hard, but telling me what happened is important if I'm to help you.

[23-second pause, then CB mumbles]

SA: Sorry, I missed that. What did Matty say?

CB: Before he got hurt, he said if I woke him up that night he would help me catch Limey Stan.

SA: So he wanted to help you?

CB: Yes. I didn't force him to get out of bed like the policemen said I did and I didn't make him come downstairs and hide with me. It was his idea as well.

SA: The hiding place was a good one. I've seen a picture of your front room and the curtains were very thick and very long.

CB: That's why I said go behind them.

SA: Did you have to hide for long?

CB: I don't know. It felt like a long time. Matty started giggling and wouldn't be quiet.

SA: I think I might've been scared hiding in the dark like that. Were you?

[13-sec pause, no response from CB]

SA: Did you and Matty have a plan for what you were going to do once you caught Limey Stan?

CB: No. I just wanted to tell him to stop waking me up and to go away.

SA: You never got to do that in the end.

CB: No, because he hurt Matty and I got in trouble for it. [Cries again. Tape continues for 2.06 min with only sound being CB upset, followed by pause for 31 sec]

SA: I have an idea. Why don't we talk about what happened that night as though you are telling me a story? I know you like stories, because you just told me you like *Aladdin* and *The Worst Witch* books. How about I start the story off, then you take over? If you get stuck along the way, I can help. Does that sound good?

CB: Okay.

SA: I'll start then. Once upon a time, there was a little girl called Cara, who lived with her mummy and daddy and her brother, Matty. One day, Cara said she was very tired because something was waking her up in the night.

CB: It was a ghost called Limey Stan, who would knock on the walls and make noise coming up the stairs, and Cara wished he would go away. [CB sounds excited retelling the story]. It went on for a long time. One night, Cara asked her brother Matty to help her catch Limey Stan and he said yes. They went downstairs in the middle of the night and hid behind Mummy's new curtains in the front room. Matty said it was an adventure and she was the best big sister ever.

[15-sec pause]

SA: Cara and Matty thought they could jump out and surprise Limey Stan?

CB: Yes, they did. Matty thought it was funny hiding at first, but then they heard creaky noises on the stairs and in the hallway and he got scared and started to cry and he tried to get out from behind the curtain, but he was all tangled up. [Sounds upset, but not crying] Cara tried to pull him out, but her arms got tangled too and it was so dark, she couldn't see what she was doing properly.

SA: Cara then tried to call for help?

CB: No, she was too scared to. It was like her voice got stuck in her mouth and wouldn't come out. All she could think was that Limey Stan was getting closer and she had to rescue Matty. But she was too late. Limey Stan was standing in front of the curtains and Matty made a horrible noise, like he was trying to cough, and then he fell on the ground.

[19-sec pause]

SA: Then what happened?

CB: Cara thought Limey Stan would get her next, so with all her might, she pushed her way out from behind the curtains and ran upstairs and locked herself in the bathroom until Mummy and the police came to find her.

[26-sec pause. CB breathing heavily]

SA: Is that the end of the story, Cara?

CB: I don't want to play telling stories any more. Can we stop now?

70

Chapter Fifteen

Cara

Anne takes my arm and pulls me away, but it's not until we are outside the gates to the cemetery that I stop shouting and my body stops trembling from the sudden and violent release of rage, the emergence of which surprised me as much as it did Jim. I have been so adept at containing my upset all these years that I had not realised quite how livid I am about what happened to me until now. I was nine years old, a kid, and I was locked up in hospital like I was a dangerous psychopath when I did nothing wrong.

I pitch forward, panting heavily, and put my hands on my knees to steady myself. Anne stands beside me and gently rubs my back between the shoulder blades.

'Don't let it get to you,' says Anne. 'It's a pointless waste of emotion.'

I straighten up, still thrumming with anger.

'How can I ignore it? You heard what he said.' My body shudders again. 'I can't believe he expected me to stand there and admit to something I didn't do. The bastard thinks he knows what happened, but he couldn't be more wrong.'

Anne doesn't flinch from my wrath. She's been on the receiving end of so many outbursts as a foster carer that she knows not to take it personally.

'No, he doesn't know what happened, which is why you should ignore him. He's not important.'

'But he is, in a way, because he's the sum of every other person in this town who thinks I'm the girl who killed her brother and spun a stupid ghost story to cover it up. But it wasn't a story,' I snarl, my fists curling involuntarily at my sides. 'I know what I heard and I know what I saw.'

For a split second, Anne's expression shifts, like a light bulb suddenly dimming, then flickering back to full brightness.

I reel back, my anger rapidly abating as I'm filled with dismay. Not her too, not Anne.

'You still believe me, don't you?' I whisper.

'Don't be silly, of course I do.'

'No, you don't – I saw your face just then. You think I made it up, like everyone else.'

She reaches for my hand, but I step backwards. I don't want her touching me.

'Please, Cara. I do believe you.' Where a moment ago her expression showed doubt, now there is desperation. Anne knows how seismic the fracture will be in our relationship if she can't convince me in the next few seconds that she means what she's saying. 'I've always believed you never hurt your brother,' she says.

'But you never believed me about Limey Stan,' I state, aghast.

Anne flounders for a reply.

Tears fill my eyes and I hold up my hand to stop her bothering.

'One of the few things that's kept me going all these years is knowing that you believed my side of things, you and John,' I manage to say, though my voice is strangled with grief. This feels worse than finding out my mum was dead. For twenty-three years, Anne's been my mainstay, my protector and my friend. If I can't count on her, who can I count on? 'You're the only grown-ups who ever cared enough to listen to me. I thought you believed me. I need you to believe me still.'

Anne is close to tears herself now. 'You've misunderstood me. I never doubted your story, not once, and nor has John.'

'So you agree it was Limey Stan then?'

My body is taut with apprehension as I wait for Anne to answer. The air shifts around us as the wind picks up and the rustle of leaves in the trees towering over the entrance to the cemetery grows louder, but I bet you could still hear a pin drop, so dense is the silence between us.

Seconds tick by, until I start to lose patience and prompt her. 'Well?'

Anne's face fills with anguish. 'When you first came to live with us and told us all about Limey Stan and what he'd been doing all those nights before your brother died, you spoke with such conviction that we knew you believed he was real and that was good enough for us.' She wavers for a moment, then ploughs on. 'But did we question whether a ghost could have been responsible? Yes, I'll admit we did. I mean, the idea of it—'

The enormity of what she's saying hits me squarely, like a sledgehammer to the guts.

'I don't want to hear any more,' I say, knowing that if I let Anne continue talking, I might blurt out something I'll regret forever. 'I need some air.'

'We're already outdoors,' she says despairingly. 'Please, Cara, let me explain properly what I mean by that.'

I shake my head, my heart aching with sorrow. 'It's clear what you meant. And you know what, I've questioned it myself. Gone over and over that night in my head, trying to remember every last detail.' I gulp down a shuddering breath. 'And the thing I always come back to is that I was the only other person there. So if you think there couldn't have been a ghost called

Limey Stan in my house that night, what you're actually saying is you think it was me who did it.'

Anne gasps. 'No, that's not what I'm saying at all. You're twisting my words. We know it wasn't you who smothered Matty with that curtain. The police got it terribly wrong.' She dissolves into tears, but instead of going to comfort her, I start to back away. 'Where are you going?' she pleads.

'I need to be on my own. Just for a bit. I'll see you back at the hotel.'

'No, wait, don't go off like this, Cara, not when you're so upset.'

I pause for a second. Part of me wants to stay and have her reassure me that everything's going to be okay, like she used to when I first went to live with her and John. It was only after leaving the Peachick that I finally felt free to grieve for Matty, and Anne would sit with me as I cried myself ragged thinking about him dying and how it was my fault and I should never have got him out of bed that night. But I can't bring myself to seek comfort from her now. It feels like a huge void has opened up between us and I don't know how to bridge it.

Ignoring her pleas not to go, I turn my back on her and walk away, and as I do, it's impossible to tell which of us is crying the hardest.

Chapter Sixteen

Daily Mirror

12 NOVEMBER 1994

EXCLUSIVE: Belling babysitter: 'I caught Cara hurting her brother'

The babysitter who regularly looked after the 'Heldean Haunting' children told police that nine-year-old killer Cara Belling often lashed out at her little brother – and on one occasion seriously injured him.

Detectives interviewed student Daisy Carmichael, from Chapel Road, Heldean, two days after six-year-old Matty Belling was found dead at his family home in Parsons Close in the early hours of Saturday 16 July. A police investigation has since concluded Cara suffocated him behind a curtain after they argued about her waking him up in the middle of the night.

The transcript of Miss Carmichael's police interview, exclusively obtained by the *Daily Mirror*, reveals Cara broke Matty's wrist three months before his death, while their parents Anita and Paul were drinking at their local pub.

Miss Carmichael, 20, had put the children to bed and was

downstairs watching television when she heard Matty screaming.

'I went upstairs and found Matty lying on his bedroom floor clutching his wrist. He said Cara had wanted to give him a Chinese burn, but he refused, so she bent his hand right back at the wrist and he heard it crack,' Miss Carmichael told officers.

An X-ray confirmed Matty's wrist was fractured. Asked if Cara had shown any remorse for hurting her brother, Miss Carmichael said the girl became angry when confronted.

'She said Matty was putting it on and that she hadn't pulled his hand like he said. She didn't like me telling her off,' said Miss Carmichael.

The children's identities became public knowledge after details of the police investigation were leaked to newspapers – including Cara's outrageous claim that a ghost called Limey Stan was responsible for killing her brother.

Miss Carmichael confirmed in her statement that Cara had tried to hoax her about the 'ghost' too.

'She kept going on about Limey Stan coming into the house at night and creeping up the stairs. I knew it was a silly ghost story she'd made up to scare Matty and I told her not to say it in front of him because he'd wet the bed at night. But Cara wouldn't stop going on about it. She was trying to trick everyone.'

The police have been criticised in some quarters for implicating Cara in the absence of conclusive forensic evidence. While fibres from her clothing were found on the curtain used to smother Matty, fibres matching a dressing gown owned by her father, Paul, were also found. Nor could they retrieve any clear fingerprints from Cara from the curtain material.

However, as Mr Belling was away working at the time and therefore had an alibi, the presence of Cara's clothing fibres and the history of violence towards her brother convinced detectives to conclude she was to blame.

Miss Carmichael also believed Cara was capable of killing her brother – and blamed herself for not speaking up to save him.

'I stopped babysitting as much because I couldn't control her,' she said. 'Now I wish I'd made it clearer to Anita and Paul how concerned I was about her behaviour. I will never forgive myself for not speaking up more. Matty might still be alive if I had. His sister is truly wicked.'

Cara has been detained indefinitely at a children's psychiatric hospital in London. Her age means she is too young to be charged with any offence.

Chapter Seventeen

Cara

I really did have no intention of ever setting foot in my childhood home again. No sane person would experience what I did, then knowingly put him- or herself in harm's way again by returning to the scene of such a traumatic episode. But Anne's reaction changes everything. She and John were the only people I could rely on to reassure me that I did not lose my mind over Limey Stan and the thought of them sharing their doubts behind my back all these years is devastating. Yet it has also solidified a thought that's been kicking about the back of my mind ever since I found out Mum died: the only way I'll ever silence the disbelievers and live a normal life without hiding who I am is to prove beyond a shadow of a doubt that I wasn't lying then and I'm still not lying now. So that means going back to the house where it started. It's mine now and I shall rip it apart brick by brick to prove my innocence if I have to.

From here, the journey to Parsons Close will take me ten minutes on foot if I cut up a lane from the main road, then cross the railway bridge to reach the estate where the house is. My stride lengthens, the faster I walk, but as I round a corner to rejoin the main road, I lose my balance, my limbs still loosened by the alcohol I drank earlier. Suddenly I have a craving for more – call it Dutch courage, if you will – so I dart across the road to where there's a general store and select a cheap bottle of white wine from the chiller cabinet.

I don't normally drink to excess, certainly never in the day-time, but after that confrontation with Jim, the crushing hurt of Anne showing her true colours and the fear of what awaits me at the house, I need the cushioning effects.

Back across the road, I undo the screw cap and take a swig without removing the bottle from the plastic bag the shop assistant put it in.

By the time I reach the mouth of the lane, I'm feeling calmer, but no less determined. The bottle of wine is already a quarter empty.

Halfway along the lane, I expect to come across the primary school where I was a pupil before I went away. However, I already know from keeping up with the town's news that it was closed because of falling rolls and now occupying the site is a small estate of tightly packed modern homes.

I stop for a moment and the boxy new-builds dissipate from view as my mind replaces them with the squat, red-brick build-ing where I spent the early years of my education. Inside the main part of the school, its doors and window frames picked out in peacock blue, was the last classroom I was taught in and alongside that were three more classrooms, the main hall, staffroom and the head's office. Then, across the playground, umbilically attached to the main building by a raised corridor, was a modern annexe with more classrooms and the woodwork room.

I smile to myself as I picture the criss-crossed markings on the playground for netball, football and rounders – instinctively, we always worked out which was which. Then my recollection is assaulted by the shrill voices of my classmates taunting me as word of Limey Stan spread and I see the tree I used to run to cry behind is still on the site, absorbed into the new estate's landscaping. Quickly, I walk away and head for the railway bridge, another large swig of wine propelling me onwards.

By the time I reach Parsons Close, dusk is starting to draw a gloomy veil over the dregs of the afternoon. Some of the houses have lights already on and I hurry past, scared that if I linger for even a second I will attract unwelcome attention. The alcohol might be emboldening me, but it is also spiking my level of paranoia.

My old house is at the top end of the close from the direction I am coming in and being the last in the row meant we only had neighbours on one side of us, a lovely Asian family whose surname was Shakoor. They had three boys – Tishk, a teenager all us younger girls had a crush on, Amir, who was a bit older than Matty, and Raman, who was a bit younger – and twin girls who were toddlers back in 1994 and whose names I can't remember. Me, Matty, Amir and Raman used to play tag together in the street or we'd ride our bikes up to the Rec to use the playground if our mums let us. Scurrying past, I see their house is in darkness and I wonder who lives there now.

Suddenly I'm at the foot of the driveway next door and my insides somersault so wildly with a mixture of dread and expectation that for a moment I think I'm going to be sick.

I'm home.

Chapter Eighteen

Cara

The first person I told about Limey Stan outside of my immediate family was Evie, my best friend at school. We never saw each other outside of class – play dates structured and facilitated by parents were an anomaly back then – but from the moment we stepped inside the playground gates each morning, we fused at the hip and stayed like that until the home-time bell.

The first thing Evie said when I told her about Limey Stan was, 'But your house is so boring.'

She was right, in a fictionalised sense. Haunted houses featured in novels and films tend to be either crumbling Gothic mansions with dark corners and secret passageways or Victorian, multiple-storey terraces with ancient, creaking stairs. A 1930s-built, south-facing, bay-windowed detached suburban home with a side garage didn't scream horror then and still doesn't now. Indeed, as I stare up at the house that was for a time my childhood home, a maelstrom of emotions churning inside me, the only word that springs to mind to describe it is 'normal'.

And, if I'm honest, I shared Evie's scepticism. I hadn't actually seen Limey Stan at that point, so I could not say with any certainty what he was. It was more of a feeling that there was something in the house besides us, an insidious presence. I didn't know his name then either, that came later: I think I might've described him to Evie as 'this thing' that kept waking me up at night but that no one else in my family heard, and that was odd because they were all much lighter sleepers than me. Mum used to say it would take a truck crashing into the house to rouse me once I had nodded off, yet this thing was waking me up but not anyone else.

Slowly, I climb the driveway, then cut in front of the bay window to reach the open arched porch. I trail a hand over the familiar brickwork, a gesture of hello to the home I never imagined I'd set foot in again. The brick is cold and unyielding to my touch.

With a jolt, I see the front door has been replaced since I was last here – the day they carried me out, it was solid white uPVC, but the one I'm about to open is made from composite wood that's been painted black, with two frosted-glass panels inserted in the top half. I linger for a moment, unsure how to feel, let alone act. I don't know what I expect to find on the other side of the door, but it's certainly not anyone waiting to greet me with open arms and the thought of the house being empty fills me with sadness. I pause to drain the bottle of wine to stop myself turning on my heel and legging it out of here as fast as I can.

I set the empty bottle down on the doorstep and rummage in my pocket for the ceramic heart Mum's solicitor gave me and, with fumbling fingers, I isolate the key from the bunch that will open the door. The key turns easily and before I know it I'm inside. I shut the door quietly behind me, then bolt down the hallway, unwilling to linger there a second more than I have to. Yet as my hand reaches to yank open the door to the kitchen, I glance over my shoulder and my brain registers that the glass panels in the front door let so much light into the hallway now that the shadows where Limey Stan once hid have receded to the skirting. The pounding in my chest eases a little.

The kitchen stops me in my tracks, however. I do not recognise it at all. Like the front door, it has been updated in my absence, with shiny white cabinets and a black marble worktop replacing the oak of old. This isn't the house of my childhood, I think despairingly. It's a stranger's home and not recognising it frightens me just as much as being here does.

Yet for all its newness, the kitchen is shambolic. There are saucepans, casserole dishes and stacks of plates and utensils covering every inch of the worktop, all unused, six or seven plastic containers in a heap on the floor and some of the drawers and cupboard doors have been left wide open. Immediately, I think it is Karen's doing – she was so sure she was going to get the house that she must have started going through Mum's things to see what she could keep or chuck away. Anger nips at me as I forcibly bang shut the doors and drawers, then crouch down to pick up the plastic containers.

One in particular, an old ice-cream tub, makes my eyes widen with surprise and my 'Oh' fills the kitchen. Carefully, I prise off the cracked lid and, with trembling fingers, reach in to stroke the velvety branches of the snow-dappled fir tree and the round face of the ceramic snowman with the cheery grin and bowler hat that Mum and I used to decorate the Christmas cake with every year. There are two reindeer ornaments in the box as well, a mother and baby with matching red noses, and the sight of them brings tears to my eyes, because Mum told me she'd bought them the first Christmas after I was born as a sentimental nod to me and her. I recall Matty once asking where his baby reindeer was and being thrilled when Mum told him the cake was our special tradition and that she would think of something else for him. He was upset, but I did not rush to comfort him, because it was nice to have something that was just mine and hers for once.

Feeling the loss of them both keenly, I shut the lid and leave the box where I found it.

Rising to my feet, I glance out of the kitchen window above the sink and gasp. Even in the dying light, I can see the back garden is a tip; the once-manicured lawn is undetectable beneath waist-height weeds and they are choking the trunk of the sycamore tree at the end of the garden as well. The level of neglect shocks me: Mum always loved gardening and would shout at Matty and me whenever our ball, Frisbee or shuttle-cocks landed on her carefully cultivated borders. Now it looks as though it's been years since she was out here lovingly tending to them and my apprehension balloons: what was going on with Mum even before she became ill that her garden was in such a state?

The kitchen leads into a vast reception room that's also unfamiliar. There used to be two rooms here, one a designated dining area, the other the lounge, but the wall between them has been knocked through. A dining table still occupies the end of the room closest to the kitchen, but its surface has disappeared beneath piles of old newspapers, books and magazines. Then I walk to the opposite end of the room and my heart sinks further – this part isn't just messy, someone's well and truly ransacked it.

I turn on the overhead light so I can assess the extent of the damage. The light grey sofa, which looks fairly new, has been pulled away from the wall and its cushions upended, while the drawers from the sideboard I remember my parents buying when I was a child have been yanked from their apertures and their contents scattered on the floor. A bookcase in the alcove next to the fireplace is also missing what once crammed its shelves, novels now laid out like stepping stones across the carpet. On the walls, there are gaps where pictures must've once hung, the hooks still intact.

Then I see it, the coffee table with the black lacquered surface. It's lying on its side where it's been pushed over and my heart judders in my chest as I lift it upright and rub my hand over the smooth surface, delighting in its familiarity. Suddenly I'm a child again and it's Thursday afternoon, chips-for-tea day, and I choke down a sob as I think about Matty sitting beside me with our legs poking under the table as we watched telly and ate.

No matter what anyone else said, not my parents, our babysitter, the teachers at our school, no matter what was decided by strangers with official-sounding titles and foolscap reports who didn't know me, I loved Matty with all my heart and I would never deliberately hurt him. We bickered like normal siblings and I admit that sometimes I would get so wound up I would lash out, but Matty always pushed and hit me as hard as I did him and the wrist fracture he sustained was not my fault – we were playing and he fell. To say I did it on purpose is wrong.

Minutes tick by as I sit there thinking about him. All this time later and I still miss him so much it hurts. I think about him constantly. I try not to acknowledge the day of his death because it feels too much like the anniversary of when my life was ruined, but, instead, every year on his birthday, I take the day off, unless it falls on a weekend, and visit the tree I had planted in his memory at the nature reserve near my home. I sit beneath it and pop open a can of lemonade, the fizzy drink he loved the most when we were little. Then I toast him and have a good cry, which is what I'm on the verge of doing now. Being back in this house without him is even harder than I imagined it would be and it's unleashed a torrent of grief that is impossible to control, so I give in to the tears and let them flow.

God knows how much later I finally stop crying. I lean against the sofa and wipe my damp cheeks on the sleeve of my coat and that's when I hear a noise in the hallway – the faint but distinct squeak of a shoe pressing down against a floorboard. I freeze, unsure if I really heard something or whether my mind's playing tricks on me. I've had a lot to drink and I'm jittery, being in the house after all these years, so I could've easily imagined it. I stay still, my heart thundering in my chest as I listen intently, my hands gripping the edge of the coffee table so tightly my fingertips whiten.

The second squeak is louder.

I let out a cry; the noise is coming from the hallway, just like before. Only this time, instead of moving slowly up the stairs towards my bedroom as it did most nights, it's coming closer to where I am now.

Panic surges through me, but my body ignores my brain's frantic commands to stand up and get the hell out. It's as though I'm pinned to the floor by an invisible force. When a third squeak resonates from the hallway, closer still, I try to shout a command to leave me alone, but only a wordless rasp comes out. Fear has paralysed every part of me, although the voice of nine-year-old me is screaming blue murder inside my head.

Limey Stan's been waiting all this time for us to return.

I hear the door between the hallway and kitchen swing open and then the clatter of the plastic boxes skidding across the floor. Powerless to do anything else, I squeeze my eyes shut. It seems a crazy thing to do, but it's what I did when Matty died beside me – I was too scared to look then and I am too scared to look now.

Limey Stan has reached the doorway to the lounge. I can hear him breathing, a shallow, ragged noise that is as menacing now as it was then.

He moves forward. Barely three paces must separate us now.

I squeeze my eyes tighter.

Chapter Nineteen

Cara

Yet when he speaks, Limey Stan's voice sounds nothing like the guttural growl I've committed to memory. It is softer, higher and surprisingly polite.

'Excuse me. How did you get in here?'

My eyes fly open. The man addressing me from the doorway resembles nothing of Limey Stan. For one thing, this man is dark-skinned, of Asian descent, and I've always been certain Limey Stan was white. I slump forward and bury my face in my hands, somewhere between crying and laughing, as relief courses through me.

'What are you doing here?' the man asks, his tone firmer this time.

'I could ask you the same,' I shoot back, finding my voice at last. I have no clue why this stranger is here or what his intentions are, but his presence is not threatening: if anything, he looks concerned.

'I saw the light on and came to check it out, because this place is meant to be empty.' He peers at me through narrowed lids. 'Hang on – Cara?'

To my amazement, he breaks into a grin.

'It's me, Tishk!'

He takes a step forward into the room. The sudden movement

makes me feel vulnerable in my position on the floor and I scuttle sideways like a crab. His face falls.

'You don't remember me. I'm Tishk Shakoor, from next door. You and Matty were friends with my little brothers . . .'

He stops abruptly. I use the pause to clamber ungainly to my feet.

'Of course I remember you,' I say, and I feel a flicker of something I have not felt in a long time: delight. There aren't many people connected to my childhood that I have good feelings about, but Tishk is one of the few. He was older than me, by about seven years, but it didn't stop me having a huge crush on him as a kid. I think he knew – I wasn't the only girl locally to adore him and all of us would giggle and blush profusely in his presence, even Lisa – but he was sweet about it and always chatted to us. He even taught me to tell the time because I found it confusing and my parents had given up trying. It was one of the best afternoons of my childhood when he did that.

We stand awkwardly for a moment and I don't know whether he expects me to shake his hand or hug him. In the end, I do neither and shove my hands in my coat pockets.

'I didn't know your parents were still living next door.'

'They're not. After they retired, they moved to the Midlands to live with Amir and his family. They kept the house though and I'm living there for the time being.' He hesitates. 'I'm really sorry about your mum. She was a lovely lady.'

I don't know how to respond to that, so I don't. 'How are your mum and dad keeping?' I ask.

I always envied the Shakoor kids for how their parents were. It wasn't just that they were always around, unlike our dad, who worked away most of the week, but Mr and Mrs Shakoor were present. Most of the time, Mum was impenetrable to me, a daydreamer lost in her own thoughts. Sometimes I'd have to say the same thing five times before she registered I was talking to her, let alone standing in front of her. She was never quite all there.

'They're good, thanks. Older, but healthy.' He pulls a face. 'Sorry, that was insensitive of me.'

'It's okay. So, are you living on your own next door?' It's a blunt question, but I want to know if there is anyone else I need to expect.

Tishk nods. 'Yep, it's just me. The family visits regularly and Amir often stays when he's down for work.' He pauses. 'He won't believe it when I tell him you're back. Seriously, it's such a nice surprise to see you again.'

As he beams at me, it registers that Tishk is even better-looking now than he was as a sixteen-year-old. He must be forty now, or nearing it, but his hair's still dark, to the point of almost being black, except for this one streak of silver running through his artfully styled quiff. He has a beard now too, although it's more stubble than hair, and he looms over me in height.

'How come your parents didn't sell up when they moved away?' I ask.

'They decided to keep the house as a rental investment. It's worked out well for me because when they moved, I decided to give up my job to do a PhD and I needed somewhere cheap to live while I did it. Mum and Dad said I can live there for the time being and they'll sell up when I've finished.'

Clearly there's more to the story, such as where he was living before, but Tishk doesn't elaborate. His gaze strays to the bay window and mine follows it. The curtains that hang there now are sill-length and beige in colour. I imagine the burgundy velvet full-lengths, among the folds of which my brother was smothered, were either kept as evidence or destroyed.

It upset a lot of people that I was too young to be charged in relation to Matty's death, my parents and wider family included. But, believe me, if I'd had a choice, knowing what I know

now, I would much rather have faced the inside of a courtroom and taken my chances in front of a judge than gone to the Peachick. In juvenile detention, I might've been able to stand up for myself; in the Peachick, any resistance to authority was medicated out of me. Hospital was the wrong place for me because there was nothing wrong with my mind and I told the doctors at the Peachick over and over that it wasn't my fault Matty died. Looking back, it's a wonder they ever let me out, but after two years of being there, a new doctor arrived to assess me and he declared I was well enough to re-enter society as long as it wasn't anywhere near home. I still don't know why I ended up in Morecambe of all places, though.

Tishk and I both look away from the curtains at the same time and our eyes meet. I expect to see revulsion reflected in his, as I did in Jim's at the cemetery, but instead he looks sad.

'We all missed you afterwards. It was never the same round here without either of you.' He hesitates and his lips pinch and twist as though his mouth can't quite work out how to form its next sentence. 'You know, none of my family ever believed you were responsible for Matty dying.'

I am shocked and say so. 'Everyone else did,' I add.

'In Islamic culture, we don't believe in ghosts – we recognise what's known as "jinn", a spirit that appears in either human or animal form that can be good or bad but isn't the spirit of anyone who actually existed, so not your grandparents or someone else from your family,' says Tishk. 'My parents always said your house must've been visited by a jinn that was pure evil for Matty to die.'

I am astounded Mr and Mrs Shakoor believed I didn't do it. That makes them the only adults who did.

'Why were they so sure it wasn't me?' I can't help myself asking.

'They thought you were a good kid.'

Tishk says it with such magnanimity that I am overwhelmed. If only more grown-ups had reached the same conclusion as his parents. Instead, they all believed the lies about me being hateful and aggressive towards Matty and towards other kids at school. Lies, manufactured to condemn me, because I don't remember my temper being any worse than any other child's and I'm pretty sure I was on the receiving end of as much bullying as others were. Certainly when word of Limey Stan started to spread – I blame Evie for that, because she told the other girls in our class what I'd confided to her about being woken up – I was picked on mercilessly.

'But what about afterwards, when people were gossiping and all the stories came out about me?' I ask Tishk.

At the Peachick, I was not allowed access to newspapers or televised news, so it was down to my social worker, an earnest young woman called Marie, to inform me that someone close to the police investigation had leaked the details to the press and given them my real name. The publicity surrounding the so-called 'Heldean Haunting' effectively killed off Cara Belling and forced me into a lifetime of hiding.

'My parents took no notice of what was said,' Tishk answers. 'They believed you, and so did the rest of us.'

He appears genuine, as though he really does believe I am innocent. I suddenly think of Anne and wonder if I was wrong to storm off like I did without talking it through. I at least owed her that.

'You were petrified of Limey Stan being in your house,' he goes on. 'I know that because Amir told me you couldn't sleep because you were so scared of all the noises at night and things shifting around. He said one time you were so tired you had a nap while sitting on a swing up at the Rec.'

I falter. 'Amir told you that?'

'Yes, he was worried about you. He told me what was going

on and asked me to keep an eye on your house at night.'

'How could you do that? It was happening well after midnight.'

Tishk grins sheepishly. 'I wasn't always the model Muslim son everyone thought I was. Sometimes I'd sneak out at night to meet up with my mates and stay out late. Amir knew but never said anything.'

I laugh, shocked by his confession. 'What if your parents found out?'

'That's the irony. They wouldn't have minded. Well, they wouldn't have liked me being out on a school night, because they were sticklers for passing exams, but they wouldn't have minded the friends I was hanging out with. They're third-generation Pakistanis born in England and believe we should live our lives in whatever way makes us happy. They've supported all our choices as adults,' he adds. 'Amir's wife is a white-Canadian Christian and both my sisters are unmarried and live with their boyfriends.'

'What about Raman?' The youngest brother, he was Matty's best friend out of school.

'He's single, like me.'

I make no reaction to the remark and instead steer the conversation back to that summer. 'Did you ever keep watch on our house then?'

'Only in passing, but I never saw anything.'

I want to talk to him more about what he remembers of that time, but I don't trust myself not to say the wrong thing and I certainly don't trust him yet. Yes, I knew him all those years ago, but I don't know him now. What's to stop him repeating this conversation to others? For all I know, he could be recording me right now, on the phone he's holding.

'Well, thanks for checking on the place,' I say, hoping he'll take the hint and leave.

'You didn't answer my question.'

'What question?'

'How did you get in?'

'Oh. Right. Mum's solicitor gave me the keys. She's left me the house.'

Tishk's eyebrows shoot up his forehead. 'Really?'

'Yep, and I am as surprised as you are.' I pause. 'Hang on, how did you get in?'

'Spare key. Your mum gave it to me after she had the front door changed, just in case she locked herself out, or for emergencies.'

'When was that?'

'Three years ago,' he says with a smile. 'My PhD is a slow work in progress – I actually moved back to start work on it a year before that.'

If Mum gave Tishk a key, that suggests they were on good terms. Good enough to chat regularly? 'Did she ever mention me?' I blurt out.

He shakes his head a fraction too quickly. 'We didn't speak much, only in passing really. My parents said after your dad's accident, she kept to herself. I didn't even know how ill she was until an ambulance arrived one day because she'd collapsed with pneumonia. I came round to see her after she was discharged and that's when she said she'd been diagnosed with cancer a few months before. She went into the hospice not long after.'

I think about Mum collapsing and then I remember the ambulance that came to the house for me and suddenly I'm assailed by nausea. The effects of the wine are profound now and I gulp down a deep breath.

'Are you okay?' Tishk asks, frowning.

I decide there is no point lying. 'Actually, I think I'm drunk.'

'I guessed as much.'

'That obvious?'

'The swaying is a giveaway, as is the empty wine bottle I found in the porch.' He shrugs. 'I'm not judging. It can't be easy coming back to this place after all this time and after your mum's died. Look, why don't you come next door with me and I'll make you a coffee?'

'I can't. I need to sort this mess out. I think the place has been burgled.'

Tishk reacts with shock. 'No way.' He looks round the room. 'Are you sure?'

'The house was always immaculate when we were kids. Mum worked as a housekeeper for a time and keeping things spick and span rubbed off on her. Even if she wasn't well enough to tidy and clean it herself, I would've thought she'd have got my aunt or someone else to help.' I think about the state of the back garden. 'Maybe she let her standards slip when she was sick, but this still doesn't look right, does it?'

'You're asking the wrong person. I grew up in a household with two adults and five children, so neatness isn't a concept I'm familiar with. Do you want me to call the police?'

He holds his phone aloft, but I shake my head. Suppose Mum had lived in disarray in her final weeks – how stupid would I look if I reported it? Plus, I really do not want the police poking around. 'I'll see if anything's missing first.'

'How will you know?'

I'm sure he doesn't mean to be hurtful, but his question pierces my heart. Of course I won't know, because I don't have a clue what belongings my mum had. I hate that I don't know. I turn away before he can see how upset I am and begin shoving the cushions back on the sofa.

'Do you want a hand? I can stay and help. I'm working on a fifteen-thousand-word paper at the moment and I'm in no rush to get back to it.'

'I'll be fine.'

'If you're sure.' He sounds disappointed. 'I'll be off then, but if you change your mind about that coffee, pop over.' He hesitates for a second. 'Have you thought about what you're going to do with the house now it's yours?'

The words spill from my lips before I even realise what I'm saying.

'I'm going to come and stay for a bit and get the place straight before I sell it.' Am I? 'The garden needs some serious work first.' I hate gardening. 'I'm going to ask for a leave of absence for a few weeks, unpaid if necessary. I think my boss will say yes.' She will, because Jeannie's lovely like that.

He brightens. 'So we'll be neighbours again?'

'I guess so.'

He must sense my trepidation, or maybe my expression gives it away.

'It'll be okay,' he says gently. 'Nothing bad is going to happen.'

'I know. The house looks so different now, it's not the same place.'

It is different, yes. But what I cannot bring myself to tell Tishk is that it still feels the same. Since we've been talking, the air around me has grown heavy and my body is rigid against it. I'm also experiencing the same sense of foreboding that had me cower beneath my bedclothes, waiting to hear the creak of footfall on the stairs, or the drag of a chair being moved across the floor without being pulled or pushed. It was unsettling and hostile back then and it feels exactly the same now.

'There's nothing for you to be scared of,' Tishk says solemnly. 'Not when I'm just next door.'

If that's true, why do I feel so frightened?

Chapter Twenty

Tina (Home)
online

You'll never guess who Jim from next door's just seen up at the cemetery!!!!!

Who?

Cara Belling. Bold as brass, visiting her brother's grave.

NO WAY! Did he speak to her?

Cheeky cow had a go at him!!!! Jim told her she should admit what she did instead of making up shit about ghosts.

Good for him. Can't believe she's had the nerve to come back.

Her mum just died.

Yeah, saw that in the paper. Poor cow.

The mum, not CB. Anita was lovely.

Jim said CB's as hard as nails now. Wouldn't want to get on the wrong side of her, put it that way.

I'm really shocked she's come back.

I told Jim he should tip off papers, make a few bob. But he's worried it'll be traced back to him as he was the only person there. Council wouldn't be happy. He's made me promise to keep quiet, but had to tell u of all people!

I'm glad you have!

Do you reckon she definitely did it?

Are u mad? Of course she did!

Evie always thought she was telling the truth. They were so close as kids.

E's too nice for her own good. Will u tell her about CB being seen?

I don't know. Don't want her upset with baby on way. Hopefully CB was making a one-off visit and I won't have to worry about it.

Here's hoping.

Chapter Twenty-One

Cara

Saturday sees me return to Heldean with Mustard in tow. The few days in between have been spent tying up loose ends at work, mainly because Donna's relentless probing about where I was going slowed matters down considerably. My refusal to tell her anything beyond the bare minimum – there has been a death in my immediate family and I am taking a couple of weeks off – drove her to distraction and already I have had three texts since leaving the office yesterday asking if I am okay and proclaiming that if I ever want to talk, she is happy to listen. She is the last person in the world I would confide in about the situation I find myself in, but so conflicted are my emotions at the moment that I find myself thanking her for the offer.

The house feels more hospitable today, possibly because I am sober, but more likely because the second we arrived, I turned on all the lights and pulled back the curtains as far as they will go to vanquish any shadows. A handwritten note from Tishk that I found waiting for me on the doormat has also eased my anxiety at returning: he's left me his mobile number and wrote that if I need anything to phone him at any time. It's reassuring to know there is someone I can call upon next door.

Outside, it's raining heavily and my hair and jumper are soaked from bringing my suitcase, Mustard's bed and belongings, and a couple of boxes of supplies into the house from my car. Mustard is going to miss his daily walks along the estuary, but there is a country park a five-minute drive from here that should suffice in the meantime and, when I get round to clearing it, he will be able to go into the back garden too – a treat after living for three years in a first-floor flat. Leaving him to sniff around downstairs, I haul my case upstairs so I can change out of my wet top.

My decision to stay in the house before I put it up for sale still surprises me. Never once did I think I would end up living here again. This house is not a place of comfort for me, nor is it somewhere I can relax: it represents death, loss and the dissolution of my childhood, and coming back after the will reading did nothing to change my opinion of it. Being here freaks me out. But I also know, as it dawned on me that same day, if I am to ever change people's perception of me, or rather of Cara Belling, I need to unravel once and for all the mystery of what happened in 1994. The police investigation ruled out anyone else being in the room with us when they laid the blame squarely at my door. Mum was the only other person in the house and she was asleep upstairs and only woke up when I ran screaming into the bathroom. So if it wasn't me, and it certainly wasn't her, what else could it have been but something unexplainable like a paranormal entity? So it's up to me now to find out exactly what Limey Stan was.

The day of the will reading, I ventured upstairs to use the toilet before leaving and afterwards peeped my head round the door to my old bedroom. It had been redecorated like the downstairs and it was actually a relief to see the walls painted white and the bed now a double. If I was to sleep in there again I did not want any reminders of what I'd missed out on growing up: hiding the fussy Laura Ashley wallpaper beneath posters of pop stars and actors; hosting sleepovers with Evie once we were at big school; sitting at my dressing table learning to apply make-up; daydreaming about boys as I danced to my favourite CDs. In Morecambe, I shared a bedroom with two other girls – me in a single bed, them in bunks. It meant companionship, but no privacy – I couldn't freely celebrate the milestones of adolescence as I would have done at home in Heldean.

On entering the bedroom with my suitcase, my phone, which is in my back pocket, pings with a text from Anne, wishing me good luck for today. She was so distressed when I met her back at the hotel that I did not have the heart to argue it out. I let her convince me that she'd never once doubted my story and in return I smiled and hugged her and pretended I was fine. Since then, with her back in Morecambe and me here, things have settled between us, but my trust in her is shaken. I did tell her about my plan to stay at the house for a bit, to which she reacted with surprise, but I did not elaborate further, nor did she ask. I do feel rudderless without her counsel and comfort and hopefully time will heal us, but for now I am very alone in this situation.

Somewhere downstairs, Mustard releases a volley of barks, so I shove the suitcase onto the bed and go back out onto the landing. The door to Matty's old bedroom at the other end catches my eye. It is pulled shut and still visible on the outside are the Panini football stickers he carefully positioned on it twenty-five years ago. The World Cup was staged in America in 1994 and Matty had reached the age where he'd begun to share our dad's obsession with football. I peer closer and see that no attempt has been made to peel the stickers from the door and it makes me wonder what I would find if I opened it – a refurbished guest room, like my old bedroom, or the preserved enclave of a six-year-old boy who also loved Power Rangers, *Mr Men* books and sherbet Dip Dabs? I decide I am not ready to find out yet.

When I get downstairs, Mustard is barking furiously at the

inside of the front door. He's not a particularly vocal dog as a rule, which was one of the reasons I adopted him: living in a flat put paid to me keeping a yappier breed. Through the glass panels, I see someone standing on the other side, but I'm sure the doorbell didn't ring, or maybe it doesn't work. Grabbing Mustard by his collar to stop him jumping up at our first official visitor, I open the door and, to my surprise, it is Karen, sheltering under a spotted navy umbrella. Her arm is extended and clutched in her fingers is a key. It takes me a second to realise why.

'Were you letting yourself in?' I ask, appalled.

She tips the umbrella back and looks me squarely in the eye. This is the closest we have stood since we were forced back into one another's lives and the proximity rattles me. Part of me wants to slam the door in her face but there is another minuscule part tugging at my insides that wants to throw myself into her arms – because a hug from my aunt is the closest I will ever get to being hugged by my mum again.

'I was.'

'This isn't your house.'

'I know. I thought I should check on it while it's sitting here empty. I wasn't expecting you to be here.'

Her harsh tone curdles the air between us. She looks down at Mustard, who cocks his head to one side as he gazes back at her.

'What breed is it?'

'He's a mix.'

'What's his name?'

'Mustard.'

'Is he friendly?'

'Yes, he is.'

She bends down to stroke him and he butts his head up to meet her hand, his tail wagging approvingly. As I watch them delight in one another, I steel myself by remembering it was

Karen's words and actions that expedited my estrangement from my parents and that she is not a nice person, because the temptation to drop down on all fours to be petted myself is strong.

When she finally lets Mustard be, I hold out my hand, palm up.

'I want my key back.'

Karen clutches it to her chest, like a child might their comforter. 'Why? I won't let myself in again.'

'I know you won't, because I'm taking the key back. This is my house now.'

I brace, expecting the Karen who erupted in the solicitor's office to bare her teeth at me again, but this doorstep version instead dissolves into tears.

'I know it's yours, that's what Anita decided. It's just so hard letting go of it. It's all I have of her now.'

The rain is coming harder now, driving down at an angle, and the canopy of Karen's umbrella bows against the onslaught. Mustard retreats into the hallway – for all his love of jumping in the estuary, he detests the rain – and, against my better judgement, I invite my aunt inside before she gets any wetter. There is a lengthy pause before she accepts.

'I'll leave this here,' she says, shaking the umbrella off, folding it half shut and propping it up against the wall just inside the door.

Nerves percolate in my stomach as she follows me along the hallway into the kitchen. I feel like a fraud, taking charge – she knows this house as well as I do, if not better, and she might well have racked up more time here, if you measure the hours she visited over the past quarter century against the nine years I lived here. But it's not a competition, I chide myself; it doesn't matter who has greater claim to the place – it's mine now.

I haven't had the chance to tidy the kitchen yet and Karen's face folds into a frown as she takes in the mess, which immediately confirms it wasn't caused by her sorting through the cupboards and drawers. Someone else had been in the house. But there is no time to dwell on that, because Karen suddenly asks me a question that robs me of all rational thought.

'How much will it take for you to leave Heldean and never come back?'

I stare at her, open-mouthed. Her expression remains impassive in return, but there is a flintiness in her eyes.

'It's money you want, isn't it? Otherwise you'd have told Fairlop's by now that you're giving the proceeds of the will to that hospital and fostering charity.'

Thoughts ping-pong around my brain as I continue to stare at her. How does she know I haven't spoken to the solicitors yet? Why are they discussing my financial matters with her? When did my aunt become so cold?

'So, what will it cost me and my family to make you go away?' She couldn't have said 'my family' more emphatically if she tried.

I swallow hard, desperate to quell the anguish that is surging up my throat and threatening to spill forth. I won't let her see how upset her comment has made me. But it has, horribly. I can see now that Karen will never allow me back into their lives and knowing that breaks something inside of me.

As she waits, one eyebrow hitched expectantly, a thought begins to grow in my mind like a balloon being pumped with air. It gets bigger and bigger until I know exactly how I will respond to her question.

'There isn't enough money in the world, Karen,' I say quietly. 'I'm staying put. This is my home town and I will not be driven from it again. You might have got rid of me twenty-five years ago by convincing Mum and Dad I was evil, but I won't let you force me out again.'

Karen's cheeks glow pink. She looks worried now. 'I never said you were evil. You were ill, delusional. You needed treatment.'

'I was not and I didn't. There was nothing wrong with me.'

'But you claimed a ghost killed your brother,' she exclaims. 'You can't possibly still stand by that? It's preposterous. There's no such thing as ghosts.'

I don't contradict her. 'If that's all you've come to say, there's no point continuing this conversation. I'll show you out.'

As I go to move, Karen reaches forward and grabs my arm with her right hand. I'm wearing a fairly thick wool sweater, but I can feel the brittleness of her fingers through it. She comes closer and suddenly I detect her perfume, a heady floral scent that instantly transports me back to my childhood. Mum might have been the more immaculately turned-out sister, but I always loved the way my aunt smelled.

Close to tears, I try to wrench my arm away, but her grip tightens.

'There's nothing for you here, Cara,' she says sternly. I duck my head like a child who doesn't want to be told off, still trying to pull away, but she gives my arm a shake. 'Look at me when I'm talking to you.'

I comply. Our faces are so close, our noses are almost touching. I never thought she looked much like Mum, but now, with her hair bobbed and dyed blonde, the same fringe cut into it, she could be her twin.

'You cannot stay in Heldean. I won't allow it. You being here is upsetting everyone.'

'You don't get to dictate what I do.'

My aunt appears startled, as though she wasn't expecting me to stand up to her. 'Well, in that case, I'll tip off the press,' she blusters. 'Once they find out you're here, they won't leave you alone.'

The threat throws me. I've spent enough time on social media to know what would happen if news of my homecoming got out. My notoriety would see me crucified in the court of public opinion and what would it do to Anne and John if the media muckrakes over my life? Their names might end up getting dragged into the public arena, and what if it affected their fostering? I don't want their livelihood ruined because of me.

'Is that what you want?' Karen asks me again.

I shake my head.

Satisfied that I've caved and will obey her demand, she lets go of my arm and puts her coat back on.

'We've already had the house valued by a few estate agents and Leonards' price was the most realistic. You can have the rest of the week to clear the mess up so they can take pictures for the marketing, then I expect you gone. Once the sale goes through, I want you to think long and hard about who really deserves the proceeds, because it certainly isn't you.'

Her audaciousness is breathtaking and it takes every ounce of self-restraint not to swear at her. Who the hell does she think she is? But I say nothing and nod docilely again to show her how compliant I am being.

I follow her to the door, meek in posture but raging with anger inside.

'I'll keep my key for now, just in case,' she adds, reaching for her umbrella and opening the door to a brighter sky and easing rain.

She's poised to leave, then turns back, and for a moment I'm filled with hope that she might change her mind.

'Goodbye, Cara. I hope to never see you again.'

I shut the door behind her and manage to resist the urge to slam my fist against it, because I know Karen will hear the thump as she walks away and I will not give her the satisfaction of thinking she has beaten me. Instead, breathing deeply to calm my anger, I retrieve my phone from my back pocket and open up the internet browser. It takes a few seconds to find the number I need. I dial it and a male voice answers.

'R. Smith & Sons Locksmiths, how can we help?'

'I urgently need all the locks on my house changed – doors, windows and a back gate. How soon can you come round?'

Chapter Twenty-Two

Karen

Picking through the puddles of rainwater swilling across the pavement, Karen struggles to keep the umbrella upright, her hands are trembling so much. She has never been one to enjoy confrontation and usually finds it difficult to articulate her feelings in the heat of the moment, but she is proud of how she tackled Cara. Her niece is under no illusion about how unwelcome she is in Heldean and any doubt Karen has about not supporting Anita's final wishes is being quashed by her utter conviction that Cara must not stay.

The caustic approach isn't the one Gary wants her to take and she wonders how he will react when she tells him she threatened to contact the press. Not favourably, she imagines, because he suggested she be more conciliatory, in the hope that by being nice to Cara, she will do right by Ryan and Natalie with regards to the house. Really, if he had his way, they'd be inviting Cara round for tea and making her part of the family again, a prospect that makes Karen's skin crawl. But she knows Gary has the emotional capacity to be more welcoming to Cara because his outrage over what happened to Matty has abated over the years. He remains terribly sad about his nephew's death, but the anger is not something he carries around with him constantly, as Karen still does.

One of the worst moments of her life was, and always will be, accompanying Anita to the chapel of rest for a final farewell. Personally, she would have preferred not to go, but Paul found the idea of seeing Matty laid out in a coffin too awful to contemplate and there was no way she could let Anita go alone. She still remembers her knees giving way as she walked into the dimly lit room and the horror of seeing her nephew laid out as he was. In that moment, she was overcome with hatred for Cara for what she'd done and that feeling hasn't diminished. In fact, seeing her standing in Anita's kitchen like nothing was ever the matter is making it stronger than ever, and it makes her sister's decision to leave Cara the house all the harder to bear.

It was during Anita's last prolonged stay in hospital, after she developed bronchial pneumonia because her immune system was so weak, that she suddenly brought up the subject of her will. The deterioration in her health meant getting her affairs in order had become a matter of priority.

'Please don't get cross,' Anita had ventured anxiously as Karen perched on an orange plastic chair beside the bed, 'but I've been thinking a lot about the house and I'm afraid I can no longer leave it to you for Ryan and Natalie to live there. I've had Fairlop's draw up a new will.'

Karen was dismayed, not because Anita had changed her will without telling her, but because she clearly found it a difficult conversation for the two of them to have.

'It's your house and your money, you can do what you want with it,' she'd retorted. 'I'm upset that you think I'd mind though.'

'I don't think that at all,' Anita assured her. 'But you're not going to like what I've decided. I'm going to leave some money to you, but the rest, including the house, is going to Cara.'

At first, Karen thought her sister was joking. When it became apparent she wasn't, she reacted furiously.

'Why on earth would you want Cara to have anything of yours?' she'd spluttered.

'Because it's rightfully hers,' Anita answered wearily. She sat up for a moment to readjust the headscarf covering her bare scalp, then slumped back against the mound of pillows. Karen found it almost too painful to watch; her vibrant sister looked diminished without the hair and eyebrows the chemo had taken from her and with her face hollowed out by illness. Every day she became a little thinner and every day she moved a little closer to death.

'Rightfully hers? After what she did?'

'I don't expect you to understand or agree with what I'm doing. But it's what I want to do and I'd like you to respect that.'

'I can't. I'm sorry. I haven't forgotten what happened.'

Anita turned on her, livid. 'And you think I have? How dare you! I live with it every single day,' she spat.

'I didn't mean it like that,' said Karen anxiously. With time hurtling by as Anita's condition worsened, she did not want to waste precious moments stoking a row between them.

'Do you remember what Cara was like as a child?' Anita had asked her then.

Karen's voice hardened as she remembered how objectionable her niece was. 'Of course I do.'

'No, not how she was when Matty died, I mean before that, when she was very little. Do you remember how tenacious she was? She would never relent until she'd got her way. It used to drive me mad when she wouldn't let things lie, like the time she wanted Paul to tie a swing to the tree in the back garden. On and on she went for days, until she wore him down and he gave in.' Anita fixed her gaze on Karen. 'That's why I'm doing this. Because I know that if I leave her the house she won't stop until she works out why.'

Karen shook her head in disbelief. 'I don't get it. Her actions destroyed your life – why on earth would you want to give her a single penny?'

'I've told you, it's rightfully hers.'

The steely stare on Anita's face told Karen she wasn't going to get a fuller explanation than that, so she decided not to push it. Instead, she returned to Anita's comment about Cara working out why she was doing it.

'Why don't you just explain it to her in the will,' she suggested. 'Or write a letter to be opened afterwards and leave it with your solicitor.'

'I don't want to write it in the will because it's private, between her and me, and I don't trust she'll receive any letter I write.'

'You don't trust your solicitor to pass something that important on?' Karen asked sceptically. 'They would have a duty to.'

'It's not that simple. The letter could get lost, or someone might intercept it.'

'I think you're being a bit paranoid, Neet. Your solicitor can handle it.'

'I don't want them to. Cara needs to work it out for herself.'

That baffled Karen and she said so. 'Why make it so hard for her?'

'I have to,' said Anita weakly. 'If I try to tell her in a direct way, it might backfire. I know it doesn't make much sense, but I know what I'm doing. Believe me, I've given this a lot of thought.'

'If you don't want to tell her straight out, can you at least tell me?'

'No, I mustn't.'

'But we've always told each other everything,' Karen pouted.

Anita reached over and clasped her hand and Karen was struck by how old and worn her sister's skin was to the touch. The pads of Anita's fingertips felt as though all the moisture had been squeezed out of them.

'I can't tell you, I'm sorry. You just have to trust that my reasons for not telling you are good.'

'If you don't want to say now, can't you write it down somewhere for me to read after you're gone?'

Anita had chuckled at that, until somewhere within her body, most likely in her liver where the disease was wreaking the most damage, she felt a stab of pain and cried out.

'Do you want me to get the nurse?' asked Karen worriedly.

'No, I'm fine. Just give me a moment.'

She'd closed her eyes then and Karen sat quietly holding her hand while she caught her breath. Eventually, her eyelids fluttered open again.

'I know me rewriting my will makes no sense to you, but Cara deserves to inherit my and Paul's money. We owe her.'

'Are you kidding me? You owe her nothing. She killed Matty!'

Anita reacted as though she hadn't heard Karen, gazing off into the distance. 'I used to go to see her in Morecambe. Once or twice a year at least.'

Karen's mouth gaped open in surprise. Anita had never breathed a word of those trips.

'Cara never knew though, nor did her foster parents. I would wait across the street from their house and would follow her to school. Then I'd go for a walk or sit in a café until it was home time and then follow her back. She grew up to be such a beautiful, lovely girl, but when she was eighteen, she left Morecambe and I didn't know where she moved to.' Anita turned to Karen, her face stricken. 'It was a terrible mistake to send her away. I should have let her come home after her hospital discharge.'

Karen had supported Anita's decision to let Cara be fostered after her time in the Peachick and even encouraged it, so to hear her say she wished she'd done things differently came as a shock.

'But you couldn't have had her home,' she'd offered up lamely. 'Even after she left the hospital, she still had to be monitored constantly. You weren't in the right frame of mind to do that; you were still grieving.'

'I should have brought her home and kept her safe,' said Anita firmly. 'Paul begged me to change my mind and I almost did, when she was thirteen, but the social workers said she was settled and happy with her foster parents and I didn't want to disrupt her life. I was too scared to.' Anita fixed her gaze on her sister. 'But now it's time for her to come home. The house is hers.'

It was a conversation they never repeated after that afternoon in the hospital: every time Karen tried to bring it up again, Anita simply refused to engage beyond saying her mind was made up and that Karen mustn't tell Gary or Ryan and Natalie because it was her business, not theirs. Anita got so worked up that Karen had no choice but to agree.

The rain is coming down even harder now – sheets of water that make it impractical for Karen to continue her journey without getting completely saturated. She takes shelter beneath the spreading branches of an oak tree at the end of Parsons Close to wait for the downpour to pass, and as she stands there, she contemplates how Cara is feeling about being back in the house. Is she, as Anita hoped, already trying to work out why she's been left it? Karen hopes she doesn't care and simply sells it as soon as she can.

Part of her wishes she could mull over with Gary what Cara might do next, but she daren't risk letting it slip that she'd known about the will and hadn't told him. Karen can't discuss it with Ryan either, because he is bound to tell his dad, and the same goes for Natalie, whose tearful reaction the other day showed clearly where her priorities lie.

But there is someone who might listen. Karen reaches into

her pocket for her phone and finds the contact she needs. Her heart thuds a little deeper as the number rings. Will her call be answered or will she be abruptly cut off and rerouted to voicemail, as often happens?

Today, to her relief, Lisa chooses to answer.

'Hey, Mum, is everything okay?'

It saddens Karen that her daughter automatically assumes something must be the matter for her to call and not that she's ringing just because. It puts her on the back foot and she has to force herself to sound upbeat.

'Everything's fine. I was just ringing to see how you are.'

'Good. Busy.'

The inference stings: I don't have time for this.

'Well, actually, there is something I need to tell you,' Karen begins nervously. 'Cara's come back.'

There's a sharp intake of breath down the line and when Lisa speaks again, her voice is strained.

'She's in Heldean?'

'Yes. She's staying at number 16. Auntie Neet's left her the house.'

Lisa swears loudly, then says 'Sorry' in an aside to someone. She's a senior researcher with the Justice and Social Affairs Research Unit within the Scottish Parliament, a job that inspires immense pride in Karen, but also regret that it has taken her daughter so far away to live.

'Oh, I shouldn't disturb you when you're working,' she says. 'I'm sorry, I didn't think.'

'I'm glad you did, Mum. Frankly, I'm staggered Cara's been left the house, but I'm glad she has. It's the least Auntie Neet could do.'

Karen is taken aback by Lisa's vehemence. 'Why do you say that?'

'Because Cara deserves it after what Auntie Neet did.'

Chapter Twenty-Three

https://theheldeanhaunting/blog

CARA BELLING RETURNS!

22 November 2019

Comments [3]

Well, this is certainly a post I never imagined (but had fervently hoped) I would be writing in my lifetime! It has been brought to my attention (by a well-placed source whose name I am afraid I cannot divulge) that after a quarter of a century Cara Belling has returned to the scene of her 1994 paranormal experience. Yes, she's back!

Ms Belling's return to Heldean follows the death of her mother, Anita, last month. What's more, I have learned that she is actually staying at the house where she encountered Heldean's most infamous paranormal resident, Limey Stan. In a further twist of the plot, my source also tells me that Anita Belling has left the house to her estranged daughter in her will!

This is quite the remarkable turnaround, as it has been well-documented, by others and myself, that Mrs Belling and her daughter have remained estranged since the events of 1994. We can only speculate, therefore, on what persuaded the mother to leave the property to her daughter, as my source confirmed that, sadly, no reunion took place before she died.

As avid followers of my blog will be aware, there were no further reported sightings of Limey Stan after the tragic death of six-year-old Matty Belling. However, it is not uncommon for spirits to respond only to the presence of certain people, so we must wait with bated breath to see if Ms Belling's return will prompt Limey Stan to show himself again.

I shall, as the leading expert on the legend of Limey Stan, be offering my assistance to Ms Belling, should she require it, and I will, of course, update you with developments when they happen, as I am sure they will. In the meantime, my investigative account of the Heldean Haunting is available to download as a 99p ebook if you click here.

Timothy Pitt, paranormal investigator

Chapter Twenty-Four

Cara

It is almost midnight when I finally get round to unpacking my suitcase, my sweater long since dried after getting soaked in the downpour. The locksmith came within two hours of my calling and I then spent the rest of the afternoon and evening tidying up downstairs. I tried to put things back where I thought they might belong, all the while trying to suppress how dismal I felt that I didn't know for certain if they were in their rightful places.

Equally as upsetting was what little evidence I found of my existence amongst the belongings – aside from the plastic tub of Christmas decorations, I unearthed only one framed photograph that I appear in, of the four of us dressed up for a distant relation's wedding, the buttonhole in my dad's lapel a giveaway of the occasion. I have a vague memory, prompted by the pink polka dot dress I'm wearing in the picture, of Matty and me pretending to be ice-skaters as we slid across a parquet dance floor at whatever venue it was. Because I was the taller, I'd always be Dean and would make him be Torvill, but he never minded because he was sweet like that. As a grown-up, a job in conciliation would've suited Matty down to the ground, but he wanted to be a builder like his hero, Bob.

The photograph wasn't on display but buried at the bottom

of a drawer, face down. Beyond that, there was nothing to suggest I was ever a part of the Belling family, or even once a resident of the house, which again makes me question what possessed Mum to leave it to me. If she wanted to taunt me with proof that I have been all but eradicated from their lives, then not including me in the will at all would have been a far less contentious way to do it. My omission would've spoken volumes. But by leaving me the house, she must've known I'd be compelled to return, willingly or otherwise, and I think Anne was right when she said an explanation could be hidden here. In the absence of anything relating to me beyond the photo and the Christmas decorations, I've yet to work out where or what it could be, but I shall find it, otherwise I'll drive myself mad wondering.

What I also didn't find during my tidy-up was a single thing relating to the circumstances of Matty's death. By that I mean my parents hadn't kept any news cuttings or books that mentioned what happened here on 16 July 1994. I didn't even come across his death certificate. I find this strange, because I've accumulated boxes of stuff about the Heldean Haunting. Or I had until about ten years ago, when Anne and John decided I was becoming obsessed, spending every evening poring over them, and spirited the lot back to Morecambe to store in their loft, out of temptation's way.

In what was once my old bedroom, there is a white chest of drawers and a matching wardrobe, both new additions, like the double bed. Cautiously, I pull open the doors to the wardrobe but find only some empty coat hangers, upon which I quickly place the only clothes I've brought that require hanging: two shirts and a pair of smart trousers; the rest can be folded away in a drawer. I have brought enough clothes for a two-week stay as I would take on holiday. Two weeks is also what Jeannie's given me in paid compassionate leave – if I choose to stay on beyond that, my pay stops and I'll have to put a wash on.

The last thing I remove from my case is a large Ziploc plastic bag containing half a dozen pill bottles and packets. The most potent among them is trifluoperazine, an antipsychotic I was first prescribed at the Peachick. It takes a really bad episode to force me to take it, and it has been two years since the last time – the tablets are probably out of date, I haven't even checked. I just keep them with the rest, just in case. The others are a mix of tranquilisers, sleeping tablets and antidepressants that my GP insists on prescribing me, and the last bottle, the biggest of the lot, is a super-strength, high-dose multivitamin, which I'm certain does me far more good than the rest put together. I can be an erratic eater when I am tired or stressed, often skipping meals because I cannot be bothered to cook, so I take it to counter the lack of nutrition in my diet and, placebo effect or not, it makes me feel healthier than any antidepressant ever will. I take the plastic bag and dump it alongside my underwear in the top drawer.

The bedding appears fresh and clean, but I decide to strip it anyway. I've brought my own duvet and pillows with me, for comfort as much as anything else, and Mustard watches curiously from his position on the floor as I pull the duvet off the bed and lay my own in its place. I don't usually let him sleep in my bedroom, but for my first night back in this house, I am making an exception.

He trots after me as I head for the bathroom to brush my teeth. I've left all the lights on, so the landing, stairs and hallway are brightly illuminated. I don't care what it will do to the electricity bill – if the place is in darkness, I won't be able to sleep.

As I ease the bathroom door open, Mustard suddenly runs to the top of the stairs and barks. 'What's up, mate?' I call out to him.

His bark drops to a low growl and that's when I hear it.

Tapping.

I cross the landing and crouch down next to him, putting a trembling hand on his collar. 'It's okay, boy,' I whisper.

The tapping is coming from downstairs and it's loud enough that I can hear it clearly over both Mustard's growling and the white noise of blood rushing in my ears.

This is how it started in 1994. Tapping sounds downstairs, loud enough to rouse me from my sleep and persistent enough to fill me with dread. I would tiptoe to where Mustard and I are crouched now at the top of the stairs in the hope I'd catch Limey Stan doing it and could beg him to leave me alone. But the tapping would stop then and the silence would rush up at me, squeezing the breath from my lungs. Frightened out of my wits, I'd scurry back to bed and pull the covers over my head, wishing I was brave enough to call out for my mum but not wanting to wake her or Matty because I didn't want them to be as scared as I was.

Tishk, I suddenly think. I could call him and ask him to come round: he said to, if ever there was an emergency. My breathing steadies a bit as I release my grip on Mustard's collar and reach round to my back pocket, but all my hand finds is a flat patch of denim and my heart sinks. My phone is still in the kitchen, where I left it charging earlier.

The tapping is getting louder. Now it's more like a bang and each time it reverberates, I flinch more violently. I venture down a couple of stairs, but I can't see where it's coming from. The lights are all on, I remind myself shakily. There are no shadows downstairs for anyone to lurk in.

'Come on,' I say to Mustard and he follows me down the carpeted stairs before his claws clatter onto the stripped floorboards lining the hallway. We head into the kitchen and I listen intently, but I cannot hear anything. The tapping has stopped.

Seconds later, I jolt as the noise starts up again and this time

I realise it is coming from the front room. Fear crawls up my spine. I don't want to go in there, not at this hour, even with the light on and the curtains wide open. But Mustard has other ideas and shoots into the room, barking madly. I force myself to go after him, but my legs give way as he makes a beeline for the bay window and he leaps up, claws clanking against glass.

That's when I see it.

Outside, the wind has picked up and a branch from the mature rose bush in the front garden is being battered against the window. That's what's making the tapping sound.

Nerves frayed, I exhale shakily, until suddenly I see a pair of eyes staring at me, reflected in the glass.

Mustard barks, but my scream is louder.

Chapter Twenty-Five

Cara

'I probably should've warned you Rascal likes to roam round your garden,' says Tishk, handing me the stubby glass tumbler he's poured some brandy into. He, of course, doesn't drink and instead sticks to water. 'He's nearly twelve, so it's been his territory for a long time.'

Great. Even the next-door neighbour's cat is more at home here than I am, I think to myself. Grimacing, I sip my drink.

Tishk came running as soon as he heard my screaming. Once I started, I couldn't stop, not even when I realised the yellow eyes staring back at me belonged to a big black scraggy cat and nothing more sinister.

He wasn't the only person to rush to my aid though. Standing awkwardly next to the sofa, fluffy purple dressing gown wrapped tightly around her, is Heather, who lives with her husband and children in the house directly across the street from mine. The noise of my hysteria woke her up and on peering through her bedroom curtains, she saw me through the bay window, backlit by the bright lounge light, and came straight over. Unless I'm much mistaken, I think she's worked out who I am, because she keeps casting wary glances my way.

She hasn't said anything to me though, directing all her comments and questions at Tishk. To be fair, I was too upset to engage with her when I opened the front door to the pair of them – Tishk had to hammer on it to get me to answer, his key no longer working now I've had the locks changed. The first thing I did when I calmed down was to give him a new spare.

'Is she going to be all right now?' Heather asks him.

'I'm fine, thank you,' I interject. I fix my gaze on her, but she still won't look at me and it's starting to piss me off. 'I'm sorry if I scared you.'

Her eyes widen at this and she pulls her dressing gown tighter across her ample chest. 'The screaming isn't what scared me,' she says. 'We just don't want any trouble.'

I catch the frown on Tishk's face. He knew Heather's name to introduce us, but I wonder how well he actually knows her.

'What kind of trouble?' I ask her.

She doesn't answer that and instead asks me how long I'll be staying in Parsons Close.

'A while.' Her lips purse as she absorbs my answer. 'Is that a problem?' I ask, sensing that it most definitely is.

'It's not for me to say.'

'But you want to, I can tell,' I say quietly. 'Go on, just say your piece and get out.'

'Cara, there's no need to be rude, she was trying to help,' Tishk admonishes.

His intervention appears to embolden Heather, and her stance suddenly becomes confrontational as she puts her hands on her hips and glares down at me. The front of her dressing gown begins to gape and for a second I pray she's wearing something beneath it.

'If you must know, I've got two small children and I don't know if I'm comfortable with a convicted killer living across the way from us!'

Before I can react, Tishk steps in.

'You're being ridiculous. Cara was never convicted of any crime. She didn't kill her brother.'

I am so grateful for him standing up for me that the look of outrage on Heather's face doesn't bother me in the slightest. It is about time someone in Heldean did.

I cannot articulate how utterly defenceless and undefended I felt the last time I was here. I know from what I have read since about the police investigation that the physical evidence against me was flimsy at best. It did not matter to them, though – it felt as though my guilt was decided from the moment Matty was found with his lips turning blue. Most damning was the statement my mum made, although I only found this out much later when I applied to see my medical notes. A transcript from one of my sessions with my psychiatrist, Dr Stacey, revealed she had questioned me about my feelings towards Mum after she told the police she was one hundred per cent convinced I was responsible for Matty's death. I had no recollection of being asked about it, so seeing it written down in my notes like that was like a knife to the heart. If the police were my judge and jury, my mother's testimony was the unanimous guilty verdict.

'Are you mad? Everyone knows she did it!' Heather snaps at Tishk. 'Now she's living across the road from us like nothing's happened!'

Tishk shakes his head. I am not familiar with his grown-up facial tics and mannerisms yet, but the way his jaw has clenched tells me he is really angry. More gratitude floods through me.

'I think it's time you left,' he says. 'I'll show you out.'

Heather stalks out of the room without looking in my direction and I cannot resist calling after her.

'Nice meeting you – pop round for a cuppa if you fancy another chat!'

A few moments later, Tishk returns. I'm relieved to see he's grinning. 'I have a feeling she's not going to take you up on that.'

'Shame,' I deadpan. Then I sigh. 'Word's going to get round, isn't it?'

'It already has.'

'How do you mean?'

'There's this local guy, Timothy Pitt, who lives on the other side of Heldean and reckons himself as a paranormal investigator. He's got a blog that has a fairly large following and someone tipped him off that you're back. He's put a post up about it.'

I know the blog. It was compulsive reading before Anne and John intervened to wean me off my obsession with the 'Heldean Haunting'.

'That's just what I need,' I say morosely, 'bloody spooktators turning up on my doorstep.'

Tishk comes over and sits down next to me on the sofa. Our arms are almost touching and for once I don't mind someone sitting so close to me. I feel comfortable in Tishk's presence, presumably because we knew each other all those years ago; it's as though my emotions have muscle memory, and where he's concerned, my recollection is healthy.

'You must've been prepared for the reaction you'd get when people realised who you are,' he ventures.

'That's the thing, I didn't. I never expected to set foot in Heldean ever again. Never in a million years could I have predicted my mum would leave me the house.'

'Why do you think she did?'

I'm mindful of my words now, because being comfortable in Tishk's company does not mean I trust him with my deepest thoughts yet. I may be on a mission to find out why Mum left me the house, but I'm not ready to tell him that.

'Clearly she was trying to make a point,' I say carefully, 'I'm just not sure what. It's hard for me to guess what she was thinking, because there was no contact between us after I went to the Peachick. I never saw her again.'

Tishk is stunned. 'You're joking. Not even once?'

'Nope. Apparently she and Dad came to the hospital in the first few weeks, but I was too out of it on medication to remember. Then, when I started to get better, they refused to come.'

'Why?'

'Because I said I wasn't guilty and that made them angry.' I shrug nonchalantly, but inside I am wounded all over again. The two people in the world who were supposed to love me no matter what turned their backs on me when I was at my most vulnerable. 'When I was being discharged, I thought they might come for me then, but my social worker turned up at the hospital instead to tell me my parents had signed the paperwork authorising me to go into foster care. What's more,' I add bitterly, 'my mum insisted I was sent to the other end of the country, as far away from Heldean as possible.'

'Could she do that?'

'I ended up hundreds of miles away in Morecambe, so yes, I'm guessing she could.'

'That's awful. I can't imagine my parents doing that to any of us. Even when I went through a phase of drinking and scandalised our mosque elders, they stood by me.'

I smile. 'That's because your parents are lovely.'

'But yours were too—'

We both jump as the rose branch clatters against the window. The wind is up again.

'I can prune that back if you want. I think my dad's old secateurs are still in the shed.'

'Thanks, but I'll sort it out tomorrow.' I set the drained brandy tumbler down on the coffee table. 'It's nearly two in the morning; you should go home and get some sleep.'

'I can stay if you want. I can doss down on here.' Tishk pats the sofa cushion.

The gesture inexplicably puts me on edge and my chest tightens as though I'm about to start panicking again. 'There's no need,' I say quickly.

He hesitates. 'You were pretty hysterical, Cara. Are you sure you should be on your own?'

I really don't want him to stay, but I can't say that without sounding rude. 'It was just the noise freaking me out,' I shrug, faking nonchalance. 'I couldn't catch my breath and it spiralled, but I'm okay now, really. Mustard will keep an eye on me.' We both look down at my dog, currently snoring on the floor by my feet, having not left my side since Tishk turned up.

'Are you sure that's all it was?'

Something in Tishk's expression stills me. 'What do you mean?' I ask.

'Nothing,' he says quickly and stands to leave. 'Call me any time you need me. I don't mind.'

'I appreciate you saying that, thank you.'

After he's gone, I go upstairs to sneak into the master bedroom at the front of the house. I say sneak, because that's what it feels like I am doing by entering my parents' bedroom without their permission. It's funny how some habits never leave us: when we were little, Mum and Dad's bedroom was strictly invite-only – it was their private space, they'd tell us, and we had to knock to enter. Bowling in without asking would especially irritate Mum, which seemed daft, because most of the time she was in there alone because Dad was away so much working. Yet here I am now, tentatively tiptoeing over the threshold, half-expecting to hear her yell 'Knock first!' when she sees my head peeking around the door.

The silence that greets me is a punch to the gut and I gulp down a deep breath to steady myself as I enter the room fully.

There's no Mum or Dad in here, no Matty scurrying in my wake, always full of giggles, because he was one of those rare kids who was perennially cheerful. My entire family is gone and coming to terms with that is proving far harder than I thought.

I don't dwell on the room's decor, quickly passing the foot of the neatly made bed to reach the window. The curtains are open and, as I suspected and the reason I've come up here, across the road, I can see Heather and a man I presume is her husband standing at their bedroom window staring at my house. Their blatant observation is no doubt designed to unnerve me, but, tired and numbed by the brandy, I have surpassed my limit for being rattled tonight. Let them stare. They won't drive me out of Heldean and nor will anyone else, not while I'm searching for answers as to why my mum really brought me back here.

I pull the curtains halfway shut, but not before I bid them goodnight with my middle finger first.

Chapter Twenty-Six

Cara

'The updated interior has been done really well, good use of high-end fixtures and fittings – a definite selling point we can flag up. Same with it being south-facing, detached and in a coveted cul-de-sac on the right side of town. At Leonards, we pride ourselves on the standard of the property we sell and this place fits the bill nicely.' There's a pause. 'But even I'm going to have trouble spinning that as a saleable feature.'

The estate agent tilts his head towards the French doors in the dining room and the overgrown garden beyond. I swear the weeds have grown taller in the five days I've been staying here.

'I'm going to get it seen to,' I say.

The estate agent crosses his arms. He manages Leonards, which is why I've had to wait until Wednesday afternoon for him to come round. I did tell the receptionist that anyone would do, because the agency had already valued the house at my aunt's request and all I wanted was to sort out the pictures and marketing info, but apparently it had to be the most senior member of the team who came back to make sure the valuation still stood. I doubt house prices are fluctuating so much for there to be a sudden increase or decrease in price, but I decided to humour them because I am feeling too drained to bother arranging valuations with their rivals.

Four days on from being scared witless by Tishk's cat, I am managing to sleep undisturbed at night now – but only because I'm knocking myself out with sleeping tablets. The side effect of that is the zombie-like state I currently find myself in, which is why I'm not really taking in much of what the estate agent is saying. He's prattling on regardless though, using six words for every one a normal person would utter.

'The thing is, Ms Marshall, a garden that looks like it needs a fortune spent on it to get it to even a basic level of tidiness will drive the price down. So while I can get round the problem in the marketing details by not including a photograph, when it comes to viewings, it's really going to put potential buyers off. So if it's a quick sale you're looking for, the entire garden needs to be cleared asap.' He pronounces it 'ay-sap', as though it's a word rather than an acronym. 'It would also be wise to throw in some bedding plants, give it a splash of colour,' he adds.

As I stare out into the garden, wondering how much it will cost me to put it right, a thought occurs to me. 'You came before, didn't you, when my aunt Karen requested a valuation?'

He nods confidently. 'I did.'

'When was that?'

His face scrunches as he thinks. He's an attractive man: tall, early forties at a guess, grey peppering his temples, broad shoulders that fill his well-cut suit. But the legato manner of his speech is off-putting even for me.

'It must've been almost three months ago now, because I remember it was the week after I got back from the Bahamas and that particular holiday was in early September.'

Three months ago? I was expecting him to say a couple of weeks. Why was Karen getting the house valued when Mum was still very much alive? Did Mum know?

'What state was the garden in then?'

'It wasn't great, but not as bad as it is now. I guess the Indian summer we've just had did wonders for helping it grow. I don't know what it was like where you live, but here we had a lot of rain and even some flash flooding.'

I nod, but do not venture an answer, not wishing to get drawn into a conversation about where I live. I cannot hide the fact I'm back in Heldean, but I don't have to divulge where I've been until now.

'Your aunt did say she was going to get the garden sorted herself. I even gave her the details of a landscape gardener we use a lot for our rental properties. I can give you his number, if you want?'

I nod and he reaches for a business card from his breast pocket.

'This is my card, but I'll write his details on the back. Do you have a pen?'

As I forage for a biro in the bottom of my handbag, I decide to ask him the question I've been building up to since he arrived – and it has nothing to do with how much money he thinks the house will sell for. I decide to lay it out plainly, so there is no miscommunication.

'I'm sure you're aware of what happened in this house in 1994,' I say, as I hand him the pen. 'Is that going to affect me selling it?'

He stares at me for a moment, his expression inscrutable, then he gathers himself.

'I'm not going to pretend it won't put off some people from making an offer. Knowing a child died in the property in vio-lent circumstances might be too much for some.' He pauses, as though waiting for a reaction from me, but again I don't give him the satisfaction. 'On the other hand, it's the first time the property has been on the market since the eighties and it has been altered considerably since then. This is a really nice house in a lovely quiet street – the ideal family home for buyers who want to move up the property ladder.' He breaks into a smile.

'Why don't you let me worry about that side of things – I'll even handle all the viewings personally to smooth over any concerns potential buyers might have.'

I have no doubts about his ability to persuade people round to his way of thinking. If nothing else, he'll talk them into submission.

'Okay, that sounds great. How soon can you let me know what price you'd market it for?'

'I can tell you now,' he replies, and gives me a figure. It's a bit less than I was expecting, but it is still comparable to what I've seen on Rightmove for this area.

'That's with the garden done, though,' he adds.

'I'll definitely take that gardener's number then,' I say wryly.

The estate agent smiles, scribbles the number on the back and hands the card to me face up with his own details showing, picture included.

'Ian Leonard, managing director and founder,' I read from it. 'So you don't just run the agency, you own it?'

'Started it from scratch when I was twenty-two using my own savings. Now we have three branches across the county and another in the pipeline,' he says with obvious pride. Finally I warm to him: I know how much determination and grit it takes to build a life from nothing and I am admiring of anyone who has done the same.

We discuss a few more details and he promises to send a letter of engagement via email by the end of the day.

'I don't have a spare key to give you at the moment, but I can drop one into the office in the next day or so.'

He eyes the bunch of keys on the ceramic heart key ring that I'd left by the front door then shoots me a quizzical look.

'I had to get the locks changed. Those are the old ones,' I explain.

'Oh. Okay. No problem. Drop one in when you can.' He

glances at his watch. 'I've got another appointment straight after this. Can I please use your toilet before I go?'

'Sure.'

When he goes upstairs, I look out over the garden again. From the state of it, I'm guessing it could take weeks to clear it and get it looking nice again – but I don't mind if it does. Contrary to what I'm telling Leonard, I'm in no rush to get the house sold. This is a going-through-the-motions exercise to deflect my aunt and everyone else from my real intention: that I won't give up this house until I've unearthed the truth about it. It's all I've thought about since being spooked by the tapping noise and Tishk's cat. I need to establish why Mum left it to me and, at the same time, I'm also looking for evidence of what forced me out in the first place. Proof of Limey Stan, in other words. The more I mull it over, the more convinced I am the explanation as to what killed Matty is also still within these four walls. If I can show it really wasn't me who hurt Matty, I can clear my name. Needless to say, the nine-year-old Cara in my head thinks it's a terrific idea and it's her badgering me to do it.

I hear Leonard coming back down the stairs when he's done with the toilet and go into the hallway to let him out of the front door. He shakes my hand, then launches into another spiel.

'Please be assured, Ms Marshall, that Leonards will get you the best possible price for your property and will facilitate a smooth sale. I appreciate this is a difficult time for you and the circumstances are a tad unusual, but my firm is on your side and I shall work tirelessly to make sure the house is sold as soon as possible.'

'Good. I just want to get it sold and get out of here,' I fib.

'I expect you do.'

He gives an involuntary shudder as he glances back at me, then smoothly covers it by pretending to adjust his cuffs. I feel deflated. He's just like all the rest.

Chapter Twenty-Seven

Cara

The landscape gardener's name is Jason and when I phone, he says he is free to come round at noon tomorrow to give me a quote and if I find the price reasonable, he can start immediately. I'm guessing the time of year is a factor in his availability – how many people want their gardens done at the approach of December?

I spend the next hour or so picking through the drawers of paperwork I've already searched through four or five times, looking for even the tiniest reference to Matty's death or Limey Stan. Should I really be surprised there's none, though? My parents seemed to wash their hands so effectively of me that it stands to reason they would avoid any reminder of why they did. Eventually, I give up, frustrated, and stuff the papers back in the drawers. Then I go into the hallway and kneel down to run my hands over the skirting boards on the left-hand side, where the shadows that hid Limey Stan used to stretch across from. I don't know what I expected to find, but the focused act of examining the walls and flooring calms my agitated mind a fraction.

Part of me wants to call Anne to talk it through with her, but I'm not ready for another conversation with her in which Limey Stan is referenced. The blow-up between us still feels too raw. Instead, I prowl about the house, poking through more drawers and riffling through cupboards to no avail, and as I do, I become worked up again, because the longer I spend here, the angrier I am becoming that I was sent away in the first place. I was a child, for crying out loud. Why didn't anyone intervene and stand up for me? Where was the compassion, the attempts at understanding? I know my parents must have been devastated by Matty's death, but they knew me. I was no naughtier than any other child my age – how could they have been so quick to believe I was guilty of such a violent act? Why did they never reclaim me when the Peachick decided I was well enough to leave?

Those questions and more continue to pirouette through my mind as I move restlessly from room to room until I find myself on the landing upstairs. There is one room I haven't searched yet and that's Matty's bedroom. I've been putting it off, out of fear of what I'll find in there, so before I can talk myself out of it again, I throw open the door and step inside.

A sob escapes my lips: the room is completely unchanged from how it was a quarter of a century ago. I had a feeling it would be, which is why I hadn't dared open the door before now. I wasn't ready to confront my past in such an emotive, devastating fashion.

My breath catches as my gaze falls first on the Power Rangers duvet cover and then on the bedside-table-cum-toy-chest that is covered in the detritus of a nineties childhood: dozens of Pog discs scattered randomly, two Teenage Mutant Ninja Turtle action figures and a green Power Rangers one (Matty's absolute favourite), a yo-yo and a Tamagotchi key ring. Stacked on the floor beside the chest, on a rug designed to look like a football, are the board games Matty and I played with endlessly: Twister, Operation and Hungry Hungry Hippos.

Gingerly, I sit down on the bed. On the one hand, it breaks

my heart that Matty's bedroom has been frozen in time by my parents' grief, but on the other, I am upset his was preserved while mine was redecorated. It's yet another slap in the face and I speculate how quickly my parents cleared mine out after I went into the Peachick – was it weeks, months? I wish I knew.

I expected Matty's room to be dank, but it doesn't smell of anything in particular. Dust lingers in places, but not in large enough quantities to suggest it was never visited or cleaned. Mum must have ventured in here regularly to banish the dust, or maybe there were times when she just did as I am doing now – sitting on the bed with tears rolling silently down my cheeks, wishing Matty wasn't dead and missing him so much it hurts. I reach my hand out and stroke his pillow and think about how I used to ruffle his hair to wake him up when Mum would ask me to get him ready for school. Straight away, my throat starts to thicken and tears well in the corners of my eyes.

There is one saving grace when I think about Matty dying and that's in the moments before it happened, he was as happy as he had ever been. I was certain I had worked out a pattern to Limey Stan's comings and goings and thought that if we crept downstairs after midnight and hid in the bay, we would catch a glimpse for sure. Matty was so excited when I woke him up – I set my alarm clock to wake me up at 12.30 a.m. and hid it under my pillow – and it was an effort to keep him quiet once we had taken our places behind the curtains. When I finally got him to stop giggling, Matty whispered to me that this was the best adventure he had ever had and I was the best big sister in the world. Those were the last words he ever said and it comforts me to know that they were positive ones.

When the moment of his death came, suddenly, violently, and with little warning, I am ashamed to say I did nothing to help him. I didn't even scream. Feeling the near presence of this thing that had terrorised me for so long stunned me into silence. I became tangled in the curtain too and began to panic, but still I was physically unable to scream for help. Then, after what mercifully must have been only a few seconds, Matty's body slumped against mine and the curtain went slack and that's when I managed to free myself and run upstairs and lock myself in the bathroom.

I have relived the moment many times over the years, wishing I had reacted differently, wishing I had saved him. It was my fault he was there and my fault that he died. Now, reliving it once more in the house where it happened, I am crying so hard, I cannot see straight. I fall sideways onto Matty's bed and bury my face in his pillow. My body heaves as I cry and cry, until eventually I've exhausted myself. Then I slide under the duvet and pull it tight around me and soon I've fallen into a fitful sleep, plagued by dreams of shadowy figures climbing the walls and the face of my little brother screaming at me to help him.

When I awake a couple of hours later, I feel no better. The half-light between afternoon and evening has dimmed the room and it takes me a moment to realise where I am, until I spy a film poster for *Super Mario Bros.* stuck on the wall by Matty's wardrobe. The film was released the summer before he died and he and Ryan loved it so much that Uncle Gary took them to see it three times. As I stare up at the poster, my gaze is slowly drawn to three medium-sized cardboard boxes neatly stacked against the wall directly beneath it. Each has something written in marker pen on their side. I scrunch my eyes to read the lettering, then sit up, stunned. It's my name.

Scrabbling out of the bed, I dash across the room to them. I am not mistaken: each box has my name written on it in block capitals. I take the first one off the pile and set it on the carpet. It feels light. I need something sharp to cut the tape with, so I leg it downstairs for a knife. Mustard is asleep in the kitchen when I thunder in but scrabbles to his feet and wags his tail as he picks up on my excitement.

Back upstairs, Mustard at my heels, I slice easily through the tape and pull back the lid of the box. It occurs to me that the box looks new and the cardboard has a stiffness you wouldn't expect if it were decades old. That suggests they've been packed fairly recently.

I open the box to find a pile of clothes staring back at me. My clothes, from when I was a kid. I take the first item out – a denim pinafore dress Mum bought me at Adams and that I loved so much I wore it endlessly. Next in the pile are some stripy T-shirts, a grey sweatshirt with a transfer of a cat ironed to the front that's all creased and faded, and a flowery pink and blue skirt that I instantly recall as being the one I wore to the funfair the day I heard Limey Stan say his name. I drop the skirt to the floor as though my hand has been scalded, then I sit back on my haunches, fighting back tears.

It's not the sight of the clothes that's upsetting me, but that Mum kept them. I have no recollection of what belongings were sent to the Peachick with me, but I always assumed the clothes I wore there were ones from home. Now, judging by the contents of this box, I must have been provided with new clothing, while my parents held on to these. I cannot fathom why though. If I had come home after my discharge, I would have outgrown them by then and needed new stuff. Or did they simply decide to store them, knowing they would never be worn again? I push the box to one side and set down the next one. This contains toys and books I recognise as mine from my childhood, as does the final box. I don't get it: why keep all this stuff but not keep me?

At the very bottom of the third box, I find a small ceramic box. I do not recognise it and it looks fairly new. I open it up and I am surprised to find two hospital ID bracelets nestled together on a bed of white tissue paper. Examining them closer, I see both have the name 'Baby Belling' printed on both of them and my heart catches: these must be mine and Matty's from when we were born. Gently, I take the first one out and I can tell it is mine because it has my date of birth on it and the weight I was. I turn it over and over in my palm, marvelling at how tiny my wrist once was.

Matty's band contains the same details, but there is also something written on the inside of the band, in tiny printed capital letters: HL72QR, presumably a hospital reference number. With a sigh, I return both bracelets to the box and put the lid back on. I suppose I should be happy that my parents kept my bracelet – as keepsakes go, it's a lovely one.

I stack the boxes back where I found them, then leave Matty's bedroom, pulling the door firmly shut behind me. I decide to go downstairs – all that crying has left me parched and I am craving a glass of water. I also need to put all the lights on – the onset of dusk means the house is now shrouded in gloom and I don't like it.

But as I trudge downstairs, I notice the door between the lounge and the hallway is ever so slightly ajar and I stop. This is a door that was never used when I was a child and still isn't now – to maximise the space in the front room, the sofa is pushed up against it, so if you tried to enter from the hallway you'd walk straight into the back of it. The only way to access the extended lounge now is to go through the kitchen – yet while I've been asleep, the door has been opened a fraction from the hallway side.

Unease creeps over me as I inch towards it, my brain searching for a reasonable explanation as to why it's open, but knowing there is none. There are no windows open downstairs that could've facilitated a gust of wind blowing it ajar and while

Mustard has been known to open the doors in my flat, it's only because they have lever handles he can lean his paws on. But in this house the handles are round – there is no way the door could have opened without someone turning the knob to do so.

I am shaking from head to foot and barely managing to breathe as I reach the bottom stair and cross the hallway to the door. I peer through the gap and what I see causes me to let out a cry of shock. The coffee table with the shiny black lacquered top has been moved into the middle of the lounge from its position next to the sofa . . . and it's upside down.

Chapter Twenty-Eight

Karen

Eight months on from taking early retirement, Karen still isn't used to being at home during the day. She'd been in employment since leaving school at sixteen, breaking only for a year both times after Lisa and Ryan were born, then returning on a part-time basis until they were at secondary school. Her final position before retiring was on the front desk at a building society in town and she still hankers for the daily interaction of talking to customers, especially the pensioners who came in every week at exactly the same time, regular as clockwork.

Her decision to quit work was driven by Anita's illness. She wanted to spend every moment she could with her sister and it was inconceivable for her to be at work every day while Anita faded away. Karen needed to be with her. It left things a bit tight on the financial front and she sensed Gary wasn't happy at the amount of time she spent in Parsons Close, but he was sensitive enough not to say it out loud. Karen supposes it was because he knew that once Anita had gone, he wouldn't have to share his wife any more.

She's spent most of today doing housework, but now she's ready for her usual Wednesday afternoon coffee break. While a fresh cafetière brews on the hob, she nibbles on a second biscuit, taken from the plate she laid out on the table earlier. Tishk is running late again, which is par for the course.

Their Wednesday get-togethers began a couple of months ago, when Anita was in the last stages of her life. Tishk had been keeping an eye on Anita since living next door again and he and Ryan had also become friends, the decade age-gap between them no longer feeling as pronounced as it did when they were children. One week, Tishk unexpectedly turned up at Karen's house to see how she was holding up being Anita's full-time carer and from there they segued into a 'same time next week?' routine that had quickly become a highlight of her week. Tishk is a good listener, and thoughtful, and Karen is grateful for the kindness he's shown her since her sister died.

Today, though, she wishes he'd hurry up and arrive. This is their second catch-up since Cara reappeared in Heldean and Karen is desperate to know if Tishk has seen her at all since Saturday. She knows they are already reacquainted: Tishk told her he'd found Cara in the house on the day of the will reading, although he didn't say much else beyond that it was lovely to see her again. It surprised Karen how much she minded him saying that. In fact, it bothered her more than Lisa saying on the phone the other day that Cara deserved the house. Karen has grown used to her daughter's little digs at Anita over the years, which she puts down to Lisa still being upset with her aunt that Cara was sent away like she was.

Suddenly the back door opens and Tishk appears.

'Sorry I'm late,' he says sheepishly. 'I dozed off. One minute I'm working, the next I wake up with a textbook over my face.'

'Just as well I've made the coffee strong,' she laughs. 'Come in, sit down.'

Tishk takes his usual seat at the table and helps himself to a biscuit. He wolfs it down, then takes another, and not for the first time, Karen wonders if he's feeding himself properly.

His mum, Nura, was a fantastic cook but, in that way that was traditional in many Muslim families, passed down her skills to her daughters but not to her sons. Tishk reckons it's because she thought he'd have a wife by now to cook for him. Instead, single again after a broken engagement, he's done nothing to remedy his lack of kitchen skills in the four years since his parents moved away and there isn't a single meal he eats that doesn't begin life in a tin, jar or packet.

Karen doesn't want to jump straight into the subject of Cara, so they chat for a bit about the progress of Tishk's PhD – or rather the lack of it, as he is an arch procrastinator, as well as tardy.

'I need to knuckle down and get it finished,' he says, snaffling a third biscuit. 'Otherwise I'll lose my funding. The Bank of Mum and Dad is only open for a limited time,' he adds with a grin.

It works in Tishk's favour that he is a nice, genuine person, Karen observes, because otherwise it would be very easy to think he is taking advantage of his parents by using their pension pot to gain a qualification he doesn't really need and staying in their house rent-free while he earns it.

'Perhaps you could get a part-time job to earn yourself some extra cash?' she suggests.

'I could, but I prefer to work through the night; it's the way I've always studied. If I had a job during the day, I couldn't catch up on my sleep and I'd be shattered all the time.'

'Best hurry up and finish your thesis then.'

'I will. I'm just a bit distracted, with everything going on next door at the moment.'

Karen's fingers tighten on the handle of her coffee cup. 'Why's that?'

Tishk regards her with a grin.

'Come on, Mrs J' – try as she might, she can never get him

to call her Karen – 'you know exactly why. Because of Cara.'

'Hasn't she left yet? I told her on Saturday she needs to go.'

'It's not really your decision whether she stays or not,' says Tishk carefully. 'It's her house now.'

'I know it is, but she's not welcome. No one wants her here.'

'She's not causing any harm.'

Karen scoffs at that. 'Cara was responsible for the death of her brother, and her returning to Heldean is raking up painful memories for the rest of us. To say she's causing no harm is plain wrong.'

'Okay, let me reword it then. She's not trying to cause more trouble. She didn't ask to be left the house.'

'She could easily rectify that. Anita added a clause that if Cara doesn't want the money, she can give it to charity.'

Tishk pauses for a moment. 'What about redemption, Mrs J? She was a nine-year-old child when she was last here; now she's a woman of thirty-four. She's not the same person. Doesn't she deserve the chance to make amends?'

'She doesn't need to be in Heldean to do that.'

Karen doesn't like how harsh she sounds and hates that Tishk might think badly of her because of it, but she will never embrace what he's saying. Cara doesn't deserve her understanding and if Tishk had seen Matty's broken little body laid out in the chapel of rest, he'd agree with her.

'I think, if you took the time to get to know her again, you might like her. She reminds me a lot of her mum.'

'I find that hard to believe,' Karen says, rising from her seat and taking her mug to the sink so she can stand with her back to him. She doesn't want him to see how upset he's making her, because she knows it's not deliberate.

'If you made the time to talk to her properly, you'd see it too,' he adds.

Crossly, she rounds on him.

'What do you expect me to do, Tishk? Welcome Cara back into our lives as though nothing ever happened? You of all people know what Anita was like after Matty died because you grew up next door to her and saw it with your own eyes. She was a shell, broken beyond any hope of recovery. The cancer might've killed her, but she was dead inside long before that and I can't forgive Cara for that.'

Tishk nods. 'I do understand now is an emotional time for you and that you're grieving. But I can't stop thinking about what life must've been like for Cara growing up in foster care, knowing her family didn't want her. It must've been horrendous.' He pauses. 'She still maintains she never killed Matty and, if I'm honest, it's hard not to believe her.'

Karen is astounded. 'She was the only person with him when it happened. There was no one else downstairs. You can't possibly believe that ridiculous ghost story she came out with. Thanks to her, our family became an international laughing stock, with every aspect of our lives ripped to shreds by the press. I haven't forgotten all the TV crews camping out here, the constant knocks on the door by reporters, even if you have.'

'I'm not saying that,' he answers slowly.

'You didn't know how she really was. The months before Matty died, she was an absolute horror. She bullied other children, as well as him.'

'I know what Amir's told me and it sounds like her behaviour was down to her being terrified and exhausted from being awake all night because she was convinced she was hearing things.'

'Exactly!' Karen crows triumphantly. 'She thought she heard noises, but no one else in the house did. It was her illness, the delusional disorder.'

'If she was ill and couldn't help herself, isn't that even more reason to show her some compassion?'

Thrown by his comment, Karen slumps back down into her chair. 'I can't believe you're taking her side.'

'I'm not trying to pick a fight, Mrs J. It's just that Cara's not in a great place either. She's vulnerable and she's got no one.'

Karen shakes her head. 'I can't help her. Not in the way you want me to.'

Tishk sighs and she is grateful when his phone suddenly rings, puncturing the moment.

'Hello?' he answers.

Even from where she's sitting, Karen can hear the caller is hysterical and instinct tells her that it's Cara.

Frowning, Tishk leaps to his feet, asking what's wrong but seemingly not getting any sense from her. 'The table's upside down? How?'

Karen gets to her feet too. 'What's happened?' she mouths.

'I have to go,' Tishk mouths back, pulling his coat off the back of his chair. Then he speaks firmly into his phone. 'Cara, I'm on my way. I'll be two minutes. Stay on the line and keep talking to me.'

Karen grabs his arm. 'Wait, what's going on?'

His frown deepening, Tishk holds the handset away from his mouth for a second. 'It's something about some furniture being moved downstairs.'

'Why has that upset her so much?'

'She's saying Limey Stan did it.'

Chapter Twenty-Nine

Cara

We are going round in circles, Tishk and I. He is trying to come up with a plausible reason for why the coffee table is upside down in the middle of the front room and I keep telling him there isn't one. His refusal to accept that while I was asleep the furniture was being rearranged is infuriating. Why is he persisting in not believing me?

'Are you sure you didn't tip it over without realising?' he asks me again.

I shoot him another exasperated look. 'I told you – I would've remembered that. Plus, it's been moved into the middle of the room.'

'Have you been drinking today?'

Embarrassment floods through me and colours my cheeks. My drunkenness after the will reading was a one-off, but Tishk obviously now thinks I get so wasted during the daytime that I regularly stagger round the house sending furniture flying. 'No I haven't. The table was upended on purpose and it wasn't me who did it,' I reply hotly.

Tishk made me tea with lots of sugar after he arrived and I'm clutching the mug with both hands for warmth. The adrenaline surge triggered by my discovery of the table has subsided and now I'm shivering like I'm freezing cold. We're in the kitchen, sitting at the small table that's pushed against one wall. The room really isn't big enough to accommodate a place to sit and dine and I should move the table and chairs out of the way when the estate agent returns to take the pictures.

The fact I can even make a mental note shows I'm calming down. Yet the question of who moved the table niggles away at me: if I didn't knock it over (and I know damn well I didn't), who did? When I called Tishk, I blurted out it must've been Limey Stan again, but I've since convinced myself, and him, I only said it because I was upset and not thinking straight. As I silently remind the nine-year-old me who is currently screeching in my head that he's returned to haunt me again, Limey Stan only ever showed up at night and this was four o'clock in the afternoon. It's someone playing a trick, it must be.

'Karen's behind it, she has to be,' I declare. 'She wants me gone and she's trying to freak me out so I'll pack up and leave.'

'It wasn't her. I was with her when you called.'

I stare at Tishk, shocked. 'What?'

'I'm friends with the whole family. I go round every Wednesday afternoon at the same time for coffee.' He says it glibly, as though it shouldn't have any bearing on my feelings, but it jolts me to hear he is close enough to my aunt that he visits her house once a week. 'So I was there when you say this happened,' he adds.

'It'll be one of the others then. Uncle Gary.'

Tishk shakes his head. 'He's at work, as are Ryan and Natalie before you ask. Look, they wouldn't think to stoop to something like this. It's trespassing for a start, because you changed the locks, so they couldn't use their key. It's also harassment, trying to force you from a home that's now legally yours. I can't see any of them risking getting into trouble with the police. They're not like that, trust me.'

Trust. Now there's a word. I don't know what or who to

apply it to right now. Certainly not Tishk now I know he's cosy with my aunt. How do I know he won't rush back round there after this and tell her everything I've said? 'If it wasn't Karen, my uncle, my cousin nor his girlfriend, who else could it have been?'

Was it Tishk?

The intrusive thought startles me. Why on earth would he be the culprit? He's my friend, he's been nothing but supportive. Yet I can't help myself asking him what time he went round to Karen's. I was asleep in Matty's bed for a while, so there may well have been a window of opportunity for him to somehow sneak in here first.

Tishk sighs and crosses his arms. 'I've told you, it wasn't her,' he says, and I realise he's misunderstood me and he thinks I'm trying to suss out if there was time for Karen to have crept in before their meeting. The fact he didn't react as though I was accusing him lessens my unease. If it was him, surely he'd have reacted more suspiciously? 'I think you knocked it over and didn't realise,' he adds.

Nine-year-old Cara chooses that moment to launch a foot-stamping tantrum in my head. You know who did this, she's shouting at me. I grip my mug tighter, my pulse quickening, as I dare to contemplate the unthinkable, that she's right and it was something, rather than someone, who moved the table – the same something that preyed on our house twenty-five years ago.

I glance across the kitchen to the hallway door. Next to it there used to be a set of steps with a seat on top – not quite a chair, not quite a stepladder, but a contraption somewhere in between. Mum used to sit us on it to administer Savlon and plasters to grazed knees, but my mind drifts back to one night in particular when it was about three in the morning and she'd sat me on the steps and given me a mug of hot chocolate to calm me down after another night-time scare.

'It was just a bad dream, sweetheart,' I remember her saying as she stroked the crown of my head and encouraged me to take small sips of my drink so I didn't spill it down my nightie.

'But Mr Blobby was by my bedroom door and I couldn't get out,' I'd protested. 'Limey Stan put him there to scare me.'

Mr Blobby was an enormous Swiss cheese rubber plant that sat in a pot on the upstairs landing, named after the TV character whose eponymous pop song had been a favourite of mine and Matty's that year. That particular night the usual tapping and creaking noises had woken me up, but when I'd gone to investigate, I'd opened my bedroom door to find Mr Blobby blocking my path. I was so terrified to see him there, I screamed the house down, then ran back to bed and hid under the covers. When Mum came to see what the matter was, she said I must've had a nightmare because Mr Blobby was in his usual corner at the top of the stairs and nowhere near my bedroom door. She even opened the door again to prove it. But I know what I saw and it was that plant, leaves the size of my head, spread across the threshold so I had no means of escape. Something had moved it there and moved it back before Mum got up . . .

The same something, the nine-year-old me shrieks in my ear, which upended the coffee table.

'Are you okay?' asks Tishk.

I take a deep breath to bind myself to the present and nod at him reassuringly. I dare not share my suspicions based on a rubber plant called Mr Blobby – he'll assume I'm losing the plot, like I'm starting to think I am. I will the voice in my head to shut up and, thankfully, it does.

'Yeah, I'm fine. I was just thinking I wish this was hot chocolate rather than tea,' I say, pasting on a smile.

'Sorry, tea was all I could find. Your cupboards are a bit bare.'

'I know, I need to go shopping.' I thought I had brought

enough supplies for at least a week, but they are dwindling fast and Mustard is also running low on reward treats.

'Why don't you do an online order, save you the trouble of going out?'

'I like food shopping. I find it oddly relaxing, even when it's busy.'

Tishk looks troubled. 'Do you really want to venture out in public though? Not that I think you shouldn't,' he adds hastily, 'but I'd be worried about people's reactions if they recognise you.'

'I've been concerned about that too, but I can't lock myself away indefinitely or only take Mustard out in the early hours when everyone's still asleep. It's not fair on him. But nor do I want to have to deal with dozens of Jims shouting in my face.'

When I told Tishk about my encounter at the cemetery, he said I should make a complaint. I'm realising he can be rather officious and has very clear ideas about what's right and what's wrong, which is a far cry from how he was as a teenager, breaking his curfew and sneaking out at all hours.

'But I've also been thinking about something my foster mother said to me before the will reading: who's going to recognise me really? You did because you knew me from living next door, but the man at the cemetery only guessed who I was because I was standing by my family's grave. If he'd met me in the street, he wouldn't have had a clue.'

Tishk nods. 'True. If I'd met you in passing, I don't think I'd have guessed straight away that you were Cara Belling. Your hair is much darker and short now and your face is thinner.'

'Exactly. So I think I'll be okay doing a supermarket run.'

'I can come with you if you want.'

I want to say yes, but something's stopping me. I've grown to like Tishk in the short amount of time we've spent together.

Maybe it's because he's that bit older, but he's different from the men I usually gravitate towards – he's funny and kind and doesn't appreciate how attractive he is, which is attractive in itself. In different circumstances, I might've made it known I like him, but discovering he's friendly with Karen means I won't be throwing caution to the wind any time soon. For the time being, I shall keep him at arm's-length, until I know for sure what his motives are.

'No, I'll go alone. If we bumped into anyone you know, it could be awkward. I've got enough stuff to see me through until morning, so I'll go then. Is there anything you need while I'm there?'

'Actually,' he grins, 'can you get me some hot chocolate? You've given me a craving for it and I don't think I've had any since I was a kid.'

'Sure, I can do that.'

He pauses and I can see he's weighing something up, so I tell him to just say whatever's on his mind.

'Actually, I was wondering what it was like growing up in foster care.'

I shrug as though the question is no big deal, but a hard ball of tension immediately forms in my stomach.

'I was one of the lucky ones. The couple I was put with were lovely to me. Are lovely to me,' I correct myself. 'I'm still close to them.'

'You must have really missed your parents though.'

The ball tightens.

'At first, I suppose. Then I got used to being away from them.'

He pauses again, taking in my answer. Then he leans forward across the table. I inch backwards in my seat in response.

'You asked me the other day if your mum ever mentioned you.'

The ball expands now, pushing up against my lungs and rendering me breathless. I nod at him to continue.

'Well, she did. Often. She would ask me if I remembered you and then we'd talk about what it was like growing up around here. She liked to reminisce.' He hesitates. 'When you asked me the other day, I didn't know whether to be honest, in case it upset you. But she didn't forget about you.'

The ball explodes, hollowing me out. Knowing she used to talk about me is far worse than thinking she didn't. How could she discuss me like that with Tishk, like I actually mattered, after she and Dad sent me away?

'Did she ever say why they left me in foster care?' I ask with evident bitterness.

He leans even closer. 'I asked her once. I don't know why, but one day we were chatting and I suddenly got angry that she could be so casual discussing her memories of you, when we both knew where you'd ended up.'

'What did you say?'

He looks abashed. 'I asked her why she'd left you to rot in foster care like an unwanted puppy. I didn't mean to be that rude, it just came out.'

'I'm glad you were. What was her response, then? Why did they leave me to rot?'

He leans away from the table and rakes his hand through his hair. 'I don't think she answered me,' he says unconvincingly.

'Yes she did. I can tell by your face. Go on, what did she say?'

'I don't want you getting upset again,' Tishk says, looking pained.

'There's nothing you can tell me about my mum that would upset me more than her and my dad placing me in foster care in the first place. I just want to know why they left me there.'

'I'm sorry, Cara. She said it was for your own good.'

Chapter Thirty

The New York Times

10-18-94

World News Briefs

England – The county of Essex, situated east of London, is typically synonymous with girls called Sharon and Tracy wearing strappy white stiletto shoes as they dance around their handbags at infamous nightclubs like Tots in Southend. But presently it is the backdrop to an altogether more fascinating breed of being – ghosts.

The British media is gripped by a tragic killing involving two children . . . and a paranormal entity that goes by the name of Limey Stan. Six-year-old Matty Belling was found suffocated in his home in the Essex town of Heldean in July and police held his nine-year-old sister, Cara, responsible for his death. She is currently hospitalised. Yet in police transcripts leaked to the media, Cara has denied culpability and claims her brother died at the 'hands' of a ghost called Limey Stan that had been haunting their three-bedroom family home for many months. It is this aspect of the story – whether a ghost is capable of committing murder and whether the 'Heldean Haunting' is a hoax

– that has inflamed reporters and caused a stampede of TV crews from around the globe to descend on the small, landlocked town, including one from CBS, which will air a special news report this evening at 10 p.m. ET.

Chapter Thirty-One

Cara

The next morning, I drive to Morrisons on the outskirts of town. There are a couple of supermarkets nearer, but this is one of those vast superstores with a zillion parking spaces and it means I can pull into one farthest away from the store, with no other vehicles nearby. Mustard, familiar with the drill, settles down on the back seat to await my return.

I venture warily up the first aisle, clinging to the trolley handle as though it's a swim float. I am still feeling shaken by the incident with the coffee table and I barely slept last night, churning over my conversation with Tishk, and the anxiety both have triggered is not combining well with how vulnerable I feel coming out in public like this. I probably should have waited until I felt calmer to go shopping, or ordered online as Tishk suggested, but, in truth, I wanted to escape the house and its memories for a couple of hours . . . except now I am here, all I want to do is hide away again.

Yet pretty quickly it becomes obvious that my fellow shoppers are more engrossed in the produce and products they are selecting than other customers milling around them and I begin to relax as I fill my trolley with fresh fruit and vegetables, then swing into the next aisle, meat and poultry.

It takes me a good forty-five minutes to complete my shop.

It's always slower when you're in a new store with an unfamiliar layout and this particular Morrisons also stocks clothing, electrical goods, books and magazines, so I browse those aisles as well. Then I turn a corner to be confronted by shelves heaving with Christmas decorations and related paraphernalia, which pulls me up short. Usually I spend Christmas in Morecambe, but I honestly don't know how I feel about that after what happened with Anne at the cemetery, but I do know she and John will be terribly hurt if I don't go.

I leave the aisle and head to the checkout. Standing still as I wait to be served makes me nervous and my eyes dart from side to side to check whether anyone has noticed me. But, again, everyone is engrossed in their own actions and the till operator barely looks at me as she scans my shopping and takes my payment.

Outside, I breathe a sigh of relief and my mood lifts as I push my laden trolley in the direction of where I left my car. As I draw closer, however, I notice there is a cluster of people standing next to the vehicle and, from their expressions, they are not happy.

Heart hammering in my chest, I pick up my pace and when I am a few metres away, one woman turns on her heel and points at me.

'Oi! Is this your car? You should be ashamed of yourself!'

The crowd parts and I see Mustard lying on the ground, panting heavily. A man is kneeling beside him and is slowly pouring water from a plastic bottle onto his tongue and into his mouth and Mustard is gratefully lapping it up.

I let go of my trolley and roughly push through the bystanders, my trainers crunching on glass fragments from where the front passenger window of my car has been smashed in.

'Is he okay?' I ask frantically, crouching down. Mustard is pleased to see me and wags his tail.

'No thanks to you,' the man snaps. 'I heard him barking –
he was in distress because there were no windows open.'

Stunned, I stare at my car. Aside from the window that is
broken, the others are firmly shut. But I always leave one of the
back ones open a crack to let air in, even when the temperature
outside is cold, and I did today . . . didn't I? 'I swear I left the
window open,' I tell my accuser.

'You should never leave a dog unattended in a car full stop,'
snaps another man standing behind us. 'The poor thing was
gasping for air.'

The thought of Mustard suffering makes me feel wretched
and I bury my face in the furry cuff of his neck and whisper
how sorry I am. After a few moments, I raise my head and see
a couple of people in the crowd are holding phones up and
appear to be recording me.

'Please don't film us,' I plead. 'I know I left the window open
before I went into the store. I would never hurt my dog.'

Not one of them looks like they believe me, nor do they
lower their phones.

'People like you shouldn't be able to keep pets,' an elderly
woman says loudly. 'Bloody irresponsible.'

'You need to take him to the vet's, and get him checked out,'
says the man knelt beside me. His tone has softened a fraction
and I thank him for coming to Mustard's aid. 'It's okay,' he says
gruffly. 'Just be more careful next time.'

'Don't let her off the hook,' crows the pensioner. 'Report
her to the RSPB.'

'That's for birds, love,' says someone else and the crowd
bursts into laughter. Phones are lowered and they begin to dis-
perse, the drama at an end.

With the help of his rescuer, I guide Mustard onto the back
seat again. 'I really did leave a window open.'

'No, you didn't,' he replies peevishly. 'They were all shut.'

I open my mouth to protest, then close it again. I want to convince him, but I don't know if I can even convince myself.

As he walks away, I climb into the driver's seat and close my eyes for a moment. I replay driving into the car park, getting out, making sure Mustard is settled in the back seat . . . and pressing the key fob to lock the door as I walk off. The man was right: I didn't lower the window before I left Mustard in the car.

I burst into tears, horrified. My poor dog could've died if the man hadn't spotted him. I've allowed myself to become so distracted by the voice of my nine-year-old self crowing in my head about Limey Stan that it is drowning out all rational thought. But I mustn't lose my grip on what is real and what is not. If I do, I will be readmitted to hospital and this time I'll end up staying there.

I cancel the gardener coming round before I leave the car park. He's understandably annoyed because it's last-minute, but I appease him when I tell him the job is his regardless of the quote and ask him to start first thing tomorrow. Foolish, perhaps, but I am too frazzled to consider the implications, plus I've got a pile of money coming to me from Mum's will, so it's not like I can't afford it.

Mustard rallies by the time we get home and bounds out of the car and into the house. I fret about whether to take him to a vet to be looked over – the thought of leaving the house again fills me with trepidation – but judging by the way he troughs his dinner and the treats I keep offering by way of apology, I don't think he's in any way injured by his ordeal. I'll keep a close eye on him for now and will take him in tomorrow if I think he needs it.

Seeing him happily bound around the kitchen does not negate my guilt though. More tears flow as I contemplate what might've happened if that man had not spotted him barking inside the car and broken the window to release him. Losing Mustard would destroy me.

Wiping my tears away, I head upstairs to my bedroom, resolute: I need my pills. There's no shame in it. I am struggling, obviously brought on by my coming back here, and for my own sake as much as Mustard's, I need to get myself back on an even keel. I don't think I am bad enough to need the trifluoperazine, but a couple of days on diazepam should settle me down.

As I open my bedroom door, my brain takes a second to register the scene before me. Then I gasp. Laid out on my bed, ranked in order of size, are the toys from Matty's bedside.

Chapter Thirty-Two

MEMORANDUM

To: Dr Patrick Malloy, head of clinical services
From: Dr Stacey Ardern, consultant child and adolescent
  psychiatrist
Date: Tuesday 23 May 1995
Subject: Cara Belling

I have an urgent matter we need to discuss – are you available at 3 p.m. today for a case conference? Cara Belling's progress has stalled and I am deeply concerned she is slipping back into the catatonic state she was in at the time of her admission, thus undoing all we have achieved so far. The issue is her parents and their decision to cease all contact, bar her father's weekly phone call to me to update on her welfare, of which Cara remains unaware, at his request.

While I do have the utmost sympathy for what the parents have been through, I feel it is imperative that we again implore them to be involved in the process of her recovery and I was hoping that entreaty could come from you this time. Much of Cara's reluctance to engage has stemmed, in my view, from her immeasurable confusion and hurt over the absence of family visits. She wants to see her parents and asks repeatedly why they are staying away.

Chapter Thirty-Three

Cara

I close my eyes, convinced I am seeing things. Yet when I open them again, the scene before me remains unchanged. Displayed neatly across my bed in a straight line are my dead brother's favourite toys.

I back out of the room, hands clutched to my chest, legs turned to jelly. My breath comes in gasps and when I try to gulp down more air, nothing happens – my lungs have seized in panic. I put out my right hand to grab the balustrade at the top of the stairs to steady myself, but I miss and fall to the carpet. I am choking now, my body desperate for oxygen but getting none, and the last thing I think I hear as I slip into unconsciousness is the slow creak of footsteps in the hallway down below.

What feels like only moments later, Mustard brings me round by licking my face repeatedly until the roughness of his tongue and the drench of his slobber rouses me enough to push him away. My chest hurts like hell from heaving to catch my breath when the panic attack struck, but other than that, I am okay. As I gingerly get to my feet, I wonder how long I was unconscious for, but there is no way of telling; I did not check the time when we arrived back from Morrisons.

The first thing I notice when I'm back on my feet is that the door to my bedroom is shut now. Fear ripples through me again: I know I left it open after seeing the toys on the bed. I am tempted to flee downstairs and call Tishk to come round, but I fear he will tire of me contacting him so often, and should an occasion arise when I really need him, he may not come. I need to deal with this on my own, however terrified I am.

Slowly, I move forwards and open the door. I look across the room, expecting to see Matty's toys on the bed, but they are no longer there and the duvet has been smoothed flat.

I am stunned. 'What the hell?'

Mustard looks up at me enquiringly.

'Did you see anything?' I ask, but, of course, he has no answer for me.

I stumble across the landing to Matty's bedroom and a quick look inside confirms the toys are back in their rightful places on his beside chest.

Mustard nudges my leg with his snout.

'I know. They were on my bed,' I say to him. 'Laid out in a row in order of size. I did not imagine that, I know I didn't.'

Mustard woofs supportively.

I return to my bedroom and retrieve my bag of pills from the top drawer. My hands are shaking so violently, it takes me three attempts to pop the diazepam tablet from its blister packet. I swallow it down dry, almost gagging as it drags against the inside of my throat, but immediately I start to relax. It will be at least half an hour before my senses actually begin to dull and my body unclenches, but the placebo effect is instant.

Emboldened, I go back to Matty's bedroom and carefully examine each of the toys, but I find nothing to indicate how they came to be somewhere else. As I place the green-suited Power Ranger back down, I remember I thought I heard creaking footsteps in the hallway in the seconds before I blacked out and so I head downstairs. I cannot see any marks on the floorboards to suggest someone trod on them and all the windows and doors remain locked, so it can't have been someone breaking in . . . as much as I would love it to have been.

More than anything, I want it to be an intruder. I want word to have spread that Cara Belling is staying at the house where her brother died and someone's said, let's break in and teach her a lesson so she'll freak out and leave Heldean again. Nothing would make me happier than discovering that and I wouldn't even press charges, because the alternative explanation for what's happening fills me with a horror I cannot even begin to process – that the voice in my head is right and Limey Stan has returned because I am here again and he's no longer waiting until the small hours to torment me.

Chapter Thirty-Four

Cara

As my medication kicks in, however, so too does the analytical part of my brain, the side that makes me good at accountancy and a reasonable thinker. The side that reminds me Limey Stan only ever visited in the middle of the night, so moving the toys in the daytime had to be an actual person's doing. I also need the culprit to be human for the sake of my mental state, because the idea that Limey Stan has re-emerged since I moved back in terrifies me, and I can't live through that again, no matter how much I want to prove what killed Matty and to clear my name. No, it has to be a person who wants to see me gone from this house and is mimicking my past experience to do it . . . and it's far more likely to be someone I already know.

I go downstairs and settle on the sofa with my phone. Using a notebook app, I make a list of all the people who I think might hate me enough to risk breaking into the house to scare me in the hope I'll leave. It's not a particularly long list, admittedly, because I don't know many people in Heldean now, but compiling it makes me feel like I'm taking back control.

Karen heads the list, followed by Gary, Ryan, the girlfriend with the red hair, Heather from over the road, Heather's husband and Jim from the cemetery. Then, after a moment's hesitation, I add Tishk's name. He's shown me nothing but kindness since I arrived, but he's also a friend of the people who want me gone the most. How can I be sure he's not helping them? He also lied to me about discussing me with my mum; he said it was because he didn't want to upset me, but I have no way of knowing if he's being genuine. Until I can be certain, Tishk stays on the list.

There's another name I'm debating whether to add to it: Timothy Pitt, the man behind the Heldean Haunting blog. Pitt of all people would benefit most from Limey Stan returning to haunt me – he's made a career out of writing about him, after all. But would he really risk lingering downstairs while I discovered the toys? Whoever did it had no inkling I would have a panic attack and faint, it was pure luck they were able to come back upstairs while I was passed out and put the toys back in Matty's room. The others, even Tishk, I can imagine doing that, but Pitt? Reluctantly, I dismiss his name.

Although familiar with his earlier blog posts, I haven't looked at his site for a couple of years and for the next hour my right thumb is continually scrolling as I read his take on the event that took away everything I held dear as a child. Pitt remains utterly convinced that a ghost called Limey Stan possessed our house and took Matty's life. He even now claims to know the identity of Limey Stan before he died.

Americans called British servicemen 'Limeys' during World War II, perhaps in retaliation for being labelled 'Yanks' by us. Although it has been around a lot longer than that – limey is shortened from the phrase lime-juicer, a nickname ascribed after the British navy began watering down their sailors' daily rum ration with lemon juice to counter outbreaks of scurvy during the nineteenth century.

I have looked into the background of Parsons Close and have discovered that an RAF serviceman called Wilfred S.

Smith lived there and it is my belief he was given the nickname Limey Stan during his service in the war and that
Stanley could be the 'S' of his middle name.

I sit back, surprised. It has never occurred to me to dig into
the provenance of Limey Stan. To nine-year-old me, he was
simply the ghost who would not leave me alone, not the ghost
of someone who had previously lived. It is such a strange name
that to learn it might be based in reality is eye-opening. I was
only three months old when we moved into the house, so I
have no recollection of my parents ever discussing who owned
it before us. They can't have known though – my first mention
of Limey Stan surely would have triggered a connection in their
minds?

Pitt's most recent posts are a rehash of information I have
already digested over many years of reading books and other
online essays on the subject of hauntings. I click on 'About' to
learn more of Timothy Pitt, but his bio is still disappointingly
brief: he's Heldean born and bred and became a paranormal
investigator in the late 1980s. What prompted it, he doesn't say.

Below his bio, however, there is a contact form. My thumb
hovers over the screen, ready to scroll on, but I stop myself,
thinking. There is one glaring omission in his blog, a thorny
question he hasn't tackled yet or is deliberately dodging. Or
perhaps he simply hasn't been asked the question yet.

I fill in the required details using my own email address, which
is obscure enough for me to hide behind: pixie426@gmail.com.
The 426 relates to my patient number at the Peachick, a salutary
reminder of what I survived. Then I begin to type.

Dear Mr Pitt,
I have read your blog with interest and you throw up some
interesting theories about Limey Stan, i.e. who he was and

how he came to haunt the Belling family's house. But one thing you haven't addressed, and what I would love to hear your take on, is how can a ghost kill when it's not of actual physical substance?

I don't know what name to use to sign off, so I leave it blank. Whether he answers me privately or via his blog, I don't mind – I just want to know what he thinks happened all those years ago.

Chapter Thirty-Five

Karen

Friday night for Karen and Gary means a fish-and-chips take-away and a few drinks each in front of the telly, their former habit of going to the pub scuppered by the closure of their local a few years back. Normally, Gary fetches the food on his way home, but just after six, Karen pulls on her coat and sends him a text saying she is going to pick it up herself to save him the trip. He'll be back by six forty-five at the latest, so that gives her enough time to take a quick stroll past Anita's house on her way to the fish bar. She's heard nothing from Tishk since he dashed off to see Cara two days previously and she is desperate to know what's going on with her niece. The idea that Cara is still blaming Limey Stan for things going wrong has incensed her.

It is a two-minute walk between her house and Anita's, if that, and as she turns into Parsons Close, Karen is assailed by a wave of grief. How many millions of footsteps has she trodden between her house and here over the years? With her sister gone, it suddenly feels like nowhere near enough.

The first thing she notices as she nears number 16 is that it is ablaze with light. The porch light has been left on and through the glass panels in the front door, she can see the hallway is also illuminated, while the lounge and the two bedrooms at the front of the house are lit up, with the curtains still wide open. Slowing her pace, she stares up at the windows but can't see Cara anywhere. She must be in the back of the house, perhaps in the kitchen . . .

Then it hits her.

The lights.

Turning on every light in the house is what Cara did in the weeks before she killed Matty, even when it was daylight outside. Anita would shout at her to turn them off, but the child would run round flicking them back on again, insisting they had to stay on so there were no shadows anywhere in the house. The pattern of behaviour continued in the days after Matty's death as well, before the police investigation had yet to categorically conclude her guilt. Only then, Cara had confined herself to her bedroom, where she lay on the bed, catatonic, with her bedside lamp and the overhead light on. She would not sleep; she just lay there, eyes wide open, but every now and then would shout 'You can come out now, Limey Stan' at the top of her voice. The doctors at the Peachick told Paul and Anita the obsessive behaviour with the lights was a symptom of her being unwell.

Karen chews her bottom lip anxiously as she burrows her chin into the collar of her coat to stave off the evening chill. If Cara is keeping all the lights on again, should she intervene? It might be a way to get her to leave Heldean after all. Yet Tishk's comment about giving Cara a second chances needles her and she hasn't forgotten either that it was at her urging that Anita called a doctor out to examine Cara in the days after Matty's death. The doctor took one look at her and suggested an immediate psychiatric referral, which the police agreed to as they were getting nowhere with their questioning. How would it look if she were the one who has Cara carted off again?

Karen stares up at the house, contemplating whether to seek help again for her niece and knowing it probably wouldn't be welcomed if she did. What would Anita want her to do in this circumstance? On that thought, she exhales a long, tremulous sigh. The truth is, she has no idea how her sister would want her to react. Cara's hospitalisation was a topic Anita would not discuss with anyone, not even Karen, no matter how hard she tried to get her to open up. It was almost as though Anita did not want to acknowledge it was a psychological illness that had caused Cara to hurt Matty.

Yet, in the immediate aftermath of Cara's admittance to the Peachick, Anita and Paul would catch the train to London every other day to visit her. The doctors treating Cara told them that, with the right treatment and support, she should make a good enough recovery to lead a normal life into adulthood, albeit one underpinned by necessary medication. Paul, although distraught by Matty's death, had been fully committed to welcoming Cara home when she was deemed fit for release – he told Karen he couldn't bear the thought of losing her as well and he accepted it was her illness that had made her commit such a terrible act of violence.

A couple of weeks in, however, Anita stopped going and then announced she was done with her daughter. Cara would never be returning home to them. Not even Paul's suggestion of a move away from Heldean, a fresh start, could persuade her to rethink her devastating proclamation. Where they lived wasn't the problem, Anita told him, it was Cara. She could not be her mother any more, not now, nor in the future. If he insisted on Cara coming home, she would leave him.

A desperate Paul had relayed this to Karen, thinking that if anyone could change Anita's mind it would be her. But she actually agreed it might be better for Anita to grieve for Matty without Cara's presence being a continual reminder of her loss;

it was obvious Anita was never going to be able to forgive her daughter.

Karen shivers into the depths of her collar again as she remembers the conversation she and her sister had about it, when she said she would support her decision to have Cara fostered. It wasn't an easy thing for her to say, but she truly felt that it was in everyone's best interests – Cara's included. Living with a parent who hated her guts was surely worse than being fostered by people who could properly care for her? That Anne who came with Cara to the will reading did seem nice, Karen thinks.

It left Paul facing a dilemma of monstrous proportions: keep his child or lose his wife. In the end, he chose Anita, for reasons he never articulated to Karen, their relationship strained from that moment. But it was obvious the guilt of giving up Cara needled him like a rash, never giving him a moment's peace, and when the accident investigators ruled there was no mechanical reason for his car to have veered across the motorway into the side of an articulated lorry one March evening six years later, Karen knew in her heart he had crashed it deliberately. As much as he loved Anita, he could no longer live with himself for agreeing to banish their daughter.

Karen wipes a tear away. Her and Paul's relationship was never the same after she sided with Anita – he was staggered she had so little empathy for Cara and would rather see her cast out of the family than support her recovery. Now, on reflection, with Tishk's comment about how Cara must have suffered being parted from her parents ringing in her ears, Karen realises she was wrong not to care. She should've thought more about her niece's experience: instead, her personal anger at Matty's death meant her focus was always on Anita and how she was coping and feeling.

She stares up at the illuminated house again. The lights all being on does feel like an ominous warning sign that more trouble is approaching. Should she give Cara another chance, as Tishk suggested, and try to help her this time before it's too late again?

Wiping another tear, Karen pulls her phone out of her pocket, her intention being to call Gary and ask him to come straight to Parsons Close instead of going home. He knows all about Cara's obsession with the lights and might have an idea what they should do now about it. But before she can make the call, a car suddenly roars into the close and screeches to a halt outside number 16. A suited man with lightly greying hair climbs out of the driver's seat and in his hand he is holding a large, white foolscap envelope. Karen frowns as the man heads towards the house.

Pocketing her phone again, Karen retreats a few doors down to a house with a lofty hedge growing along its perimeter that can shield her from view. The man is in the porch now, ringing the doorbell. He appears agitated and twice checks his watch before ringing the bell again. A few moments later, the door opens a fraction and Cara peers nervously through the gap, her eyes darting from side to side. Karen is shocked by how dishevelled she is, her hair a tufted, unwashed mess and dark circles underlining her eyes.

Karen steps into full view of the front door, all thoughts of hiding herself evaporated. Cara sees her and frowns.

'Are you spying on me?' she hollers over her visitor's shoulder.

The man turns round and his eyes narrow as he stares at Karen, as though he is trying to place her.

'Of course I'm not. I was just passing,' she says, stepping forward to the foot of the driveway.

'I don't believe you,' Cara snarls.

She pulls the front door wide open and comes out into the porch. The man, who looks perturbed, shuffles to one side to make room for her.

'I know what you're doing,' Cara continues, her voice still raised. 'It's you, isn't it? You're the one coming into my house and trying to scare me.'

Karen shakes her head. 'I haven't set foot inside since the day you wanted to take my key off me.'

'I don't believe you. I know what you're trying to do. It's because I haven't left like you told me to.'

The man clears his throat. 'I think it might be better if you went,' he says to Karen. 'Ms Marshall is obviously upset about something and you being here seems to be making it worse.'

'Who are you?' Karen asks him, annoyed.

'Not that it's any of your business, but he's the estate agent,' says Cara. 'And he's right – I want you to leave me alone.'

Karen ignores her. 'Are you from Leonards? This was my sister's house and I arranged the valuation with your office a few months ago. My husband Gary showed you around.'

The man comes down the driveway after saying 'Leave this to me' in an aside to Cara.

'Yes, I'm Ian Leonard,' he tells Karen, shaking her hand. He glances back at Cara, who is watching them, arms folded, face as thunderous as storm clouds. 'Your niece really would like you to leave,' he says apologetically.

Karen nods. 'Can I ask you a favour before I go? I'm worried about Cara. If I call you tomorrow, will you let me know if she's okay? It's because of all the lights being on—'

The estate agent interrupts her worriedly. 'The lights?'

'It's hard to explain, but the lights being on is significant.'

'Ms Marshall is my client and while there is no professional law that requires me not to discuss my dealings with her, I am not comfortable telling tales on her,' says Leonard awkwardly.

Cara chooses that moment to remind them both that she's still there. 'What is she saying?' she shouts, her tone brittle with anger.

'I should go. I'm sorry,' says Leonard, and he scurries back up the driveway. Cara marches into the house and he follows her, pulling the door closed behind them.

Fighting back fresh tears, Karen crosses the road to go home. She has a knot in her stomach that's left no room for appetite, so Gary will have to get the fish and chips himself if he wants them.

Suddenly, behind her, she hears someone call out her name. Turning round, she sees Heather, the woman who lives in the house opposite Anita's, bearing down on her.

'I'm glad I caught you,' says Heather breathlessly as she chugs down the path towards her. 'Have you got a minute?'

'Um, I guess.' Karen doesn't know her that well and is surprised she wants to talk to her.

The neighbour pulls her cardigan tightly around her middle. She's wearing it over legging-style pyjamas and her feet are burrowed inside booted slippers. 'Blimey, it's nippy out here,' she says with a shiver.

Karen doesn't want to get drawn into a chat about the weather. 'Is everything okay?' she asks.

'No, it's not. It's your niece. I know it's not your problem now as the house is hers, but she's driving us mad. The lights are left on all night and the brightness keeps us awake, then she keeps yelling in the middle of the night and that sets that bloody dog of hers off. Between the lights, her and the barking, we're not getting a wink of sleep.'

Karen is alarmed. 'Yelling what?'

'Dunno. We're too far away to make out what she's saying and it's so late we don't like to go over. But it's loud and it's getting out of hand and I was hoping you could have a word with her.'

'I'm sorry you're being disturbed, but as you said, it's her house now. There's nothing I can do.'

'Why not?' Heather huffs. 'We're not the only ones getting fed up. I think the only person not bothered out of the entire street is Tishk, because he's friendly with her. She's your niece, why won't you speak to her about it?'

'We're not close. She won't listen to me.'

Heather's lips pucker with obvious annoyance. 'Look, I'm trying to be nice about this, because I always got on with your sister. She was a nice woman. But letting her daughter return was a terrible mistake. We're all scared of what she might do. We all know what she's capable of.'

Heather's words hang in the cold air between them, the unpalatable truth out there for all to hear.

'That was a long time ago. Cara spent a long time in hospital being treated,' says Karen falteringly. 'The doctors said she was better—'

'Your sister didn't think so,' Heather scoffs. 'Why wait until she was dead and out of the way to invite her back otherwise?'

The woman has a point, Karen thinks uneasily. Anita did make a song and dance about wanting Cara to return to Heldean – but only after her death. Had she suspected it might be problematic and that's why she didn't want to be around to witness it? What had she hoped to achieve by Cara coming back anyway? Anita swore it was because she wanted to make amends, but what if, it suddenly occurs to Karen, her sister was lying and she's now an unwitting part of making Cara suffer for what she did all those years ago? Being back in the house might be triggering a repeat of her behaviour – the lights suggest so – yet this time there would be no leniency. Cara is an adult now, not a child below the age of criminality. If anything were to happen, she wouldn't escape punishment so easily – she'd either be recommitted to hospital or imprisoned, and as much as Karen wants Cara out of Heldean, she wouldn't wish either scenario upon her.

She begins to back away from Heather, who is still in full flow, complaining about the noise.

'I have to go,' she says weakly.

'What? No, wait, I haven't finished—'

Karen turns and flees, but she can't outrun the unspeakable thought coursing through her mind – what if Anita's plan all along was to see Cara locked away again?

Chapter Thirty-Six

Cara

Ian Leonard follows me into the kitchen. I do not ask him if he wants a glass of wine, I just pour it anyway. If he doesn't drink it, I will.

'What did my aunt say to you?' I ask, thrusting the glass at him. He accepts it, but puts it straight back down on the counter.

'She asked me to let her know how you were. She said she was worried about you. I said no,' he adds hastily. 'I don't want to get in the middle of a family dispute, if that's what this is.' He holds up a large white envelope. 'I only came round because the electronic signature document you emailed back to the office corrupted, so I thought, to be on the safe side, we should do it the old-fashioned way. This is the contract for you to sign in person.'

'I could've come into the office.'

'It's no trouble, it's on my way home.'

I take the envelope from him, then waggle my glass of wine at him. 'Are you sure you won't join me? It is Friday night, after all.'

He hesitates and I imagine he's wondering what my motive is in asking him. I'll flatter him by not explaining the truth: it's not that I want to have a drink with him; I just don't want to drink alone. He could be anybody, frankly.

His face breaks into a grin. 'Okay, but just the one, otherwise I won't be able to drive home.'

An hour and two large glasses later, he resolves to leave his car and get a taxi back.

To be fair, as drinking companions go, I could have picked worse. Leonard is easy on the eye and while he does have that annoying way of speaking, he's entertaining with it. He's been regaling me with amusing stories about the horrors he's come across while valuing houses and I splutter a mouthful of wine down my front when he tells me about an elderly woman who was selling up to go into a nursing home, who, an hour before completion, told him she hadn't packed up her house to move because she thought selling included the entire contents as well.

'What did you do?' I ask, wiping my mouth.

'I couldn't get professional movers at such short notice, so I booked the buyers into the best hotel in town for the night, hired a lorry and paid everyone in the office triple time to work through the night to get it packed.'

We both laugh and, after pouring us both more wine, I thank him.

'What for?'

'This. Being normal. Chatting.' I pause. 'For not treating me like I'm the Antichrist.'

It is thanks to him that I am calmer now. Seeing Karen standing in the street like she owned it made me so angry I couldn't help but lash out.

Leonard shifts in his seat, causing his suit jacket to slip on the back of the chair where he'd hung it. He doesn't notice and the jacket remains coquettishly draped from one shoulder.

'I just want to sell your house,' he says matter-of-factly. 'Anything else is irrelevant.'

I am not disappointed this is purely a business transaction for him. It makes it easier. I'm still in no rush to get the house on the market, though. Not before I get to the bottom of why Mum left it to me, which I'm still drawing a blank on despite turning the house upside down again and even venturing into the loft, where I found nothing but rolls of fibrous insulation laid between the joists.

I've managed to swallow my fear about delving further into Limey Stan too, although, admittedly, that hasn't progressed much either beyond a trawl of the internet for the latest scientific explanations of paranormal events. I've been too exhausted to do more, because despite taking my medication, I have managed only three hours' sleep in total since Wednesday when I found the table upside down. No matter what I take, I can't sleep. So, as a consequence, I'm shattered and can barely think straight, let alone try to piece together proof of what killed my brother.

Mustard trots into the kitchen from the front room, where he's been asleep himself for the past couple of hours. He goes straight to greet Leonard, tail wagging.

'You should be honoured, he doesn't like most men,' I say, smiling.

'I grew up owning dogs,' Leonard answers, ruffling Mustard's ears with both hands. Then he looks up at me. 'Can I ask you something?'

I shrug a yes.

'Your aunt mentioned she was concerned all the lights were on . . .'

Panic flutters up inside me and I fight to keep a straight face. I know why my aunt brought it up with him. She remembers.

'Anything that woman says is a lie,' I say, hoping my voice sounds normal. 'She never believed me and she wants me gone again. She even asked me how much it would take me to leave.'

He ignores the last remark. 'She never believed you about what?'

'That I was being honest.'

'About what?' he presses.

I swallow hard, the irony of what I'm about to say to the man selling my house not lost on me. 'About thinking the house was haunted.'

Give him his due, he doesn't react in the slightest. Not even a twitch.

'When I was admitted to hospital after my brother died, I was diagnosed with delusional disorder brought on by stress,' I plough on, 'and my psychiatrist said it was the illness which made me think I'd seen and heard a ghost. It didn't feel like that at the time, though – it felt real.'

I don't know why I am telling Leonard this. Possibly because he has the kind of face that invites you to open up and makes you think he will be receptive, but also I think it's because I really need to talk about it to someone, anyone. Since I wrote my list yesterday, I've kept Tishk at arm's-length, not inviting him in when he pops round and ignoring his texts.

I take a sip of my drink. 'How much do you know about the Heldean Haunting?' Setting my glass down, I make speech marks in the air with my fingers, my pretence at making light of it.

'Same as everyone else, I imagine. I didn't pay much attention at the time because I was a teenager and more interested in hanging out with my mates and meeting girls, but my mum told me some things based on what she'd heard from friends and neighbours, the rest I read about afterwards.'

'Where did your family live at the time?'

'Right across the other side of Heldean,' he says.

Word of Limey Stan really did spread far that summer, I realise. No wonder the press later accused me of trying to hoax the entire town.

'Did you really hear "Limey Stan" being said aloud?' he asks, aping my airborne speech marks.

'Yes. I'll never forget what night it was either because earlier that day we'd been to the funfair and I went on the waltzers for the first time.' Leonard smiles, as do I. 'It's funny how things like that stick in your mind,' I say. 'Anyhow, it was gone two in the morning, I'd been woken up again and was listening on the landing and I heard a voice in the hallway downstairs say very clearly "Limey Stan". Except it was more like a low growl and not really human.'

This time he does react and the corners of his lips tug upwards.

'I know what you're thinking,' I grin back. 'It does sound crazy. And, believe me, I've gone over it a million times since, thinking I must've imagined it. But how else would I have come up with such a distinctive name if I hadn't heard it? I was a clever kid, but not that clever.'

'But a ghost hurting a child . . . I mean, come on.'

I'm not offended by the way Leonard says it, because I'm sure it's how I would react if our roles were reversed.

'I know what you mean, but what other explanation is there? I know I didn't kill my brother, whatever anyone else thinks.'

He looks uncomfortable and shifts in his chair. 'I'm not saying you did, Ms Marshall. I'm sorry if I gave you that impression.'

'It's fine,' I say, batting away his apology. 'And, please, call me Cara. More wine?'

He shakes his head. 'I should get going. I've got an early start. Saturday is our busiest day for viewings.'

He gets on his phone to summon an Uber as I continue to sip my drink.

'One should be outside in four minutes,' he announces. He gets to his feet and slips on his jacket, then pats down the pockets as though he's looking for something. 'The contract,' he exclaims.

I quickly extricate it from the envelope and sign it after checking it is the same version I was sent via email.

'Thanks for the drink,' says Leonard, taking the contract from me.

'You're welcome. It was nice to talk to someone friendly for a change. I haven't exactly been welcomed with open arms since I returned.'

He nods. 'Are you going to be okay?'

'I'll be fine, thank you.' I show him to the door and we shake hands.

'Actually, I have a confession to make before I leave,' he says, shifting awkwardly on the spot. I tense, fearful of what's coming next. 'The reason I brought up what your aunt said about the lights was because I thought there was a problem with the electrics that might affect the sale . . .'

I'm still laughing as his taxi pulls away.

Chapter Thirty-Seven

Cara

Most likely it was the combination of medication and alcohol knocking me out, but that night I sleep soundlessly for almost ten hours. Saturday and Sunday are the same, although I drink less both evenings because I no longer feel the need to wipe myself out. The conversation with Ian Leonard has shifted my perspective a bit: there are people out there who are willing to believe that I was not responsible for Matty dying. That matters to me hugely.

There have been no further disturbances either. No footsteps in the hallway, no tables upturned, no toys from Matty's room being rearranged across my bed. I wonder how Leonard would've reacted had I told him about those bizarre, unfathomable incidents – he might not have been as confident about selling the house if he knew.

Jason the gardener did not work over the weekend, but he's back this morning. He estimates it will take him at least another eight days to finish clearing the garden, lay new turf, weed the beds and replant them, paint the fences and prune back bushes, before it will be presentable enough for the marketing pictures to be taken. I tell him not to worry about rushing it.

Mid-morning, I ring Jeannie in the office to update her on my return to work. I hold my breath, hoping it's not Donna who answers because I don't fancy the interrogation that will inevitably follow, but thankfully it's Leo, the junior, who picks up.

'Jeannie's not in today, but I'll leave a message saying you called,' he says. 'Or you could just email her. She's checking her emails at home.'

'I'll do that.'

I end the call before he has a chance to question me about when I'm coming back. The truth is, I don't know when that will be. I'm hoping Jeannie will give me three weeks off unpaid, then I'll see after that.

But before I draft and send the email, I make another call, one that I've been putting off for days.

Anne answers after only two rings.

'Oh kiddo, I'm so pleased you've called,' she says.

'I'm sorry I haven't before now.' I mean it too. I'm so happy to hear her voice, I tear up. 'I should've rung you sooner.'

'It doesn't matter. What's important is that you've called now,' she says, and I can hear the vibration of unshed tears in her voice too. 'What happened at the cemetery—'

I cut her off. 'Let's not talk about it. I don't want another argument.'

'No, we need to discuss it. I want to explain. You thought I reacted because I didn't believe you about Limey Stan, but that wasn't it. I was scared.'

'Scared? Of what?'

'Of you having another episode.'

My stomach somersaults as she says that. 'What do you mean?' I splutter.

'You know what I mean, Cara,' she says gently. 'The obsessive behaviour that flares up whenever you become fixated on Limey Stan, when you stop eating, start drinking too much and stay up all night rereading all the press cuttings. When I saw your reaction to what that man said at the cemetery, I feared the worst.'

'I was upset because he was rude,' I correct her, but her words strike a chord. I have gone through stages in the past where I have been preoccupied thinking about Limey Stan and what happened to me and I've obsessed about it, but I'm better at stopping myself now, hence me drawing up a list of people who could've overturned the table and moved Matty's toys and not immediately assuming it was him.

'I know he was rude, but the look on your face when you were shouting about Limey Stan . . . I'm just worried about you, Cara. I wish you'd come and stay with us for a bit. We can look after you.'

'I don't need looking after – what I need is answers.' Suddenly I have an idea and I don't know why I didn't think of it sooner. 'Do you still have all my stuff in your loft?'

'Cara, have you listened to a word I've said? It's reading those books and cuttings that makes you ill.'

'I don't want the books – I want my medical file from the Peachick.' Anne and John took it back to Morecambe when they packed up all the paranormal-related material, out of concern it too was fuelling my spiralling mood. 'I want to read my discharge report, the one which said I was well enough to leave.'

'Why do you want to read it now?'

There's a lull as I decide how to frame my next sentence, knowing what Anne's probable reaction will be. 'I want to make sure they really did think I was better.'

She gasps. 'But of course you were!'

'Sometimes I'm scared they got it wrong,' I say, and I mean it. Taking my pills again fills me with concern that my disorder never really went away.

'Cara, why would you say that? Has something happened?'

I think about the coffee table and Matty's toys and I know I can't tell her about them, because she already sounds worried enough. Even if I said I'm convinced an actual person was responsible, she's still going to assume I secretly think it was Limey Stan.

'No, everything's fine,' I lie. 'It's just being back in this house – it's brought up loads of unanswered questions that I'm trying to make sense of and I guess I'm looking for reassurance.'

'What else is bothering you?'

'Well, one question I keep asking myself is why did I end up being fostered in Morecambe and not somewhere closer to Heldean? Whose decision was it to place me so far away from home?'

'It was your social worker's suggestion, actually. Marie trained in this area before she moved down south and we'd worked with her on a number of previous cases. She knew we specialised in long-term placements for adolescent girls so she contacted us to see if we'd be willing to foster you. So it was nothing to do with Morecambe as such, but rather what John and I could offer you.'

'Long-term? You mean from the outset it was decided I would be with you for a while?' I ask, perturbed.

'I suppose so, yes. And we were happy to have you, Cara.'

'Did my parents know that's why I was fostered by you?'

Anne hesitates. 'I imagine they did. Parents are usually informed.'

I am distraught. I thought I was sent to Morecambe because it was a decent distance from Heldean, not because it had been decided even before I arrived that I'd stay there for years.

'I don't understand how my parents could've agreed to that,' I say. 'It's like they knew I was never going to return to them.'

'I imagine they thought it was the best thing for you at the time. Securing a long-term foster placement gives children a

186

sense of continuity and security they've been lacking in their home lives.'

'But I wasn't lacking either of those things,' I protest. 'Up until Matty died, our home life was happy.' The conversation is making me tense and I feel a stab of pain in the side of my head that marks the beginnings of a headache. I need to get off the phone. 'Look, can you please just send me my medical file? I can cover the postage if you let me know how much it is.'

'If you're absolutely sure you want it, yes, I'll get John to fetch it down from the loft. He might not be able to get up there until tomorrow though – his back is giving him gyp. He strained it getting the Christmas decorations down yesterday.'

With a pang, I realise I've been so wrapped up in myself and how I'm feeling that I haven't asked Anne how either of them are. 'I don't want him hurting himself,' I say. 'It can wait until his back is better. There's no rush.'

I wrap up the call by promising I will definitely be at theirs for Christmas. From Anne's joyous reaction, I can tell she's been fretting that our row in the cemetery would deter me going this year.

'That's marvellous news, I'm so pleased and John will be too. In the meantime, try not to let yourself become overwhelmed while you're sorting out your mum's house. I know that's easier said than done, but you've got to take care of yourself.'

But it's too late for that. I am already overwhelmed and finding out that my parents agreed to me being fostered long-term while I was still in the Peachick tips me over the edge. Call ended, I sink to the floor, my phone still in hand, and begin to cry.

Jason is spreading sand on the ground where he's removed the old turf, ready to lay the new. He's brought a radio with him today that's turned up high and he doesn't hear me calling his name over the music until I'm standing a metre away. My presence, when he does notice it, makes him jump and he drops the rake.

'Sorry, I didn't mean to startle you.'

He trots over to the radio and clicks it off. 'Didn't realise I had it on so loud.'

'It's not a problem.'

His face scrunches as he peers at me, the sun-scored wrinkles around his eyes become even more pronounced. 'Are you okay?'

My face feels puffy from crying, I haven't showered yet and my hair is flattened with grease. I must look a state.

'I'm not feeling very well,' I fib. 'Would you mind finishing up today and coming back in the morning?'

He checks his watch. 'It's not even lunchtime.'

'I know.'

'Is it the music bothering you? I can turn it down . . .'

'It's not that. I think I'm coming down with a virus and I need to sleep it off, but I want to lock the door if I'm upstairs, so you won't be able to come in to use the tap or the toilet.'

He nods slowly. I am probably coming across as a bit odd, but I don't care. I want him to leave so I can lock myself away.

'You reckon you'll be okay tomorrow?' he asks.

'I'm sure I will be.' I force a smile. 'You're doing a great job, it's going to look terrific when it's done.'

The praise pleases him and as I retreat inside, he is whistling to himself as he gathers up his tools. I lock the back door and make sure the front is secure too, then I head upstairs to the bathroom.

I spend a long time standing beneath the showerhead over the bath, letting the force and the heat of the spray persuade my muscles to unclench. Eventually, I turn off the water and reach out from behind the shower curtain to grab my towel from the rail. My prolonged shower has caused a warm, clammy fog to envelop the room and the mirror above the sink has misted over. I am about to climb out of the tub when something on the mirror catches my attention. I double take. Then I freeze.

Written in the steam, in thick, plain lettering, are the words I AM LIMEY STAN. I AM HERE.

Chapter Thirty-Eight

https://theheldeanhaunting/blog

16 PARSONS CLOSE UP FOR SALE

1 December 2019

Comments [22]

How would you like to own Heldean's famous haunted house? Yes, you read that correctly! I have it on very good authority that Cara Belling has instructed Leonard Estate Agents to begin the process of selling 16 Parsons Close. While a part of me wishes Ms Belling would keep the property, as she is as much a part of its legend as Limey Stan is, I do respect her wishes to move on following her mother's death. Plus, the prospect of a new owner experiencing the same paranormal phenomenon is too exciting to disregard!

My most favoured outcome, however, and I'm sure avid readers of this blog will agree with me, is for Heldean Historical Society to purchase the property and preserve it for the benefit of the townspeople. It is a property of worldwide renown, and Heldean could benefit enormously from the many visitors it would attract. Needless to say, I have already contacted the HHS to put my suggestion to them and I shall report back when they reply.

In the meantime, I would like to answer a question sent in to me by a reader. They didn't give their name, but I shall refer to them as 'Pixie' in a nod to their email address. Pixie asked 'How can a ghost kill when it is not of physical substance?' Well, the answer is quite easy, Pixie. Copious paranormal investigations over many years have proved that poltergeists, of which Limey Stan is one, have the capability to move objects using invisible force. Therefore, while a ghost won't be able to touch you with its bare hands, so to speak, it can and will pervade items to use as weapons – in the case of Matty Belling, the curtain used to smother him. If you want to find out more about how Limey Stan was able to kill, read my investigative account of the Heldean Haunting – available to download as a 99p ebook if you click <u>here</u>.

Timothy Pitt, paranormal investigator

Chapter Thirty-Nine

Cara

I stumble forward, banging both shins on the side of the bath in my haste to get out. Without bothering to towel myself dry, I struggle back into the same clothes I had on earlier and throw open the bathroom door. I am dangerously breathless again, my chest burning with pain as I heave to take in more air against my lungs' will. But it is a battle I must force my body to win because I need to remain conscious and get as far from the house as I can run.

By the time I reach the front door, though, I'm already seeing stars. I force myself to take shorter gulps to squeeze in some air and it works and I'm able to unlock the front door. Down the driveway I run, my feet bare, and as I hit the street, my breathing begins to steady — but my terror remains sky-high.

Who can help me?

I pause for a millisecond, then pelt along the path towards Tishk's. He had texted to say he was going away for the weekend to visit his parents, but he should be back by now. Yet as I near his house, I cannot see his car parked outside and I falter, at a loss what to do next. The words on the mirror swim before my eyes.

Limey Stan was there, in the room with me.

My lungs leap into panic mode again and this time I cannot

force them to stay operable. I drop to the ground, barely reg-
istering the sting of bone against concrete as my knees crunch
heavily against the pavement, and I'm crying and gulping and I
don't think I can stay upright—

Suddenly, hands grip my upper arms, pulling me up.

'It's okay, we've got you.'

Then a whisper that's loud enough for me to hear.

'It's her.'

My sight's blurred and I can't make out who is supporting
me on either side, but I feel their solidness and let them take my
weight as they lead me over to the patch of grass outside Tishk's
house and sit me down.

'It looks like a panic attack. Has anyone got a paper bag for
her to breathe into?' I hear a woman's voice ask.

There's low murmuring and then an empty brown paper
McDonald's bag is thrust into my hands. I gratefully wrap it
over my nose and mouth and begin to take deep breaths, finding comfort in the scent of the few random fries still in the
bottom.

My sight clears as my panic subsides and I look up to see a
disparate group of people watching me keenly. Four are elderly,
a man and three women, and standing next to them is a young
woman all dressed in black, and behind her is an overweight
man wearing a *Beano* T-shirt beneath a brown leather jacket
with a sheepskin collar. Last in line, I am surprised to see, is
my neighbour Heather. Although, when she talks, it becomes
apparent she's not with the group, just standing with them.

'Where did you find her?' she asks my rescuers.

Beano Man points back towards the street. 'Over there, on
the pavement, on all fours.'

'Was she screaming again? She's been doing that a lot . . .'

Weakly, I let the bag drop. 'Mustard. My dog. Have you
seen him? I left the front door open, he'll have got out . . .'

'I'll go and look for him,' says the tallest of the three women. She is wearing an anorak and for a moment I am reminded of Anne and I want to cry. I would give anything for her to be here now.

The older man steps forward. 'Are you able to stand, Ms Belling?'

It's only as I shakily get to my feet with his and the girl-in-black's assistance that it dawns on me what name he called me. I stare at the man, dismayed. 'Who are you?' I croak.

He glances at the others, who nod at him encouragingly. Then he turns back to me with a full-wattage smile stretched across his face.

'I, Ms Belling, am your greatest admirer. Allow me to introduce myself. I am Timothy Pitt, Heldean's leading paranormal investigator. You may know my blog—'

'Oh God, no, not you! Get away from me!'

They are spooktators come to gawp at me, led by the man who has forged a career off the back of my family's misery and grief.

Pitt was clearly anticipating a warmer welcome and is ruffled by my obvious rancour.

'Ah, well, our timing is indelicate, I can see. However—'

'I want you to leave,' I snap. 'And take the other parasites with you.'

Beano Man steps forward. 'We just want to talk to you about Limey Stan, Cara.'

'Seamus, please, let me deal with this,' says Pitt sharply.

'I don't want to talk to you,' I yell at him. 'Leave me alone!'

None of them move. They all stare at me, dead-eyed.

Then the girl-in-black steps forward. 'I have a message for you from your mother,' she says.

'You what?'

'Jenny is a medium,' says Pitt quickly. 'You should listen to her.'

'Are you serious?' I admonish him. 'You should be ashamed – exploiting a kid to be a part of this.'

'Please listen to me, Cara,' says Jenny urgently.

I shake my head at her, horrified. Between this ambush, Anne's revelation about why I ended up in Morecambe and Limey Stan's message on the mirror, I am done. I need to get away from here before I go insane. I start backing away from the group, my mind already picturing the place where I can find temporary refuge.

Jenny, a wisp of a thing with skinny limbs and long straggly blonde hair, takes a step towards me, then another.

'Cara, your mum says you mustn't ignore what is precious from the very beginning,' she tells me in an unsteady voice.

I roar at her to stop talking, but she carries on, becoming more flustered by the second. I start walking away from her.

'Don't ignore what is precious from the very beginning,' she incants, raising her voice so it follows me down the street. 'Because that's the road you should take to put things right. Your mum wanted you to know that.'

Chapter Forty

Cara

By the time I reach the cemetery gates, my bare feet are blood-ied and bruised, but I am too agitated to think about stopping or even slowing my pace. I limp through the gates and head for the far corner where my family lies. I have come here because it was the first wide, open space that came to mind when I was escaping Pitt and his followers. I need to be outdoors, away from people, away from that house.

I come to a standstill at my family's graveside, which is shrouded in shadow beneath the spreading branches of the giant oak that stands next to it. It looks the same as it did the last time I was here a couple of weeks ago, but the flowers from Mum's funeral have been removed and a fresh spray of yellow roses has been left in their place, presumably Karen's doing.

I flop down onto the grass next to the headstone and give in to the tears that have been building on my journey here. The last time I felt this helpless and frightened was the day my social worker told me I would be going into foster care and in the same breath said there was nothing I could do about it. My wishes counted for nothing and I was impotent to stop it hap-pening. And that's how I feel now, impotent, with no control over what's happening to me.

But it's not just me I'm crying for. Knowing Matty is buried just metres beneath where I'm sitting fills me with remorse. Right now, I would give anything to go back to the night he died and, instead of forcing him out of bed, I would tuck him back in and whisper that it was okay, he should go back to sleep, that I would tell him all about it in the morning. I will never forgive myself for not doing that.

Eventually, my tears dry and I start to shiver as the cold begins to penetrate, starting at my exposed feet and working its way up my body. The jumper I am wearing is no shield against the plunging temperature, so I pull my knees up and wrap my arms around my legs for comfort. I sit there for a while, until I sense someone watching me. I look up, expecting to see Jim or another worker from the cemetery, but instead I see a woman in a green-and-purple checked overcoat, with red hair too vivid to be natural, standing a few metres away. The frames of her chrome wire-rimmed glasses are so large they make her eyes appear owl-like.

'You'll catch your death sitting out here with no coat or shoes on, Cara. Although, I suppose you're in the right place for it,' she says with a wry grin.

Her face is achingly familiar. My mind swirls like shifting sand until it lands on the image of a teenage girl with mud-coloured hair and a semi-permanent frown.

'Lisa?' I gasp.

The woman flashes me a tearful smile and swallows hard as she nods.

'Long time no see, little cousin.'

I clamber to my feet and launch myself at her with a sob. I hug her fiercely, not wanting to let go, as years of grief flow out of me in a torrent. Lisa turning up now, with everything that's been going on, cracks a fault line through my heart.

Eventually, I loosen my grip and she stands back and holds my shoulders at arm's-length.

'Christ. What have they done to you?' she asks, her own cheeks wet with tears.

Close up, she, of course, looks the age I know her to be, not the age I remember her as. There are tapering cracks around her eyes and lines between her nose and mouth, but she still looks glorious to me, my darling, brilliant cousin.

'I look a mess, I know,' I half-laugh, half-sob. 'It's a long story.'

'I want to hear it. But let's get you indoors first.'

I shake my head. 'I don't want to go back to the house. Not yet.'

'No problem, we can go for a coffee first.'

I look down at my bare feet and she follows my gaze. We both laugh.

'What size are you?' she asks.

'Six.'

'Snap.' Lisa links her arm companionably through mine. 'My car's parked outside the gates. I've got some shoes in my suitcase you can borrow.'

'And socks?'

She grins. 'Socks too.'

At my request, Lisa drives us to the next town, twenty minutes away. I want to be somewhere I can feel anonymous. I do feel a bit guilty asking her – she's already been on the road for eight hours, after setting off from Edinburgh at six a.m. – but Lisa says she doesn't mind. We don't chat much beyond small talk about her journey and the weather; it's as though we're both storing up what we need to say for when we are sitting face to face again. On the way, Tishk texts to say Mustard is with him and asking if I'm okay. I reply I'll be back soon and thank him for taking care of my dog while I'm gone.

Lisa's satnav guides us to a retail park with a coffee chain. I find a table tucked away at the back, while Lisa pays for two lattes and a sandwich for her, because she hasn't eaten since stopping in Doncaster at eleven and now it's gone three. Beneath the table, my toes are pinching in a pair of bright purple suede pixie boots and I smile to myself. It's an eye-opener to see how vivacious adult Lisa is, because child Lisa was far more conservative, in both appearance and manner. Already I like this version more, and that's saying something, because I adored the previous one.

This Lisa looks nervous as she puts the tray down on the table and takes the seat opposite me. I reach over to squeeze her hand, wanting to reassure her that she does not need to be apprehensive around me and that she's the only person in the world I care about right now.

'How did you know I'd be at the cemetery?' I ask.

'I didn't. I went to leave some flowers, then I was going to meet with a friend who I'd arranged to stay with tonight. My plan was to come to yours tomorrow.' My disappointment is crushing and must be written all over my face, because she adds empathically, 'But seeing as we've run into each other like this, I'll call my friend in a bit and let him know I'm staying with you instead. I'm so glad I ran into you, but why the hell were you in the cemetery with no shoes on?'

I grimace as I rake my fingers through my mussed-up hair. 'I had to leave the house in a rush.'

'Why?'

I hesitate. How will she react if I tell her about the message on the mirror? Will she think I'm crazy? I decide it is worth the risk.

'There's been some stuff going on since I've been staying at the house. Weird stuff.'

'Limey Stan weird?'

She says it so casually, I almost spill my coffee. Then I take a deep breath and tell her everything that has occurred so far, right up to the words on the mirror that made me flee the house in my bare feet, and Pitt and his merry band of followers waiting outside to exploit me. Lisa doesn't interrupt, but listens intently, nodding occasionally.

'I've been wracking my brain for rational explanations for what's been going on,' I say. 'I actually thought your mum and dad might be behind it, or even Ryan, because they're furious I've been left the house when Mum had promised it to them. But they'd have had to force entry to get in, so it doesn't stack up.' I let out a groan and rub my temples with my fingers. 'I feel like I'm losing my mind again.'

'You never lost it the first time,' says Lisa, so quietly she's almost inaudible.

'I think the psychiatrists at the Peachick would disagree with you there.'

'They got it wrong. Everyone did.' Lisa's eyes begin to gloss with unshed tears. 'I'm so sorry, Cara, I truly am.'

'What have you got to be sorry about?'

'I could've stopped you being sent to the Peachick. I mean, I tried to, but they wouldn't listen to me—'

I interrupt her, baffled. 'What do you mean?'

She exhales shakily. 'I knew all along you weren't guilty, Cara. You should never have been sent away and it's my fault that you were.'

Chapter Forty-One

Cara

Lisa dissolves into tears and as I reach across the table to take her hand again to comfort her, my mind races. What does she mean it's her fault I was admitted to the Peachick? Who wouldn't listen to her?

Her sobs catch the attention of the baristas behind the counter and one comes over and asks if she is okay. I thank him for his concern and say she'll be fine. A couple of minutes later, he returns and slides two fresh coffees and a few serviettes onto our table.

'On the house,' he mouths.

Lisa continues to cry and I start to get impatient. 'I'm confused,' I say edgily. 'Why is it your fault I was sent away?'

She snivels into a serviette, then blows her nose.

'That night, do you remember? I promised I'd come to the house and hide with you and Matty—'

I cut her off. 'I know, but you didn't. Christ, I'm not angry with you about that, Lisa, if that's what you're worried about,' I exclaim. 'I know you were only humouring me when you said it.'

The day I decided we should hide behind the curtains in the bay window to catch Limey Stan once and for all, Lisa had taken Matty and me to the Rec after school. Until that point, I didn't think she believed what I was saying about Limey Stan, so I was thrilled when, upon hearing my plan, she agreed to sneak round to ours when everyone else was asleep and join mine and Matty's stakeout. But she never turned up and much later on, when I was at the Peachick and my psychiatrist was helping me clarify my recollection from that night, I realised Lisa had been joking about coming round.

'That's the thing, Cara – I was there.'

Everything around us seems to freeze: the baristas, the other customers, the gurgle of coffee machines, the loud hiss of the milk-heating element – it's as though they've ground to a halt and it's only me and Lisa who are still in motion.

I withdraw my hand from hers.

'You made it to the house?' My voice is strangled with surprise.

She exhales shakily. 'I did. Do you remember how heavily it was raining that night? It was chucking it down – like, thunderstorm-heavy. So I waited for it to ease a bit before I set off to yours, because I was worried that if I got soaked Mum and Gary would know I'd snuck out and would go mad.' She pauses for a moment, then plucks one of the serviettes from the table and pats dry her cheeks and the delicate skin beneath her eyes. 'It was gone two in the morning by the time I got there.'

I start to tremble.

'I came through the back way like we agreed,' she goes on.

A flashback: I left the back gate unlocked for her, her secret passage in.

'I used the key you'd left under the flowerpot in the porch to let myself into the kitchen and that's when I heard noises coming from the front room. I was so scared,' she says, her voice lowering.

'What exactly did you hear?' I ask.

My heart is hammering nineteen to the dozen as I wait for Lisa to answer me. She can barely get the words out, but she does, to my horror.

'Cara, I heard everything . . . I heard Matty being killed.'

Part Two

June 1994

Chapter Forty-Two

Anita

The staircase up to Dr Stephens' surgery was so narrow that had another person been coming down at the time she was going up, Anita Belling would have had to reverse all the way to the bottom to allow them to pass. As it was, she managed to get to the top without any bother, although her path was tracked by drips of water from the hem of her rain-soaked dress, the unpredictable weather of the past week catching her out on the walk there.

She gave her name and the time of her appointment to the reception clerk, then tried to hide her annoyance behind a nod when the woman said Dr Stephens was running at least half an hour behind on his consultations. No apology was forthcoming, only an instruction to take a seat in the waiting room next door and a slow look up and down at the bedraggled state of her.

There were three other occupants already in the waiting room: an elderly gentleman with a walking stick, coughing politely into a cotton handkerchief, and a young woman with a toddler asleep across her lap, the boy's cheeks rosy with a fever from the look of him.

Sweeping her sodden fringe off her forehead, Anita took a seat across the room, next to a table laden with magazines and leaflets. Putting her handbag on the floor beside her feet, she twisted round in her chair to tidy the magazines, a force of habit instilled during her last job housekeeping for a woman who liked everything kept neat and straightened and threatened to dock her pay when they weren't.

The magazine on top was a three-year-old issue of *Family Circle* and Anita's eye was drawn to a small headline in the bottom left corner.

Mending A Marriage
When he seems weak and she seems cold

Anita grimaced. Had the writer been spying on her and Paul? She picked up the magazine and flicked to the start of the feature, then immediately dropped it back on the pile as though the pages had pricked her fingers, a quick scan of the intro confirming she didn't want to read on.

If your marriage is in a rut, don't despair. Here are 10 foolproof ways to pull you out of it.

What if there was no way to pull you out? What if the rot had always been there? What if the doubts you had on your wedding day, which you dismissed as jitters, had solidified into absolute certainty that you married the wrong person? Anita shifted in her seat again so her body was angled away from the table and the magazine no longer in her eyeline.

Paul wasn't a bad man. A decent earner in a profession that, touch wood – and she did, reaching down to touch the leg of her chair – had emerged relatively unscathed from the recession, she knew she could count on him to keep a roof over their heads. His wage covered their sizeable mortgage, the remaining bills and their outgoings for the children, which meant she was able to keep whatever wage she earned to spend on herself, and when she wasn't earning, like now, Paul would slip her extra in the housekeeping.

His commitment to being the main breadwinner didn't make him a good match for her, though. He was undemonstrative and insular and in the course of their marriage had lapsed into treating Anita not as a person in her own right but simply as an extension of himself. He behaved as though her sole purpose in life was to make his easier, that she should put up with his endless work trips and minimal contribution to their home life because he brought in the most money. In the early days, she would've happily forgone luxuries for some genuine affection from him, but not now. The rot was too entrenched.

Anita shivered, as much from apprehension as from feeling chilly sitting there in a damp dress. She was concerned Dr Stephens would refuse her request, even though she had a compelling reason to make it and had been rehearsing for days the speech she planned to deliver to him. Paul knew nothing about the appointment and had he known he would be devastated, which is why she didn't tell him. Fortunately, he was away again for work, flogging pens, stationery and other office supplies to firms in Yorkshire over a five-night stretch. If she was careful enough, he might never find out.

Her appointment clashed with the end of the school day, but her sister Karen had offered to cash in a lieu day she was owed by the building society to collect the children for her. This was after Anita had lied and said the appointment was about getting a specialist referral for Cara — Karen was only too eager to help because hers was the loudest voice demanding that Cara's emotional outbursts could not go unchecked for much longer.

There was a calendar hanging on the wall by the door of the waiting room and Anita felt her pulse quicken as the month of June loomed at her. It was Cara's ninth birthday in two weeks and she had done nothing to plan for the party she had promised her other than issue the invitations. Cara wanted it Barbie themed, predominately to show off the Golden Dream Motor Home she'd been given for Christmas and which none of her friends had yet. Anita had tried to explain that bragging and one-upmanship were not attractive personality traits, but, as always, it fell on deaf ears. Not Cara's – Paul's. He wanted both children to have their hearts' desires, because nothing made him happier than knowing his children were happy, even if that happiness was almost always bought. He wasn't even going to be there for the party, as his boss had scheduled a trip away that clashed with it and Paul claimed it couldn't be changed and nor could anyone else go in his place. Cara didn't know yet and Anita was dreading telling her.

Maybe she could get away with icing the cake pink and chucking up a few pink balloons, she mused to herself. It wasn't the branded decor Cara was demanding, but it might suffice.

Anita turned back to the magazines and flipped through the pile, looking for inspiration. She found it in another issue of *Family Circle*, in a feature entitled Easy Children's Party Food. Anita waited until the elderly man was called for his appointment, then slipped the magazine into her handbag. The young mum opposite didn't notice, she was as exhausted as her child was feverish, her eyelids half shut in a semi-doze.

Forty minutes later, after the woman and toddler were seen, Anita was called into Dr Stephens' office. He didn't look up as she entered and she slipped into the seat next to his desk without waiting to be offered it.

She had been a patient of Dr Stephens since birth. He knew everything there was to know about her, from a medical point of view, and also about Paul, Cara and Matty, because they too were his patients. His intimate knowledge of her family put an awkward spin on the conversation they were about to have, but at least Anita had the Hippocratic oath on her side.

Dr Stephens looked up and smiled. His wiry grey hair was particularly flyaway today, as were the bushy eyebrows growing up his forehead to meet it. His eyes were sharp, though, and bored into her as he asked what was the reason for today's visit.

Anita cleared her throat. 'I'd like to be referred for sterilisation, please.'

'I see,' he replied, the beginnings of a frown rippling his forehead.

'I don't want any more children, and nor do I want to rely on contraception for however many years until my menopause, which could be at least fifteen. I've given it a great deal of thought and I know this is the right course of action for me to take.' The words she had rehearsed over and over in her mind sounded stilted as Anita said them aloud, but she did not pause or falter as she recounted them. 'Sterilisation feels to me to be the most effective solution to my situation.'

'Yours and your husband's situation, you mean.'

Anita's eyes narrowed. 'No, this is up to me.'

'Female sterilisation is a very invasive procedure, Mrs Belling, whereas a vasectomy, while painful in recovery, is far more straightforward,' said the GP solemnly. 'If you really don't want any more children and there is no contraception you will consider using long-term, I suggest your husband comes and sees me about having the snip.'

Anita knew Paul would never agree to that in a million years – it was because of his insistence that they try for a third child that she wanted the operation. Yet it would be irresponsible to bring another child into a marriage she dreamt of escaping and if she were to fall pregnant accidentally, Paul would expect her to keep it. She could not take that risk.

'This is about me, not Paul,' she said, her eyes filling with tears. 'At least refer me to a surgeon so I can find out the full implications of being sterilised. That's all I'm asking.'

The GP regarded her for a moment, then nodded. 'Fine. I shall put in for a referral.'

Anita quietly exhaled with relief. 'Thank you.'

'Do you wish to continue the pill in the meantime? I see your prescription is due.'

Anita nodded fervently. 'I do.'

After a few more questions about her general health, the doctor took her blood pressure. She sat silently as he did so, not wishing to invite further discussion. A few minutes later, prescription in hand, she rose to her feet and thanked the doctor for his time.

'My pleasure,' he answered. 'The hospital will contact you directly with an appointment time.'

She gave thanks again, then quickly left his consultation room. So eager was she to escape that she didn't pay attention to the next patient hovering by the reception desk. It was only when the receptionist said 'Mrs Lawler?' to catch the woman's attention that Anita realised she was being stared at. As her gaze met the woman's, she quailed, but forced out a 'Hello, how are you?' for politeness.

Anita's former employer, Nina Lawler, shook her head in disgust. 'Don't talk to me like we're friends.'

The receptionist's eyes widened as her gaze darted between them.

'I – I . . . I should go,' Anita mumbled, her cheeks flaming.

'Yes, you should. And don't you dare think about phoning me again for your last month's pay,' Nina spat. 'You're damn lucky I didn't report you to the police for what you did.'

'I didn't do anything illegal,' said Anita quietly.

'You betrayed my trust!'

Nina's face mottled as she spoke. A decade older than Anita, she was an impeccable dresser, as evidenced by the pure white, drop-waist linen dress and Chanel-logoed ballet flats she was wearing, but the anger coming off her in waves made her appear unkempt.

'I let you into my home, put my trust in you, and you took advantage of that. Have you told your husband what I caught you doing?' Anita flinched at the question. 'No, I thought not. Well, unless you want him to find out, you stay far away from my family and me. If I catch you anywhere near my home, I will tell your husband what a nasty, conniving bitch you are.'

Anita knew it wasn't an empty threat – this wasn't even the angriest Nina had been with her. Their exchange when Nina had thrown Anita out of her house had been blisteringly ugly. Afterwards, Anita had told Paul she'd resigned from working for the Lawlers because she was being overloaded with duties beyond the job description of housekeeper and she wanted to look for a new position. Were he to find out the truth, he would almost certainly leave her and try to take the children and she simply could not allow that to happen. Their marriage might be flagging, but if it was to end, she wanted it to be on her terms.

'I'll stay away,' she said. 'I promise.'

Really she wanted to defend herself against the slur – that what Nina caught her doing wasn't as bad as it appeared and definitely didn't warrant the police being called and had Nina calmed down long enough to listen, she would've seen that – but she was fearful of inflaming the situation, not to mention the receptionist was still listening to their every word.

Nina's eyes drilled into hers. 'Good, because I don't ever want to see you again.'

Chapter Forty-Three

Anita

When Anita let herself into Karen's house through the back door, she could hear yelling coming from the front room – the kids squabbling over which television programme to watch by the sounds of it. The next second, she heard her sister's voice rise above the yells.

'Cara, what have I told you about hitting the boys? Give me the remote control now.'

An all-too familiar, high-pitched petulant whine echoed through the downstairs and Anita fought the urge to put her hands over her ears to block it out. It had taken her the entire walk home from town to finally stop trembling after her confrontation with Nina Lawler and she had no desire to enter into a new fray with her daughter.

She put her bag down on the side, making sure it was tightly zipped so the pill packets from the chemist were hidden, and filled the kettle with fresh water.

Karen appeared in the kitchen a moment later, looking harried.

'Bloody kids,' she said. 'They bickered all the way home and they're still at it. They were kept in at break time because of the rain and now they're like caged animals.'

'What was Cara doing?'

Karen grimaced. 'The usual.'

'I hope you made her say sorry.'

'I did.' A pause. 'What did Dr Stephens say?'

Anita busied herself, taking two mugs off the wooden tree on the counter, then reached in the cupboard above her head for the teabags. She and Karen treated each other's homes like their own and always helped themselves without asking.

'Same as before – be patient, she'll grow out of it.' Anita could almost hear her sister frowning behind her and dared not turn round.

'That's not helpful. Her behaviour's getting worse, not better.'

'Maybe she needs to reach peak-Chucky before it starts improving,' said Anita airily.

'It's not a joke, Neet.'

'I know it's not, but you were the one who let Lisa watch that film.'

'She found it funny,' said Karen defensively. 'And stop changing the subject. You need to do something about Cara because it's not only Matty she's lashing out at. She just walloped Ryan on the head with the remote.'

Anita turned to face her sister. 'I'm not trying to make light of it. I know it's bad. But we're trying our best with her.'

'Can't Dr Stephens give her something?'

'She's not sick and there's nothing wrong with her,' Anita replied, a tightness creeping into her tone. Their GP saying there was no obvious behavioural disorder or learning difficulties causing Cara to misbehave was a topic she and her sister had already covered many times.

'These outbursts are happening too often to be normal, though.'

'Dr Stephens said he thinks it's a reaction to Paul being away so much. She's playing up for attention.' The GP had said that about Cara, just not during today's appointment.

Karen nudged her sister to one side to take over making the tea.

'There's a big difference between playing up and being a right madam,' she sniped.

Any other mum might feel compelled to defend their child from name-calling, but Anita was so worn down by Cara's antics that she didn't have the energy. And in this instance the cap fitted.

'Is Lisa home yet?' she asked. 'I want to ask a favour.'

Karen glanced at the clock on the kitchen wall. 'She should be back in the next half-hour, unless she's been kept behind for something.'

'Detention?'

'No, play rehearsals. Although she keeps threatening to pull out.'

'Why? She loves performing. Aren't they doing *Blood Brothers*?'

Karen gave a wry smile. 'You know what she's like at the moment. She's decided it's not cool.'

Lisa was nearly fourteen, the product of a disastrous relationship Karen had when she was only nineteen herself. It was the only time in the sisters' lives where they weren't close despite both still living at home: Anita, the older by eighteen months, couldn't identify with Karen's single-mum status and struggled to find common ground with the sleepless nights and endless feeds. It was only when she met Paul, and Karen met Gary, that they regained their pre-Lisa closeness.

'She's taken down all her PJ and Duncan posters,' Karen confided.

'Seriously?' Anita laughed. 'But she loves them.'

'Not any more; it's all Kurt and Courtney now.'

'Who?'

214

Karen rolled her eyes. 'Kurt Cobain. You know, that singer who shot himself a few months ago?'

Anita shrugged. She knew Nirvana's music and had read about the suicide, but that was as far as her interest went.

'Lisa's become obsessed with him and his wife Courtney Love now he's dead. She wants to throw away all her clothes and buy slip dresses to wear with Doc Martens.'

'What's Gary's reaction to that?'

'Guess. He still hasn't got over her outgrowing My Little Pony.'

Anita laughed. She had always admired Gary for the way he had treated Lisa as his own from the moment he and Karen became a couple. Lisa was four at the time and her father a non-entity – a married man, he chose to stay with his own family and paid Karen a nominal amount each month for the daughter he never once met. Gary had slipped seamlessly into the role of father figure and Lisa quickly took to calling him Dad. Recently, however, friction had begun to build between stepfather and stepdaughter, and more than once Lisa had thrown in Gary's face that he wasn't her real father and couldn't tell her what to do. Naturally, he was hurt, but his reaction had been to clamp down even harder with rules, making their household at times as fraught as Anita and Paul's.

'Anyhow, what do you want to ask her?'

'I need a babysitter for Friday. I thought she might fancy the extra pocket money. If that's okay with you?'

'She already babysits Ryan, so she's old enough. What about Daisy, though?'

'She can't make it.'

'Can't or won't?'

Anita accepted the mug of tea her sister was handing her.

'Won't.'

'Because of Matty breaking his wrist?'

215

Anita nodded as she blew on the surface of the scalding liquid. 'We told her it was an accident and not her fault, but she still felt responsible and said it didn't feel right to keep babysitting if she couldn't keep the kids safe.'

'Keep Matty safe,' Karen corrected.

Anita was firm. 'It was an accident.'

'Well, I'm sure Lisa will be happy for the money. Where are you off out?'

'Remember when I temped for a time at that office in Charlton Street? I bumped into one of the girls who worked there and we got chatting and she suggested meeting for a drink.'

Karen frowned. 'That was ages ago you worked there.'

'I know, but I was there for a year and always got on well with her. I don't get to go out much, with Paul always away, so it's nice to be asked.'

'You don't need to go out with some stranger. You could come out with us.'

Anita detected a hint of jealousy in her sister's reply and was irritated by it. 'Much as I enjoy a night at the Fleece with you and Gary, it'll be nice to go somewhere else for a change.'

'Where are you going?'

Anita named a newly opened wine bar on the other side of town.

'Bit of a trek isn't it? The cab'll cost you.'

'Paul's paying. He feels bad he won't be back until Saturday evening.'

'Lucky you.' Karen's smile didn't quite meet her eyes and Anita knew why. The disparity in their family incomes was a topic she and her sister studiously avoided. Gary was currently working as a warehouse operative, his third career in eight years. His inability to stick to one thing affected his earning potential and it meant Karen also needed to work full-time to keep their heads above water. Usually, it was Anita who collected Ryan from school and took him back to theirs; without her sister's help with wraparound childcare, Karen would be limited to the part-time roles that Anita took on for pin money and they couldn't survive if she did that.

'Ryan could stay at ours too, if you were getting Lisa to mind him while you went out.'

'He's already going to Gary's mum's for the night. Lisa doesn't like going any more, she says it's boooor-ing.'

Anita grinned at her sister's mimicry, but the smile quickly slipped from her face when there was another yell from the front room, followed by the sound of one of the boys bursting into wracking sobs.

'I'll go,' she said, setting down her mug.

She found Cara perched on the sofa, remote control tightly clutched in both hands, brown bobbed hair ruffled from the fight that had obviously just ended, a picture of feigned innocence. Ryan was sitting on the floor with his face buried in his palms as he cried, while Matty crouched next to him, patting him gently on the back.

'What happened?' Anita directed this at Matty, not Cara. She didn't trust her daughter to be honest.

'She hit Ryan because he wanted to turn over.'

Anita glared at Cara and held her hand out. 'Give me the remote.'

'No.'

'Pass it here.'

'No.'

'Cara, I'm warning you. Give it to me now or I will take you home and you can go to bed without any tea.'

Reluctantly, Cara held the remote out. But just as Anita's fingers reached to grab it, she let it fall to the laminate floor. The back burst open and the batteries toppled out like spent bullets.

'For crying out loud—'

Her tirade was stunted by Matty tugging at her dress. 'Mummy, Ryan's hurt.'

She looked down at her nephew and let out a cry of shock. He had taken his hands away from his face and his palms were covered in blood, as were his nose and chin.

'Christ, Cara, I think you've broken his nose!'

But Cara wasn't listening. Her eyes were trained firmly on the television set, on the programme she wanted to watch.

Chapter Forty-Four

Lisa

Friday afternoon after school saw Lisa in her favourite spot in the house: face down on her bed, plugged into her Discman with 'Smells Like Teen Spirit' blocking out everything and everyone. So she didn't hear the rat-a-tat-tat on the door, or the footsteps shuffling across the carpet, and the unexpected tap on her shoulder that followed sent her body jolting towards the ceiling.

'You made me jump!' she screeched as she yanked the headphones off, her heart thundering in her chest.

'You'll ruin your ears having it that loud,' said Karen, nodding to the headphones in Lisa's hands, where the mournful voice of Kurt Cobain could clearly be heard.

'What do you want, Mum?'

'It's nearly six-thirty. Auntie Neet's expecting you.'

'Shit, I didn't realise the time.'

'Language,' admonished Karen, but Lisa could see she wasn't cross really. Her mum was pretty laid-back about stuff like swearing, probably to counter the fact her stepdad was a stickler for not doing it.

Lisa scrabbled off the bed. She was excited about her first paid babysitting gig – she was going to put the money towards a pair of DMs, reasoning her stepdad could hardly object if she paid for them herself. Auntie Neet said she'd give her the going rate too, rather than a lesser 'we're family' fee. Lisa grabbed her trainers by the door and was stuffing her feet into them when Karen announced she was going to walk her round.

'Why do you need to come?' asked Lisa, annoyed. This was her arrangement with Auntie Neet, nothing to do with her mum.

'I need to ask your aunt something.'

'So ring her.'

'I'd rather ask in person.'

Lisa knew what her mum really wanted to do was check up on Auntie Neet before her night out. It was all she'd talked about for the past few days – who was this ex-colleague she was going out with, why were they going to a wine bar right across the other side of town, wouldn't it be better if they came to the Fleece with Karen and Gary and made a night of it? She was obsessed.

'Can't it wait until tomorrow? I don't want you there while Auntie Neet's showing me where everything is and telling me what to do.'

Karen's laugh came out like a bark.

'You know where everything is already. All you've got to do is sit the kids in front of the telly, then send them up to bed when it's time.'

Lisa flushed with anger. This was an important job for her and she wanted to take it seriously – and be taken seriously.

'Auntie Neet might have special instructions for me,' she said hotly.

Karen's face darkened. 'Well, if Cara gives you any trouble going to bed, you call us at the Fleece and your dad or me will come back. Tessa behind the bar won't mind you ringing their phone.'

'Cara's always fine with me.'

'Hmm. You know what she's been like lately.'

Lisa rolled her eyes. 'She's a bit grumpy, so what? You all act like she's going mad or something.'

'It's more than grumpiness,' said Karen darkly.

'It'll be fine. We're going to watch a film and then go to bed.' Lisa was going to stay over on a camp bed in Cara's room so Auntie Neet didn't have to worry about getting her home late at night. 'I was thinking we could watch *Wayne's World*.'

'What certificate is it?'

Lisa went over to the row of VHS cassettes on her bookshelf. They were stacked alphabetically and it didn't take her long to find the film starting at the back.

'It's a PG.'

Karen appeared surprised. 'Is it? I thought it would be a 15 because it's a bit rude in places.'

'Mum, it's not rude,' said Lisa peevishly.

'Even so, I think it's too old for Matty. It's not appropriate viewing.'

Lisa sighed resignedly, then slid the case back onto the shelf.

'You're better off watching one of their Disney films,' her mum added. 'One that'll keep Cara calm.'

Auntie Neet was dolled up and ready to leave when they arrived. She was irritated to see Karen, which pleased Lisa enormously.

'Lisa didn't need you to come with her,' she snapped. 'She's been walking to ours on her own since she was seven.'

'Mum said she needed to tell you something,' said Lisa impishly, putting her mum on the spot.

'Oh? What?' asked Anita.

Lisa could tell her mum hadn't thought ahead and was now scrabbling to come up with a reason why she was there.

'Um, actually, I was going to see if you wanted a lift. Gary's boss has offered him overtime and he won't be back until eight now.'

Lisa frowned. Her stepdad was doing a lot of overtime at the moment, but him and her mum still kept going on about being skint. 'Are you sure he's at work?' she blurted out.

'Of course he is,' said Karen, bemused. She turned to her sister. 'Do you want a lift, then?'

'My taxi's on its way,' said Anita in a tight voice. 'Honestly, Karen, why are you making such a big deal about my night out?'

'I'm not,' replied Karen hotly. 'I'm just offering you a favour.'

'No, you're not. You're trying to muscle in. I know what will happen – you'll give me a lift, then when we get to the pub, you'll ask to say hi to my friend and then you'll end up hanging around for the evening. I can read you like a book, sis.'

Karen's eyes reddened and Lisa suddenly felt sorry for her mum. She didn't have any female friends to go out with for an evening: her social life amounted to drinks with Gary at the Fleece, or occasionally with him and Anita and Paul. She's probably a bit lonely, Lisa thought, and impulsively she reached for her mum's hand and squeezed it.

'Thanks for walking me round, Mum.'

Karen flashed her a grateful smile, then turned back to Anita. 'Well, the offer's there if you want it.'

'I don't,' came the sharp reply.

Karen, clearly upset, made for the back door, but Lisa managed to grab her before she reached it. 'I'll see you in the morning, Mum.'

Her mum hugged her back, then whispered in her ear so Anita couldn't hear: 'Don't forget you can call us if Cara plays up.'

Lisa grinned and nodded, then left the sisters saying a tetchy goodbye while she went into the lounge, where her cousins were. Both were sitting on the floor in front of the television: Matty playing with his cars and Cara kneeling by the coffee table, drawing with felt-tip pens. She looked up and beamed as Lisa entered the room, which made her relax a little. Despite her mum's concerns, Lisa had never experienced any problems herself with Cara and they'd always got on well despite the four-year age gap. Babysitting her was going to be fine.

And it was, at first. Anita left at seven, after enveloping the two younger children in a cloud of perfume as she hugged them goodbye. She left the number of the wine bar where she was going written down for Lisa, along with instructions about what snacks they could have before bedtime. Matty usually went up first, at eight, but tonight he was allowed to stay up until half-past as a treat. Cara's bedtime was normally 9 p.m., but Auntie Neet said it could be pushed to ten to give the girls more time to hang out.

Until Matty went to bed, they watched the Nickelodeon channel and Cara seemed content enough with that. But when Lisa came back downstairs after tucking Matty in and reading him a story as he dropped off, she found Cara fiddling impatiently with the video recorder beneath the TV, trying to insert a tape in the slot at the front, but it wouldn't go in.

'What are you doing?'

'I want to watch one of Dad's tapes.'

'Which one?'

'It was a pretend programme that was on telly when I was small. Dad taped it and he says it's really good.'

'A pretend programme?' echoed Lisa. 'What's that?'

'It was pretending to be real.'

Nonplussed, Lisa went over and took the tape from her. On the spine, in her uncle's handwriting, was the words *Ghostwatch* – NOT FOR CHILDREN!

'It's about ghosts?'

'Yes. Dad said it's about some famous people off the telly pretending to look for ghosts in a haunted house.'

'Your dad's written it's not for children.'

'That was for when we were really little. I'm old enough now.'

'I still don't think we should watch it.'

'But I need to!' Cara flared up. 'Give it back.'

Lisa folded her arms defiantly, holding the tape down by her side beyond Cara's grasp.

'No. We're not watching it.'

Cara stood up, her little hands balled into fists. 'I have to watch it,' she said through clenched teeth.

'Why?'

'Because.'

'Because what?'

Cara started crying, much to Lisa's surprise. Usually it took a lot to upset her cousin; she wasn't the weepy kind.

'Hey, what's up?' she asked.

Cara's response was to cry even harder. Lisa dropped the tape on the carpet and rushed to her.

'What's wrong?'

'I have to watch that tape,' Cara sobbed, as a trail of snot escaped her left nostril.

'Why, though? What's so special about it?'

Cara wiped her cheeks with the backs of her hands. Her left one glistened as the snot spread with her tears.

'Because I need to know what to do about ghosts.'

'Is it something for school? Are you doing a project?'

'No, it's for here.'

'I don't understand.'

For a moment, Cara said nothing as she stared at her cousin. Then, in a small, quavering voice, she said, 'I think we've got a ghost in our house and I need to know how to get rid of it.'

Chapter Forty-Five

Lisa

Lisa burst out laughing. She couldn't help herself. 'Oh, Cara, don't be daft.'

'But it's true. I've heard it.'

Cara was trembling, so Lisa led her over to the sofa and sat her down. She hooked her arm around her cousin's narrow shoulders, noticed how clammy her skin was and wondered if she should get her a fizzy drink for the sugar, like grown-ups did with sweet tea. Cara refused the offer though, which surprised Lisa because her cousin normally never said no to anything loaded with sugar.

'You said you've been hearing things – like what?' she asked.

'Tapping noises, downstairs.'

'What kind of tapping?'

'Like someone knocking on the wall.' Cara demonstrated, holding up her hand and tapping the air with her knuckles. She gazed imploringly at her cousin, eyes still wide. 'I'm not making it up.'

'I'm not saying you are,' Lisa said carefully, fighting hard to contain the giggles threatening to erupt from her throat, 'but the noise might not have been made by a ghost. It was probably your mum or dad.'

'Everyone else was asleep,' said Cara. 'What else could it have been?'

'Older kids, then, mucking around.'

'Who would do that?'

Lisa could think of one. Tishk, who lived next door and who Lisa fancied. He was older than her by three years and was always out late. But would he really break into someone's house to play a silly trick like this? No way, she decided. He was too cool for that.

'It has to be a ghost,' Cara reiterated.

Lisa gulped down a deep breath to quash her giggles completely. Her cousin was clearly frightened and she should try to be more understanding.

'When was this?' she asked.

'It started a while ago.'

'Started? You mean it's been more than once?'

Cara nodded. 'Yes. First it was knocking, then I've heard footsteps and creaking. Not every night, but on and off since . . .' She paused for a moment and bit down on her bottom lip as she thought to herself. 'I think it started after Christmas.'

Lisa's arm fell from Cara's shoulders. 'Christmas? That long ago?'

'Yes.'

'And you reckon you've heard someone walking about?'

Cara nodded. 'In the hallway and on the stairs.'

'Has anyone else heard these noises?'

'I think it's only me.'

Lisa shivered. She didn't believe in ghosts, but what Cara was saying still scared her and her heartbeat accelerated as she looked across the lounge to the door that led to the hallway that her aunt and uncle always kept shut. What if something was lurking on the other side right now, waiting until they ventured upstairs . . .?

She shook her head as though to dislodge the thought. 'Ghosts aren't real,' she said firmly.

'How do you know that?' asked Cara.

'Because I've never seen one.'

'That doesn't mean they're not real. It just means one hasn't showed itself to you.'

Lisa bristled. Her cousin had lately developed an infuriating, know-it-all way of challenging everything other people said and it was no wonder she drove Auntie Neet up the wall at times. Lisa's stepdad said Cara was precocious, a word she had to look up in a dictionary because she didn't know what it meant, but when she read the definition, it made perfect sense.

'I don't believe in ghosts and you shouldn't either.' She got up from the sofa, bored of the conversation. 'Let's put *Grease* on,' she declared. It was an old favourite, although her preference had shifted from Good Sandy to Bad Sandy now she was older.

'I don't want to watch it,' said Cara stubbornly. 'Why won't you help me get rid of the ghost?'

'How do you expect me to do that?' Lisa scoffed. 'Wave a magic wand?'

'We could ask it to go away. We could use a Ouija board again to talk to it.'

Lisa stared at her cousin. 'How do you even know what a Ouija board is?' She only knew herself because she'd watched a horror film that featured one when she was round at her friend Claire's house.

'Evie told me about them. Evie, my friend from school,' Cara added on seeing Lisa's blank expression. 'I told her about the noises and that I thought it was a ghost and she said her nana used to talk to dead people using a board with the alphabet on, so I asked our teacher if she knew what it was called and she said it was a Ouija board but that they weren't toys and we shouldn't even be talking about them; she got really cross. But Evie said I could make my own at home, so I did. I made it out of paper and it wasn't very good, but me and Matty played with it and I think that's why the ghost started coming more often.'

Lisa laughed at the silliness of Cara's statement, but the girl didn't seem to care.

'Then Matty drew all over it, so I had to throw it away. Can we make another one now, to ask the ghost to go away?' she asked hopefully.

'No, we can't.' Lisa hated craft and wasn't about to start cutting and sticking things. Suddenly a thought popped into her head unbidden. 'Are you sure the ghost isn't your sister Michael back from Australia?' she smirked.

Cara frowned. 'Who?'

'Don't you remember? When you were about three, you had this imaginary friend called Michael, only for some reason you insisted he was your sister. You used to play with him and talk to him all the time.'

'I did not,' said Cara indignantly.

'Yes, you did. You even got your mum to make him extra fish fingers for tea. Ask her if you don't believe me. He was around for ages, then all of a sudden you said he'd gone on holiday to Australia and you didn't know when he'd be coming back. Do you really not remember? He went everywhere with you, even on our holiday to Southsea. You stole a stick of rock from a shop and said Michael made you do it.'

Cara's face lit up. 'I do remember him! I remember the stick of rock too. Dad got really cross with me and made me take it back.' She paused, thinking. 'Michael had red hair and always wore stripy shorts.'

'I bet that's who's making the noise,' said Lisa, stifling a yawn. It was nearly ten o'clock and she was ready for bed herself. 'Michael's back from his travels.'

'It's not. I know it's not.'

'How can you be so sure?' Lisa asked idly, not actually caring what the answer was, then freezing on the spot when Cara gave it.

'Because Michael was a boy the same age as me and this ghost is a grown-up like Daddy.'

Chapter Forty-Six

Anita

The sisters and their families ate lunch together every other Sunday. It was a tradition that began shortly after Anita and Paul moved into their house round the corner from Karen's; they would alternate hosting, and this Sunday it was Anita's turn. Thankfully, Paul was home to help her with the preparation that went into feeding all eight of them. He'd arrived back late the previous evening and was presently next door in the dining room showing Matty how to lay the table, while Cara was in the kitchen with Anita, lining up the ingredients for the pavlova they were going to serve for dessert.

'Is that everything, Mummy?'

Anita cast an eye over the worktop. 'Eggs, caster sugar, strawberries, cornflower, vanilla essence, icing sugar, double cream . . .' She stopped. 'You've forgotten the white wine vinegar.'

Cara's face creased. 'Yuck. Why are we putting vinegar in it? I hate vinegar.'

'It's what the recipe calls for, sweetheart. It's only a tiny bit though.'

Cara contemplated her mother for a moment, then went to the larder cupboard to fetch the bottle without further complaint. Anita smiled with relief, then in the next breath scolded herself for doing so. Her daughter wasn't some monster she needed to be on tenterhooks around – most of the time, Cara was as calm as she was now, and while her outbursts had heightened over the past couple of months, Anita chose to believe Dr Stephens when he said Cara would grow out of them.

Cara skipped back across the kitchen, bottle in hand. She was in a good mood and Anita suspected Paul's return was at the root of it.

'Are you happy Daddy's home?'

Cara nodded. 'I like it when he's here.'

'I know it's tough for you and Matty when he goes away.'

'Daddy says it won't be forever, just until he gets his new job.'

Anita had been annoyed when Paul told the children he was angling for a promotion that would put an end to his travels. He might not get it, she'd pointed out, which had annoyed him because he thought she was being unsupportive. She wasn't – she was simply struggling with the idea of him being at home a lot more and the inevitable increase in conversations about them having a third child.

'Do you miss Daddy?' Cara asked.

The question was unexpected, and it wrong-footed her. 'Um, I . . . well, of course I do,' she lied.

Cara beamed, as though nothing made her happier than to know her parents hankered after one another when they were apart.

Anita's eyes pricked with tears and she quickly turned her face away.

'Are you okay, Mummy?'

'I'm fine, just a bit tired today.'

'I'm not, I had the best sleep ever!' Cara threw her arms out wide and twirled on the spot, giggling as she did. Anita laughed at her exuberance.

'Wow, it looks like you really needed it,' she chuckled.

The twirling stopped and Cara's arms dropped to her sides. 'I did,' she said solemnly. 'I've been very tired from being awake.'

Now she thought about it, Anita could see the dark half-moons usually visible beneath her daughter's eyes were not as pronounced and she had colour in her cheeks. Was that just down to sleeping better though? she wondered. Maybe Cara had been sickening for something and that's what had also been causing her mood swings? For a moment, Anita felt elated, then guilt pricked at her: what kind of mother was she to hope her child was ill as a means of justifying how badly she behaved?

Pushing the ugly thought from her mind, Anita gathered Cara into an embrace, smiling as the girl hugged her back with all her might. Their home life had been so strained lately that sometimes she struggled to be affectionate and with a pang she realised Cara may have picked up on that. Burying her face in her daughter's hair, breathing in the comfortingly familiar scent of Vosene, Anita vowed to make sure Cara never doubted she was adored.

'I love you, sweetheart,' she said, her voice cracking.

'I love you too, Mummy,' came the muffled, joyful reply.

Anita was carving the lamb, ready for serving, when Karen and her family arrived. Brief kisses and hugs all round, then Paul ushered them out of the kitchen into the lounge to give her room to continue. It was only after a few moments she realised she wasn't alone.

'Brought some wine for a change,' said Gary, easing two bottles of red out of a carrier bag and setting them down on the side. 'Where's the corkscrew?'

Anita frowned at him. Drinking alcohol during the day when the kids were about was something they never did as a rule, the legacy of her and Karen's painful upbringing with a father who daily drank himself into rages and a mother who was blinkered to the effect it had on them.

'I don't want any,' she said abruptly. 'Karen won't either.'

Gary shrugged. 'It was her idea.'

'I don't believe you.'

'Ask her. I think she's decided it shouldn't be you who has all the fun.'

'What's that supposed to mean?'

'You went out with your mate on Friday and didn't invite her. Now, where's that corkscrew?'

'Top drawer beside the sink,' said Anita huffily, not happy Karen was still moaning about her going out. It wasn't like she did it every weekend.

Gary whistled under his breath as he found the utensil and set about opening both bottles. Anita was about to comment that one would be enough, but something about his manner stopped her and as she resumed carving the meat, her hands trembled slightly. Her brother-in-law's presence in the kitchen was making her uncomfortable and she wished he'd go next door to join the others.

'Wine glasses?'

She tilted her head to the right, her hands otherwise occupied with knife and carving fork. 'In that cupboard.'

He moved past her to open the cupboard door, still whistling. Then he filled a glass to the rim and proffered it to her.

She shook her head. 'No thanks.'

'Just have a sip.'

'I really don't want any.'

'Come on, it'll help you relax. I know you've had a tough week, with Paul being away.' He said it so soothingly that Anita found herself parting her lips as he held the glass to them. As she swallowed down the mouthful of wine, she realised he was standing so close she could feel the warmth of his breath upon her face and was uncomfortably reminded of another moment when they had been alone like this and a line was crossed.

'Stop,' she said, pulling away. She put the knife and carving fork down with a clatter and wiped her hands on a tea towel.

Gary grinned at her. 'I don't know what you mean—'

Lisa coming into the kitchen just then was a timely interruption.

Gary's expression hardened as he clocked the mutinous look on his stepdaughter's face. 'What's up with you?' he asked.

She said nothing, but glowered at him.

'Dinner won't be long,' Anita told her, hoping to break the tension. 'Cara and I've made pavlova for afters, your favourite.'

Lisa turned her death beam on her aunt. 'I don't want any.'

'Don't be so rude,' Gary admonished.

'It's okay,' said Anita. 'Let's not make a big deal out of it. There's ice cream in the freezer for those who don't want it.'

Lisa stomped out of the room.

'What's all that about?' Anita asked Gary, who shrugged.

'Beats me.'

Karen did want the wine and by the time the pavlova was brought to the table by Cara with a cheery 'Ta-da!' she was on her third glass. It put Anita on edge to see her sister becoming tipsy – what was going on with her to make her want to drink like this? The obvious answer was the enmity between her husband and daughter, but Lisa was being fine with her mum, responding to Karen's comments with smiles. It was only when she turned her gaze to Gary that her demeanour became brittle.

It was a bit of a squeeze around the table with all eight of them seated and Anita didn't like the fact Gary had plonked himself down in the chair next to hers so they were forced to sit arm against arm. She liked it even less when he turned to her and asked how her job was going, when he knew full well what the answer was.

'I resigned, remember,' she answered him in a tight voice.

'Oh yeah, I forgot. Karen did say. But why did you leave again?'

'I felt like a change.'

Paul, at the head of the table and matching Karen drink for drink, butted in. 'Her boss took liberties, that's what. All that extra work she suddenly expected Neet to do for no more money.' He took a slug of his wine. 'I told Neet to quit back at Easter, but she wouldn't listen.'

Anita nodded awkwardly to endorse the lie, yet contrary to Paul's interpretation, it had been an easy job – her duties included a little light cleaning (an actual cleaner came in twice a week), running errands, such as taking packages to the post office, providing access for tradesman and deliveries, picking up groceries additional to the weekly shop Nina did, putting out the rubbish and arranging flowers and taking care of indoor plants. She was employed five days a week around school hours, so it had been the perfect gig, plus she got to see how the other half lived. Nina and her husband owned a seven-bedroom house on one of the most exclusive streets in Heldean, their son was privately educated and Oxbridge-bound in a year's time and Mr Lawler had a job in the City that saw his monthly pay reach five figures. Anita and Paul considered themselves comfortably off, but compared to her former employer, they were impoverished.

Sometimes she would stand in the Lawlers' kitchen and pretend the house was hers. It was a mental escape from her reality living in Parsons Close and in her fantasy life she had no children and a husband who didn't want them either. She tried to rationalise that didn't mean she didn't want Cara and Matty now – it was simply her subconscious demanding a break from being a parent and for that she blamed the societal shift of the past few years that now insisted parents put the needs of their children first.

She would never dare admit it to anyone else, but she longed for the halcyon days of the previous decades when children were ushered outside to play first thing in the morning and told to return only when they were hungry, and when relatives admonished you for raising a weakling if you praised your kids, instead of hinting you were a bad mother for not. Hers was the first generation of mothers expected to be hands-on all the time and it left her feeling drained and frustrated. Her pedestrian marriage only amplified the discontent she felt standing in Nina Lawler's kitchen, until she'd found the most unexpected way to distract herself.

'I thought you left because of a row,' said Gary.

Anita faltered. What exactly had Karen told him? Then she caught herself, remembering she had been economical with the truth when she'd told Karen why she'd left the job as well, so she did not need to worry about what Gary knew. Karen liked to think they shared everything as sisters, but it was far from the case.

'We did row, because of the extra duties she wanted to foist on me.' Desperate to change the subject, Anita looked around for inspiration and her gaze settled on her niece. 'Thanks again for babysitting on Friday, Lisa. We'd love you to do it again.'

'Not while there's a ghost in your house,' the teenager snickered.

Paul laughed. 'A ghost?'

'That's what Cara reckons.'

All eyes landed on Cara, but she kept hers trained on the contents of her dessert bowl. Anita could see the spoon in her hand was trembling.

'Cara reckons she's heard a ghost tapping on the walls and creeping up and down your hallway.'

Anita exchanged a bemused look with her husband. This was the first they'd heard of it, yet it also didn't surprise her that Cara had come up with a fantastical story to impress her cousin – she had a vivid imagination and would come up with the most elaborate stories while playing make-believe with her toys. Then there was Michael, the imaginary friend who Anita was freaked out by when Cara would say he was standing right beside her.

'When did you hear the noises, sweetheart?' she asked.

Cara looked up from her bowl and Anita was taken aback to see how frightened she looked.

'In the middle of the night, when everyone's asleep.'

Paul laughed and Karen joined in. 'You're probably dreaming it,' said her aunt.

'I'm not. The noise wakes me up.'

'I bet you were still asleep and you just thought it had,' said Paul airily, topping up his glass and Karen's, then passing the bottle to Gary. It was the second bottle and it was almost drained. 'Might have to open one from our stash,' he grinned sloppily at Anita, clearly relishing the unexpected daytime drinking session.

She raised an eyebrow disapprovingly, gave a quick shake of her head, then reverted her attention to Cara.

'The noise woke you up? When was this?'

'It's happened a few times.'

Anita swallowed hard. Cara was being very convincing. The others were all ears.

'I've seen him too. I crept to the top of the stairs one night and saw him moving in the shadows in the hall. He was mumbling to himself.'

All the grown-ups apart from Anita chuckled at that.

'You never told me that,' said Lisa accusingly.

Cara stared at her defiantly. 'So?'

'You're making it up,' said the older cousin. 'You told me you'd only heard noises, now you reckon you've heard him speak? You're a liar.'

Cara jumped to her feet, her cheeks mottling. 'I am not! He lives in the shadows downstairs, and he taps and bangs and he makes the house go cold!'

Anita reached out to her daughter, fearing she was on the cusp of an almighty tantrum that would take hours to burn out.

'It's okay, honey. Don't get upset.'

'She called me a liar, but I'm not making it up, I'm not!'

Lisa couldn't help herself. 'Yes, you are.' Then she shot Anita a look. 'Everyone in this house lies!'

Anita had no time to process the remark before Cara let out a howl of anger. Then she picked up the quarter-full gravy boat that hadn't been cleared from the table yet and flung it in a wide arc so the liquid splashed across everyone sitting opposite and the gravy boat itself fell to the floor and smashed. Matty and Ryan both screamed and burst into tears.

Paul reacted first, jumping to his feet and grabbing Cara by the upper arm to yank her away from the table. She was going to her room, he shouted, and she could bloody well stay up there for the rest of the day while she thought about what she'd just done. A livid Gary nodded approvingly as he pulled Ryan onto his lap to comfort him.

Using their serviettes, Lisa and Karen began wiping the gravy off themselves and a sobbing Matty. Anita knew she should say something to calm her son, but she couldn't drag her gaze away from the wallpaper behind their heads, where blobs of Bisto arced across it like muddy brown blood.

Chapter Forty-Seven

Lisa

Lunch at an abrupt end, Karen and Gary decided not to stick around for coffee as they usually did and walked Ryan and Lisa back to theirs. Lisa went ahead with her brother, but they were near enough to their parents still for her to make out snatches of their furiously whispered conversation.

'Can you imagine either of ours doing that?'

'I'd have done more than just send her to her room . . .'

'I swear she's getting worse . . .'

'Anita babies her too much . . .'

'Bloody ghosts? I've heard it all now . . .'

'She did look scared . . .'

'She's wrong in the head. I've always thought it and don't pretend like you haven't too. The way she stares at people is creepy . . .'

'She is a bit intense, I'll give you that . . .'

'She needs to see someone and I don't mean that old codger of a GP . . .'

Ryan stopped in his tracks and swung round, prompting Lisa to do the same. 'Are you talking about Cara?' he asked.

Karen, eyes glazed from drinking, quickly pasted on a smile. 'Oh no, just someone at work that Daddy knows.'

Lisa rolled her eyes. Even Ryan wouldn't buy that. But her

little brother did, or rather his mind immediately switched to matters more pressing for a six-year-old. 'I didn't get to eat my pudding.'

Karen held out her hand for him to take. 'Well, let's rectify that once we're back home and changed out of these mucky clothes. How about a big bowl of ice cream?'

'Raspberry ripple?' asked Ryan hopefully.

'I think there's some left.'

The pair of them walked ahead and Gary fell into step with Lisa, which annoyed her intensely as she had nothing to say to him right now.

'Why didn't you tell us about Cara's ghost story after you babysat?'

She shrugged.

'She's obviously making it up, like she made up her imaginary friend.'

Lisa was in no mood to engage with her stepdad, but on the other hand, she was desperate to discuss Cara. She wrestled with the dilemma for a minute, until the desire to spill her guts trumped her desire to ignore him for being an idiot.

'She thought Michael was real and now she thinks the ghost is real,' she said.

'She's making it up for attention,' said Gary. 'It's what kids her age do.'

'Did I?'

'No, not like Cara does. But you used to say funny stuff to make people take notice of you,' he smiled.

'Do you really think she's wrong in the head?' Lisa asked. 'I heard you say it to Mum just now.'

Gary frowned. 'What have I told you about earwigging conversations between adults that have nothing to do with you?

That made her blood boil. 'Why, worried what I might hear?'

'No, it's just rude.'

'You should be worried,' she blurted out, unable to stop herself. 'I know all sorts.'

Gary's pace slowed and she hung back too, not wanting her mum to get wind of what they were talking about.

'Why should I be worried, Lees?'

She hated it when he abbreviated her name. He only did it when he was trying to be all matey and win her round. Look at him now, all smiles, like there was nothing wrong.

'I could tell Mum,' she spat.

Now he appeared genuinely puzzled, which threw her. 'Honestly, Lees, I have no idea what all this is about. Why don't you just tell me?'

Did he really have no idea she saw what he did at that party last year? Seeing the confusion on his face as their eyes met, a similar shade of brown even though they weren't biologically related, Lisa hesitated. Once she said it, there would be no taking it back – and what if she was wrong? Things might never be the same between them again and she wasn't sure if she could bear that. She was only cross with him because she loved him.

She let out the breath she'd been holding in. 'It doesn't matter. It's not important.'

Gary stared at her beadily. 'Are you sure?'

'I am.' She wasn't really, but the fallout would be too immense, and despite how annoyed she was with him, she didn't want him and her mum not to be together.

'You know you can talk to me about anything, don't you? I'm always here for you and I always will be.'

She nodded, the lump in her throat making it difficult to swallow, and when he put his arm around her shoulders, she didn't pull away.

'Do you really think Cara's not right in the head?' she asked again as they continued along the pavement.

Gary looked sheepish. 'I shouldn't have said it like that. What I meant was she's always away with the fairies, like she's not paying attention to the real world. A dolly daydreamer, as your nan says.'

'What's wrong with being like that?' asked Lisa.

'Nothing, I suppose, but the outbursts, the screaming and the violence that goes with it, that's not right. Look what she just did – if that gravy boat had hit you, Matty or Mum in the face when she threw it, it could've really injured you. She hurt Matty's wrist too.'

'I don't think she meant to.'

'That's the point, Lees. She can't help the way she is.' His expression darkened. 'If I had my way, I'd keep you and Ryan away from her, for safety's sake. But your mum being so close to Auntie Neet means she won't hear of it. But, between you and me,' he squeezed his stepdaughter's shoulders conspiratorially, 'the sooner they get Cara properly seen to, the better, before she really hurts one of you.'

Chapter Forty-Eight

Anita

Cara was allowed out of her room an hour after Lisa and the others had left, but only after she'd received a blistering lecture from Paul about her behaviour and been handed down a punishment of no sweets, treats or TV for a week. The child accepted it without argument and said nothing when, after ham sandwiches for tea, Matty was allowed a Kipling Country Slice by his dad and she had to make do with a satsuma. Anita said nothing, in an effort to present a united front with her husband, but later, when they were getting ready for bed, she voiced her disagreement.

'You know how she gets about Matty having more treats. She thinks we favour him as it is, and it felt like you were rubbing her nose in it.'

'Tough. He's not the one being punished for lobbing a gravy boat. It wouldn't have been fair to say no to him having the cake.'

Paul sat on the edge of the bed to remove his socks while Anita perched on the stool in front of her dressing-table mirror and wiped her make-up off with cleanser and cotton wool.

'I just think we should choose our battles,' she sighed. 'Things are difficult enough with Cara as it is.'

'You don't need to tell me that. I spent half an hour trying to get rid of those gravy stains. The wallpaper's bloody ruined.'

'All I'm saying is, let's not antagonise her.'

They were speaking in lowered voices because the children were asleep in their rooms next door. But the expletive Paul uttered in response to her comment was said at normal volume, making Anita flinch.

'Please keep your voice down,' she hissed.

'I will if you stop making ridiculous statements. Let's not antagonise her,' he repeated with a scoff. 'You act like you're scared of her.'

Anita spun round on the stool and glared at him, a nerve hit. 'Of course I'm not.'

'So stop acting like you are.'

'I'm not scared of her,' she seethed at him, 'but I am concerned about her behaviour.'

'I am too. Saying she thinks she heard and saw a ghost . . .' he tailed off. 'It's not right, is it? First that bloody friend Michael, now this. I think we need to take her back to see Dr Stephens and ask for a referral to a specialist. I'll get the day off to come with you.'

Anita was taken aback. Paul never normally bothered with any appointments relating to the children. Admittedly, his working hours precluded his attendance on pretty much all occasions, but it was often a struggle to get him to engage with the children when he was at home. He didn't seem bothered that he was missing Cara's birthday party or that she'd be devastated when she found out. They'd been putting off telling her, hoping that the closer it got, the more excited she would be and the less his absence would bother her. So this new-found concern of Paul's irritated Anita, as did the thought of him leading the discussions with the specialist, as he would invariably try to do. It was all very well taking charge now, but where was he when Cara was disrupting the household with her outbursts?

'That said, maybe the house is haunted,' he said with a wry grin.

'Don't be ridiculous.'

'It happens. There are stories in the papers all the time.'

'Paul, our house is not haunted,' said Anita exasperatedly. 'Next you'll be telling me you want to get a priest round to perform an exorcism.'

'Maybe Cara's possessed and that's what's wrong with her,' he chuckled, taking off his jeans.

'Well, if her head starts spinning and she vomits green sick, I'll be sure to call the vicar at St Mary's.'

Paul laughed, then removed his shirt and climbed beneath the covers. She slipped into bed beside him and prayed he was too tired to try anything.

'Damn, I forgot to bring a glass of water up,' he said. 'Want one?'

'Yes, please.'

He threw back the covers and went downstairs, leaving her alone in darkness. Within seconds, she was drifting off, until a noise downstairs jarred her awake. What the hell was that? Then she realised it was Paul shutting the door between the hallway and the kitchen and she laughed to herself. Cara's story about the ghost must have spooked her more than she realised.

Settling back on her pillow, she was just closing her eyes again when she heard the creak of footsteps as Paul came along the hallway and up the stairs and it was in that moment that Anita's brain made the connection between what she had just heard and what Cara had said about being woken up in the middle of the night by noises and she sat up, panicked. Footsteps on the stairs, someone talking in the hallway . . . what if Cara really had been woken by someone else in the house – someone who wasn't Paul . . .

Chapter Forty-Nine

Anita

The next morning, Anita awoke in turmoil after a restless night spent tossing and turning. There was no way she could say anything to Paul about what was troubling her and she could barely look him or Cara in the eye as the two of them sat down in the dining room for breakfast with Matty, an act in itself which threw her, because Paul rarely ate with the children before leaving for work. But it was clear, after he helped himself to a bowl of their Coco Pops, that he had an agenda.

'Mummy and I were talking last night and we think we should go to see Dr Stephens again,' he addressed his daughter. 'Just for a chat to check how things are.'

Anita could see he was being deliberately ambiguous, but he was underestimating Cara's level of comprehension.

'You think I'm making the ghost up,' she scowled at him.

Anita, who was standing in the doorway listening to them, readied herself for another row.

'It's not that,' said Paul hastily. 'You just don't seem very happy, you often get angry, and we want to get to the bottom of why.'

'It's because I'm tired!' Cara cried. 'I get woken up all the time.'

'By a big scary ghost,' breathed Matty, his eyes widening.

Then he broke into giggles, but his remark made Anita's insides churn.

'What, have you heard it too?' Paul asked their son.

'Cara always wakes me up too late and it's gone by then.'

Cara shot a furious look at her brother and tried to kick him under the table.

Anita's insides churned even more. 'You wake Matty up?'

'I get scared on my own.'

Paul looked puzzled. 'Why don't you wake Mummy if you're frightened?'

'She's always fast asleep and snoring.'

Anita looked at him helplessly. 'I've never heard her come in or call for me.'

He reacted as though he didn't believe her and she didn't blame him. What kind of mum was she to sleep through her children being upset?

'There's no point getting Mummy to come and help, though,' Cara added, 'because grown-ups can't see ghosts.'

Anita caught Paul's eye again and she was relieved to see his annoyance of a moment ago had been supplanted by amusement. Their daughter really did have an answer for everything.

'Who told you that, sweetheart?' he asked.

'Evie. She said that's why you haven't heard Limey Stan either. It's because you can't.'

'Sorry, who?' Anita asked.

'Limey Stan. That's his name.'

There was a moment's silence, then Matty giggled again. 'It's a silly name.'

'It is,' Anita agreed. She eased into the room and set her coffee cup down on the table. 'How do you know it's called that?'

'He,' Cara corrected. 'He's called that. Because I heard him say it.'

247

'You heard the ghost speak?' Paul was trying hard not to laugh. Anita glared at him.

'He whispered it at the bottom of the stairs.'

Anita had to give credit where it was due: it was a heck of a name her daughter's imagination had conjured up. She was probably having nightmares and dreaming about noises and voices in the house, thinking she was awake, and was still too young to work out what was real and what wasn't. Anita was overcome with relief, because it meant the fears that had driven her demented throughout the night were unfounded. She'd never heard of the name Limey Stan in any context before now, so all this ghost nonsense with Cara couldn't be her fault and the next breath she exhaled was released with a tremble. Her secret was still safe.

'Why didn't you tell us he was called Limey Stan when Lisa brought it up yesterday?' Paul asked.

Cara scowled again. 'You were all laughing at me, so I didn't want to.'

'Honey, if you go around saying you're talking to ghosts, people will laugh,' he said pointedly.

'Evie thinks it's brilliant,' she pouted.

'Have you told anyone else?' asked Anita worriedly.

'Evie told everyone,' Matty piped up. 'The whole school knows about Limey Stan.'

'She shouldn't be spreading stories like that, she's meant to be your friend,' said Paul harshly. 'People will think you're weird.'

Cara's expression shifted and Anita could see she was about to blow. Eager to stave off the impending tantrum, she clapped her hands briskly.

'Right, you two, upstairs to brush your teeth.'

Thankfully, Cara did not protest. She shoved her chair back and rushed from the table in an effort to beat her brother to the bathroom.

Anita sighed. Another crisis averted.

'You need to ring the doctor today,' said Paul, rising from the table, where he'd left his empty bowl for her to clear away. 'This is getting out of hand. I don't want people thinking my kid is a fantasist.'

'I will,' she reassured him. 'I'll call for an appointment after I've dropped them off.'

The floodgates opened, Cara talked about Limey Stan non-stop on the way to school. It was a struggle for Anita to concentrate, but she did, because it was the first time in ages she could remember her daughter being so enthused about something. Cara might claim to be spooked by Limey Stan's nocturnal 'visits', but she was also excited – this was her experience, no one else's. She also revelled in the retelling of it to a captive audience: Anita was so conscious of giving Cara her full attention that a couple of times she ignored Matty tugging at her hand, which made Cara's smile spread even wider.

The school was a ten-minute walk from their house, through the estate and across the bridge spanning the railway line, then down a lane. They were early for a change and among the first to arrive in the playground. Yet as the minutes ticked by, Anita began to notice that, as more families arrived, hers was still standing alone. The mums who normally came up and said hello were giving her a wide berth as they entered the playground and a couple threw looks of ill-disguised contempt in their direction. Why were they being unfriendly? She tried to pretend she hadn't noticed and chatted brightly to the children, until, to her relief, Karen came tearing in with Ryan in tow.

'Can you see him into the queue?' her sister panted. 'I'm going to be late for work and I'm already on a warning.'

Anita wanted to say 'No, wait with me and shield me from

the dirty looks I'm definitely not imagining,' but that wouldn't have been fair on Karen, who was clearly harassed and couldn't risk losing her job.

'Of course, you shoot off.'

At least Ryan was a good distraction for his cousins from the obvious shunning that was going on around them. Anita tried to catch the eye of Jane, whose daughter was among Cara's circle of friends and who she'd always got on well with, but the mum shifted position so her back was to them. Upset, Anita was debating whether to go over and ask for a word when she saw Susie, mum of Abigail, another girl in Cara's class, bearing down on her. Anita smiled with relief – finally someone was coming to say hi.

On reaching Anita, Susie thrust a sheaf of papers at her. 'These are for you.'

The pieces of paper were bright pink and covered in glitter that rubbed off on her fingertips as she took them from Susie. Anita recognised them immediately as the invitations she and Cara had made for her birthday party.

'Everyone's RSVP'd,' Susie went on, her expression set. Over her shoulder, the other mums were watching them.

Anita leafed through the invites, her dismay ballooning as she checked each one. 'They're all ticked "unable to attend",' she said.

'That's right. None of the kids can make it.'

Anita cast a panicked eye down at Cara, who was thankfully absorbed in examining a snail she, Matty and Ryan had found on the ground.

'But why?'

'You'll find out soon enough.'

Susie turned on her heel and strolled back to the others, who swarmed around her like worker bees protecting their queen. Anita couldn't see Susie's expression, but it must have been pretty animated, if the reaction of the other mums was anything to go by.

Anita quickly stuffed the invites into her cardigan pocket so Cara wouldn't see them. She didn't know how, but she would try to salvage the party somehow, once she got to the bottom of what was going on . . .

'Mrs Belling?'

Anita looked up to see the head teacher, Mrs Colman, approaching. The woman did not look happy and Anita's stomach pitched in alarm.

'Do you have a moment to come to my office?' the head asked.

'What for?'

Anita didn't mean to respond so bluntly, but she was conscious of Susie and the other mums watching them. Why did the head have to single her out today of all days?

'It's about an incident that happened in school on Friday that I've just been informed about.'

'And?'

'It involves one of your children.'

'I suppose it's too much to hope it's Matty,' Anita faintly laughed.

Mrs Colman's lips thinned to the point of evaporation.

'No, it is not your son we must discuss.' She addressed the children sharply: 'Get into your class lines ready to go inside.'

'You don't want Cara to come with us?' Anita queried after the three of them hugged her goodbye and shot off to join their classmates.

'It will be better dealt with between us first.'

Anita meekly followed the head inside, feeling horribly exposed as dozens of pairs of eyes tracked their journey across the playground. Once inside her office, Mrs Colman wasted no time detailing the latest allegations being levelled at her daughter.

'Cara pushed another girl to the floor and stamped on her leg when the children were collecting their bags at the end of Friday. The incident was only reported this morning because the child waited until she got home to tell her parents what happened.'

Anita waited a moment before responding, knowing it wouldn't help Cara if she did not keep her calm.

'It sounds as though you're stating what happened as fact.'

'There is incontrovertible evidence the incident occurred. The child in question has a bruise the shape and tread of a shoe sole on her thigh.'

Mrs Colman had never been particularly warm during any of Anita's previous dealings with her – trained in an era where discipline was meted out with a cane at the school's discretion, this new era of increased parental involvement clearly irritated the hell out of her – but today she was glacial.

'Do you have proof Cara did it?' Anita shot back, trying to keep her voice steady. It sounded like a horrible assault that deserved a severe punishment and she couldn't bear the thought that Cara might be responsible, but she wasn't going to concede her daughter's guilt until the head had convinced her she really was the culprit.

'There were a number of witnesses who've confirmed it was Cara. The child who was hurt also identified Cara as the person who stamped on her.'

'But they could be ganging up to blame her!' Anita protested, thinking of how she had just been singled out herself by the pack in the playground.

'They could,' Mrs Colman acknowledged, 'but in this instance I have no reason to disbelieve their compelling testimony. Nor is this the first occasion where Cara has been in trouble for causing physical harm to her classmates. As you are well aware, there have been incidents of her pushing children over and slapping them.'

'I'm sure she didn't mean to hurt Abigail,' said Anita desperately.

She knew the victim had to be her because of Susie's performance just now – throwing the invites in Anita's face felt like a personal retaliation and not something she would've done on behalf of someone else's child.

'I feel I have no choice but to impose a period of suspension on Cara. She can complete today at school, then she must not return until Friday.'

'Three days?' Anita was filled with dread at the prospect.

'I consider it a lenient punishment. A harder stamp could easily have resulted in broken bones,' said Mrs Colman, at which Anita paled. The head rested her forearms on her desk, clasped her hands and leaned forward. 'I cannot impress upon you enough how Cara's behaviour needs to drastically improve, Mrs Belling. These attacks and the disruption she causes in class cannot continue.'

Anita was close to tears now. 'We're trying our best. Our GP said there's nothing wrong with her and that she'll grow out of her moods.'

'I hope your doctor's prognosis is correct, Mrs Belling. This is her first suspension – two more and I shall have no choice but to expel her for good.'

Chapter Fifty

Anita

The three days were a living hell. Cara did not react well to her punishment and Anita was largely left alone to deal with it. Paul had already been away overnight on Monday and Tuesday and then a sudden demand from his boss on Thursday morning meant he had to head back up north again for another two nights. Before his departure he inflamed the already volatile atmosphere by telling Cara they were cancelling her birthday party . . . It wasn't enough that the school had punished her, he said, as her parents they needed to discipline her too. A part of Anita was relieved, because it absolved her from trying to convince the other mums to override the party ban laid down by Susie, but she also knew Cara wouldn't react well to the news and she was right.

On being told the party would not be happening, Cara had spun into an uncontrollable rage and had wrecked the front room, breaking an irreplaceable vase that had belonged to Anita's late mother in the process. Then she'd raced upstairs, locked herself in the bathroom and wailed like a wounded animal for an hour.

Tonight was the last evening of the suspension and Anita had arranged for Karen to come over once the kids were in bed.

Shortly before nine, her sister arrived, brandishing a bottle of wine.

'That bad?' she remarked, after Anita broke down the moment she stepped into the house.

'I've had enough. I can't deal with her any more. She's awful.'

The children were finally asleep, but only just. Cara's bad behaviour was rubbing off on Matty and it had been a battle to get him to clean his teeth and into his pyjamas. Anita had become so riled that she'd refused to read him his usual bedtime story and now felt guilty that he'd cried himself to sleep instead. Cara, meanwhile, wouldn't budge off the sofa until Matty was in bed and Anita had had to manhandle her upstairs kicking and screaming. Thank God their house was detached and their neighbours, the lovely, quiet Shakoor family, couldn't hear them.

Anita fetched some wine glasses and the pair of them went into the lounge.

'Bloody hell, it looks like a bomb's gone off in here,' said Karen.

'Cara wouldn't go to bed when I asked,' said Anita wearily, picking up the sofa cushions from the floor and ramming them back into position. She turned to her sister, eyes brimming with fresh tears. 'I'm sick to death of her. She causes me so much grief, I can't bear to be around her.'

'I don't blame you. I don't know what to suggest to help things improve though, apart from giving you this.'

Karen poured a generous helping of wine into a glass and passed it to Anita, who knocked it back in one, then held out the glass to be refilled.

'Getting me drunk will help, trust me,' she grimaced.

She flopped down onto the sofa and propped her feet up on the lacquered coffee table. Her feet looked grubby, her red toenail polish chipped. She'd been wearing the same outfit of faded blue capri jeans and a white T-shirt for three days now, too worn down to bother with showering or putting a wash on so she had clean clothes to change into.

'This weather isn't helping. It's too wet to do anything, so we can't even escape the house.'

The rain was relentless. If it wasn't coming down in sheets, it was a muggy grey drizzle.

Karen sat down beside her. She was still wearing her work clothes – smart black pencil skirt, cream blouse with shoulder pad inserts and natural tan tights. Anita envied her sister for dressing up every day to work at the building society and for the sense of purpose her job gave her. Then she caught a whiff of something stale as Karen slipped her feet out of her heels and propped them up next to hers and felt a stab of satisfaction that her sister wasn't as perfect as she appeared.

'I watched the forecast earlier and John Kettley reckons it could end up being one of the wettest summers on record,' said Karen, stifling a yawn.

'Really?' Anita was horrified. The thought of being stuck indoors with Cara for weeks on end made her want to hyper-ventilate. They hadn't booked a holiday yet because Paul didn't know when he could get leave and his boss was being evasive every time he asked. For now, it was looking as though she would be stuck at home with the kids for the entire six weeks, unless she called upon the kindness of Mrs Shakoor and off-loaded them at hers for afternoons at a time. She never seemed to mind when her younger sons Amir and Raman piled indoors with the rest of the neighbourhood children in tow and Anita was even prepared to risk exposing Cara to the eldest, Tishk, if it meant having some time to herself. Maybe she should have a word with him first, warn him what was at stake if he didn't behave around the little ones. His parents were still oblivious to his slipping out at all hours and she could use it as leverage if she had to.

'That's what he said. Obviously, they don't always get it right, but it's looking like a wet one.'

'Give me that.' Anita took the bottle of wine from her and topped up her glass.

'Steady on, there won't be any left for me.'

'So we'll open another.'

Karen turned to look at her. 'Drinking yourself into a stupor won't help, actually. For one thing, it'll be ten times worse dealing with Cara when you've got a hangover. When's the appointment to take her to see Dr Stephens again?'

'It was meant to be next Friday, but Paul's got a conference that day now and because he's insisting on coming with us, I'll have to rebook it for the week after. I'm at my wits' end, sis,' said Anita tearfully. She faltered for a moment, wondering if she dared say what she was thinking aloud and whether her sister would think her a monster if she did. Bugger it, she thought. 'I've reached the point where I just want to pack my bags and leave. God, that sounds awful, doesn't it?'

'We all have moments like that,' Karen reassured her. 'Being a mum is bloody hard work these days, not like it was when we were kids. Now we're guilt-tripped if we leave our kids to their own devices, but in the same breath we're told women should be out working to set an example to them. How can we work and not leave them alone at the same time?'

'I'd happily leave Cara alone right now.'

'So get another job.'

'That isn't going to help. Moving to Scotland might,' Anita sighed.

'You don't mean that. I know things are tough right now, but you love Cara and Matty and you couldn't leave them.'

'Don't be so sure. Loving them doesn't stop me wanting to run away and leave Paul to it.'

Karen's expression soured. 'There's your problem,' she said.

'Paul does his best. He can't help that his job takes him away from home all the time.'

'He could look for another one that doesn't involve travelling.'

'He's going for a promotion and if he gets it, he'll be at home a lot more,' she said, neglecting to add that a part of her hoped he wasn't offered the role, because the thought of him being around all the time and there being nothing for them to talk about filled her with dread.

Karen sipped her wine. 'Being at home is one thing, Neet. Helping out at home is another. How many times have you complained to me that Paul doesn't help with anything when he is here? He needs to pull his weight.'

'Gary's hardly dad of the year,' Anita sniped.

'I'm not saying he is. But he does his fair share. We take turns cooking, he hangs the laundry out if I ask, and he'll do the shopping too.'

Anita fell silent. It annoyed her when Karen eulogised Gary as though he was the patron saint of husbands.

'How's everything else between you two at the moment?' Karen asked pointedly.

Anita squirmed. It was during another wine-drinking session that she'd mentioned to her sister how infrequently she and Paul had sex, and now Karen brought it up every time they were alone together as though it was a bad thing.

'Fine,' she lied. 'What about you?'

'Actually, we've hit a bit of a purple patch,' Karen giggled. 'Gary bought me some underwear from Ann Summers and it's working wonders.'

As Karen went into more detail than was necessary, Anita simmered with resentment. She couldn't help it. She was the fitter, more attractive sister – she should be the one having great sex in racy knickers, not Karen with her badly styled mouse-brown hair and a figure that could do with shedding a few pounds, she thought bitchily.

The conversation drifted on, but Anita tuned her sister out as she downed another glass of wine. Then she got up, cutting Karen off mid-flow, and fetched another bottle of wine from the cupboard. As she stuck it in the top drawer of the freezer to chill, her frustration began to mount. It wasn't fair that this was her life, stuck indoors with a horror of a daughter, a son who wanted to be babied all the time and a husband who bored the crap out of her when he was there. She wanted excitement, adventures, to be with someone who desired her. Tears pricked her eyes.

She wanted him again.

Two months had passed since Anita had ended her affair. A shiver rippled through her as she allowed herself a moment's indulgence to think about their last time together, then just as quickly, she forced the memory back into the deep recess from where it had sprung. That last time had to be the last time, she reminded herself. She'd made a promise.

But as she returned to the lounge and Karen launched into a dull line of chat about a problem she was having at work, Anita knew she was about to go back on her word. She might hate the sneaking around, the lies she had to feed her family so she could escape to see her lover and the pervading sense of guilt, but after years of being in a marriage where she felt so lonely, to be really seen and heard by someone she never imagined would be interested in her was too intoxicating to ignore. His door was always open, that much he'd made clear, so where was the harm? A happy Anita was a happier mum, surely, she tipsily tried to rationalise.

Her mind made up, she told Karen she was exhausted and wanted to go to bed.

'What about that other bottle?'

'You were right; dealing with Cara will be much worse with a hangover.'

Karen followed her into the kitchen, where Anita took the bottle from the freezer drawer and put it in the fridge.

'Shall I come round and help you drink that tomorrow?' Karen asked.

'Oh . . . I, um, want to catch up on a programme I recorded at the weekend.' Anita could feel the heat building in her cheeks and hoped Karen wouldn't notice. 'But maybe the evening after?'

'That works for me.'

As soon as Karen had pulled the back door to behind her, Anita darted down the hallway and snatched up the phone receiver from its cradle. Heart in her mouth, she dialled the number as familiar to her as her own. To her relief, it was him who picked up.

'Heldean 27947,' came the answer.

'It's me,' she said.

Silence.

'I know I said I didn't want to see you again, but I've changed my mind. I miss you. I need to see you,' she babbled nervously.

More silence.

'Please say something,' she pleaded.

Finally, he answered.

'When's Paul's next trip?'

Relief cascaded through her. She hadn't blown it. 'He's away at the moment. He's not back until Saturday morning.'

'Tomorrow night?'

'Yes, that would be perfect.'

A noise suddenly rang out in his background.

'Who's that you're talking to?' Anita heard a woman say.

'Wrong number,' came his nonchalant reply before the line went dead.

Chapter Fifty-One

Lisa

The third week of July, right before the summer holidays began, saw Lisa allowed home early on the Friday after competing in her school's sports day. With a first place in the 4×400m relay to boast about and not wanting to go home to an empty house, she decided to meet Ryan from school as a surprise. Auntie Neet usually collected him, along with Cara and Matty, but apparently the new job she'd recently started meant she couldn't get there in time, so the children had been walking home alone every Friday for the past month. Lisa hadn't seen Cara or Matty much since the gravy boat incident – her stepdad and Anita had agreed they should hold off on the Sunday lunches for a while – and she thought her cousins might appreciate her coming to get them.

Matty's class was the first to empty out into the playground. His teacher had been on the staff when Lisa attended the school and was happy to let Matty go home with her. He, on the hand other, didn't appear that pleased to see his cousin. He took his time walking over to her, dragging his satchel along the ground behind him by the strap.

'What's up with you?' Lisa asked.

He shrugged, head bent forward so she couldn't see his face properly.

'Matty? Did something bad happen today?'

'No.'

'So what is it?'

'I'm tired.'

He finally looked up at her and Lisa could see how exhausted he was, his skin pale beneath his sparrow-egg freckles. Before she could say anything, Cara had joined them and Lisa noticed she was similarly rumpled.

'I thought I'd walk you home,' she said.

'I want to go up the Rec,' Cara immediately answered. 'Can we?'

Matty brightened at the suggestion. 'Yes, can we please, Lisa?'

She squinted skywards. It didn't look as though it might rain – the sky wasn't bright blue, but blue enough, and there were only a few clouds visible for a change. 'Okay, we can go.'

Matty jumped excitedly on the spot. 'Yes!'

'Have you got anything to eat?' asked Cara.

'No, but my mum gave me my pocket money this morning so we could stop at the corner shop on the way.'

She scanned the children still massed around their respective teachers, waiting for their parents to collect them. Ryan was among them, even though he could clearly see her waiting.

'Ryan, come on!' She gestured to him, but he shook his head.

Annoyed, she instructed Matty and Cara to wait there and went to get him.

'What's the hold-up?' she asked her brother.

'I don't want to walk home with her.' He pointed at Cara and scowled.

'Why? Has she hit you again?'

'No, but Danny is being horrible to me because I'm her cousin and he says she's loopy.'

Lisa had a vague idea who Danny was: a gobby kid with curly jet-black hair who made Ryan cry during last year's Christmas Nativity when he tripped him up with his shepherd's crook on stage.

'Why would Danny say that?'

'Because Cara keeps saying Limey Stan is still living in her house.'

Lisa could tell Ryan was het up – the lisp he'd spoken with since he babbled his first word became more pronounced when he was upset and right now it was particularly obvious.

She glanced over her shoulder at Cara. Why was she still going on about that nonsense? Her cousin glared back at her sullenly, as though she knew what they were talking about.

'Look, ignore Danny,' Lisa said, turning back to Ryan. 'He's just being silly.' She held out her hand. 'Want some sweets? I've got some money to go to the shop.'

'With Cara?'

'Yes, with Cara,' said Lisa firmly.

Ryan looked torn for a moment, but the lure of sweets was too strong to resist. 'Okay.'

They were walking away when a group of boys, around Cara's age, came bowling past them yelling at the tops of their voices.

'Limey Stan, Limey Stan, Cara loves the Shadow Man!'

'Bugger off!' Lisa yelled at them, forgetting where she was for a moment. Then she spun towards Cara, fearful of how she would react to the chants. But her cousin just smiled as the boys ran past.

Four packets of Chewits purchased, the cousins arrived at the Rec and made a beeline for the playground. Ryan and Matty dumped their bags on the floor before clambering onto the roundabout, where they would stay, spinning themselves dizzy, until it was time to leave. Cara sat on one of the swings but made no attempt to move and instead rested her right temple against the chain holding it up. Lisa plonked herself down next to her.

'Ryan says you've been telling people at school that Limey Stan's still haunting your house,' she said. Maybe if they played along with it, Cara would get bored and would find something new to be obsessed with.

Cara didn't move a muscle.

'Well, is he?'

Her cousin gave the tiniest of nods.

'Have you seen him again?'

'I keep missing him,' Cara said, stifling a yawn. 'I hear him making noises, but when I get up, he's always gone.'

'He's waking you up every night?'

'No, but I can't sleep even when he doesn't come because I'm scared.'

Lisa thought for a moment. 'What time does he usually come? Do you ever check your clock?'

Cara nodded. 'It's always after one in the morning that I hear him.'

'So there's a pattern to him showing up.' Lisa pushed herself backwards, then scuffed the toes of her shoes along the ground as she swung forward. 'If you want to catch him, you need to be hiding somewhere before he comes, not wait until afterwards.'

'What, you mean lie in wait?' Cara sat up straight, eyes sparkling with excitement. 'That's a great idea. We could hide downstairs!'

'It would have to be somewhere you can't be seen though.'

Lisa knew that even if Cara spent the whole night hiding, she still wouldn't see anything, because – duh – ghosts weren't real, but she was happy enough to encourage her cousin, because someone had to humour her. As Cara began to consider suitable hiding places, chattering away as she swung back and forth, Lisa smiled to herself.

Cara was still yabbering when Amir and Raman Shakoor turned up ten minutes later. The brothers were on their BMXs, which they unceremoniously dropped to the ground upon reaching the playground. Lisa looked hopefully past them to see if Tishk was with them, but the boys were unaccompanied. Amir came over to the swings, while Raman, the younger of the two, went over to the roundabout and waited patiently as Ryan slowed it down long enough for him to hop on.

'Is it true, Cara?' Amir asked breathlessly. 'Do you really have a ghost in your house?'

'Where did you hear that?' Lisa asked.

'At school. Is it true, Cara? Is his name really Limey Stan?'

Lisa felt a stab of alarm. Her cousin's tall tales were getting seriously out of hand if they were starting to spread across town – the faith school that Amir and Raman attended was a good three miles from Cara's.

'Yes, it is, and tonight I'm going to catch him,' said Cara, her chin jutting purposefully.

Amir stared at her in wonderment. 'How?'

'I'm going to hide behind the curtains in the front room. They go right down to the floor, so I won't be seen. Then, when I hear him, I'll jump out.'

'But if he's a ghost, you won't be able to catch him,' Amir pointed out, and he mimed the action of trying to catch something in thin air and missing. 'Same if you tried to take his picture. The photo'll just be blank.'

Cara huffed grumpily. 'Matty can hide with me so he sees him too.'

'You need a proper ghost catcher,' said Amir.

Lisa had heard enough and hopped off her swing.

'I'll tell you what, how about I sneak round to your house

tonight and hide with you? Then, if I see him too, that's three of us who can say it.'

Her intention was really to put a stop to the silly story about Limey Stan spreading further and making her family the laughing stock of the entire town. Imagine the grief she'd get if anyone found out at her school. It was bad enough that Tishk probably knew by now. What if Jake Thompson in the year above her, who she also had a crush on, found out too? She would die. No, if it meant putting an end to this ghost nonsense, Lisa was willing to sit up all night to prove to Cara she was imagining it.

'What, you'll walk round to Cara's house in the middle of the night in the dark?' breathed Amir, his eyes like saucers.

Lisa wasn't easily scared, but the thought of venturing out in the middle of the night when everyone else was asleep did make her stomach churn. She could suggest a sleepover with her cousins, but Gary would most likely say no because he was being weird about her being around Cara after the gravy boat incident. He'd go mad if he caught her sneaking out, though. Was it worth the risk? She pictured Jake Thompson's face for a moment and decided it most definitely was.

'Tishk goes out in the dark,' Amir said. 'He never gets scared.'

'Where does he go?' Lisa asked.

'He won't tell me, but I think he's got a girlfriend because he's got a bottle of aftershave hidden under his bed and he uses it before he goes out. It stinks,' said Amir impishly.

Aftershave? Lisa was floored to hear Tishk was sneaking out to see someone and all thoughts of Limey Stan evaporated as she swung morosely on the swing and tried to work out who the girlfriend might be.

Chapter Fifty-Two

Anita

Anita's insides fluttered in expectation as she sat at her dressing table and applied the crimson-red lipstick she reserved for special occasions. Then she doused herself liberally with perfume, readjusted the straps of her cream satin slip to lower its neckline and smiled at herself in the mirror.

She was ready for him.

Tiptoeing along the landing so as not to disturb the children sleeping in their rooms, she flinched as she passed the enormous rubber plant that took up the corner at the top of the stairs. Cara had been terrified to find it looming outside her bedroom door when they accidentally roused her from her sleep the other night, but instead of rushing to her, Anita had laughed as she watched him manhandle it back into position. It was wrong, she knew, but her happiness at seeing her lover again made it easier to ignore her misgivings about feeding into Cara's fears about the house being haunted. It had taken a week after the resumption of his visits – always after midnight, under the cloak of darkness, and never for the whole night – for Anita to realise her initial suspicions were correct and what Cara thought was Limey Stan was the sounds of him sneaking in and out of the house. Those previous nights when he'd tapped on the front-room window or back door as her cue to let him in;

the footsteps on the stairs and in the hall after he'd crept up to use the toilet; whispers into the telephone receiver when he called a taxi one night, misheard by a sleepy child's ears; fleeting glimpses of him in the shadows of the hallway as he prepared to creep out. Limey Stan's provenance was obvious when Anita strung those moments together – she just hadn't wanted to face up to the fact she'd caused the problem all along, by inviting him into the house.

Of course, he thought it was hilarious and was now playing up to his spectral alter ego, hence the increase in tapping and footsteps and the moving of the plant. Anita had implored him to scale it back a bit, conscious of how tired Cara was becoming through being constantly woken, but he'd persuasively argued that if spooking the children into staying in their bedrooms meant they weren't disturbed downstairs, where was the harm? It wasn't like it was every night, just the occasional one when Paul was away. He'd also pointed out that catching them having sex would cause her daughter far more psychological damage than thinking there was a ghost in the house, and she had to accept he had a point. Not to mention that Cara would tell Paul and Anita didn't want that, because she didn't plan to leave him over this affair. There was an expiry date in place, an autumn deadline when she and her lover would part company again, and she was happy with that. He wasn't someone she could feasibly consider a future with.

As she stepped into the kitchen, she heard the fierce patter of rain hitting the window and wondered if the downpour might delay his arrival, because he usually walked to hers. However, only fifteen minutes later, she heard tapping on the front door. She said nothing as she opened it to him, words redundant as she took his hand and pulled him towards her. They began to kiss, deeply and urgently, but when she tried to manoeuvre him down the hallway as she always did, he resisted.

'No, upstairs,' he whispered.

'We can't,' she murmured, as he began nuzzling her neck. She would not desecrate her and Paul's bed like that.

'Come on, it's boring always doing it on the sofa or the floor.'

That stung, because the last thing she wanted was for him to think sex with her was uninspired. She already felt under pressure to perform, because he was naturally in better physical shape than her. Thoughts of how Paul would feel about them doing it in the marital bed quickly vanished.

'Okay, but be quiet,' she hissed.

They soundlessly made their way upstairs and once inside the bedroom, she jammed a chair up against the door in case either child woke and tried to get in. By the time she turned round, he was already stripped off and under the covers.

On the chest of drawers at the end of the bed was a photograph of her and Paul on their wedding day. Anita turned it face down, then climbed in beside him.

It had not been her intention to fall asleep, so when Anita awoke with a jolt to discover it was gone two in the morning, she grabbed his arm in a panic and shook him awake as well.

'You need to go,' she whispered. 'Get dressed.'

His eyes remained closed. 'Why can't I stay a bit longer? I'm tired.'

'That's not the deal and you know it. You can't stay the night.'

'For fuck's sake,' he grumbled, opening his eyes and pulling back the covers.

She forced herself to look away from his nakedness and the temptation it offered. It was late and he really did have to go.

'Can I at least go to the loo first?' he asked, to which she nodded.

Still naked, he crossed the room and unhooked Paul's robe from behind the door and slipped it on, an action that made her stomach constrict with unease. She wanted to tell him to take it off but knew it would most likely cause a scene if she did, so she watched him leave the room without comment. While he was in the bathroom, she sat up on the bed with her legs pulled up and her chin resting on her knees. Was it really worth it, this sneaking around, putting her home life in jeopardy for the sake of a few stolen moments with someone who will have forgotten her in a few months?

He was grinning when he returned to the bedroom.

'Your kids are both awake.'

Anita was horrified. 'Did they see you?'

'No, I can hear them downstairs. They're trying to be quiet, but they're giggling and making a racket.' The grin stretched wider. 'I think they're waiting for Limey Stan to show himself.'

Anita groaned despairingly. 'That bloody ghost is the bane of our lives. Where are they downstairs?'

'Lounge. Don't worry, I can sneak out the back, they won't see me.'

'No, it's too risky. I need to get them into bed first.'

'You better be tough on them, otherwise they'll be getting up every night now.'

She bristled at the unsolicited parental advice. 'I know how to handle my children, thank you very much.'

'Is that why they're both out of bed at two in the morning and hiding downstairs?' he baited her.

'I'll tell them off,' she said. She left the satin slip in a puddle on the carpet where he'd tossed it and fetched her own robe from behind the door.

'Or I could go down and give them a little scare so they'll think twice about getting up again,' he said laughingly.

She stopped, frowning. 'You mean go into the front room

270

pretending to be Limey Stan? No, that would frighten them too much.'

'Isn't that the point?' He reached for her waist and pulled her towards him so their groins pressed. 'If the kids don't stay in their beds, I won't be able to get into yours.' He slowly ground his hips into hers. 'Is that what you want?'

Anita's face flushed. 'Of course not.'

He took a decisive step back. 'Good. Now wait here, I won't be long.'

She stood with her ear pressed against the bedroom door, the creak of the stairs signalling his descent. After that, a heavy silence fell, as though the house was holding its breath with her—

A child's scream rent the silence, then another. Gasping with shock, Anita yanked open her bedroom door as frantic footsteps pummelled the stairs and she burst onto the landing just in time to see Cara disappearing into the bathroom and slamming the door behind her. Seconds later, there was a click as the door was locked from the inside.

Anita slapped her palm against it. 'Cara, what's the matter?'

There was no reply, only the sound of her daughter sobbing uncontrollably. Beside herself with terror, Anita charged downstairs, bare feet slapping against the floorboards and then the kitchen tiles as she ran towards the front room. It was still in darkness and when she flicked on the light, the scene that greeted her there brought her to a shuddering halt.

The curved curtain rail above the bay window had been ripped from its fixings and the burgundy velvet drape it previously held up was spooled in a heap on the carpet – and lying unconscious next to it was Matty.

Chapter Fifty-Three

Anita

She cried out in anguish as she stumbled across the room and fell to her knees next to her son. She shook his shoulders to rouse him, then let out another sob as his head lolled to the side. She could see his lips were starting to turn blue and when she placed her palm on his chest, she couldn't feel any movement.

'He's not breathing,' she cried. 'Why aren't you helping him?'

He was standing next to them but didn't react, his unbroken gaze trained on Matty as he clutched Paul's robe around him.

Anita walloped him hard across his bare calf, the closest part of him she could reach. 'Don't just stand there, call an ambulance!'

The slap jolted him from his trance. 'It's too late,' he said, his voice low and mechanical. 'He's dead.'

'Don't you dare say that,' she cried, trembling with panic. She put both hands on Matty's chest and began to pump, not knowing if she was doing it right and praying she was. She did five pumps, then pinched the little boy's nose and breathed deeply into his mouth. 'Come on, honey, breathe for Mummy,' she begged. 'Breathe.'

'Anita, stop it. It's too late. He's dead.'

'It's not fucking too late,' she howled at him. 'We just need to get help. Call an ambulance,' she ordered.

She continued pumping air into her son's chest, then blowing into his mouth. His Spiderman pyjama top and his face were soon soaked with her tears, but still he didn't move.

'Matty, it's time to wake up for Mummy,' she sobbed. 'I need you to wake up now.' She could barely see what she was doing, her tears were coming so thick and fast. Then she felt her lover's hand cover hers.

'Anita, stop. He's gone.'

She shrugged his hand off. 'No he hasn't.'

But after a few more minutes of trying, she knew he was right. Matty remained lifeless and his lips were even bluer. Letting out a plaintive wail, Anita removed her hands from his chest and gathered him in her arms. As his body flopped against hers, she could feel his skin was still warm.

'What happened?' she cried, looking up at him as she rocked Matty on her lap, as though that alone would will him back to life.

'He was tangled up in the curtain when I came in and was in distress and I was helping him get free, but he started yelling and Cara screamed and then he saw my face and I panicked.'

'What did you do?' asked Anita in a horrified whisper.

'He saw my face, Anita! He would've told everyone about us.'

'What did you do?' she repeated slowly.

'I wrapped the curtain around him again so he'd stop making such a racket and then he went quiet.' He pointed a finger at her accusingly. 'You said you wanted me to scare them.'

'I didn't tell you to suffocate him!' she screamed.

His face was drained of colour. 'I didn't mean to, I swear. I only wanted to make him be quiet.'

She stared down at her son. He looked peaceful, like he was sleeping. She leaned down and pressed her lips against his forehead, breathing in the sweet scent of his skin that had been freshly bathed only a few hours previously, and as she did so, she became aware of Cara's cries echoing down the stairs. Her daughter sounded hysterical now and Anita sat up, torn, knowing she should go to her but not able to let go of Matty.

He heard her too.

'You need to get her to shut up,' he said, fresh panic creeping into his voice. 'She's going to wake the whole bloody street.'

Anita gulped down a huge, shuddering breath. 'I'll go up to her in a minute, once I've called the police.'

He shook his head, horrified. 'You can't bring the police here.'

'But Matty is dead,' she said, incredulous. 'We have to report it.'

His expression suddenly shifted and it was like looking into a stranger's face. Anita recoiled in fear and she hugged Matty's body even tighter as fresh tears rolled down her cheeks.

'I am not having this pinned on me,' he said, his voice manic. 'This is on both of us. You were the one sneaking me into the house, telling lies to your family and scaring your kids shitless because you didn't want them to interrupt us on the sofa downstairs. I shut him up to protect us – it's as much your fault he's dead as it's mine.'

'What do you want me to do?' asked Anita, sickened by his stance. 'I can't cover up the fact he's dead.'

He paced for a moment, Paul's robe flapping against his bare legs. 'Here's what's going to happen. I'm going to go upstairs, get dressed and leave. When I've gone, you can call the police.'

'And say what?'

'Tell them it was an accident. Matty got caught up in the curtain and couldn't breathe. It's not even a lie – that's how I found him when I came down. Him and Cara had wound the curtain too tightly around themselves and he couldn't escape.'

Anita was numb with shock. She couldn't believe what he

was asking of her. But there was no way she was letting him get away with this. A plan forming in her mind, she gently lifted Matty off her lap and laid him on the floor. 'Go and get dressed,' she told him. It was a struggle to keep her voice steady, but she knew she had to play along.

'So you won't call the police until after I've gone?'

'You leave and then I'll call them,' she lied.

Relief lifted his features. As Anita slowly got to her feet, she fought hard to stay calm, even though every fibre of her being wanted to scream for her dead child. But she had to stay in control for just a little bit longer.

She waited until he'd gone back through the kitchen and upstairs to change into his clothes. Then she crept along the hallway and, as quietly as she could manage, lifted the receiver to dial the emergency number.

He came at her out of nowhere, punching her in the side of her head and sending her flying across the hall. As she dropped the handset, he yanked the phone lead out of the socket.

'Which bit of keeping your mouth shut don't you understand?'

His voice was fraught and his expression wild and when she saw something glinting by his side, she looked down and gasped. Gripped in his right hand was the carving knife from the kitchen. He must have taken it from the drawer on his way upstairs to change.

'Put the knife down,' she pleaded.

He advanced on her, blade aloft. 'Not until you give me your word you won't tell the police about me.'

'I can't do that,' she said. 'You killed my son!'

She watched as he gathered himself to his full height. Suddenly his presence seemed overpowering to her, the hallway tiny compared to him.

'Either you promise to never tell anyone it was me or—' He broke off and looked about wildly, as though seeking inspiration.

Then his eyes swivelled towards upstairs, where Cara could still be heard crying. Anita's stomach lurched in terror. 'Or she's next,' he finished.

Anita let out a strangled cry. 'No!'

Without thinking, she stepped forward to grab the knife from his hand, but he thrust it towards her so the tip was dangerously close to her chin. His hand wobbled and the knife with it.

'This would slice through her body like butter,' he hissed. 'One stab is all it would take.'

'Please don't hurt my daughter,' she whimpered, her face awash with new tears, her jaw throbbing from his fist.

He took her by the arm and dragged her to the foot of the stairs. Cara's howling had subsided to wracked sobs. Anita was desperate to get to her and comfort her, but under no circumstance would she risk Cara unlocking the bathroom door now. It was too late for her to save Matty, but she would do whatever it took to protect his sister.

'Call her to come down.'

The wild look on his face terrified her, but she shook her head. 'No, I won't.'

'Then I'll go up.' He stepped onto the bottom stair, but she managed to hold him back.

'Okay, I'll do as you say!' she said in desperation. 'I won't tell the police you were here. Just leave Cara alone.'

'How do I know you'll keep your word?'

More tears streaked her face. 'I promise you on my life I will.' She meant it too. She would rather he escaped unpunished than see Cara harmed.

He thought for a moment. He was perspiring heavily and the effect of the sweat glistening on his face in the darkness of the hallway made him seem even more menacing. Anita began to sob.

'If you ever tell anyone about this,' he began, raising the

tip of the blade level with her chin again, 'I'll make sure Cara doesn't see her next birthday and you'll be burying her next to her brother. I'll make it look like an accident too, so you'll never know when it will happen or even if it was my doing. But I will kill her if you dare mention my name to the police.'

Still sobbing, Anita pleaded with him. 'This isn't you talking. You're not this person.'

He faltered for a second and she tried to take advantage by seizing the knife. She saw a flash of metal, then an intense pain seared the back of her hand and she looked down to see blood bubbling up through a gash in her skin. Anita cried out in shock and his eyes widened as though surprised by what he'd done, but then his expression hardened. 'Now do you believe me?'

She clutched her hand over the wound. Despite the blood, she could tell it wasn't deep. But she now knew, looking into his eyes, he was capable of hurting Cara. It devastated her to think he would get away with killing Matty, but she would not let him take her daughter's life too. 'I do believe you,' she nodded, tears drenching her cheeks. 'I won't tell on you.'

He lowered the knife. Above them, Cara also continued to cry.

'You should tell the police it was her fault, that she was the one who wrapped Matty in the curtain. The police won't charge her, she's too young.'

Anita was repulsed. 'I can't do that!'

'You've been saying for months you think there's something wrong with her.' In the darkness, his eyes were almost black as they bored into hers. 'The police are going to want to blame someone for what's happened. If they think it's you, you'll go to prison.' Anita flinched at that. 'But if they think Cara did it while playing a game and it was an accident, chances are she'll be let off with a slap on the wrist.'

Anita was too dumbfounded to reply and he took that as his

cue to make a run for it. He was almost at the back door when she caught up with him and grabbed his arm. He gave her a disdainful look as he tried to shrug her hand off, but she clung on.

'You might have bought my silence now, but trust me when I say I will not take this secret to my grave,' she said, her face ablaze with emotion.

He wavered. 'You don't mean that.'

'I do. When the time comes, the whole world will find out you murdered my son.'

Part Three

Now

Chapter Fifty-Four

Cara

I slam my palm down hard on the table, furious at what Lisa has just admitted. The barista who brought over the free lattes casts a worried glance in our direction.

'You heard Matty die?' I hiss. 'Why have you never told me this before? More to the point, why didn't you do anything to stop it happening?'

Lisa gulps back fresh tears. 'I was terrified. I didn't know what to do. For weeks you'd been saying your house was haunted and then I hear—'

I cut her off, disgusted. 'I can't believe you didn't help us.'

'I know it sounds awful, but you need to listen to me carefully, Cara. You need to hear the whole story. There's more to it.' She looks so earnest, it halts my tirade.

'Go on,' I order her gruffly.

Lisa takes a deep breath, then begins, her voice low and considered.

'I let myself in the back door and was in the kitchen on my way to find you in the front room when I suddenly heard Matty yelling and you screaming. Then there was this awful, horrible choking sound and I didn't know what it was.' Lisa swallows hard. 'I know I should've come to help, but I panicked and hid in the cupboard under the stairs. I left the door open a crack and I watched you run past into the hallway and heard you bang the bathroom door shut, then Auntie Neet came rushing downstairs and that's when she found Matty. She was crying so much and I was about to come out of the cupboard and go to her when I heard him too.'

'Who?'

'Limey Stan.'

I stare at her, astonished.

'You heard Limey Stan in the room where Matty died?'

Lisa nods and I don't know whether to laugh or cry. For so long I've wanted validation that I wasn't going crazy and imagining Limey Stan, and now my cousin has just confirmed I wasn't – but twenty-five years too late.

'Did you get a glimpse of him?' I ask wonderingly.

'No. I just heard his voice.'

I sit back, stunned. Then something in me snaps.

'You never said a word!' I yell at her, not caring if I'm over-heard. 'You heard him and yet you let everyone believe it was me and that I'd made it all up. I was shut away in the Peachick for two years because of you and sent to live hundreds of miles away from everyone.' Angry tears stream down my face. 'You let people think I killed Matty.'

Lisa reaches for my hand, but I snatch it away.

'No, you don't get to play the supportive cousin now,' I spit at her.

'I understand why you're angry, but you need to hear me out,' she says imploringly. 'Before I tell you what happened next, please know that I am so, so sorry I didn't help you that night. I will never forgive myself for not stopping what happened. But it's not true to say I never spoke up about it until now. I did, so many times—'

Her words are flying at me like machine-gun fire and it's

making my head swim. 'Slow down,' I say. 'Explain what you mean.'

After another deep, shaky breath, she begins. 'I did hear another voice besides your mum's in the front room.'

'Limey Stan's,' I intone dully, but my body and brain are ablaze with fury. Every inch of me thrums with it.

'Yes, but when I say I heard Limey Stan's voice, what I mean is I heard whoever Limey Stan was. There wasn't a ghost in your front room that night, Cara, it was a man – and he was talking to your mum.'

I lurch in my seat, dizzy with horror. 'No, it can't have been.'

'It was. I heard them talking after Auntie Neet came down-stairs and found Matty's body.'

I let out a low moan. My mind is spinning so much I can't see straight. Lisa jumps out of her seat and kneels beside my chair.

'Cara—' She reaches for my hand and this time I let her take it.

'She can't have . . . She wouldn't . . .'

'I didn't want to think it either and, believe me, I've gone over it a million times since, wondering if I was mistaken, but I'm certain that's what I heard. Limey Stan, whoever he was, started saying something about not getting into trouble and then I heard Auntie Neet agree he should leave before the police arrived and then I heard him coming towards the kitchen and I was so petrified he'd find me, I slipped out the front door and ran all the way home.' Lisa begins to cry again. 'The next morning, everything was such a blur after Mum told me that Matty was dead that I couldn't be sure if what I'd heard actually happened. At one point, I convinced myself that I hadn't even left my bed and I'd dreamt it all.'

I don't acknowledge I'm hearing her, so she swings back into her seat and leans across the table towards me, her voice lowered again. I keep my gaze firmly trained on the surface of the table, because I cannot bear to look at her. Lisa could've saved both Matty and me from our different fates that night, but instead she saved herself.

'Two days after it happened, I tried to talk to Auntie Neet about what I'd heard. She got hysterical and said I was lying to stir up trouble and that I was making her suffering worse, which is a horrible thing to be accused of when you're a kid,' Lisa says. 'Mum and Gary wouldn't listen to me either and when police officers turned up to question them, Gary sent me to my room before he even let them in the house. I didn't know what else to do. Everyone was so convinced of your guilt, they refused to entertain the idea someone else could've attacked Matty. Then the hospital diagnosed you as being delusional and I started to panic that I wasn't well either and became convinced they'd take me away too. So I kept quiet. But when they told me you were coming out of hospital and going into foster care, I tried to talk to Auntie Neet again, but she told my mum I was shit-stirring and it got really nasty between us for a while and I started to doubt myself again.'

She pauses and I finally force myself to look at her and I can see she is as devastated telling me all this as I am listening to it.

'After I went to university in Scotland, I didn't come home that much, but every time I did, I'd go to see your mum and would ask her again about the voice, and every time she'd say I was either making it up to cause trouble between her and your dad or I'd imagined it.'

Something about her account doesn't make sense, and I say so.

'You've had all these years to share your suspicions with the police but you haven't. Why not? If they knew you were in the house at the time Matty was killed, they'd have interviewed you as a witness.'

Lisa nods. 'Lots of times I thought about going to the police station to report it, but at the end of the day I had no proof. I didn't see anything, I just heard talking.' She looks shamefaced. 'I'm so sorry.'

My voice clamps in my throat. How can I respond to that? Lisa merrily got on with her life afterwards. I didn't have that luxury.

'I also loved your mum. If I'd have gone to the police and it turned out I really was mistaken, she'd never have forgiven me for dragging her through more stress,' she adds.

I swallow hard. 'What about my dad? Did you ever try talking to him about it?'

'A couple of times, but the thing with your dad, he was a closed book after Matty died and you went. Conversation with him was impossible.' Her eyes fill with fresh tears. 'He missed you so much.'

'Not enough to get me out of foster care.'

Silence settles over us for a moment. Then I clear my throat.

'So, Limey Stan was a real person and not a . . .' But I can't bring myself to finish the sentence. The already shaky foundations of my childhood are being razed to the ground as we speak and my mind is filled with only one thought: Mum put the blame on me.

'There was no ghost in your house that night,' Lisa says emphatically, finishing my sentence for me. 'Limey Stan was a real person and Auntie Neet knew it all along.'

Chapter Fifty-Five

Cara

I remember little of the journey back to Parsons Close, or the hours that follow. I do know Lisa helped me upstairs and into bed, where, my mind blanked with shock, and shivering uncontrollably, I curled up on my side under the duvet. Tishk must've brought Mustard round when he saw Lisa's car in the driveway because my dog bounded into the room just as I got into bed, as relieved to see me as I was to see him, then settled down on the floor bedside me, one ear cocked, my consummate guard.

I do not sleep though. I simply lie like that for hours, staring into space, until I hear a tentative knock at the door and Lisa comes in bearing a mug of tea, which she sets down on the bedside table. Then she hesitantly perches on the edge of the mattress and smoothes back my hair from my forehead.

'How are you doing?' she whispers.

I close my eyes tight to stop the tears coming, but it's no good, they're too dense, too demanding.

'Do you want to talk about it?' she asks.

I shake my head. Where would I start? My mother sacrificed me, her nine-year-old child, apparently to save her own skin. Her treachery and her lies condemned me to two years in a hospital being treated for a condition I wouldn't have had but for her manipulation of my mental state, and then she ensured I was sent far away from home, away from everyone and everything I loved, so she didn't have to live with her guilt. Really I should be incandescent, but I'm too heartbroken to be as angry as I should be. My mum was one of two people whose job it was to protect me from harm, my dad being the other. For his part, I have to believe he didn't know what she did to me. I don't think he'd have allowed it, so instead she let him think his only daughter took the life of his only son.

And they called me the wicked one.

I gesture to Lisa that I want to sit up and she helps me, propping up the pillows against the headboard. She lifts the tea to my lips so I can take a sip and pats my back gently when I cough it straight back up. I lean back against the pillows and look at her. I can tell she's been crying again and there's a tiny fraction of me, hardened like a kernel and buried deep inside, that doesn't care she's upset, because despite her excuses, she had the power to stop me being sent away and did nothing. But, really, I do not blame her. I know what it's like to be the child who can't make themselves heard by the adults around them, whose version of events is shot down every time without question. My mum told Lisa she'd got it wrong – as a thirteen-year-old taught to respect her elders, what else was she meant to think? Punishing her for not having the guts to pursue the truth isn't fair of me and, right now, I think I prefer her as an ally rather than an enemy.

'I need to ask you something,' I say. 'Why tell me now about Limey Stan? I mean, you didn't have to – you could've carried on letting everyone, me included, think he was the famous Heldean ghost.'

Lisa reacts as though she's been preparing for this question.

'It was after Auntie Neet left you the house that I knew I had to say something. It was such a huge, unexpected gesture after you two being estranged for so long that there had to be a reason for it, and I suspect it was because I was right all along – there was someone else in the house with her the night that Matty was murdered and rather than speak up and admit it, Auntie Neet let you take the blame. I think giving you the house was her way of trying to make amends.'

'So you think it must have been this man who killed Matty and not me?' I watch my cousin keenly for any sign that she thinks I was responsible. Because, when you think about it, a strange man being in the house doesn't necessarily mean I'm innocent.

'He must've done it. You said someone grabbed Matty through the curtain and I saw your mum come downstairs afterwards, so it can only have been whoever was in the front room.' Lisa takes a deep breath. 'I think he was her lover and your mum had been sneaking him in late at night while your dad was away and it was him making all that noise while you were in bed.'

Finally, someone in my family believes I didn't kill Matty. Gratitude floods through me and I lean forward to hug her. 'Thank you,' I whisper. She starts to apologise again, but I shake my head. 'Please, enough. You tried to get my mum to confess – it's not your fault she didn't.'

'I should've tried harder.'

'I'm not angry with you, Lisa,' I say firmly.

No, that emotion is reserved for my mum and what she did, for my dad for being so blind and weak he didn't see what was happening in his own house, and for the police for assuming my guilt just because I'd had a run of bad behaviour at school and had accidentally hurt Matty's wrist once. It's also reserved for the bastard who killed him after torturing me at night for months on end.

'I won't let him get away with it,' I tell her. 'I'm going to find out who he was.'

My eyes smart as I say it. Truth be told, I am bereft to discover Limey Stan was almost certainly a real person. Like it or not, my entire identity and who I am is tied up with being the girl from the Heldean Haunting and not even a surname change helped me escape the notoriety of that. To discover it was all a lie perpetuated by my mum is something I shall never get over.

'But it happened twenty-five years ago and the only person who knew who it was has just died,' Lisa points out.

'Well, it's definitely someone who's still in Heldean because they've been breaking into the house pretending to be Limey Stan again.'

'It might not be the same person.'

My laugh is brittle. 'Oh, come on, who else is going to write I am Limey Stan on a mirror or move Matty's toys about?'

'Someone who wants to wind you up? One of those spook-tators you were telling me about – it would give that blogger something to write about.'

I can feel myself getting annoyed. I don't need her doubting me about this. Then I notice the high spots of colour that have appeared on her cheeks and I realise she's agitated too.

'Do you have any idea who he might be?' I ask her curiously.

'No, I don't.' She reaches down to pat Mustard, a classic diversionary tactic if ever I saw one. With a start, I realise she does have a suspicion about who Limey Stan was. But rather than push her on it and risk her becoming defensive and clamming up completely, I opt for a different tack.

'Whoever he was back then, he wasn't an intruder,' I say. 'Why would Mum ask him to leave before the police came otherwise? If it had been a stranger, Mum would've wanted him caught. It must've been someone she had feelings for, because otherwise why protect him over me?'

The spots of colour on Lisa's cheeks deepen a shade. Her gaze remains averted as she continues to pat the dog.

'I think we should ask your mum,' I plough on. 'She was the closest person to mine, they told each other everything. She might have an inkling who it was.'

'No! Leave her out of this.'

'Why? If anyone can help me, it's most likely her.'

'Please, Cara, you can't ask her.'

'Why not?'

'Just drop it.'

I throw back the covers and get out of bed. 'No, I won't. I'm going round there right now to ask her.'

I'd gone to bed fully dressed so all I need are my boots, which are downstairs. Determinedly, I make for the bedroom door, but Lisa stands in the way and blocks my path.

'My mum doesn't know anything and if you go round there now and say all this to her, she won't react well.'

'Why not? It proves it wasn't me.'

'She's never going to believe us if we say Auntie Neet was behind this, you know she won't.'

That gives me pause, because I know Lisa is right. Karen will always believe my mum over me. But something isn't sitting right with me.

'You're protecting someone too, I can see it in your face,' I state, to which Lisa flinches.

'I'm not.'

'Yes, you are, and if you don't tell me what else you know, I'm going straight round to your mum's house to ask her.'

Defeated, Lisa moves out of the doorway and sinks back down on the edge of the bed.

'I don't want this to be true, which is why I've never said a word about it to anyone.' Every syllable is strained, forced from her lips with an almighty effort. 'Cara, I'm scared my stepdad might be Limey Stan.'

Chapter Fifty-Six

Karen

Karen drops a raw potato into the saucepan already on the boil, then yelps as a splash of water rebounds and scalds the back of her hand.

'How many times have I told you, put the potatoes in first, then pour the water on top,' says Gary from his vantage point at the breakfast bar.

Ignoring him, she gives her skin a rub, but that makes it sting even more, so she goes over to the sink to run her hand under the cold tap.

'One of these days you'll listen to me,' he grins.

Karen returns a forced smile. Her husband has been under her feet for most of the day and it's getting on her nerves now. He says it's a head cold keeping him off work, but she's seen no sign of sniffles or sneezing and suspects he just fancied the day off. At least she hopes it's that and it's not him clashing with his boss and beginning to tire of the job again – this one has lasted longer than most and she couldn't bear it if he began talk of handing his resignation in again.

The mince for the cottage pie she is making is simmering in a frying pan, along with some onion, celery, carrots and seasoned stock. She gives it a quick stir, turns the heat right down, then asks Gary to keep an eye on it.

'I need to put some antiseptic cream on this burn,' she says.

He doesn't look up from the article he's reading on his tablet.

As she roots around the bathroom cabinet for a tube of cream that hasn't already been squeezed flat, her phone goes. It's Tishk, back from visiting his family in the Midlands.

'Hey, how was your trip?' she asks, cradling the phone against her ear with her left hand as she continues rooting with her right.

'Good, but I'm not ringing for a chat, Mrs J. I know you're keeping your distance from her and I understand why, but something's up with Cara and I don't know who else to speak to.'

Karen stops rooting and perches on the edge of the bath. Her niece has been on her mind constantly since she saw all the lights on and the new-found worry that Anita's true intention in leaving Cara the house was to this time punish her properly and have her locked up indefinitely hasn't gone away. She's even walked past the house a few times, hoping she might bump into Cara to see how she is.

Nervously, she listens as Tishk recounts being confronted by a group of strangers outside his house, led by that blogger Timothy Pitt, who claimed Cara attacked him after being frightened by another Limey Stan episode.

'Pitt said Cara ran off somewhere without her shoes on and they didn't know where she'd gone. One of the women got hold of Cara's dog after he escaped when she left the front door open, so I took him back to my house. I dropped him round because I saw she was back, but she's not alone – Lisa's with her.'

'My Lisa?' says Karen, astonished.

'Yes. She's at the house with Cara now.'

'What's she doing there?'

'I don't know. She answered the door when I took the dog back, and when I said I was shocked to see her, she went all weird and shut the door on me.' Tishk sounds peeved at Lisa's refusal to engage with him, but Karen's upset trumps his.

'Why is Lisa at Cara's and why didn't she tell us she was down?'

'I don't know, you'll have to ask her.'

'How did she seem?'

'Upset, actually. I think she'd been crying.'

Karen hangs up without another word and goes into her bedroom. She slips out of the comfy trousers she wears around the house, pulls on a pair of jeans, then goes downstairs. Gary hears her retrieving her coat from the cloakroom by the front door and comes into the hallway.

'Where are you going?' he asks, frowning.

'I've got to nip out.'

'Where to?'

Karen thinks quickly. She knows Gary will want to see Lisa too, but she wants to get to the bottom of why she's at Cara's first, because she's pretty sure they're not going to like the explanation. Better that she sees Lisa alone, then tells him.

'Chemist. We haven't got any cream and I think I've burned my hand quite badly. It's starting to blister.'

She cups her uninjured hand over the other to hide the red mark that is actually fine and fading fast.

'What about dinner?'

'Turn the potatoes and the mince off and I'll finish it when I get back. I won't be long.'

'But I'm hungry,' he moans.

'For God's sake, have a biscuit or something,' she snaps. 'You won't starve waiting an hour.'

She's gone before he can respond.

293

Cara is not in the least bit perturbed to find her aunt standing on the doorstep. If anything, she appears pleased, which makes Karen feel conflicted because this is someone she is supposed to detest and yet part of her appreciates the warm welcome.

Lisa is in the front room, seated on the sofa clutching a balled-up tissue, her glasses removed and on the coffee table in front of her. Tishk was right about her being upset: the second she clocks Karen, she buries her face in her hands and begins to cry again. Alarmed, Karen goes straight over to her, shooting a look at Cara as she does in the hope she might offer an explanation as to what's going on, but her niece has an oddly beatific expression on her face and says nothing as she waits by the fireplace.

'Darling, whatever's the matter?' Karen asks Lisa. 'Why are you here? Why didn't you tell us you were visiting?'

'Oh, Mum . . .' Lisa says it as though her heart has splintered.

Holding her tight, Karen's panic mounts with every sob her daughter releases. She turns again to Cara.

'What the hell's going on? Is this your doing?'

'No. I didn't ask her to come, she just turned up.'

'But why?'

Cara pauses for a moment, as though waiting for Lisa to start, but when it's obvious her cousin is too upset to talk, she addresses Karen herself.

'Do you remember Lisa trying to talk to you in the days after Matty died?' she asks.

Karen stiffens at her nephew's name being spoken by the person who, in her mind, lost the right to say it a long time ago.

'She told you she knew something about Limey Stan and that she should tell the police, but you and Uncle Gary wouldn't listen to her.'

Somewhere in the back of Karen's mind, a distant bell clangs, but she shakes her head, unwilling to play along. 'I don't remember.'

294

'Really? You don't recall Lisa telling you she heard a man's voice in the house that night which definitely wasn't a ghost's?'

Karen gapes at her. 'What?'

Lisa wriggles out of her hold. 'It's true, Mum,' she says, sitting up. She blows her nose noisily on her tissue. 'I was here. I came round because I told Cara I would hide with her and Matty to catch Limey Stan. There was a man in the house that night, Mum, and I heard Auntie Neet talking to him.'

Karen swallows hard. She does recall Lisa saying something about a man being at the house, but she and Gary thought she was spinning them a line because she was upset about Cara getting into trouble and misguidedly believed it would help her.

'I do remember,' she says gently, 'but there couldn't have been anyone else in the house. Auntie Neet would've known and said something.'

Lisa shakes her head sadly. 'There was, Mum. I wasn't making it up. Do you also remember I asked to speak to the police who came to the house, but Dad wouldn't let me?'

The vague memory of Lisa begging Gary to let her speak to the police sharpens in her mind. Instead, he sent her to her bedroom, out of the way.

'You must've misheard,' Karen says firmly. 'Anita would have told the police and the rest of us if there was anyone else in the house.' She glances warily at Cara, who still has the same, odd expression on her face, then turns back to Lisa. 'I don't know what Cara's been saying, but we all know what happened that night and we know whose fault it was.'

'That's the thing, Mum, you don't. It wasn't Cara.'

'Why are you saying this?' says Karen, growing upset.

'Cara deserves for the truth to come out. I heard what happened and I stupidly let all you grown-ups make me think I was imagining it, but now I can make sure everyone knows,' says Lisa.

Karen angrily stabs her finger in Cara's direction. 'What non-sense have you been filling her head with? This is coming from you, I know it is.'

Cara looks wounded. 'I haven't said anything.'

'Rubbish!' Karen retorts. 'My poor sister was destroyed because of you and now you're back causing more trouble. When are you going to start owning up to what you did?'

Cara's face crumples and, exasperated, Lisa shakes her head. 'Cara isn't making me say any of this.' She grasps Karen's hands between her own. 'Look at me, Mum.'

Karen does so, properly for the first time in years, taking in every inch of her daughter's face. When do we stop really look-ing at our children? she asks herself. As babies and toddlers, we drink them in, committing every eyelash, freckle and dimple to memory. When does that stop?

'You need to hear this,' Lisa adds. 'For your own sake as much as mine and Cara's.'

Finally, Karen nods. 'Tell me.'

The two of them hold hands as Lisa describes her involve-ment on the night Matty died, what she heard coming from the front room and how Anita had kept quiet all those years about someone else being there. Karen sits rigid as she listens, but inside a storm has whipped up and it's battering her heart against her ribcage, because she knows from her daughter's expression that every word of what she's saying is true. At the same time, aspects of Anita's behaviour that had bothered Karen back then suddenly start to make sense – the shockingly damning statement she gave to the police, her refusal to visit Cara in hospital, abandoning her into the foster system against Paul's wishes. Sending Cara away like that ensured Anita would never get found out.

Eventually, Lisa finishes, worn out with emotion. A devastat-ed Karen lets go of her hands, her mind whirling with confusion.

For so long she's held on to the belief Cara was responsible for taking Matty's life and now, all of a sudden, she's expected to dismiss the notion? Then she catches the terrified look on Cara's face as she waits for Karen to react and in that expression she glimpses the little girl she once was and the whirling suddenly stops, as though someone's pulled a plug. Slowly, Karen gets to her feet, stiff from sitting still for so long, and crosses the room to Cara, who shrinks back from her as she approaches.

'I am so sorry,' Karen says, her voice cracking. 'I blamed you and I shouldn't have done. I had no idea about any of this. What your mum did to you is unforgiveable.'

'You believe it wasn't me?' Cara whispers.

'I do.'

Cara's eyes fill with tears. Karen thinks about hugging her, but she can't quite bring herself to step forward to close the gap between them and Cara remains equally rooted to the spot. They may never reach a level of familial closeness, but in that moment Karen vows to spend whatever life she has left making up for what was done to her niece.

She turns to Lisa. 'I always knew Auntie Neet could be selfish and sneaky, but this?' She breaks down before she can finish, the enormity of what her sister did sending shockwaves through her body. 'How could she do such a despicable thing? She lied to me, to Paul . . . she tricked us all.'

Lisa stands up and holds her mum as she cries. Eventually, Karen's tears begin to ease and she accepts the tissue Cara offers her.

'I don't think Auntie Neet tricked all of us, Mum,' says Lisa.

Karen stares at her, bewildered. 'What's that supposed to mean?'

'I think you'd better sit down again.'

Chapter Fifty-Seven

Cara

The three of us talk long into the night. Earlier, Karen excused herself from returning home by calling Gary and telling him the chemist had advised her to get the burn seen to at the local A & E. It was at least a three-hour waiting time, she informed him. He moaned a bit about his dinner and then said he wouldn't wait up. I marvelled at how she kept her cool on the phone after what Lisa had told her about suspecting he could be Limey Stan.

'It sounded like his voice,' explained Lisa, when Karen demanded to know how she could possibly think such an awful thing of her dad, let alone say it aloud. 'I don't want it to be him, Mum, but I swear that's what I heard.'

'But why on earth would he have been sneaking around Anita's house in the middle of the night?' was Karen's next reaction to Lisa's bombshell. Then, as the implication of what that meant slowly dawned on her, she recoiled in horror. 'No, absolutely not – they were not having an affair. I would've known. Gary's many things, but a cheat isn't one of them. Nor would Auntie Neet betray me like that.'

So Lisa shared another secret she'd been keeping back all these years.

'I think something was going on, Mum,' she said, looking

pained. 'I caught them outside during that New Year's Eve party you threw when I was thirteen. They were at the bottom of the garden and Auntie Neet had her arms around Gary. From where I was standing, it looked like they were kissing. He got all flustered and said he was trying to warm her up because she was shivering, but it was obvious that's not why they were hugging. That's why I got so mad with him and stopped calling him Dad. I was so angry with him and Auntie Neet for going behind your back.'

Karen was devastated to hear Lisa's account but still refused to accept Gary was guilty of infidelity. She did admit my mum might've strayed though, her words laced with fury as she said it.

'I knew she wasn't happy with your dad and I suspected there were times when she was keen on other men, but my husband?' she raged. 'No, I don't believe it's true. Anita liked to flirt, but she didn't have full-blown affairs.' Then, when she'd calmed down, Karen told me a little of what my parents' marriage was like. 'Your dad was a generous man, but he treated your mum like a paid employee, expecting her to do all the housework and never lifting a finger to help. He spent so long on the road for work that sometimes I think he forgot this house wasn't a hotel as well.'

That piqued my curiosity. 'If Mum hated being a skivvy so much, why did she work as a housekeeper for other people?'

'She left school with barely any qualifications and never trained in anything, so housekeeping was all she felt fit for, I suppose. She earned good money though, working for some very wealthy families. The last one had a huge house in a street off Middle Lane. It was like a palace.'

Then Karen had turned to Lisa. 'You do realise what you're accusing your dad of, don't you? If you think it was his voice you heard and he was in this house that night, you're saying he's the one who . . .' She broke off, distraught. She couldn't bear to say it aloud.

Lisa had nodded miserably. 'I know.'

Three hours later, exhausted from all the talking, I reach a decision. 'There's no point confronting Uncle Gary, because if he is guilty of pretending to be Limey Stan and killing Matty, he'll deny everything,' I say. 'I need to catch him in the act if I want to prove it.'

Lisa nods in agreement, but Karen just looks desolate. I know I should probably be wary of her given how she's treated me since I've been back in Heldean, but I am certain that after everything we've discussed this evening my aunt won't go running to Gary to tell him we suspect him. What she's been told tonight has hurt her immeasurably and despite her historic hostility towards me, I take no satisfaction in that. She's promised she will go along with whatever plan I come up with, because if her husband has been pretending to be Limey Stan all this time, she wants him to pay for what he did back then and is doing to me now. Earlier, I told her how distressed I was after finding the table turned upside down and Matty's toys on my bed and the writing on the mirror and she was horrified I'm being tormented again.

'Why do you think he's started it up again?' she asked me, and I could hear the fear in her voice. It must be terrifying for her to think of what her husband might be capable of.

'Presumably it's to make me leave Heldean. The longer I stay, the more risk there is of him being found out. If he makes me think Limey Stan has returned and I'm delusional again, it would be the last place I'd want to stay,' I speculated. 'Plus he wants me to give the house to Ryan, so forcing me out has two advantages.'

Now Lisa pours herself some more white wine as she asks me

how I plan to catch my uncle pretending to be Limey Stan. She and I have drunk a few glasses each as we've talked and I can see she's past tipsy. Karen's abstained because Gary thinks she's at the hospital and would ask questions if he smelled alcohol on her breath.

'Hidden surveillance. I'm going to set up cameras all around the house so when he comes back pretending to be Limey Stan again they'll record him.'

'Do you think that will work?' asks Karen tightly.

'I hope so.'

'You should ask Tishk to help you,' she says. 'He's good with things like that.'

'I don't know if I can trust him,' I admit, and I tell Karen about him lying about the conversations he had with my mum about me.

'Tishk is a good man,' she responds. 'If he lied it was probably because he was trying to spare your feelings.' Then she fixes me with a look. 'I know life's been hard for you, Cara – I can't begin to imagine how hard. But you need to learn to trust people again. Tishk is trying to be your friend, so let him. He cares about you.'

'It's a wonder Tishk never saw my dad coming round here late at night,' Lisa remarks. 'He used to sneak out at all hours, going to parties he wasn't meant to. We should ask him.'

'No!' Karen and I both say it at the same time. 'I don't want anyone outside us three knowing about this,' says my aunt, trembling at the thought.

'I agree, let's keep it between us for now,' I say.

Lisa nods. 'Okay. What about selling the house though? You can't really have viewings if you've got cameras set up. Someone might spot them.'

'The house isn't on the market yet, but you're right. I can't risk people traipsing through it now. In fact,' I inhale deeply, unsure what the reaction will be to my next statement, 'I think I might stay here a while longer.'

Lisa whoops and raises her glass, but it's not her backing I need. I look to my aunt and, to my relief, she nods. 'You belong here,' she says simply.

Putting her glass back down on the table, Lisa wonders again how her stepdad came up with the name Limey Stan. Earlier, we agreed that he must've whispered it downstairs in the hallway so the nine-year-old me would think the 'ghost' was saying it. The thought of him and my mum laughing about how adeptly they were tricking me makes me seethe and the only thing that's stopping me marching round to Karen's house to have it out with him is the thought of being able to capture him on tape. Undeniable proof: the only guarantee I have of clearing my name.

'Limey is what Americans used to call British soldiers during the war,' I say. 'Timothy Pitt wrote on his blog that an RAF pilot lived here before my parents bought the place, so maybe that's what made Uncle Gary think of it.'

Karen looks perplexed. 'That's not true, though. They bought this house off another couple just a bit older than themselves. They were selling up to emigrate.'

'Maybe he was the person before them,' I shrug.

'It doesn't matter who the person was,' says Karen shrilly, as her distress gives way to anger. 'It's too late to bring my sister to account for what she did to you, but he's not going to get away with it.'

Chapter Fifty-Eight

MEMORANDUM

To: Dr Patrick Malloy, head of clinical services
From: Dr Tamil Gent, consultant child and adolescent
   psychiatrist
Subject: Cara Belling
Date: Thursday 22 August 1996

Patrick, as per your instructions, I've been reviewing Dr Ardern's caseload since assuming her position and we need to talk about Cara Belling. It is my clinical opinion that the child is no longer showing symptoms of delusional disorder that warrant a continued stay here. We can discuss this further; however, with your permission, I would like to begin the process of arranging for Cara to be discharged under medical supervision. Her social worker, Marie Thompson, is fully in the loop and ready to make the necessary arrangements for Cara to go into foster care – I called her parents myself yesterday and sadly their position of refusing to allow her to return home to live with them appears to be immovable. Regards, Tamil.

Chapter Fifty-Nine

Cara

Heeding my aunt's advice, I contact Tishk to ask if he minds helping me set up security cameras around the house and he agrees without question, accepting at face value my reasoning that I will sleep sounder with them installed. In fact, as we browse the shelves of an electrical store two days after Lisa's arrival in Heldean turned everything on its head, I get the distinct feeling he's enjoying the spy aspect of our expedition, not to mention it excuses the arch procrastinator from working on his PhD again.

What he does question is the sudden ceasefire between Karen and myself, as twice in two days now he has spotted her leaving my house. I tell him it is not me she's come to see but Lisa, who is staying with me for a few days, but that brought a new raft of questions about why Lisa's in Parsons Close and not round the corner with her parents. While I cannot share it with him because of what I agreed with Karen and Lisa, the explanation is straightforward: Gary is unlikely to attempt any further Limey Stan scare tactics while Lisa is staying with me, so her being there buys me time to set up what I need to catch him in the act.

Fortunately, browsing for indoor security cameras quickly diverts Tishk's train of thought from why Lisa isn't staying with her parents.

'They're quite bulky. I'm not sure how well we can hide them,' he says, examining a clunky one that looks like something you'd use to project messages into outer space.

He's right, the cameras are not exactly inconspicuous, which is probably the point if you want intruders to know they're being watched. I want the opposite, however – something that can be tucked away, out of view, ready to record by stealth.

'You might be better off looking on Amazon. They have all kinds of spyware on there,' Tishk adds.

'How do you know?' I ask with a chuckle. 'Fancy yourself as the next James Bond?'

'Ha ha,' he responds drily. 'No. I know because my PhD is on the psychology of stalking and effective treatment for offenders.'

I experience a flutter of discomfort when he says that, but I remind myself what Karen said about trusting him. I do like having him as a friend.

'That sounds interesting,' I say. 'What made you choose that subject?'

'One of my sisters was stalked as a teenager by a customer who used to come into the café where she waitressed on Saturdays. He seemed normal and nice, but then he started following her home, waiting outside her school for her and sending her letters. Mum and Dad eventually got the police involved and he was arrested and cautioned. It got me interested in what drives people to stalk someone.'

'Poor girl. That must've been awful.'

'Actually it was for both of the twins. He couldn't tell them apart, so at one point he was stalking them both.'

His voice suddenly drops to a whisper.

'Talking of which, there's a guy over there that keeps staring at you. He followed us into the store. Don't turn round straight away or he'll see. But he's in the light brown suit, purple tie. Young guy, in his twenties.'

I give it a few moments, then turn round on the pretence of looking at some cameras across the aisle. From the corner of my eye, I can see the man Tishk is referring to: he's doing his best to pretend he's not staring, but the surreptitious looks he throws my way in quick succession are a giveaway.

I turn back to Tishk. 'Who do you think he is?'

'I don't know, but I think we should leave. Let's look for cameras online when we get back.'

'Good idea.'

We're outside the store when the man in the light brown suit sidles up and announces himself as a journalist.

'John Baker, ENS. Sorry to approach you out of the blue like this, but I understand you're Cara Belling, the girl from the Heldean Haunting, and I was hoping we could have a chat.'

I'm too stunned to respond and helplessly look to Tishk to intervene.

'What's ENS?' he demands to know.

'Essex News Service. We're an agency that supplies stories to the nationals. Ms Belling, it is you, isn't it? Can I have a quick word?'

'No, you can't,' snaps Tishk. 'Leave her alone.'

'Wait,' I say, quickly gathering my thoughts. 'Who told you who I am?'

'We had a tip-off.'

'From who?'

'I can't say, I'm afraid. I have to protect my source.'

I realise it doesn't matter even if he tells me. It will not change the fact that I am about to be exposed. I should be feeling panicked, but a strange calm has settled over me and as the reporter wields his phone in my face to record our conversation, it dawns on me this could be an opportunity to force my uncle into revealing himself as Limey Stan.

'What do you want to ask me?'

Tishk's mouth drops open. 'Cara, don't.'

'It's okay, honestly. My return to Heldean was going to get out sooner or later. I may as well try to control what's said about it.'

The reporter is almost beside himself with excitement. 'Shall we grab a coffee?'

'No. You can ask me a few questions now and that's it.'

People going in and out of the store eye us curiously as they pass, but thankfully no one stops.

'What brought you back to Heldean?' Baker asks.

'My mother died and she left me her house.'

Tishk stands next to me, his face tortured with concern. I reach down and squeeze his hand.

'It's okay,' I say in an aside. 'I know what I'm doing.'

'Does it bother you that your presence here is upsetting locals?'

'I wasn't aware that many people knew I was back. But I don't wish to upset anyone – I just want to be left alone.' I take a deep breath. 'But I understand why they might be upset. I am, after all, the woman who as a child was blamed for causing her brother's death. But I loved Matty with all my heart and I never hurt him. I still stand by that.'

'What about Heldean's infamous ghost, Limey Stan? Do you still stand by saying he existed?'

I hesitate, knowing that how I respond to the question will shape what happens next.

'No, I don't. Limey Stan was a figment of my imagination – I know that now. As a child, I was mentally unstable and I spent two years receiving treatment in hospital before being discharged. I feel no shame in admitting that, because there shouldn't be any stigma surrounding mental illness and psychiatric disorders.'

'Well, no, but—'

'There's no but. Demonising a child who isn't well is wrong. I don't deserve to be vilified any longer for an illness I had no control over as a nine-year-old. I deserve understanding.'

'But you're still saying you didn't kill your brother?'

'I am. It wasn't me.'

'So who did it?'

'I don't know, but I'd like to find out.'

The reporter flounders, wrong-footed by my answers and clearly not believing me when I say I'm not Matty's killer.

'Is that all?' I ask him.

'Um, I, yes – I mean no. I have one last question. Are you planning to stay in Heldean?'

This is the question I hoped he would ask. My response should hopefully inflame Gary into doing what I want him to do.

'Oh yes. Heldean is my home town and I see no reason for me not to stay,' I say. 'I now plan to live in the house that my mum left me in her will. For the first nine years of my life, it was a loving family home and while I wish I could change what happened, I am happy to be back there.'

Before he leaves, the reporter asks if he can take a picture of me on his phone and I oblige, much to Tishk's alarm.

'I can't believe you spoke to him and let him photograph you,' he says as we walk back to my car. 'Now everyone will know who you are. You'll be all over Twitter by teatime.'

I wish I could explain to Tishk why I've gone on record, but I can't. The less he knows about what I'm trying to provoke, the more protected he is.

Starting the engine, it hits me the first thing I must do when I get home is ring John and Anne to warn them. But I think that if any journalist does approach them for a comment they should talk positively about how fostering turned my life around.

Maybe The Fostering Network can help them with that and we can spin some good out of this notoriety of mine.

'I think you've made a terrible mistake,' mutters Tishk as he fastens his seat belt beside me.

I don't, I think, smiling to myself. I've done exactly what was needed. If I want to expose Limey Stan for the person he really is, it's time I stepped out of the shadows myself.

Chapter Sixty

The Heldean Advertiser

8 HRS AGO

The Heldean Haunting: Cara Belling finally admits Limey Stan was 'all in my head'

By Beth Jenkins, Senior Reporter
@Beth_HelAdv

Accused killer Cara Belling has finally confessed she DID invent Limey Stan – a quarter of a century on from blaming the 'ghost' for smothering her six-year-old brother.

Belling, who was nine at the time, has admitted she invented the ghost after becoming unwell with a mental health condition.

'Limey Stan was a figment of my imagination – I know that now,' she told a reporter from ENS. 'I feel no shame in admitting [I spent time in hospital], because there shouldn't be any stigma surrounding mental illness and psychiatric disorders.'

It is the first time Belling, 34, has publicly addressed the death of her brother, Matty. The six-year-old boy was found suffocated in the front room of her family's home in Parsons Close, Heldean, in the early hours of 16 July 1994.

However, despite admitting to faking the Heldean Haunting, as the incident famously became known, Belling still denies she was responsible for what happened to her brother.

'I loved Matty with all my heart and I never hurt him. I still stand by that,' she said. She also said she wanted to find out who had killed him.

Belling is currently staying at the house in Parsons Close, following the death of her mum, Anita, in October this year. Her dad, Paul Belling, died in a road traffic accident in 2000 at the age of 42.

After being treated in a London children's psychiatric hospital for two years, Belling went into foster care, where she remained until the age of 18.

A source told the *Advertiser* that, as the main beneficiary of her mother's will, Belling was putting the property up for sale. However, she confirmed to ENS she now plans to continue living at the house, adding, 'Heldean is my home town and I see no reason for me not to stay.'

One of her neighbours, who asked not to be named, said they were furious to learn she was no longer selling up.

'None of us are happy she's here because we've got children ourselves and we know what she's capable of,' said the resident. 'We want her gone.'

Belling said she understood why her return to Heldean had caused feelings to run high. 'But I don't want to upset anyone,' she said. 'I just want to be left alone.'

Belling was never charged over her brother's killing because being only nine years old put her below the legal age of criminality. A spokesman for Heldean Police confirmed today they are not looking for anyone else in connection with Matty Belling's death and that the case remains closed.

RELATED STORIES

- 16 Parsons Close: inside Heldean's famous haunted house
- Is Limey Stan the ghost of a World War II hero? Local paranormal expert claims to know true identity
- The Heldean Haunting: mother dies 25 years after infamous hoax

Chapter Sixty-One

Cara

The doorbell rings for the third time in an hour and Lisa lets out a groan. It's four days since my impromptu press conference outside the electronics store and I've been doorstepped by reporters offering me money to talk, emailed by researchers for TV talk shows and rung up and offered the chance 'to tell my side of the story in a sympathetic way' to women's magazines promoting themselves as the nice guys of journalism. I've said no to them all, in the hope they'll soon give up.

The story sent out by the reporter from ENS had a ripple effect and was picked up across news outlets and online. I wouldn't go as far as to say the reports were positive – there was much tawdry rehashing of the events of the night Matty died – but my comments about being unwell were reported in full and in context. It was the best I could hope for, really. So far there have been no direct mentions of John and Anne, who, bless them, have been nothing but supportive since I called to warn them they might be approached by journalists. Both said they would willingly tell any reporter who asked what a lovely, well-adjusted young woman I grew up to become while in foster care – that's their description, I hasten to add, not mine.

The doorbell peals again.

'I'll get it,' says Tishk with a sigh, getting up from the sofa.

'Tell them she won't talk for anything less than £10,000, like those supermodels,' Lisa calls after his retreating back.

'What?' I laugh.

'It was a famous quote – one of them said they wouldn't get out of bed for less than ten grand.' She gives me a look. 'Aren't you tempted to sell your story? The money would come in handy while you're not working.'

'No way, I couldn't profit from Matty's death like that, it would be wrong,' I say with a shudder. Quickly, I change the subject. 'How was your mum this morning?'

Karen's been staying away while the reporters have been swarming around and we decided it would raise Gary's suspicions if Lisa stayed at mine any longer, so for the past two nights she's also been at home with her parents. We figured the press attention should put him off sneaking in as Limey Stan for the time being.

'She's doing her best to hold it together, but it's really hard. She hates being around him, it's crucifying her.'

'It can't be much fun for you either.'

'It's not. I'm scared to be in the same room as him. I know you want proof, but part of me wishes we could just go to the police. I think Mum's wishing the same.'

'They won't believe it,' I say. 'They'll say I'm making it up. I know this is hard for you both, but I need you to let me do this.'

Tishk comes in holding a box. 'It's the spy cameras you ordered.'

I sit up, excited. 'Brilliant. Open it.'

'Were there any reporters out there?' Lisa asks.

'Nah, they've obviously moved on to something far more interesting than Cara.'

I smile, not in the least bit offended by Tishk's remark. I've grown to love his company and every day we spend together is better than the previous. I never thought returning to Heldean would bring into my life new friendships I would want to treasure, but he's making the painful truth that I was unjustly banished for twenty-five years a fraction easier to bear. I only hope he can forgive me when he finds out what we're keeping from him.

'Good,' says Lisa firmly. 'Let's hope they leave you alone now, and that bolshy estate agent too.'

Ian Leonard hasn't reacted well to being told I don't want to continue with the sale. First he'd tried to cajole me into changing my mind when I rang to tell him, but when that didn't work, he turned up on the doorstep ranting that I'd signed a contract and had to honour it and I should sell up as I had committed to doing. If it hadn't been for Lisa telling him to leave, I don't think he'd have backed down until he'd bullied me into changing my mind.

He hasn't quite relented though – the steady stream of emails and texts I am receiving are a testament to that. He says at the very least I owe him his fee. If I do decide to sell again, it certainly won't be through his agency.

But, for now, I am very happy to stay put in Parsons Close. As devastated as I am about my mum letting me take the blame and Limey Stan not being the ghost I thought he was back then, the knowledge has also brought with it a sense of peace. I have no reason to be frightened of being here now – there is nothing lurking in the shadows any more for me to fear. My only wish is that Matty was here so I could tell him that. I wish I could say sorry for making him hide with me that night.

Blinking back tears, I watch as Tishk finishes unpacking the cameras. These ones are perfectly tiny, barely the size of a thumbnail, and will be easily hidden. They have a night-vision function too, but the downside is that the battery might drain after about 90 minutes of recording. However, if I'm prepared to wait up, I should be able to activate them using my phone the moment I hear Gary step inside the house, meaning I won't waste precious minutes recording thin air.

I am prepared.

Chapter Sixty-Two

Cara

Tishk and Lisa offer to stay with me overnight, but I decline, knowing that if there are people in the house with me I cannot bring this nightmare to an end, as 'Limey Stan' will not come. Besides, this is my ending to my story, not theirs, and I need to see it through alone. I tell them I will call them if I need help and, reluctantly, they each depart: Tishk next door and Lisa to the friend's place she was originally meant to be staying at. She doesn't want to stay with her parents tonight because if she hears Gary leaving, she might not be able to stop herself confronting him first. Karen, meanwhile, dropped it into conversation with Gary that the press has dispersed and I'm staying on at the house. She said he didn't react, but the point is he knows I'm alone now.

I while away the hours until bedtime looking through my old belongings stored inside the boxes in Matty's bedroom. I've decanted them onto my bed though, as I find it too upsetting to sit in his room. I am grieving for both of us now – for his death and for the life we should've had growing up together.

Among the contents are some of my old schoolbooks and it amuses me to see I had an aptitude for maths even back then. I do not recover any English work though, because the stories I wrote in class were sent to the Peachick as evidence of my febrile imagination. I know this because there is mention of it in my medical notes.

I once again lift out the little box containing my and Matty's hospital ID bracelets. As I delicately hold each one, I wonder why Mum packed Matty's with the rest of my things and why it's not amongst his. I can understand why mine is here, much as it pains me to say it – all my other belongings were dumped in boxes, why would this be any different? But Matty's? A precious memento like this, I would've expected her to—

My mind suddenly fizzes as it connects the thought I've just had to something said to me a few days ago. The girl in black who was with Timothy Pitt, the one called Jenny, who claimed to be a medium, what was it she said? My face screws up as I force myself to piece her comment together, all the while cursing myself for not paying more attention at the time. I know it was something about not ignoring what is precious from the beginning and something about a road. I turn Matty's ID bracelet over in my palm again. It was given to him within minutes of his life beginning and Mum left it in a place where I couldn't ignore it. But all that medium prophesising is hokum, isn't it? It's about as real as Limey Stan was.

And yet it niggles at me as I sit here, the message Jenny claimed to have from my mum. I am tempted for a moment to contact Pitt, asking him to get Jenny to call me, but I backtrack immediately, knowing it would be a terrible idea to willingly invite that man and his acolytes into my life.

I put the ID bracelets back in the box and my eye catches the lettering on the inside of Matty's again: HL72QR. When I first saw it, I assumed it was a hospital reference number, but what if it's not?

I open the search engine on my phone and seconds later I want to slap myself for being so stupid for not recognising what it was the moment I saw it.

HL7 2QR is a Heldean postcode.

With trembling fingers, I click on the first link and what I read sends shockwaves barrelling through me. HL7 2QR is the postcode for a street on the other side of town – a street called Limestone Road.

It can't be . . .

Limestone . . .

Limey Stan?

Chapter Sixty-Three

Cara

'It must be,' I say aloud, my pulse at full throttle as I read again the name 'Limestone Road'. Mustard, napping on the carpet beside me, head on his paws, does not react – then again he's used to me talking to myself. 'What if I misheard Uncle Gary saying Limestone Road and that's how I came up with the name Limey Stan?'

I grab my phone again and clamber to my feet. On my way downstairs, I call Karen. It is half past eleven, but I don't think twice about disturbing her so late. I have to ask her.

'What connection does Uncle Gary have to Limestone Road?' I blurt out as soon as she picks up.

'I don't know where that is.'

'It's on the other side of town.'

I can hear the hesitancy in her voice when she answers. 'I honestly don't know, Cara. I swear I've never heard him mention it. Are you okay? You sound upset.' Her voice drops to a whisper. 'He's here still, watching telly. I was about to go to bed and leave him to it.'

I ignore her. 'Someone wrote the postcode for Limestone Road on the inside of Matty's ID bracelet from the hospital when he was born and I looked it up and I think Limestone Road is where I got the name Limey Stan from.'

I'm aware I sound a bit manic, but I can't help it. I am elated I've finally worked out the provenance of the name. But Karen's not convinced.

'It sounds like a coincidence, Cara. The lettering on the bracelet is probably something to do with the hospital.'

'No, it's a postcode,' I say, frustrated she's querying it. 'I think it was put there as a clue for me to find.'

'By who? It won't have been your mum, because we know she wanted you to take the blame.'

'My dad?' I venture. 'Maybe he suspected all along and this was his way of helping me find out the truth.'

'If your dad thought for even a second you'd been falsely accused he would've moved heaven and earth to prove it, not leave an obscure clue that might or might not have been found decades later,' Karen reasons. 'Besides, like I said, Gary has no connection to Limestone Road.'

Is she lying or is she wondering why I am trying to connect her husband to a street she knows nothing about? I don't give her the chance to explain her thinking: I say a curt goodbye, then hang up. I have bigger concerns right now than her marital secrets.

Unable to calm myself, I pace the downstairs of the house, back and forth, up and down. When that does nothing to pacify me, I head for the fridge and the bottle of wine chilling inside it. I had decided not to drink tonight, to keep a clear head, but the frustration burning in the pit of my stomach needs extinguishing so I can think straight, and this is the only way I know how to salve it. I pour myself a medium glass, down it in one, then pour myself another. By the time that glass is drained, I am feeling marginally more relaxed. I pour another, just to be sure.

Glass in hand, I go back upstairs to my bedroom. I need to give the impression that I am asleep. I have even turned off all the lights in the house tonight. I was scared at first, my natural reaction to plunging myself into the darkness being to panic. Then I reminded myself that there was nothing to fear in the shadows now: I know who my bogeyman is and I am ready to confront him.

I settle on the bed and wait. Mustard is asleep on his. He is uncharacteristically docile tonight and it occurs to me I've been so distracted I forgot to take him to the vet's to have him checked out after locking him in the car. Feeling guilty, I lean down and ruffle the fur on his head.

'I'm sorry, mate. I'll take better care of you when this is all over, I promise.' He remains still, but his tummy expands and contracts as he breathes. I ruffle his head again. 'Mustard?'

He's unconscious, I realise with horror. I slide off the bed onto the floor and gently raise his head with both hands. As it lolls heavily to one side, Mustard emits a loud snore, followed by a sigh. He's breathing, but it appears as though he's heavily sedated. Frantically, I think back over the day. Who has had access to him to administer a sedative? My only visitors today have been Lisa and Tishk. I gently lower Mustard's head back on to his paws and as he snores again, I ask myself the question I probably should have posed much sooner than this, given she's admitted she was in the house the night Matty died and it was her who first pointed the finger at Uncle Gary and convinced me and her mum that he could be Limey Stan.

Am I stupid to trust my cousin?

Chapter Sixty-Four

Karen

Karen can barely look her husband in the eye as he fusses around the kitchen preparing his usual fare of chicken paste sandwiches to take to work tomorrow for lunch. Gary's not oblivious to it though, asking her three times if anything's the matter.

'I'm coming down with a cold,' she lies. 'In fact, I think I'll sleep in the spare room so I don't keep you awake all night snuffling.'

Gary's face registers shock. In thirty years of marriage, they can count on both hands the amount of times they have slept apart. Although, Karen thinks bitterly, there have been many nights where he hasn't crawled into bed until the early hours, when she assumed he was downstairs watching television but instead could have been sneaking in from her sister's house.

Bile rises in her throat as her mind conjures up unpleasant images of Gary and Anita together. But what hurts her most isn't the thought of them being lovers but the lying that cushioned it. How they must have laughed behind her back at her naivety. Her misplaced trust in them gave them licence to do as they pleased and what really kills her is that Anita didn't care about the damage it would inflict on Karen if she found out, because she knew Karen well enough to know that Gary cheating would devastate her.

And it has. Every time she does manage to force herself to look in his direction, she wants to scream at him for humiliating her and for putting Lisa in the awkward position of catching him with Anita in the garden. Then there's what Cara went through as well, although how Karen feels about that has become conflicted in the past few days. Gary's complicity in the Limey Stan hoax seems in no doubt, yet she cannot bring herself to believe he went as far as to kill Matty. She knows he wouldn't hurt any child, let alone one he was close to, spent time with and loved. However, despite her misgivings, she is prepared to go along with Cara's plan in trying to unmask him because her niece deserves to clear her name.

She flinches as Gary places his palm against her forehead.

'You don't feel hot, so it can't be serious,' he says. 'Are you sure you want to sleep in the spare room? I don't mind if you're a bit bunged up.'

'I'll mind, because you say it's okay now, but tomorrow you'll be moaning that you've had no sleep. I know what you're like, Gary.'

She's not usually as abrupt with him and she can see he's a bit taken aback, but he shrugs it off. 'Well, if you're still feeling dicky in the morning, I'll bring you breakfast in bed.'

He gives her a wink as he says it and she wonders how many other women including Anita have been on the receiving end of that gesture over the years. She hasn't been blind to his flirting, but she trusted he would never go beyond that. Flirting was almost like a hobby he indulged in, a pastime that enhanced his life with her rather than detracted from it.

'You don't have to do that . . . I doubt I'll be hungry,' she says. 'My stomach is all over the place.'

'I thought you said it was a cold.' He eyes her warily. 'Are you sure nothing else is wrong?'

What, aside from finding out you might have killed our

nephew and let his nine-year-old sister take the blame? Oh, I'm just peachy. She bites down hard on the words she's dying to say to him and forces herself to shake her head.

'I'm fine, honestly. I'm going to go up now.'

'Are you sure I can't tuck you in?' he grins. 'Or how about a fireman's lift up the stairs?'

Jokey banter has always been a cornerstone of their marriage and normally she would laugh along with him, but not tonight. If his guilt is confirmed by the footage that Cara records during the night, she wants to be the one to call the police and report him – and when they send him to prison, she won't be visiting.

'Goodnight,' she says.

He goes to peck her on the lips, as is customary every evening before bed. The past four nights she's endured it for the sake of appearances, but now it occurs to Karen that this might be the last time they are alone together.

'Don't kiss me,' she says, turning away from him. 'You might catch something.'

Chapter Sixty-Five

Cara

I dig out the number for an out-of-hours vet. I don't care that the hidden cameras are primed: getting Mustard checked over supersedes everything I had planned for tonight. The vet I am put through to, however, seems only concerned with finding out whether Mustard has thrown up or not.

'No, he's fast asleep,' I say.

'Not whining or whimpering in his sleep?'

I crouch down beside Mustard again. 'No, but he is snoring louder than normal.'

'Do you take sleeping tablets yourself?'

'Um, I do.'

'It's not uncommon for dogs, or cats for that matter, to gobble up pills left lying around the house,' the vet says. 'Chances are your dog has eaten one of your sleeping tablets and it's knocked him out.'

I look over at the chest of drawers. There is a bottle of sleeping tablets on the top, but the lid's screwed on, so I must've dropped a tablet when I was taking them and Mustard found it on the floor. But as angry as I am with myself that it's my carelessness which has put him in this position, I'm also relieved it's dispelled my fear that Lisa might have been behind it.

'Isn't it dangerous for him to swallow a sleeping tablet?' I ask.

326

'It can be, yes, but if your dog hasn't shown any signs he's experiencing toxicity by vomiting and he hasn't had any convulsions, he's probably okay just sleeping it off. You can obviously bring him in right now if you're really worried, but I would suggest monitoring him throughout the night and then getting him checked out first thing tomorrow. I can book you in for the first appointment of the morning, at seven-thirty.'

Mustard is shifting in his sleep now, but he's still out for the count. Should I really risk waiting until morning? I'm about to question the vet's advice again when a loud bang rings out downstairs, like a window or door slamming shut. I go rigid, my phone gripped tightly in my hand, my mouth hanging open.

'Ms Marshall?' I hear the vet say in my ear. 'Are you still there?'

'I'll see you in the morning,' I manage to say, then hang up.

Crouching on the floor next to Mustard, I open the app on my phone that allows me to connect to the cameras. It takes what feels like ages to load up and in that time I can hear footsteps echoing in the hallway downstairs. Uncle Gary's not even trying to be quiet and that terrifies me, because if he wants me to be aware of his presence, he must not care what will happen if he wakes me. For the first time it hits me how naive I have been – tonight isn't just about me proving to everyone that he's Limey Stan, it's also about me surviving the night so I can. How far will he go to shut me up? Did he somehow sneak a sleeping pill to Mustard to make sure he didn't bark the house down while he does it? Or, I think, my panic accelerating, did Lisa do that while she was here earlier – is she in on this too?

The app begins to function and, shaking like a leaf, I click open the feed for the camera hidden by the doorway to the front room. Nothing else is visible in the darkness beyond the hazy outline of the sofa and coffee table. Still, I can hear noises coming from downstairs though, and my heart seizes in my chest as I hear the creak of a foot treading heavily on the bottom stair. I push against Mustard's back, hoping to wake him, but he slumbers on, blissfully unaware his owner is terrified and in trouble. I can barely hold my phone, my hands are sweating so much, but I manage to click on the feed for the cameras I have placed in the hallway. One is at the bottom of the stairs pointing upwards; the other is on the windowsill at the top pointing down.

I select the feed for the bottom camera and instantly realise I'm wasting my time: all I can see are the soles of Gary's shoes as he slowly ascends the stairs. I scrabble to open the other feed and when the screen flickers alive and focuses from above, I let out a scream.

It's not my uncle coming up the stairs.

Chapter Sixty-Six

Cara

Shock pins me to the carpet. I cannot believe what I am seeing on my phone screen. Climbing my stairs, bold as brass, is Ian Leonard.

The estate agent hesitates as he reaches the landing – the camera catches him looking at each of the closed bedroom doors, as though he's debating which one to open first. This galvanises me to my feet and before he can reach for the door handle to mine, I yank it open. He reels backwards in surprise, as though I am the last person he expects to see standing here.

'What the hell are you doing creeping around my house in the middle of the night?' I shout at him.

'Oh, thank God, you're okay,' he exhales.

'What are you doing here?' I repeat, my voice a shriek.

'Look, I know this is going to sound crazy, but I've been worried about you. You've not answered any of my messages—'

I am so livid, I might explode. 'So you thought you'd break into my house at night to bully me into selling up?'

'God, no, not at all,' he says, mortified. 'I've been downstairs ringing the doorbell for ages. Didn't you hear it?'

That calms me a fraction. 'It must've stopped working,' I say gruffly.

'No, it was definitely making the usual sound, I could hear it inside the house,' he states. 'I started to worry when there was no answer, so I tried the back door, found it was unlocked, so I came in.' His face reddens. 'I'm really sorry, Cara. I should've realised me showing up like this might scare you, but I wasn't thinking straight. I was sat at home thinking about how things had soured between us and I wanted to make amends. Crazy, really, given how late it is. Then, when I got here, I thought something must be seriously wrong for you not to answer the door. I thought you were hurt.'

My body is trembling from the shock of seeing him on the stairs, but I am calmer. He is clearly embarrassed by his actions.

'Do you often make house calls to your clients after midnight?' I ask, my voice steadying.

'Only the ones I like on a personal level . . . Which, ah, makes you the only one.' His cheeks flush an even deeper red.

It takes a moment for his comment to sink in. 'Oh. Right. This isn't a good time for me though.'

He smiles benevolently. 'No, now most definitely isn't, but what about another night? To go for a drink, I mean. Not for me to scare you walking around your house in the dark.'

On saying that he leans over and flicks on the landing light. He looks different, standing there in jeans and a casual jacket, younger than he usually does, and suddenly I feel a bit shy and don't know what to say.

'Shall we go downstairs?' he suggests.

I nod, then follow him downstairs, slipping my phone into my back pocket. I expect him to head for the front door, but instead he turns on his heel and heads for the kitchen and opens the fridge.

'Got any wine? We could have a quick drink now.'

'It's getting on,' I say. 'Let's leave it for another night.' The late hour does not bother me really, but I want him to go so I can turn the lights off again. If Uncle Gary sees us moving around downstairs, he won't risk coming inside. To emphasise to Leonard that I want him to leave, I go over to the back door to open it. But when I pull the handle, the door doesn't budge and I realise it's locked.

'That's weird. I thought you said this was unlocked?' I ask him.

'Did I?'

'Yes. You said you came in the back when I didn't answer the front door. But why is it locked now?'

'Oh, that's right, I locked the door after I came in. Otherwise anyone could get in.'

I don't say that was the whole point – I'd left it open for Gary to get in. 'Well thanks.' Then it dawns on me my keys are upstairs in my bedroom.

'There's no key down here. How did you lock it?'

I turn round and see Leonard is no longer standing by the fridge but has moved over to the sink and he's holding up a key.

'I used the spare you gave us,' he smiles.

My stomach drops to my feet. 'I never gave you one,' I say slowly. 'I had the locks changed and I was meant to drop a key off at your office before the viewings started, but I never got round to it.'

Leonard stares at me, then forces a sigh.

'You know, it would have been so much easier if you'd never come back to Heldean in the first place. Then I wouldn't have had to go to all this trouble to get rid of you again.'

I stare at him, dumbstruck, and in that moment I know.

Gary isn't Limey Stan – Ian Leonard is.

Chapter Sixty-Seven

Cara

'Do you know how frustrating it is to deal with someone who won't take a hint?' Leonard goes on. 'It's not been easy letting myself in while you've been here, but thank god for those panic attacks.' He smiles malevolently. 'You really should get help for those. And get a better guard dog. It's amazing what that mutt will eat when it's pushed through the letter box.'

'You killed Matty,' I say, my voice breaking. 'It was you.'

He says nothing, but advances towards me. A low moan escapes my lips, but it sounds distant to my ears, like a noise underwater. I try to back away, but I'm already backed up against the locked door – there isn't anywhere left for me to go. As he raises his hands, my mind gropes for a way out, a means of escape. Physically he is far bigger than me and if I try to fight him, I will lose, so I need to think of another way to stop him hurting me.

'Why pretend to be Limey Stan again?' I ask desperately. 'I was going to sell the house anyway, why go to the risk of being found out after getting away with it for all these years?'

'Because you moved in,' he answers tetchily. 'That wasn't part of the plan. You shouldn't have done that.'

'That doesn't answer my question. Why start up Limey Stan again?'

'Your dear departed mum threatened to expose me after she died and I suspected how she was going to do it was somewhere in this house. So I needed to get you out of here so I could find it myself and what better way to scare you off than to resurrect our mutual friend?' He waggles his fingers at me and makes a ghostlike wooing noise, then laughs. 'God, you're naive.'

I think about the postcode on Matty's ID bracelet. 'You lived in Limestone Road back then, didn't you?'

His eyes narrow. 'What of it?'

I was right: my sleep-deprived nine-year-old mind really did translate Limestone Road into Limey Stan. But I feel no triumph now, only terror.

'How did you know my mum?' I ask.

'How do you think?' He says this with a leer that sickens me to the core. 'She was my family's housekeeper, we got talking one day and, well, I'll let your imagination decide what happened next.'

'But you were so much younger than her,' I say, appalled.

'I was seventeen. Old enough. Anita didn't care about my age, put it that way. She was quite the teacher. We had a lot of fun together, your mother and me,' he smirks. 'It carried on even after mine caught us together. She went mad and sacked yours, obviously.'

My growing anger is making me less scared of him. How dare he stand in this house and act like what happened here was no big deal?

'Was it your idea to blame me for Matty's death and send me away?'

He pulls a face. 'The latter was nothing to do with me. The night your brother died, I said I'd kill you too if Anita ever told the police about me – I said I would come back and finish you off somehow, make it look like an accident.' He says it with such smugness, I want to smack him. 'So she decided to get you out of the way to make sure I could never carry out my threat. Quite inventive how she did it – I never expected her to go that far. But letting you take the blame for your brother was my idea, yes.'

Grief twists my insides. What a decision Mum was forced to make – to send me away like a criminal or risk losing me in an even worse way.

'I used to visit her after you'd gone to make sure she was keeping to her word. She hated me coming round, but what could she do? I even went to her funeral: I snuck in the back to make sure she really was dead.' He steps forward again. 'Now it's time I dealt with you.'

I know he's only telling me all this because he thinks it will go no further – he's going to make sure I'm silenced for good tonight.

'You don't have to do this,' I say, my back pressed against the door still. 'I won't tell anyone about you, I swear, because who would believe me if I did? I've just admitted to a reporter that I made up Limey Stan because I wasn't well and it's been printed everywhere – no one would believe me if I suddenly turned round now and said it was you.'

Doubt taints his expression for a moment, but it quickly dispels. 'All things considered, I don't think I'll take that chance. I've worked for years to build up my business and make a name for myself in this town. I am not letting you take that away from me.'

'I don't want to!' I plead.

'You want to clear your name though, and the only way you can do that is by going public with mine.'

Before I can react, Leonard grabs me by the left arm and yanks me forward with such force that I skid across the tiles and fall onto my knees. Then he drags me into the front room.

I try to resist, but fear has weakened my muscles and I am as malleable as a soft toy as he heaves me forward.

Then I hear it, a tap-tap-tap at the window. I know it can't be the rose, as I cut it back, and my heart soars: someone's tapping because the doorbell really isn't working. 'Tishk!' I scream. 'Is that you?'

There are scuffling sounds outside, then a hammering on the front door and Tishk calling out, 'Cara, are you okay? Let me in!'

Leonard is peeved at the interruption. 'Wait here,' he orders.

I am fearful of what he might do if I disobey him, so all I can do is sit and listen, petrified, ears straining, as Leonard answers the front door to Tishk. There is a low mumble of words being exchanged, then I hear them both coming along the hallway and through the kitchen together.

Tishk steps into the front room, Leonard close behind. I hurl myself at Tishk, grabbing the front of his jumper in both hands.

'It's him!' I shout. 'He's Limey Stan!'

I see the wine bottle in Leonard's hand, but there's no time to warn Tishk. A split second later, Leonard swings the bottle at Tishk's head, catching him on the temple. The bottle smashes and Tishk crumples to the floor. He's laid out cold and I can see blood seeping from a deep gash, slowly at first, then quickening as Tishk falls deeper into unconsciousness. I crawl over to him and try to stem the blood with my fingers, but Leonard pulls me away.

'Change of plan, I think. I was going to leave you down here in the bay window, make it a family tradition. But with him here,' he nudges Tishk's body with the toe of his shoe, 'the ambience is ruined. So, upstairs it is.'

I am crying so hard now I can barely see where I'm going. But I know I have to make Leonard see sense before it's too late.

'You won't get away with this,' I plead with him. 'The police will find your fingerprints on that bottle and they'll know you hurt Tishk. They'll know someone else was in the house. You broke in.'

'No I didn't. I have a key, don't forget.'

'But how did you get it?'

'Don't you know how easy it is to get a key cut from a photograph? That day I came round to do the valuation you'd just had the locks changed, but you left the new keys by the front door, so I pretended I needed to use the toilet and took a photo of them with my phone.'

He hauls me into the kitchen, where he pauses for a moment. Resting on the worktop is a coiled-up length of white electrical flex I have never seen before. Leonard grips my arm with one hand and grabs hold of the flex with the other.

'What are you going to do with that?' I ask, horrified.

'You did me a favour with that interview. When they find your body, they'll assume you killed yourself because you weren't right in the head. Admitting you made up the ghost just proved it.'

He sends me up the stairs first, pushing me when I stumble. I kick out, hoping it will send him flying backwards, but he has a solid footing and retaliates by shoving me onto the landing. My legs are so rubbery they can barely support me, but as I force myself to stand, my gaze lands on Matty's door and the football stickers that are such a reminder of him – and there and then I know I cannot let Leonard get away with this. I will not die to protect him.

I spin round, lashing out, but Leonard is ready for me. He lassoes the flex around my neck like a noose and pulls it tight. I desperately grab at it, trying to slide my fingertips beneath it to stop me choking. All the while, Leonard is pulling tighter, his face a mask of determination. Then he begins to shuffle me towards the balustrade and I realise how he plans to end this: he is going to push me over so it will look as though I hanged myself.

I have to act fast. I manage to hook two fingers of my left hand under the flex and pull it free by an inch so I have some breathing space and with my right hand I grab the slack Leonard doesn't have hold of yet but will need to tether me to the balustrade to let me hang. Just at the point he reaches down to gather up the slack, I raise my right hand and wrap the flex around his neck too and pull it tight. His eyes bulge when he realises what I am doing, but it is too late. I topple backwards – and take him over the top of the balustrade with me.

My body screams with pain as we ricochet off the opposite wall and bounce down the staircase. I have no way of telling which way is up, I just pray for it to be over quickly. My fingers yank beneath the flex and I feel them break. Then the flex around my neck suddenly loosens – Leonard has let go of it to try to save himself, but we're tumbling too fast. Suddenly we reach the bottom of the staircase, then roll across the hallway and crash into the front door – and I realise I'm the lucky one because it is he who breaks my fall and not the other way round. Groggily, I roll off him and he cries out.

'My legs,' he screams. 'I can't feel my legs!'

I look over and see they are angled awkwardly beneath him.

'Help me,' he begs.

Every instinct tells me to crawl away and leave him to suffer, but I can't. My body throbs with pain as I shuffle over to him. 'Don't move,' I say. 'You might have broken your back. I'll ring for an ambulance.'

Leonard is crying now, tears pouring down his cheeks as his hands grope his legs for any sensation but find none. His upper body slumps back against the floor. 'I never meant for Matty to die,' he sobs. 'I was trying to help him. He was already suffocating in the curtain when I got to him . . .'

Ignoring him, I drag myself away. My left ankle is swelling rapidly and I can't put any weight on it, so I half-stagger, half-limp into the kitchen and then into the front room to check on Tishk and to retrieve my phone. The blood loss from his head wound has slowed to little more than a trickle and when I stroke his face and say his name, he begins to stir.

'Cara?' he whispers with a moan.

I rest my hand against his cheek and shush him to be quiet. His eyelashes flutter as he contemplates opening his eyes, until the pain shuts them again.

'I'm calling for help. Stay still.'

'What happened?' he asks.

'It's over,' I whisper. 'I caught Limey Stan.'

Chapter Sixty-Eight

Cara

The next couple of hours pass in a blur of sirens and blue lights as police officers and paramedics swarm the house. Leonard is removed from my hallway strapped to a board to keep his spine and neck immobile, while I've escaped virtually unscathed by comparison with a sprained ankle and two broken fingers that I've already had strapped up. Tishk would accept only roadside assistance too, brushing off his injury as an inconsequential bump on the head and refusing to go to hospital because he does not want to leave my side. The two of us are in the front room now, forcing ourselves to sip the insipid tea an officer in uniform made us so we don't appear ungrateful.

'Are you sure you're okay?' Tishk asks me for what must be the twentieth time. 'Does your throat hurt?'

I rub the skin there and it does feel horribly sore, and when I swallow, it's as though the flex is still choking me. Yet the paramedic who examined me said it was superficial, like a Chinese burn.

'It's a bit sore,' I admit. 'But it could've been a lot worse.'

Tishk shakes his head, wincing in pain from the headache left by his injury, which has been glued and dressed. 'When I think about that—'

I quickly take his hand. 'Then don't. It's over. Leonard can't hurt me any more.'

We are sitting in darkness, dawn at least an hour from breaking. The house is creaking under the weight of the investigators, but I am calm. I have never felt calmer. Mustard, still dozy but awake now, is by my feet.

One of the voices at the back door seems louder than the rest and as I tune into it, I recognise the shrill female demanding to be let in. Leaving Tishk on the sofa, I go into the kitchen, where I find Karen remonstrating with the officer standing guard there.

'I need to see my niece,' she's saying. Then she spots me and bursts into tears. 'Oh Cara. Heather just called me. She said someone broke in and I knew it can't have been Gary because he's asleep, so I came straight round.'

I nod to the officer. 'Let her in, please.'

Karen stumbles over the threshold, arms open wide to embrace me. While I'm not entirely comfortable doing it, we hug, then I pull away first.

'I am so sorry we suspected Uncle Gary,' I say.

'You've got nothing to be sorry about, Cara,' says Karen tearfully. 'It's me who's the sorry one, thinking he could be capable of something so awful. I just have to pray he never finds out I thought so badly of him. It would be the end of our marriage.'

We go back into the lounge and Karen sits down after hugging Tishk.

'So who broke in?' she asks.

The police have seized the cameras from around the house, but I still have the footage saved on my phone. I play Karen the recording from the stairs camera and she gasps when she sees Ian Leonard come into the frame, his features ironically rendered ghostlike by the hazy green night-vision.

'The estate agent?' She turns to me, baffled. 'Why did he break into a house he wants to sell?'

'Karen, he's Limey Stan,' says Tishk patiently.

'But – but . . . he's too young to be. I mean, how old was he in 1994?'

'Seventeen. A year older than I was,' says Tishk.

I then show my aunt Matty's hospital ID bracelet with the postcode written on the inside. 'This is the postcode for the street where Leonard lived at the time. I think Mum wrote it on the bracelet and she put it in a box of my things so I'd find it.'

'That's her handwriting,' Karen confirms. 'So this really is the postcode for Limestone Road?'

'Yes. I always thought I heard Limey Stan whisper his name up the stairs to me, but I think what I really heard was Leonard saying his street name while calling for a taxi. Our phone was at the bottom of the stairs then.'

My aunt nods, remembering.

'I was being seen to by the paramedics when he was being loaded into the ambulance and as they were taking his details to pass to the hospital, I heard him say his surname is actually Lawler and that Leonard is his middle name,' Tishk reveals. 'Lawler sounds a bit like a solicitor's name when you think about it, so maybe that's why he used Leonard to be an estate agent.'

The blood drains from my aunt's face.

'What is it?' I press her.

'Your mum worked for a family called Lawler, but the woman got rid of her and Anita wouldn't say why.'

'Leonard said he and Mum had an affair and that his mum found out and didn't react well to her teenage son sleeping with the housekeeper. That's why she sacked her,' I say.

Tishk takes Matty's ID bracelet from me and examines the postcode.

'Why leave you a trail of breadcrumbs to find though? Why not leave a direct message telling you who Limey Stan was?' he ponders.

Karen interrupts to tell us about a conversation she had during one of my mum's hospital stays, about her wanting to atone for putting me into foster care. 'I suggested she leave a letter with her solicitor to be opened after her death, but she was adamant you had to work it out for yourself,' she adds. 'She didn't trust that if she wrote a letter it would get to you.'

'She owed Leonard nothing after he killed Matty,' Tishk remarks. 'Why not tell the police straight away it was him?'

'The night he killed Matty, he threatened to kill me too,' I reply. 'He said he warned Mum that if she ever told the police about his involvement he would come back and finish me off some other way. That's why she sent me away – to keep me safe and hidden from him. I always thought she hated me, but it was the opposite.'

I cannot stop the tears coming then and nor can Karen.

'She must have been absolutely terrified of him, and she lived with that fear right up until she died,' she cries.

I nod. 'Leonard told me he would turn up here to remind her of his threat. He had such a hold over her.' I turn to Tishk. 'It must've been him who ransacked the house before I moved in – Leonard said Mum told him she would find a way to expose him once she was gone and I think he broke in looking for evidence of it. He never found this though.' I take Matty's bracelet back from Tishk. 'Although, if it wasn't for the girl in Timothy Pitt's group, I might've overlooked it too.'

'What girl?' Karen asks.

I tell them about Jenny and repeat what she said about not ignoring what is precious at the beginning because that was the road I needed take to end this. 'She was scarily accurate,' I add. 'The bracelets were given to us when we were born, so at the beginning, and were kept as precious mementos and the postcode for Limestone Road, where Leonard lived, was written inside Matty's.'

As Tishk reacts with astonishment, Karen begins to laugh. Not giggles, but proper belly laughs. I stare at her, bemused.

'Oh Anita, you beauty,' she says, wiping tears from her eyes. 'You planned this all along.'

'What are you talking about?' asks Tishk.

Karen hiccups another laugh out, then turns to me. 'You're right, Cara, your mum did want you to find out. This Jenny, what does she look like?'

As I describe her, Karen scrolls through her phone. 'This girl?'

She shows me a Facebook profile picture of Jenny smiling widely and looking very un-Goth-like in brightly coloured clothes.

'That's her!'

'She's one of the volunteers who cared for your mum at the hospice in her final weeks and she's as much a medium as I am the Queen of England. The two of them became close and Jenny was even at the funeral. I bet, if we asked her, she'd admit your mum asked her to get that message to you after she died.'

I should be annoyed this Jenny person played on my grief by pretending to be a medium, yet I'm not. It was a brilliant ruse to get me to listen to her. At some point, I will track her down and thank her. I shall also take great satisfaction in contacting Pitt to let him know he's been duped too – by Jenny and Limey Stan.

Karen shakes her head. 'You know, when we talked about getting the house valued, Anita was adamant I mustn't use Leonards, but I thought she was being silly. They're the most popular estate agents in town, so it made sense to use them.

343

But she must've been worried it would provoke Leonard into coming out of hiding. If I'd known—'

'It's not your fault,' I assure her. 'You weren't to know.'

'What did the police say when they arrived?' she asks.

I sigh. 'They're going to take some convincing that Leonard was trying to attack me and not the other way round. It looks like falling down the stairs broke his back and they keep asking if I pushed him deliberately.'

Karen is outraged. 'How can they think that?'

'I'm the girl from the Heldean Haunting. If you were a police officer and I said to you the estate agent I had willingly approached to sell the infamous haunted house in Parsons Close was Limey Stan all along and he tried to kill me tonight after suffocating my brother behind a curtain twenty-five years ago, how would you react?' Her expression answers me plainly. 'Exactly. Don't forget I also gave an interview a few days ago admitting I was ill the first time round and the police kept going on about what medication I'm taking now. Right now I think they believe him more than me.'

'I knew talking to that reporter was a mistake,' says Tishk darkly.

'But I've got footage of Leonard prowling downstairs and then attacking me,' I remind them. 'The cameras caught everything and the police have taken them all. Leonard can deny it all he likes, but soon the whole world is going to know he was Limey Stan.'

Chapter Sixty-Nine

Karen

Gary is in the kitchen making porridge for breakfast when Karen returns home. He reacts with surprise when she lets herself in the front door.

'I thought you were asleep in the spare room,' he exclaims. 'Where have you been?'

Without a word, she crosses the kitchen to him, wraps her arms around his middle and begins to weep. He doesn't pull away to demand an explanation and instead hugs her until her tears are spent. Finally, when her eyes are almost dry again, she lets out a sigh and disentangles herself.

'What's going on, love?' he asks.

'I'm not sure where to begin,' she says. She is assailed with guilt that she let herself believe Gary might have been Limey Stan and knows that if her marriage is to continue, he must never find out. She was leaving Cara's as Lisa arrived and the two of them made a pact to never speak a word of their suspicions. Lisa is going to be interviewed by the police later to recount what she can remember of the night Matty died and thinking it was her dad's voice she overheard most certainly won't be a part of her statement.

'Is it Cara?' he surmises.

Karen nods, her eyes refilling with tears. 'It wasn't her, Gary. She didn't kill Matty.'

He is stunned. 'But the police, Anita—'

'I know. But Cara was telling the truth. It was Limey Stan all along, except Limey Stan was a real person.'

'What?'

She leads him over to the breakfast bar, sits him down, takes the stool next to his and over the next fifteen minutes narrates the events that led to their niece being attacked by Ian Leonard and almost hanged. By the time she finishes, her husband is ashen with shock.

'Bloody hell,' he breathes. 'Poor Cara. From day one she said she was innocent and none of us believed her.' Then his expression hardens. 'How could Anita do that to her own kid?'

'I'm not trying to defend her, because she could've done the right thing from the outset and told the police Leonard was responsible, but I think the impact of Matty's death, the grief she was experiencing, meant she wasn't thinking straight. Once Cara went to hospital, the whole thing snowballed and Leonard must've terrified her. He'd killed one of her children – she must've been convinced he would kill the other one too.'

Gary shakes his head. 'You're making excuses for her. She did a despicable thing to her daughter. And having sex with a seventeen-year-old. I know she was your sister and you loved her, but even you can't condone that.'

Karen wasn't planning to bring up what Lisa told her about seeing Gary and Anita together at the New Year's Eve party, but his obvious disgust at her sister's affair makes her want to. Is it because he's jealous?

'Was Anita ever inappropriate with you?' she asks. When Gary shifts awkwardly on his stool, she adds, 'It's okay, you can tell me. I won't be cross.'

His brows knit in a frown. 'Wait, you think something

happened between Anita and me? Nothing could be further from the truth, believe me.'

'But she wanted something to happen?' asks Karen. Her heart feels like cement in her chest as she waits for him to answer.

'Love, why does it matter? You adored your sister. Christ, there were times when I thought you loved her more than you loved me,' he grimaces. 'But that doesn't mean I want to ruin your memories of her.'

'She's managed that on her own, with what she did to Cara,' says Karen wryly.

Gary rubs his hand across his chin as he thinks. 'Okay, I'll tell you, but you're not going to like it.'

Karen steels herself.

'Anita made it known that if I was interested, she was available. I wasn't though. I made that very clear to her,' he adds hastily. 'We always got on well as a rule and I think she just mistook my friendliness for more. You know how fed up she was with Paul – all she wanted was for someone to pay attention to her. The reason I never told you was because she'd been drinking – when I saw her afterwards, she was so embarrassed. So I put it down to the booze talking and it was just the once it happened.'

'Was it at that New Year's Eve party we threw in 1993?'

He pauses for a moment. 'Did Lisa tell you about seeing us? She came out into the garden as I was giving Anita a hug. Anita was upset I wouldn't kiss her back and I was trying to be nice about it.'

Karen stares deeply into her husband's eyes. She wants to believe he's telling the truth, but after everything she's learned about Anita these past few days she's not sure she can trust her own judgement any more. How could she be so close to her sister and not realise she was lying to her about Cara? What if Gary's lying now and she just can't see it?

347

He leans forward. 'I'm telling you the truth, love. I've never cheated on you. Why would I? It's like that hamburger and steak joke, why go out to eat when the special's being served at home.'

This makes her smile, because she knows it's Gary's clumsy way of trying to be romantic. He's never been one for elaborate declarations of love and that's as close as she'll ever get from him. Karen decides, for her sanity, she will believe it was Anita who did the chasing, not him.

As though sensing he's off the hook, Gary asks what will happen next with Leonard.

'I suppose it depends on the extent of his injuries when the police can question him, but the fact Cara's got him on tape attacking her surely means he'll be charged,' says Karen.

'You know that if he stands trial for Matty's murder he's going to drag Anita's name through the mud. I would, in his shoes,' says Gary. 'It was her house, her son, her daughter she blamed. His defence will have a field day.'

Wretchedly, Karen nods. 'I know, but seeing what Anita did to bring him to justice, the clues she left for Cara, I don't think she would care if Leonard tries to paints her as the most terrible mother who ever lived. It's over now – she won. He'll be locked up and Cara will be safe.'

Chapter Seventy

https://theheldeanhaunting/blog

THE END

28 December 2019

Comments [873]

Sometimes in life we have to admit we have made an error of judgement because our passion for a subject might have blinded us to objectively examining it from all sides and considering different explanations. This, I write with a heavy heart, is the position I find myself in presently and is why this will be my last blog post for a while.

It is now public knowledge that Cara Belling has admitted the events of July 1994 were not related to paranormal activity, as many others and myself have long believed, but were, sadly, the direct consequence of her suffering from an illness that at the time was affecting her perception of what she saw and heard. The subsequent arrest of Heldean resident and estate agent Ian Leonard on charges connected to Matty Belling's death has also put a new slant on the subject.

In the light of this apparent confirmation that Limey Stan never existed, I have decided to pause my research on the subject of The Heldean Haunting. It is the right and proper thing to do for the time being. Having met Ms Belling in person at Parsons Close and seen the effect her notoriety has had on her, I sincerely hope she has now found peace from her tormented thoughts.

I have, after some deliberation, decided to let this blog remain public for whoever wishes to read it, however. If nothing else, I hope it is an entertaining read! That has certainly been my aim in the years I've been writing it. Likewise, my investigative account of The Heldean Haunting shall remain on sale, but I will be updating the book forthwith to include recent developments and I shall naturally be a front-seat observer when Ian Leonard stands trial next year to bring you all the details as they are revealed. The current version is still available to download as a 99p ebook if you click here.

Timothy Pitt

Chapter Seventy-One

Nine weeks later

Cara

Everything seems brighter and sharper this morning, as though a filter was applied and now it has been peeled back and I am seeing clearly for the first time in years. My devastation at finding out the truth still weighs heavy within me, but jostling for space alongside it is an excitement I never imagined I would one day feel – excitement at being given the chance to rewrite my history. No longer am I the girl who tried to hoax a town and a nation to absolve her guilt at smothering her brother: I am the woman who is bringing his real killer to justice twenty-five years after being framed.

I should be ready for this interview – I've been up pacing the house since five and have been showered, dressed and had my make-up applied since six. But as the start time fast approaches, I suddenly feel nowhere near ready and I am worried what questions they'll ask me.

'You've got to calm down, Cara,' says Tishk. 'We've been through this already: if they ask you about Leonard's arrest, tell them you're not allowed to comment or even give any details off the record. They'll understand, you're the key witness.'

'Will they though?' I fret. 'They might be expecting chapter and verse.'

'They'll have to wait until it goes to court.'

I found out yesterday that Leonard's defence team is applying to see all the notes compiled by my psychiatrist while I was in the Peachick in an attempt to prove my guilt, because he's now claiming Matty was already smothered in the curtain when he came downstairs and it was me who did it. Leonard's also saying I wound the flex around his neck first and pushed him down the stairs. Unfortunately, the camera at the top of the stairs was knocked in the melee and only the bottom halves of our bodies are visible in the footage. The solicitor I've retained to steer me through the proceedings tells me there is no chance of the request to see my medical records being granted because I am not the one on trial and the ligature marks around my neck, of which the police took photos, prove I was the victim, not Leonard.

Plus there has been a groundswell of support for me from the public since the news of his arrest broke. I spoke to the ENS reporter off the record and he used what I told him to write a piece that essentially implied Leonard had pretended all along to be Limey Stan but without emphatically stating it, so it wouldn't prejudice the forthcoming trial. Every day since then the papers have been full of stories about how I was unfairly blamed for killing Matty and the horror of me being sent away – on the first day of coverage #HeldeanHaunting and #CaraBelling were trending nationwide.

I take out a compact mirror and reapply my lipstick for what must be the fifth time in twenty minutes. But I am so nervous, I keep licking my lips and taking it off.

'You look great,' says Tishk, smiling. 'You've got this.'

I give him a hug. I am so grateful for his friendship. He has barely left my side during the past nine weeks and has acted as intermediary between me and the officers building the case against Leonard when their questions and probing have been overwhelming. I sense his feelings have shifted from platonic to something deeper and, while I am happy about that, I'm not ready to rock the boat between us. I like how things are. I like the stability and the certainty of our friendship. I just hope he will be patient with me.

I sit back in my seat. 'What time is it?' I ask.

He checks his watch. 'Nine-forty.'

'I should go up.'

He squeezes my hand. 'Good luck.'

I climb out of his car and shut the door. He's parked in a pay-and-display bay and has put enough money in for two hours and plans to sit and listen to the radio while I'm interviewed.

Nerves are making my legs shake and I wobble along the street towards the meeting place like a toddler who's only just learned to walk. I feel so unsure of myself that I have to will myself forward, instead of doing what I'd like to do, which is turn on my heel and run back to the safety of Tishk's car. Just then, my phone pings with a text from Karen.

GOOD LUCK. GIVE ME A CALL WHEN YOU'RE DONE
TO LET US KNOW HOW YOU GOT ON. X

I smile, grateful for the message. It's early days still, but I am enjoying getting to know my aunt again. We spend our time together talking a lot about my mum and how she was after I went away. I suspect Karen thinks it gives me satisfaction to know that Mum did suffer because of what she put me through, but I do not want to revel in schadenfreude. I just want to turn back the clock so none of this ever happened.

We talk a lot about my dad too, and I think I have a better understanding of the dynamic of my parents' marriage now. To the world, they presented themselves as happy and serene, like ducks crossing a calm pond. But beneath the surface Dad was paddling frantically to hold it together financially, working round the clock to provide for us, while Mum was slowly sinking into a pit of boredom and frustration. If only they'd had the guts to admit to one another how unhappy they were, all our lives might have turned out differently.

I'm getting to know Uncle Gary again too. He remains, I am glad to say, blissfully oblivious to our suspicions about him. I think he would be devastated to learn we all thought for a time that he was Limey Stan. Some things are better left unsaid.

Finally, I arrive at the place where the interview is being held. I let myself into the building, take a deep breath and step forward.

'I'm here to see Roger Grieves,' I say.

The woman behind the reception desk smiles warmly: I think she can see how nervous I am.

'What time is he expecting you?'

'Ten. I'm a bit early.'

'Is this for the accounts position?'

'Yes, it is.'

This is the first job I've applied for in Heldean and I was taken aback to receive the email asking me for an interview only a day after I submitted my CV. The position is slightly more senior to my role in Colchester, but when I rang Jeannie to give her my version of what's been going on compared to what's been in the papers and to explain that I wanted to stay in Heldean, she said she would happily write me a reference saying I was more than capable of fulfilling it and that I would be a great addition to their team. She said she'd miss me though and she also said Donna's been telling anyone who'll listen that the two of us were best friends. I don't mind – it'll give her and 'My Martin' something to talk about.

'Take a seat and I'll let Mr Grieves know you're here,' says the receptionist, reaching for her phone. 'What's your name?'

Now it's my turn to smile – with pride.

'My name is Cara Belling.'

Acknowledgements

There are two things every author needs when writing a novel: inspiration for the plot and a brilliant support team to see it to fruition! I was fortunate to have both in spades while writing *Shadow Of A Doubt*.

The idea for the book came to me one Sunday morning in April 2018, while listening to broadcaster Sue McGregor's *The Reunion* show on Radio 4. She had assembled the key witnesses to a 1977 paranormal event known as The Enfield Poltergeist and it was fascinating to listen to their recollections of the now infamous haunting. What happens in *Shadow of a Doubt* bears no resemblance to what they experienced, but I thank Sue and her team for producing such an inspiring programme and for planting the seed for the character of Cara Belling. Another point of reference was Will Storr's exploration of the paranormal, *Will Storr vs The Supernatural*, which I recommend as both an informative and hugely entertaining read. (I defy you not to howl with laughter reading the scene featuring Derek Acorah.)

I want to thank my agent Jane Gregory for championing the book from the moment I breathlessly described the plot to her in her office and also for coming up with a key plot twist! Both were game-changing moments. Thanks also to everyone at the agency, David Higham Associates, for their continued hard work on my behalf, especially Mary Jones, whose feedback on the early chapters was invaluable. *Shadow of a Doubt* is my first book with Orion and I cannot think of a better home for it. I am so grateful to Francesca Pathak for her boundless enthusiasm, acumen and for never refusing an impromptu brainstorming session! You are a dream of an editor. Thanks also to Lucy Frederick for her editorial support and to the entire Orion team, a brilliantly talented bunch that are rightly credited in full overleaf.

Thanks also to Jo Jhanji, Alison Bailey and Aimee Horton for being my beta readers – knowing how much you loved the book even in its earliest, scrappiest form gave me the impetuous to see it through. I'm also grateful for the endless morale boosting from my fellow crime fiction authors, in particular Erin Kelly, Catherine Ryan Howard and Harriet Tyce, and I also want to thank the incomparable Colin Scott for all the advice and the belly laughs. I certainly couldn't have done it without you!

Nor could I have managed without the support of my family and friends, especially my daughter Sophie and my partner Rory. Those two put up with my constant daydreaming and vagueness when I am writing the next chapter in my head, my crabbiness when I've hit a plot knot I can't unravel and my exhaustion when I've finally reached The End. I cannot thank them enough for their love and patience and for always believing in me.

Credits

Michelle Davies and Orion Fiction would like to thank everyone at Orion who worked on the publication of *Shadow Of A Doubt* in the UK.

Editorial
Francesca Pathak
Lucy Frederick

Copy editor
Francine Brody

Proof reader
Jade Craddock

Audio
Paul Stark
Amber Bates

Contracts
Anne Goddard
Paul Bulos
Jake Alderson

Design
Debbie Holmes
Joanna Ridley
Nick May

Editorial Management
Charlie Panayiotou
Jane Hughes
Alice Davis

Production
Hannah Cox

Finance
Jasdip Nandra
Afeera Ahmed
Elizabeth Beaumont
Sue Baker

359

Make sure you don't miss the new
gripping, nail-biting thriller from
Michelle Davies:

THE DEATH OF ME

Read on for an exclusive preview . . .

Prologue

I've never liked swimming in the sea. Even the slightest tang
of saltwater on my lips makes me gag. Such was my loathing of
it as a child that on holiday I would never venture further than
the shallows, primed to run back up the beach the moment I
feared the sea was getting too rough and might splash me. As an
adult I never willingly go near it.

This I am reminded of when I am shoved forward into the
next breaking wave and it hits me full in the face. I retch as
my mouth is doused and water reaches my throat. Coughing
furiously to expel it, I battle between wanting to keep my lips
tightly sealed but knowing I have to keep sucking down deep

breaths for as long as I can, for as long as I remain above the surface.

The waves are at my waist now and the further we've waded from the shoreline the more urgent they've become. The rising current pulls at the folds of my dress while the trainers he forbid me to discard on the sand now encase my feet like cement. Every step forward is a physical strain but he doesn't care – he is impatient and testy, pushing and shoving me onwards until dry land is far beyond my reach.

We shuffle onwards until the water laps my shoulders. It's here he finally unties my wrists. I beg him to let me go back, to think about what he's doing, but he's much taller than me so he's not out of his depth yet, and because of that he wants to keep going. I'm shivering with terror as much as from cold and I'm trying desperately not to cry, knowing I need to preserve every ounce of energy I have left if I'm going to survive this. And I need to survive for Daniel. I want to howl when I think about how I've let my son down. I could've stopped all this after what happened at the awards. I should've heeded the warning. But I didn't, I kept going in my pursuit of the story and this is where it has brought me, up to my neck in freezing cold sea off the Devon coast, about to be drowned.

I take another step forward but this time my foot doesn't connect with the bottom. It's a shelf break and the sudden drop knocks the wind out of me as I plunge below the surface. I want to scream that I'm not ready, that I haven't taken a big enough breath, but the water has already closed over my head and then I feel his hand upon my crown, pushing me deeper still. I claw at his skin, raking it with my nails so sharply I must be drawing blood, but he has a fistful of my hair now and I'm writhing back and forth but it's not getting me anywhere, so I grab his wrist with both hands and pull as hard as I can so he loses his footing and plunges beneath the waves with me and it works, he's loosened his grip.

But I can't fathom which way is up now. The current is pulling back and forth like I'm a rag doll and I'm trying to kick, I'm trying to get back to the surface, to fresh air . . .

Come on, Natalie, kick

I break the surface, gasping, but the next wave pummels into me and I'm under again. I keep trying to swim upwards but I'm so tired already and my eyes are stinging and I know I can't scream or call for help because I mustn't let any water in.

Kick, Natalie, kick

Then he's next to me. I can't see him in the murky darkness but I know he's there. He's grabbing at me and I'm trying to swim away but he's too strong . . .

OhmygodallIwanttodoisbreathein

My lungs are burning now and I feel dizzy and sick and my arms are heavy and everything hurts, everything really hurts . . .

Kick Natalie, kick

I'msinking . . .

lungsburning . . .

thepain . . .

Kick, Natalie, kick

needair . . .

haveto . . .

breathein . . .

So I do.